AMULET

Library of Congress Control Number: 2013957419
ISBN 978-0-545-43315-0

10 9 8 7 6 5 4 3 2 1   14 15 16 17 18
First edition, September 2014
Edited by Cassandra Pelham
Creative Director: David Saylor
Book Design by Phil Falco and Kazu Kibuishi
Printed in China   38

AMULET

KAZU KIBUISHI

BOOK SIX
ESCAPE FROM LUCIEN

AN IMPRINT OF
SCHOLASTIC

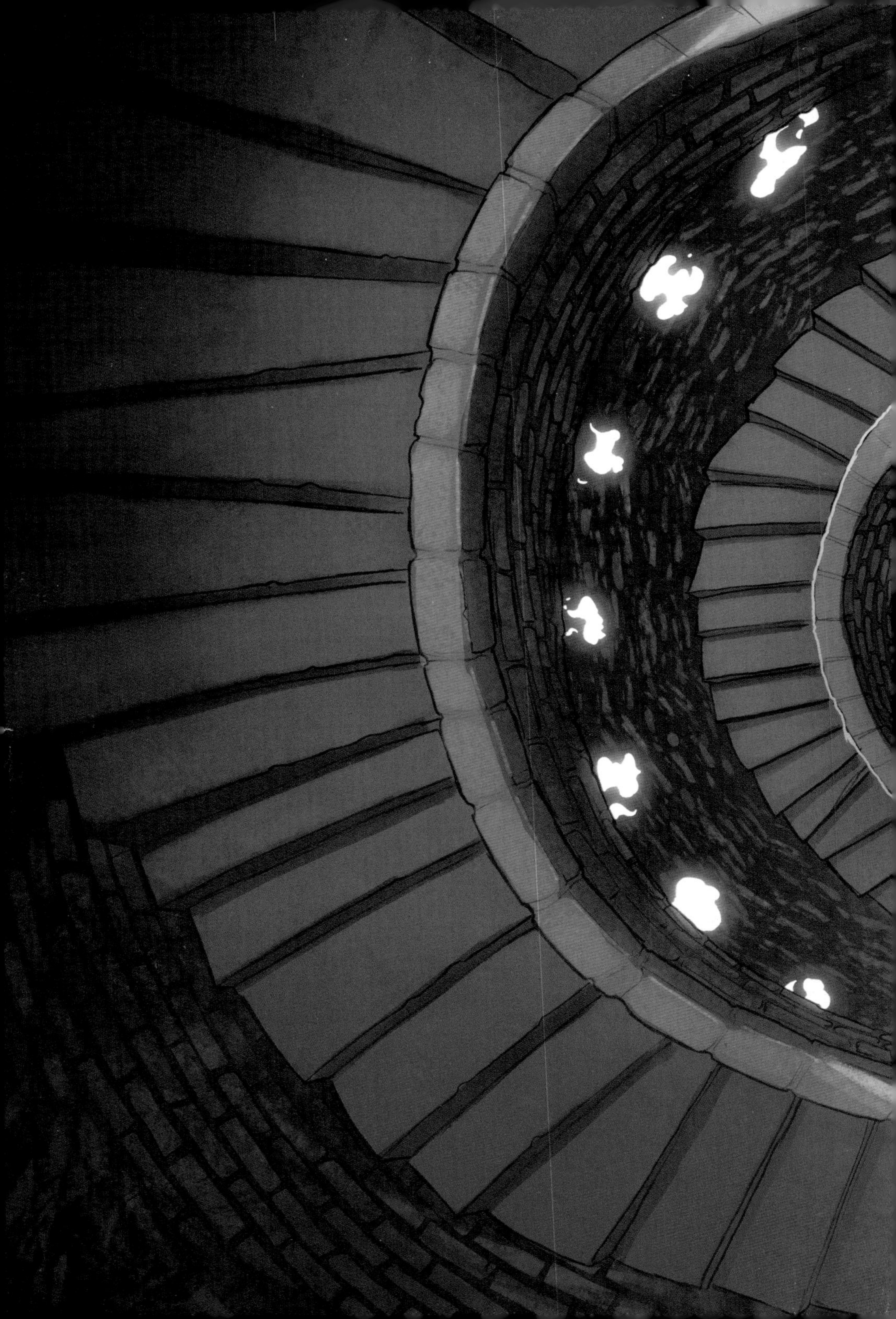

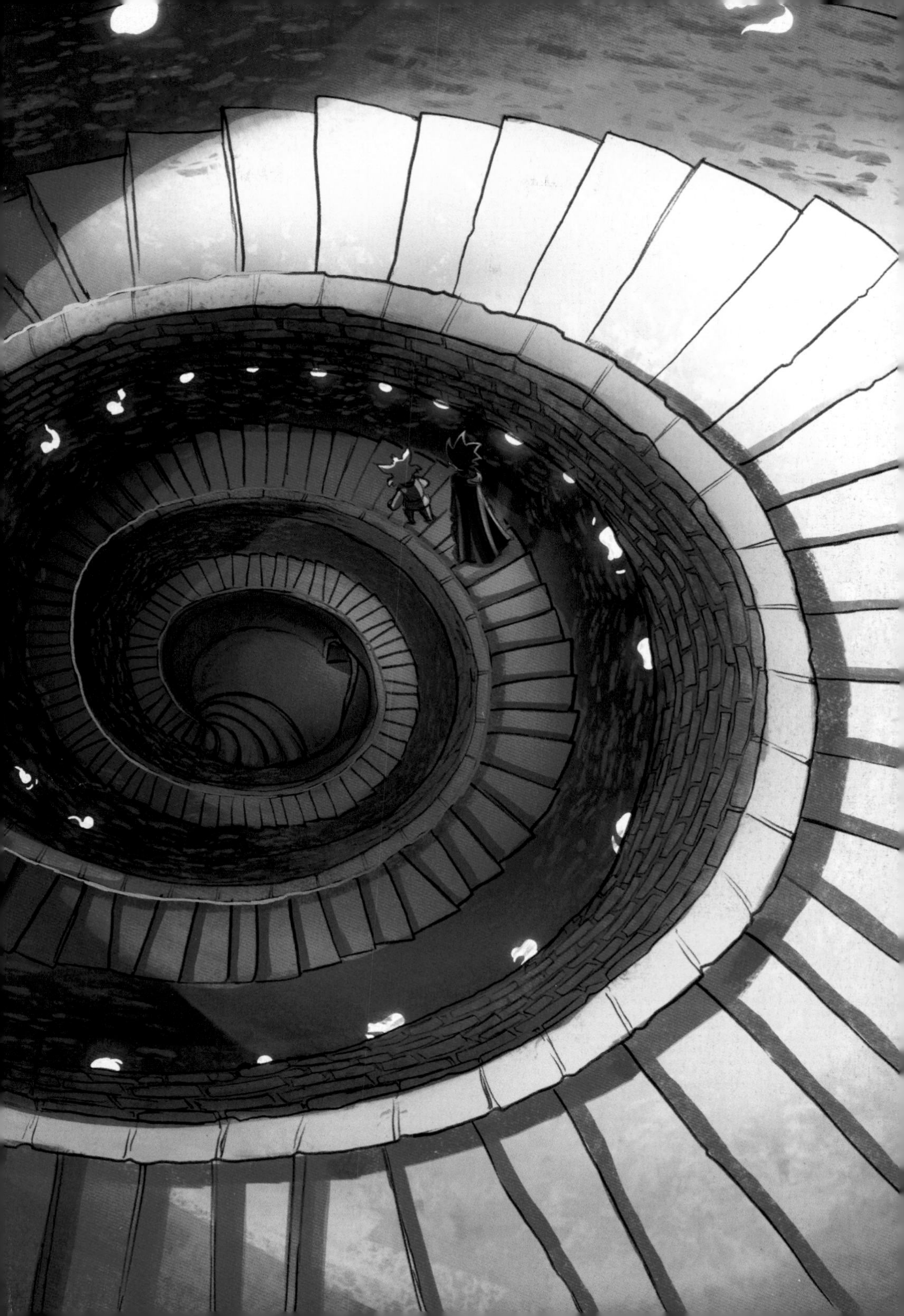

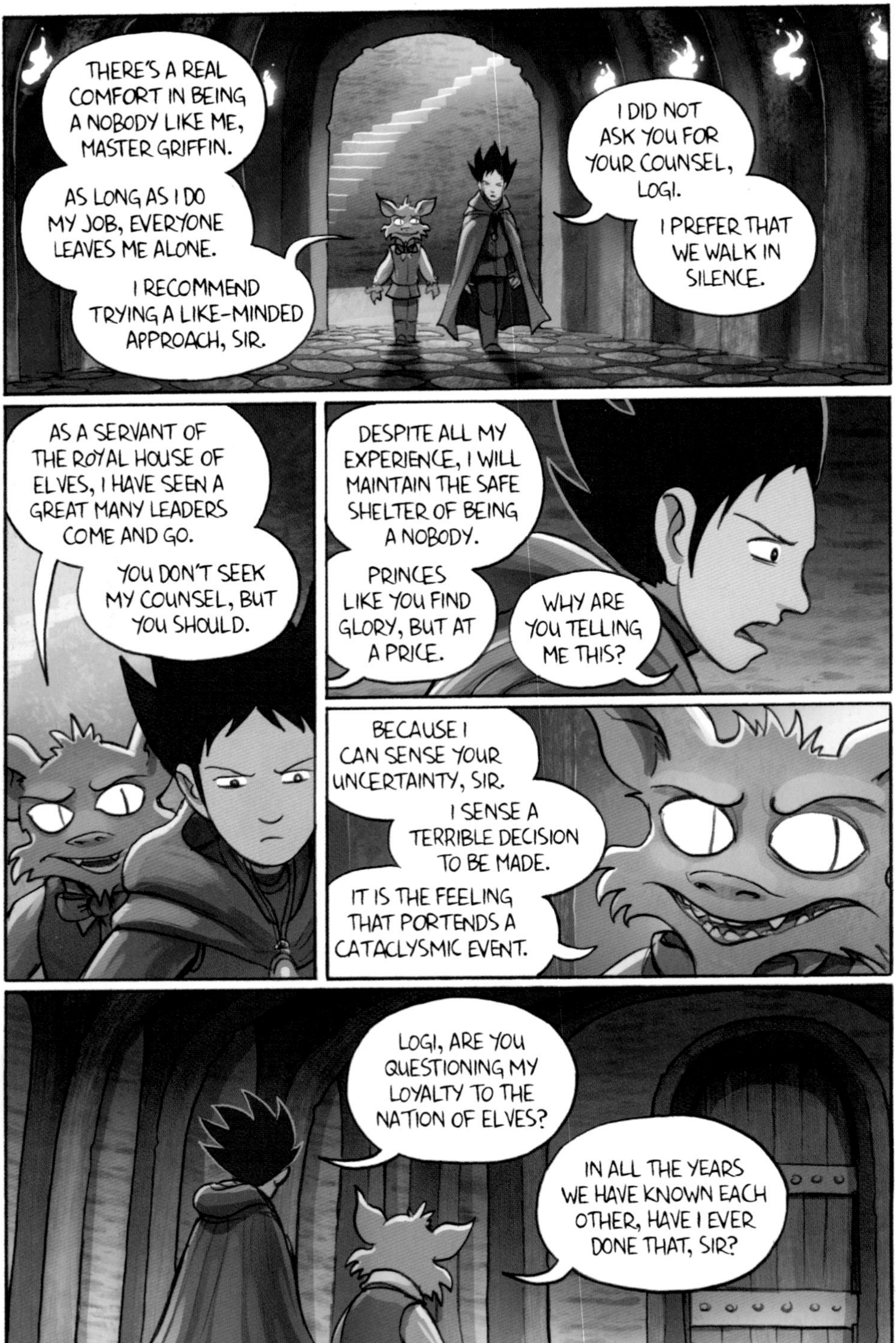
THERE'S A REAL COMFORT IN BEING A NOBODY LIKE ME, MASTER GRIFFIN.
AS LONG AS I DO MY JOB, EVERYONE LEAVES ME ALONE.
I RECOMMEND TRYING A LIKE-MINDED APPROACH, SIR.
I DID NOT ASK YOU FOR YOUR COUNSEL, LOGI.
I PREFER THAT WE WALK IN SILENCE.
AS A SERVANT OF THE ROYAL HOUSE OF ELVES, I HAVE SEEN A GREAT MANY LEADERS COME AND GO.
YOU DON'T SEEK MY COUNSEL, BUT YOU SHOULD.
DESPITE ALL MY EXPERIENCE, I WILL MAINTAIN THE SAFE SHELTER OF BEING A NOBODY.
PRINCES LIKE YOU FIND GLORY, BUT AT A PRICE.
WHY ARE YOU TELLING ME THIS?
BECAUSE I CAN SENSE YOUR UNCERTAINTY, SIR.
I SENSE A TERRIBLE DECISION TO BE MADE.
IT IS THE FEELING THAT PORTENDS A CATACLYSMIC EVENT.
LOGI, ARE YOU QUESTIONING MY LOYALTY TO THE NATION OF ELVES?
IN ALL THE YEARS WE HAVE KNOWN EACH OTHER, HAVE I EVER DONE THAT, SIR?

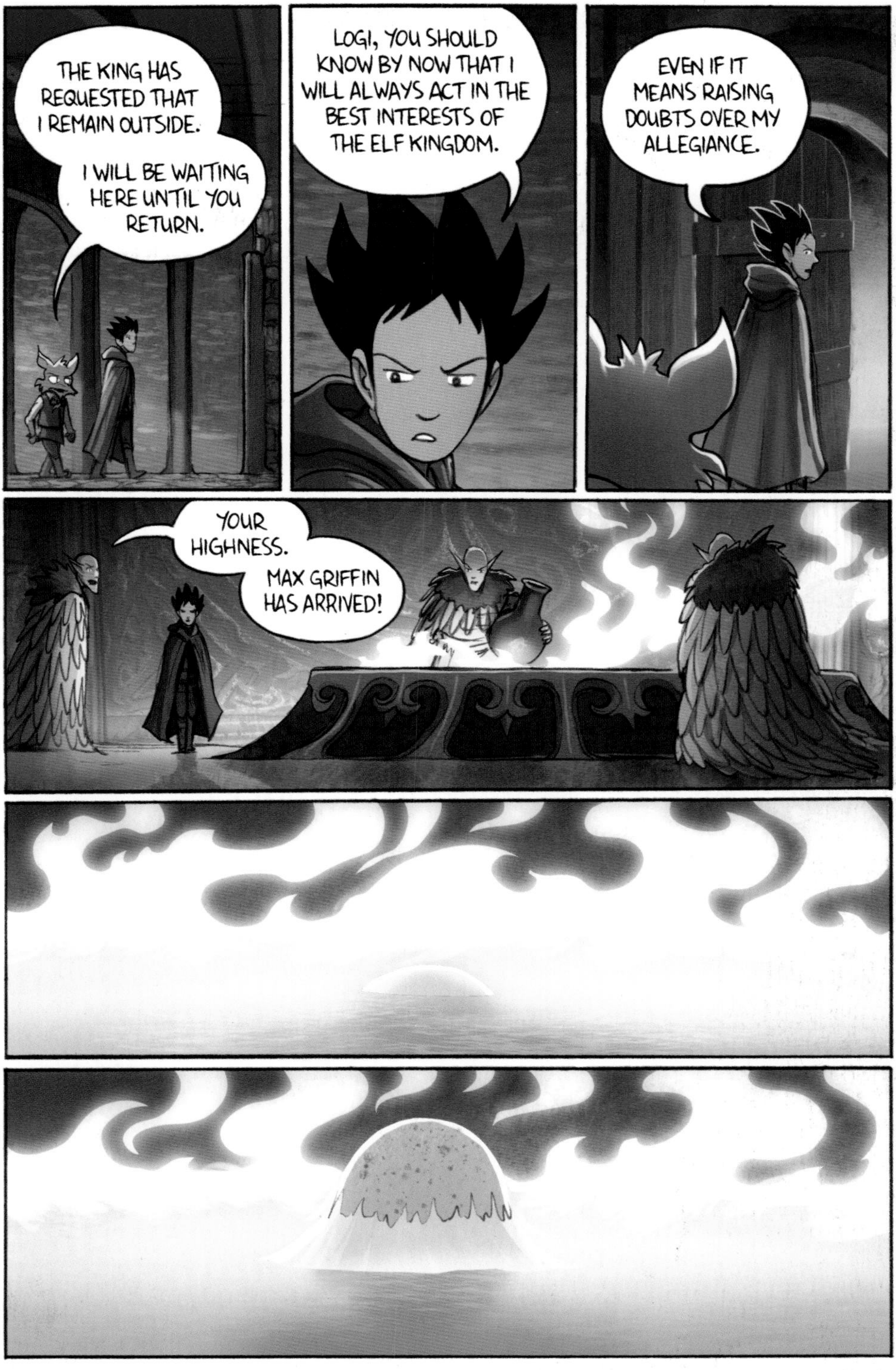
THE KING HAS REQUESTED THAT I REMAIN OUTSIDE.
I WILL BE WAITING HERE UNTIL YOU RETURN.
LOGI, YOU SHOULD KNOW BY NOW THAT I WILL ALWAYS ACT IN THE BEST INTERESTS OF THE ELF KINGDOM.
EVEN IF IT MEANS RAISING DOUBTS OVER MY ALLEGIANCE.
YOUR HIGHNESS.
MAX GRIFFIN HAS ARRIVED!

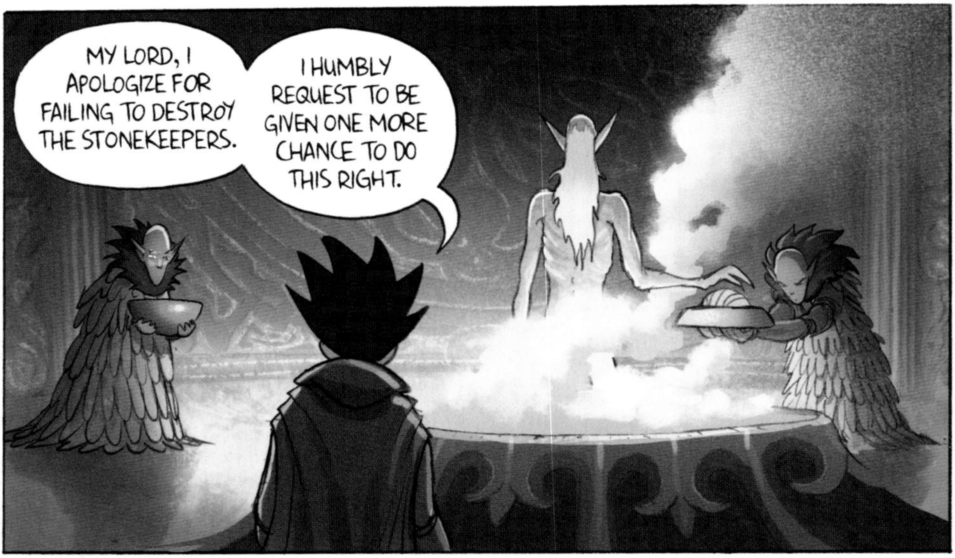
MY LORD, I APOLOGIZE FOR FAILING TO DESTROY THE STONEKEEPERS.
I HUMBLY REQUEST TO BE GIVEN ONE MORE CHANCE TO DO THIS RIGHT.

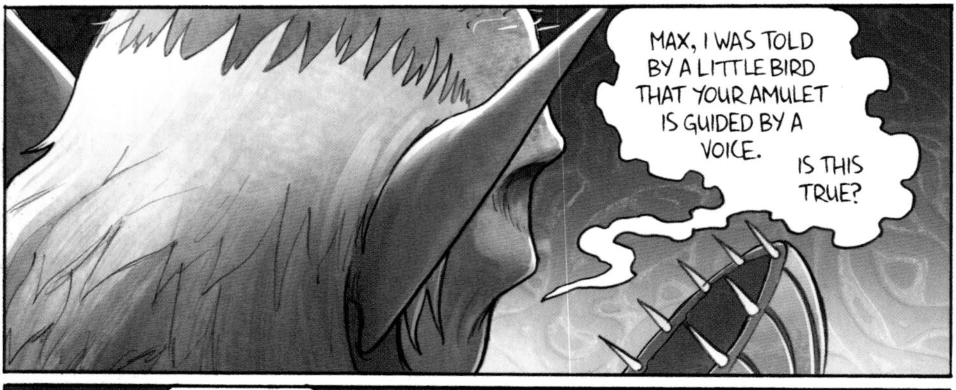
MAX, I WAS TOLD BY A LITTLE BIRD THAT YOUR AMULET IS GUIDED BY A VOICE.
IS THIS TRUE?

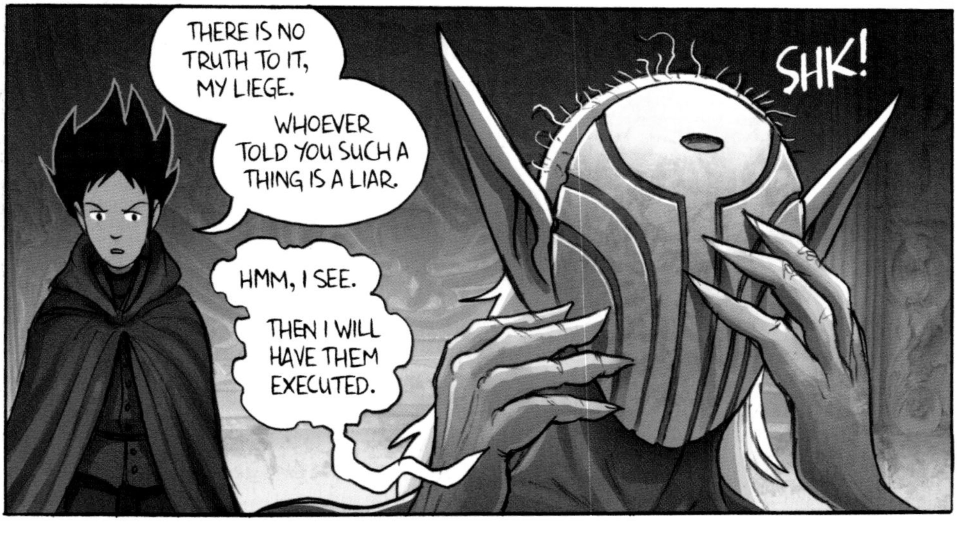
THERE IS NO TRUTH TO IT, MY LIEGE.
WHOEVER TOLD YOU SUCH A THING IS A LIAR.
SHK!
HMM, I SEE.
THEN I WILL HAVE THEM EXECUTED.

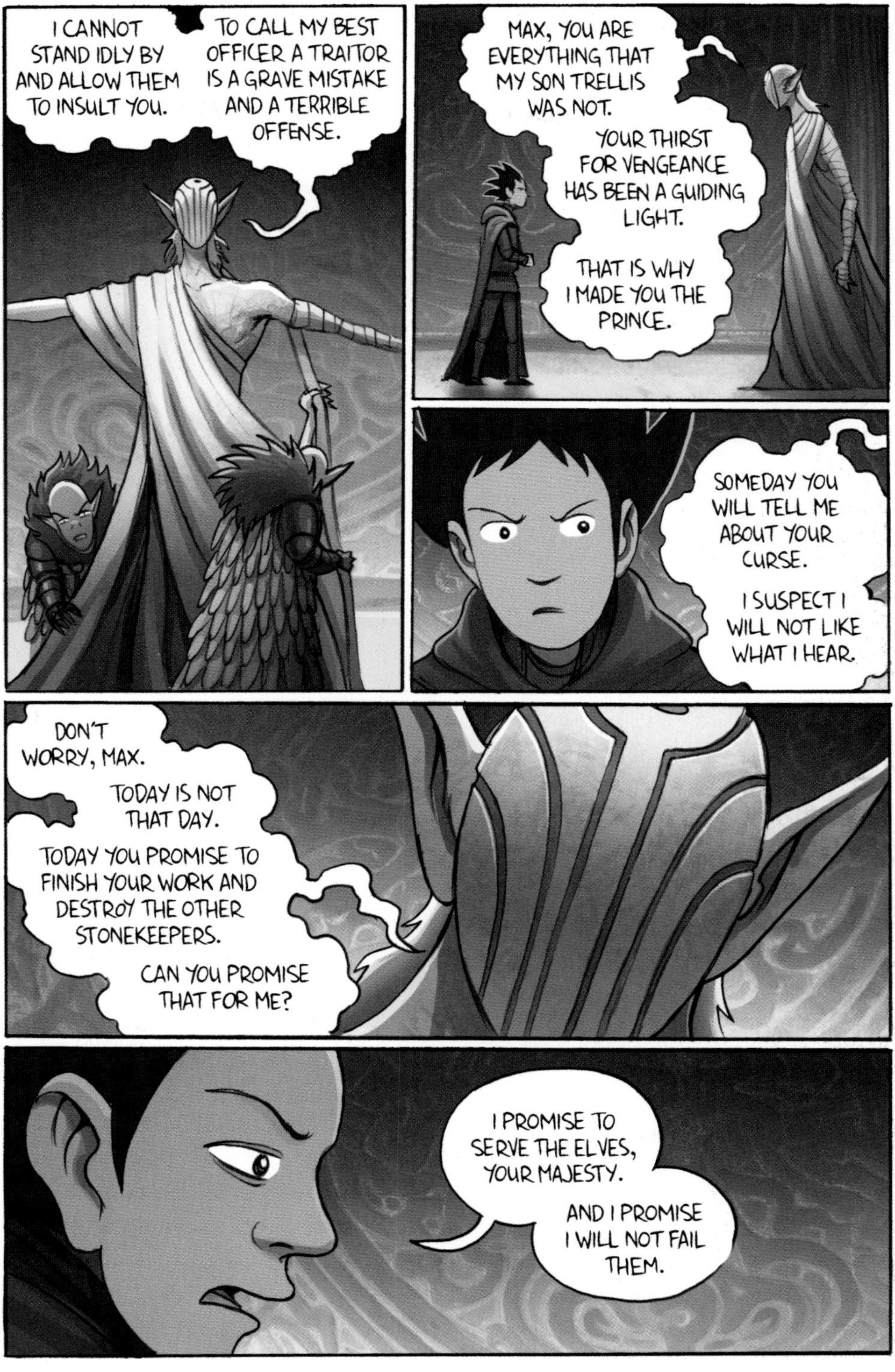
I CANNOT STAND IDLY BY AND ALLOW THEM TO INSULT YOU.
TO CALL MY BEST OFFICER A TRAITOR IS A GRAVE MISTAKE AND A TERRIBLE OFFENSE.
MAX, YOU ARE EVERYTHING THAT MY SON TRELLIS WAS NOT.
YOUR THIRST FOR VENGEANCE HAS BEEN A GUIDING LIGHT.
THAT IS WHY I MADE YOU THE PRINCE.
SOMEDAY YOU WILL TELL ME ABOUT YOUR CURSE.
I SUSPECT I WILL NOT LIKE WHAT I HEAR.
DON'T WORRY, MAX.
TODAY IS NOT THAT DAY.
TODAY YOU PROMISE TO FINISH YOUR WORK AND DESTROY THE OTHER STONEKEEPERS.
CAN YOU PROMISE THAT FOR ME?
I PROMISE TO SERVE THE ELVES, YOUR MAJESTY.
AND I PROMISE I WILL NOT FAIL THEM.

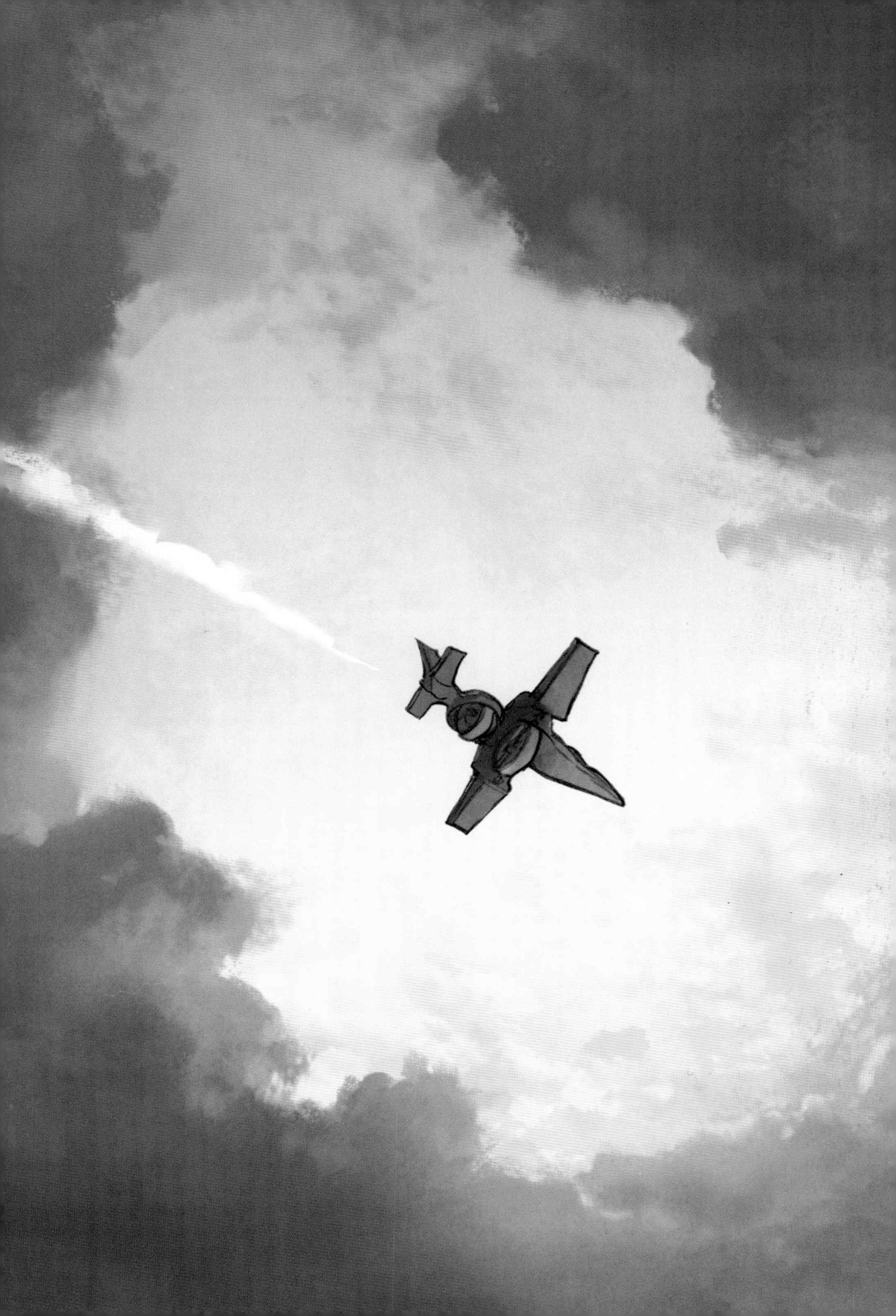

COLOSSUS TRAINING IS IN SESSION RIGHT NOW.

DID YOU HEAR WHAT I SAID?

CLASS IS IN SESSION AND WE ARE STILL JUST FLYING AROUND.

WE NEED TO GO BACK.

HOLD ON.

JUST GIVE ME A FEW MORE MINUTES HERE.

THAT'S WHAT YOU SAID A FEW MINUTES AGO.

NAVIN, WE ARE NOW A HALF HOUR LATE.

I STILL NEED TO GET A GOOD LOOK AT SOME OF THESE CLOUD FORMATIONS. THERE'S SOME WEIRD STUFF HAPPENING UP HERE.

HEY, IF WE DON'T PLAY BY THE RULES, WE'RE GOING TO GET KICKED OUT OF THE COLOSSUS PROGRAM, HAYES. AND IF THAT HAPPENS, MY DAD'S GOING TO THROW A FIT.

OKAY, OKAY. I'LL TAKE US BACK.

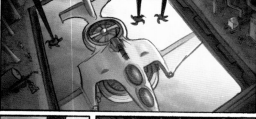

POOMF!

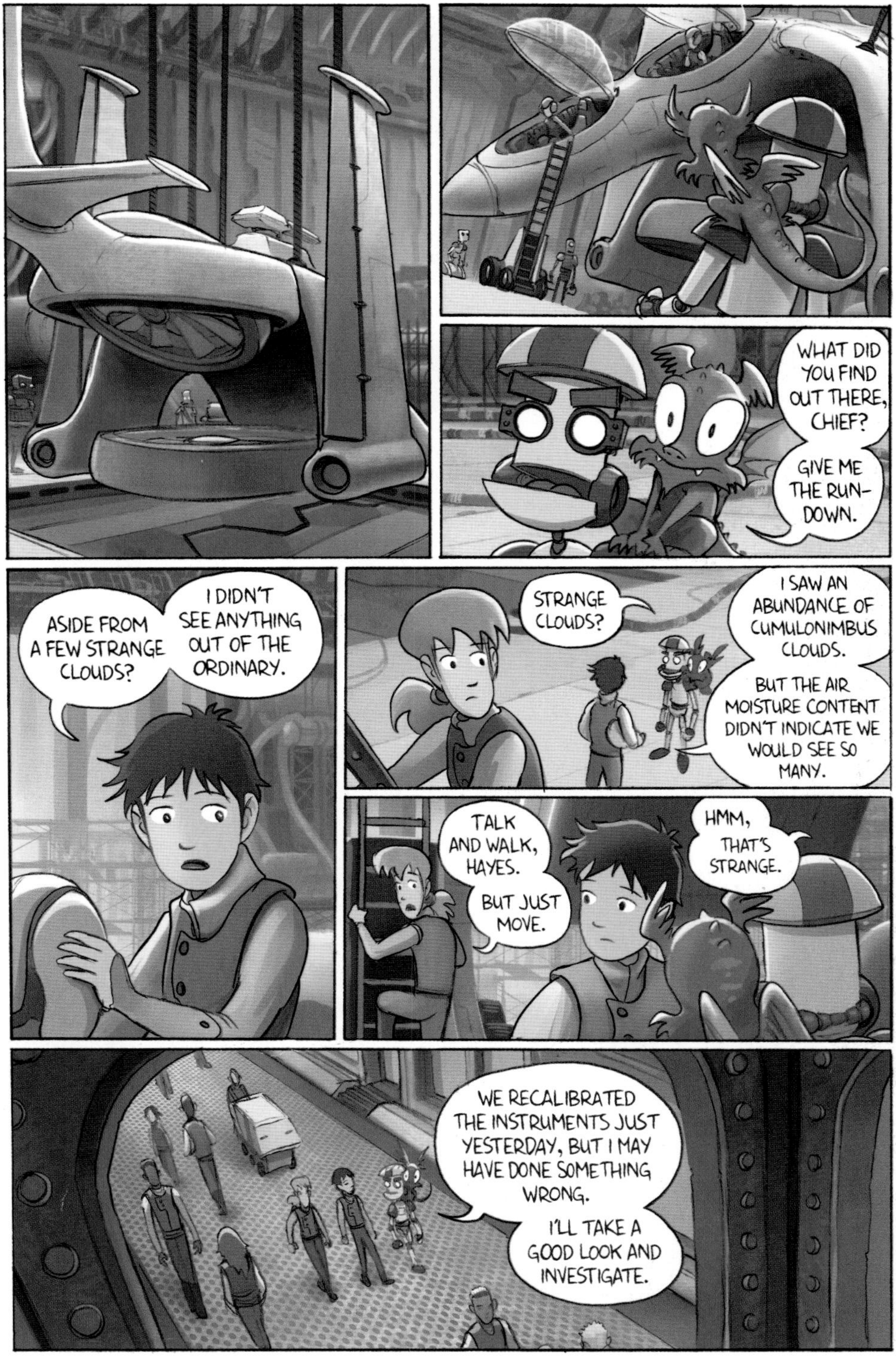
WHAT DID YOU FIND OUT THERE, CHIEF?
GIVE ME THE RUN-DOWN.
I DIDN'T SEE ANYTHING OUT OF THE ORDINARY.
ASIDE FROM A FEW STRANGE CLOUDS?
STRANGE CLOUDS?
I SAW AN ABUNDANCE OF CUMULONIMBUS CLOUDS.
BUT THE AIR MOISTURE CONTENT DIDN'T INDICATE WE WOULD SEE SO MANY.
TALK AND WALK, HAYES.
BUT JUST MOVE.
HMM,
THAT'S STRANGE.
WE RECALIBRATED THE INSTRUMENTS JUST YESTERDAY, BUT I MAY HAVE DONE SOMETHING WRONG.
I'LL TAKE A GOOD LOOK AND INVESTIGATE.

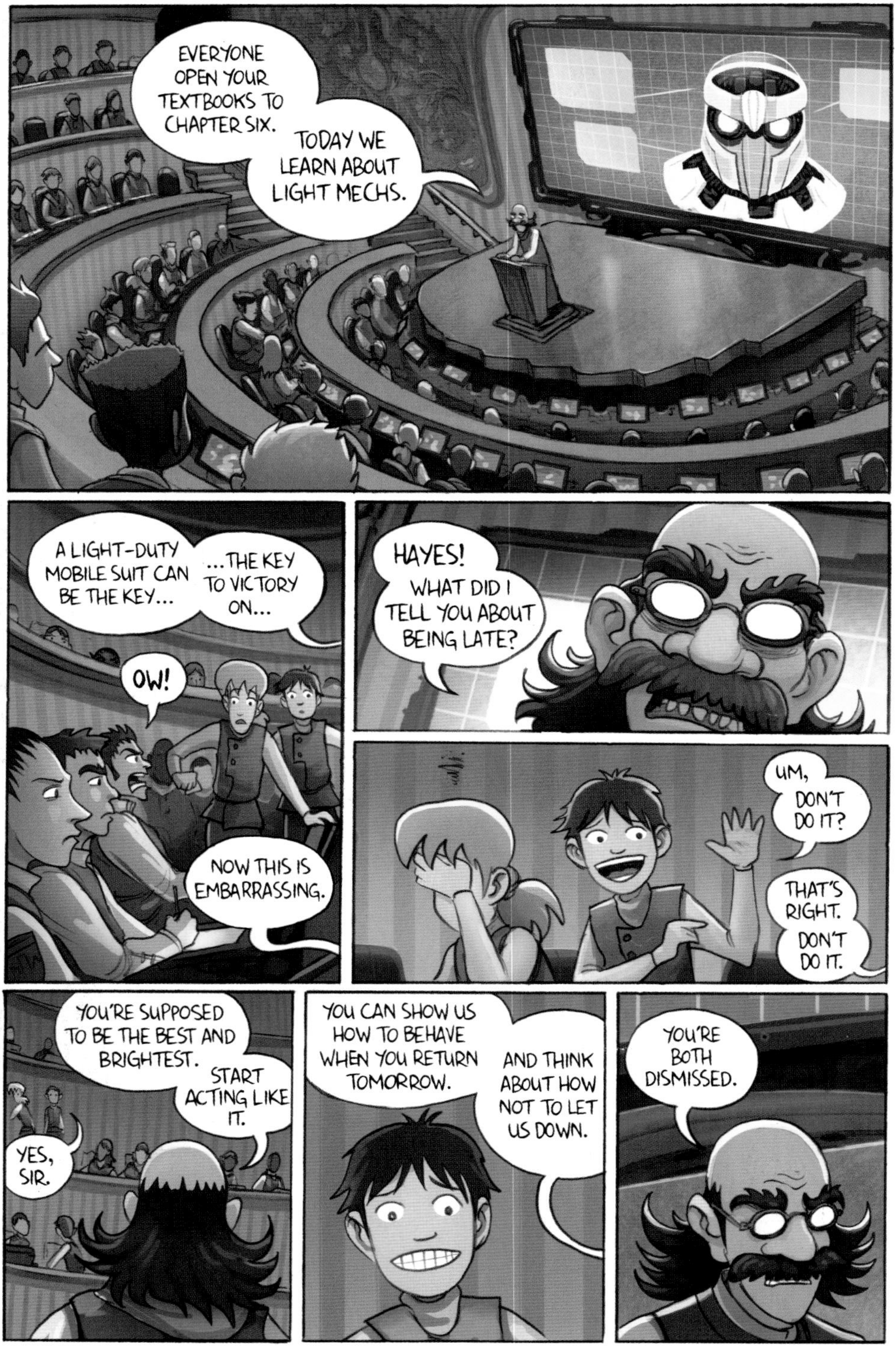
EVERYONE OPEN YOUR TEXTBOOKS TO CHAPTER SIX.
TODAY WE LEARN ABOUT LIGHT MECHS.
A LIGHT-DUTY MOBILE SUIT CAN BE THE KEY...
...THE KEY TO VICTORY ON...
OW!
NOW THIS IS EMBARRASSING.
HAYES!
WHAT DID I TELL YOU ABOUT BEING LATE?
UM,
DON'T DO IT?
THAT'S RIGHT.
DON'T DO IT.
YOU'RE SUPPOSED TO BE THE BEST AND BRIGHTEST.
START ACTING LIKE IT.
YES, SIR.
YOU CAN SHOW US HOW TO BEHAVE WHEN YOU RETURN TOMORROW.
AND THINK ABOUT HOW NOT TO LET US DOWN.
YOU'RE BOTH DISMISSED.

NAVIN, I WISH YOU KNEW HOW MUCH I LIKE ATTENDING LECTURES.

WELL, I THOUGHT HE WAS BEING A LITTLE HARSH.

THAT MAN HAS BEEN THROUGH MORE THAN WE EVER WILL.

WE'RE LUCKY HE'S HERE TO TEACH US.

HE'S WILLING TO TALK, SO WE SHOULD BE WILLING TO LISTEN.

OKAY, OKAY.

I'LL LISTEN, BUT WE SHOULDN'T BE PUNISHED FOR DOING REAL WORK.

I WAS ONLY TRYING TO HELP.

DO BOTH.

THIS WAY.

WHAT ARE WE DOING DOWN HERE?

SINCE WE GOT KICKED OUT OF THE CLASSROOM...

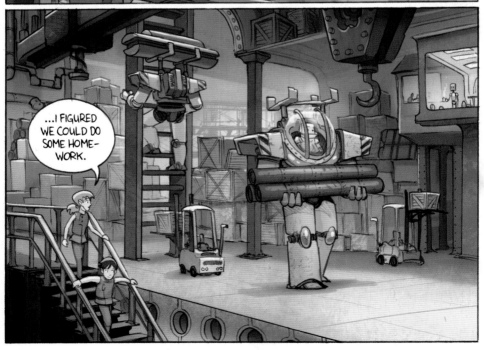

...I FIGURED WE COULD DO SOME HOME-WORK.

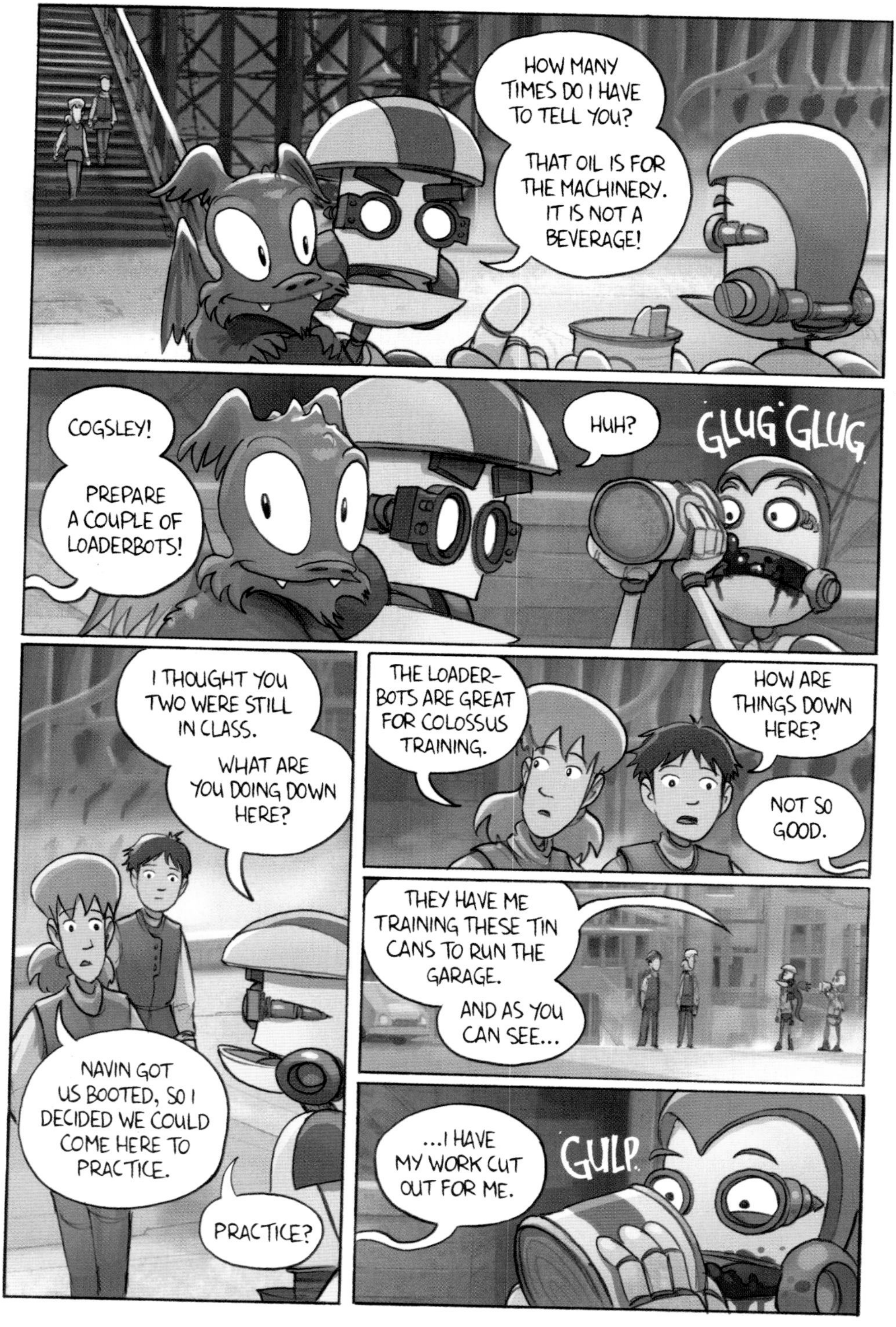
HOW MANY TIMES DO I HAVE TO TELL YOU?
THAT OIL IS FOR THE MACHINERY. IT IS NOT A BEVERAGE!
COGSLEY!
PREPARE A COUPLE OF LOADERBOTS!
HUH?
GLUG GLUG
I THOUGHT YOU TWO WERE STILL IN CLASS.
WHAT ARE YOU DOING DOWN HERE?
NAVIN GOT US BOOTED, SO I DECIDED WE COULD COME HERE TO PRACTICE.
PRACTICE?
THE LOADER-BOTS ARE GREAT FOR COLOSSUS TRAINING.
HOW ARE THINGS DOWN HERE?
NOT SO GOOD.
THEY HAVE ME TRAINING THESE TIN CANS TO RUN THE GARAGE.
AND AS YOU CAN SEE...
...I HAVE MY WORK CUT OUT FOR ME.
GULP.

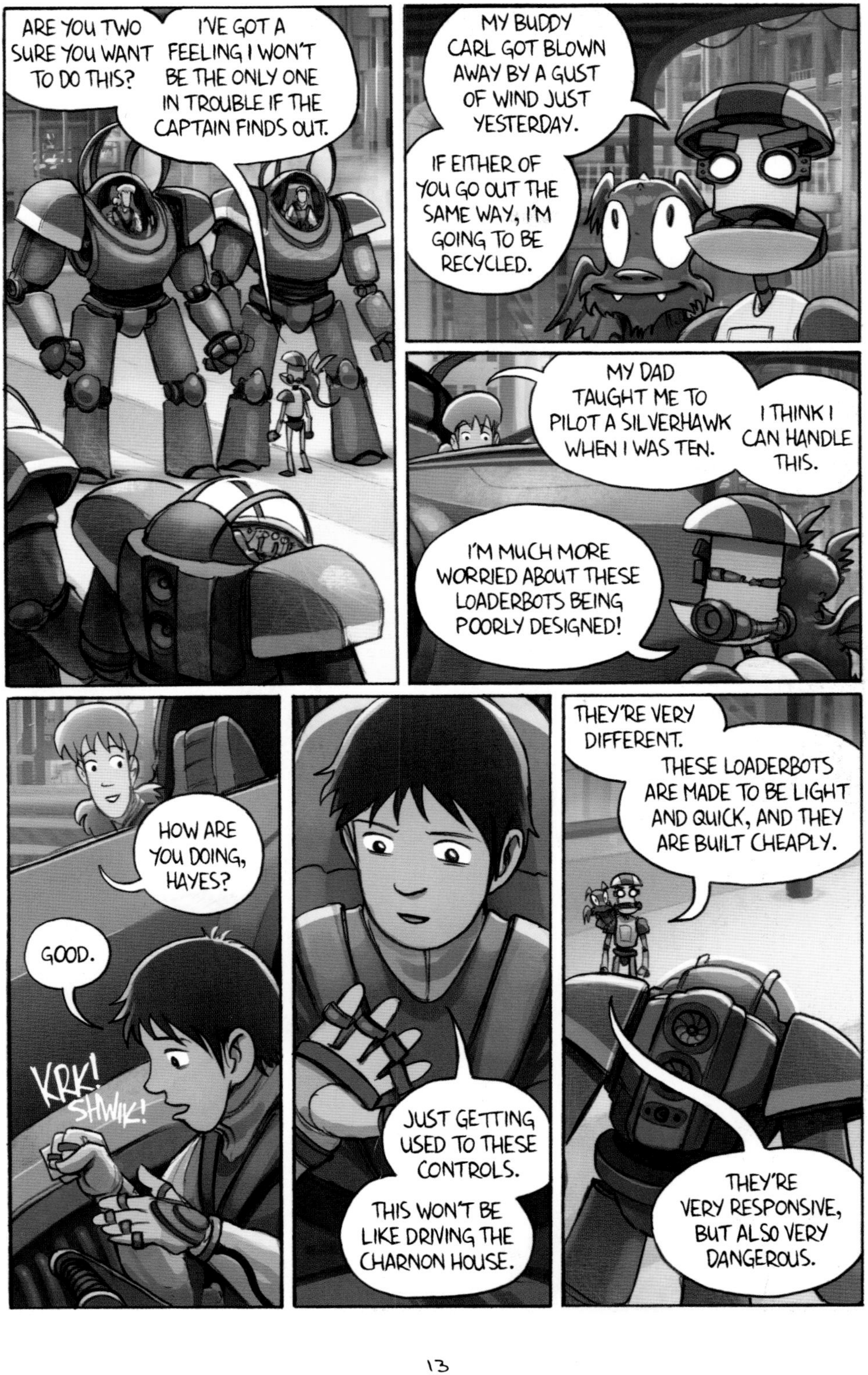
ARE YOU TWO SURE YOU WANT TO DO THIS?
I'VE GOT A FEELING I WON'T BE THE ONLY ONE IN TROUBLE IF THE CAPTAIN FINDS OUT.
MY BUDDY CARL GOT BLOWN AWAY BY A GUST OF WIND JUST YESTERDAY.
IF EITHER OF YOU GO OUT THE SAME WAY, I'M GOING TO BE RECYCLED.
MY DAD TAUGHT ME TO PILOT A SILVERHAWK WHEN I WAS TEN.
I THINK I CAN HANDLE THIS.
I'M MUCH MORE WORRIED ABOUT THESE LOADERBOTS BEING POORLY DESIGNED!
HOW ARE YOU DOING, HAYES?
GOOD.
KRK!
SHWIK!
JUST GETTING USED TO THESE CONTROLS.
THIS WON'T BE LIKE DRIVING THE CHARNON HOUSE.
THEY'RE VERY DIFFERENT.
THESE LOADERBOTS ARE MADE TO BE LIGHT AND QUICK, AND THEY ARE BUILT CHEAPLY.
THEY'RE VERY RESPONSIVE, BUT ALSO VERY DANGEROUS.

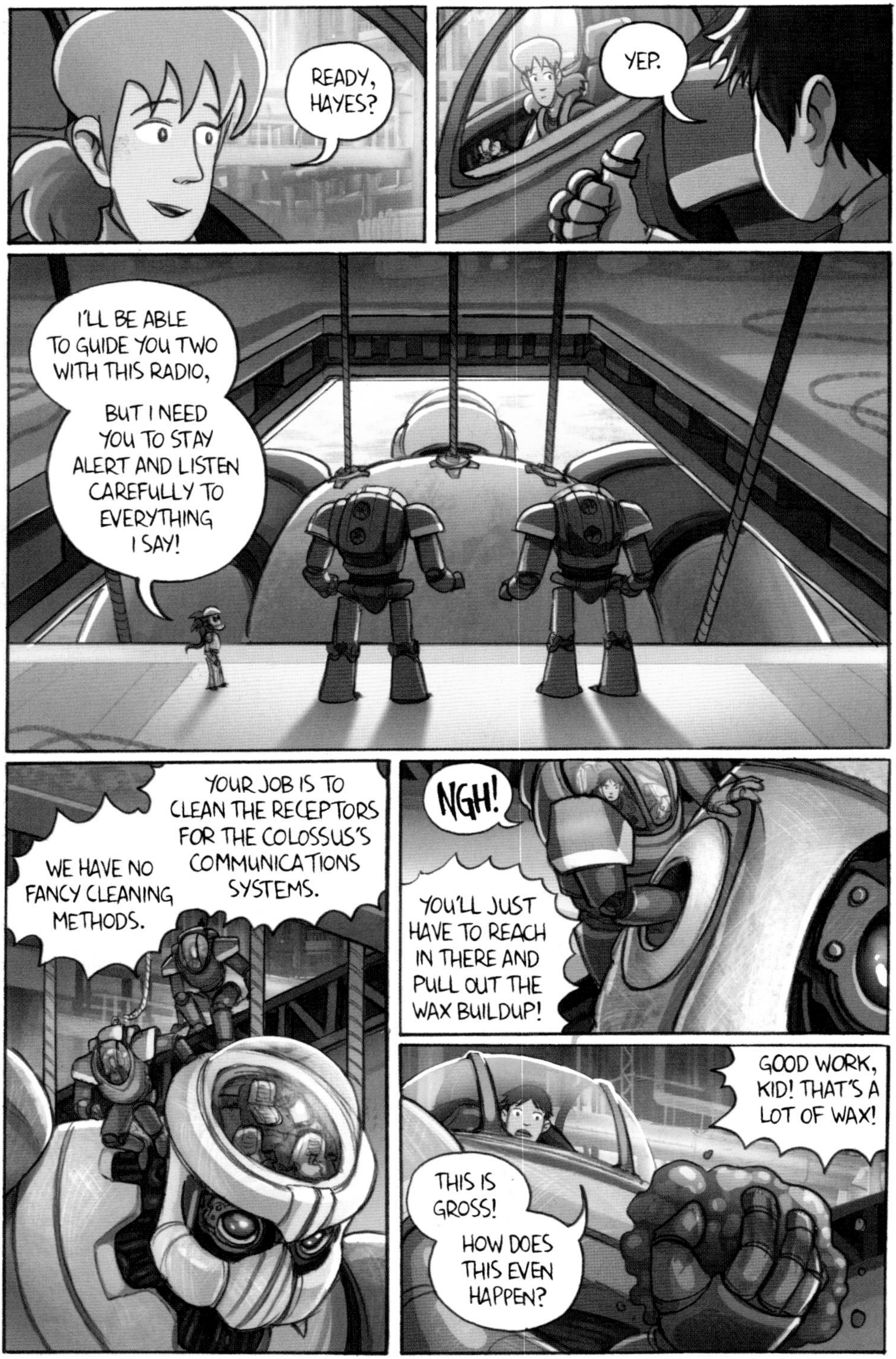
READY, HAYES?
YEP.
I'LL BE ABLE TO GUIDE YOU TWO WITH THIS RADIO,
BUT I NEED YOU TO STAY ALERT AND LISTEN CAREFULLY TO EVERYTHING I SAY!
YOUR JOB IS TO CLEAN THE RECEPTORS FOR THE COLOSSUS'S COMMUNICATIONS SYSTEMS.
WE HAVE NO FANCY CLEANING METHODS.
NGH!
YOU'LL JUST HAVE TO REACH IN THERE AND PULL OUT THE WAX BUILDUP!
GOOD WORK, KID! THAT'S A LOT OF WAX!
THIS IS GROSS!
HOW DOES THIS EVEN HAPPEN?

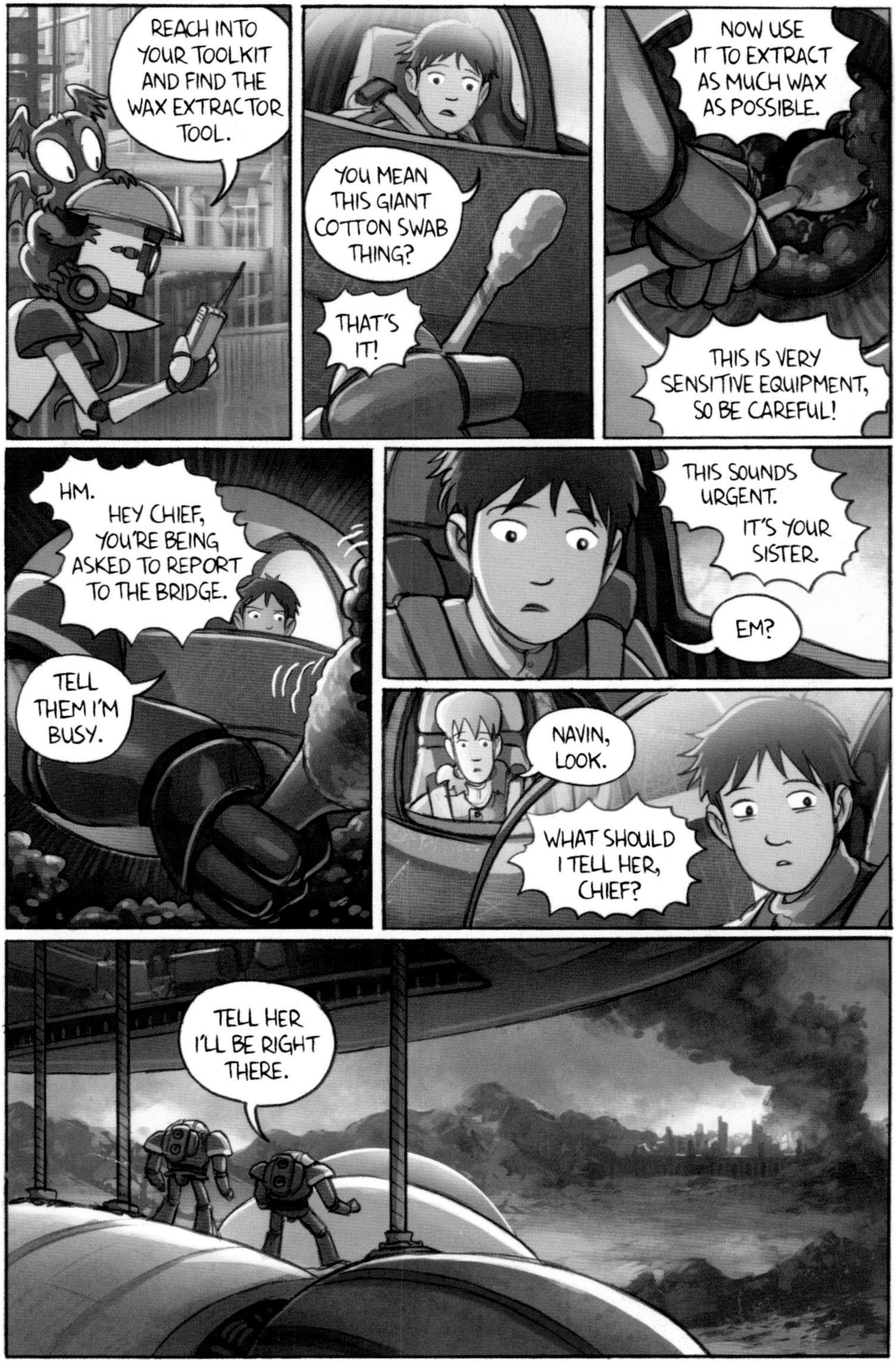
REACH INTO YOUR TOOLKIT AND FIND THE WAX EXTRACTOR TOOL.
YOU MEAN THIS GIANT COTTON SWAB THING?
THAT'S IT!
NOW USE IT TO EXTRACT AS MUCH WAX AS POSSIBLE.
THIS IS VERY SENSITIVE EQUIPMENT, SO BE CAREFUL!
HM.
HEY CHIEF, YOU'RE BEING ASKED TO REPORT TO THE BRIDGE.
TELL THEM I'M BUSY.
THIS SOUNDS URGENT.
IT'S YOUR SISTER.
EM?
NAVIN, LOOK.
WHAT SHOULD I TELL HER, CHIEF?
TELL HER I'LL BE RIGHT THERE.

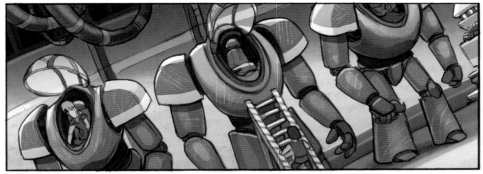

HAYES!

HUNTER!

GET AWAY FROM THOSE LOADERS RIGHT NOW!

YOU HAVE SOME EXPLAINING TO DO!

THIS IS A VIOLATION OF VEHICLE USE RULES.

YOU, OF ALL PEOPLE, SHOULD KNOW THIS, MISS HUNTER.

BUT THIS WASN'T ALY'S FAULT, SIR.

IT WAS MY IDEA.

WHAT?!

I PRESSURED HER TO COME HERE.

THAT'S NOT TRUE!

THIS WAS MY FAULT!

HM.

WE HAVE NO CHOICE BUT TO REVOKE YOUR VEHICLE ACCESS PRIVILEGES, MISTER HAYES.

NO!

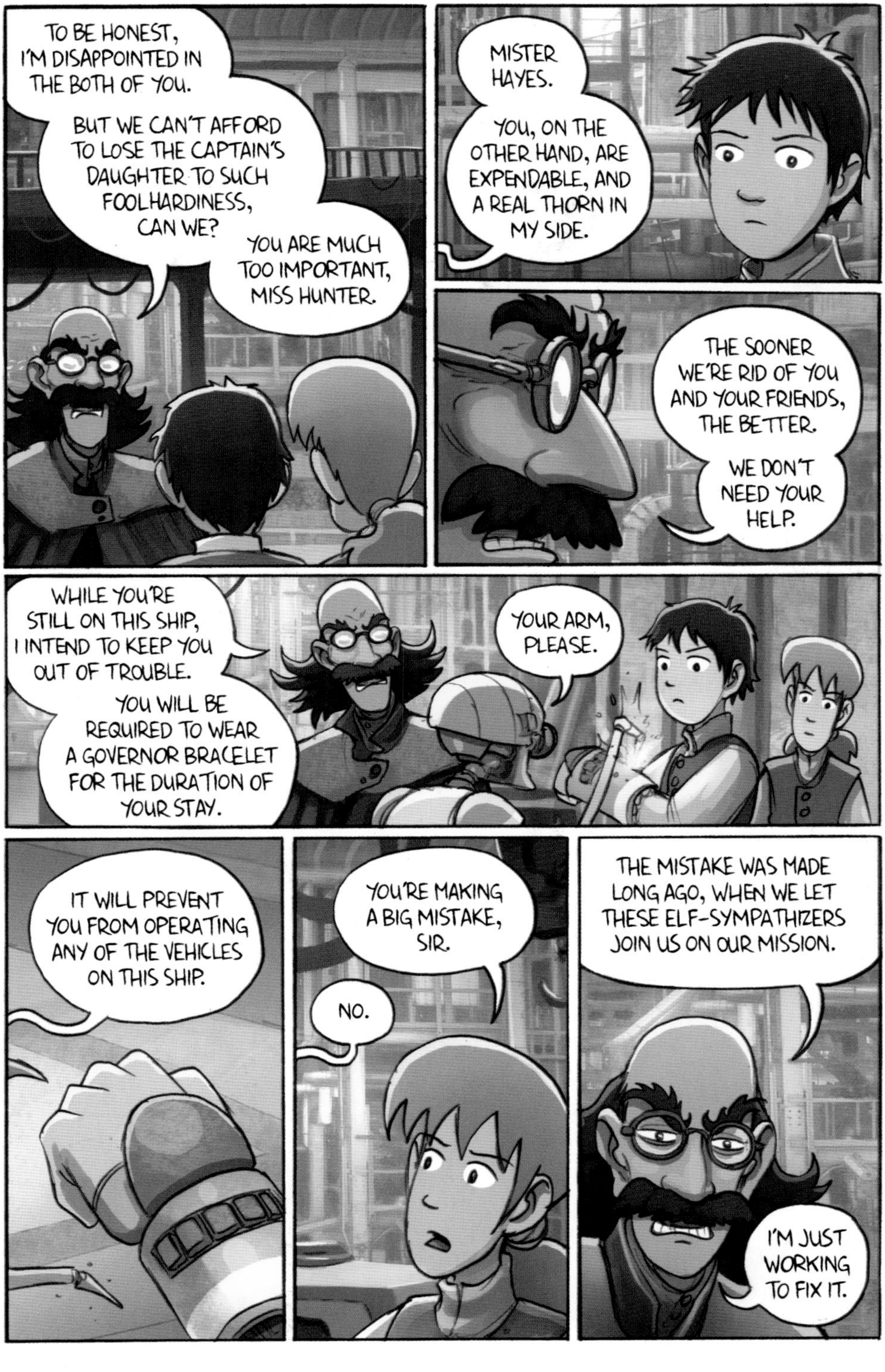
TO BE HONEST, I'M DISAPPOINTED IN THE BOTH OF YOU.
BUT WE CAN'T AFFORD TO LOSE THE CAPTAIN'S DAUGHTER TO SUCH FOOLHARDINESS, CAN WE?
YOU ARE MUCH TOO IMPORTANT, MISS HUNTER.
MISTER HAYES.
YOU, ON THE OTHER HAND, ARE EXPENDABLE, AND A REAL THORN IN MY SIDE.
THE SOONER WE'RE RID OF YOU AND YOUR FRIENDS, THE BETTER.
WE DON'T NEED YOUR HELP.
WHILE YOU'RE STILL ON THIS SHIP, I INTEND TO KEEP YOU OUT OF TROUBLE.
YOU WILL BE REQUIRED TO WEAR A GOVERNOR BRACELET FOR THE DURATION OF YOUR STAY.
YOUR ARM, PLEASE.
IT WILL PREVENT YOU FROM OPERATING ANY OF THE VEHICLES ON THIS SHIP.
YOU'RE MAKING A BIG MISTAKE, SIR.
NO.
THE MISTAKE WAS MADE LONG AGO, WHEN WE LET THESE ELF-SYMPATHIZERS JOIN US ON OUR MISSION.
I'M JUST WORKING TO FIX IT.

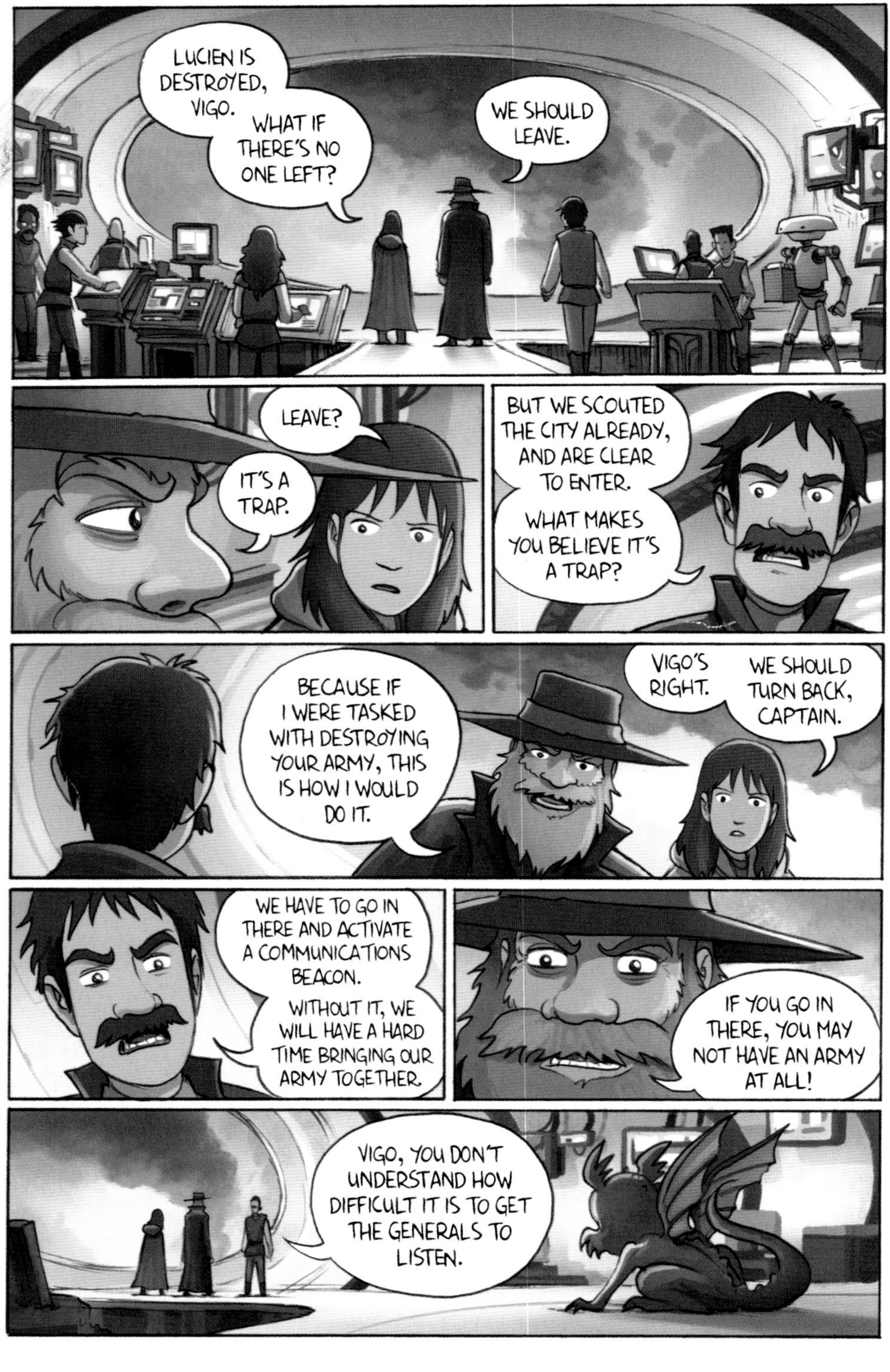
LUCIEN IS DESTROYED, VIGO.
WHAT IF THERE'S NO ONE LEFT?
WE SHOULD LEAVE.
LEAVE?
IT'S A TRAP.
BUT WE SCOUTED THE CITY ALREADY, AND ARE CLEAR TO ENTER.
WHAT MAKES YOU BELIEVE IT'S A TRAP?
BECAUSE IF I WERE TASKED WITH DESTROYING YOUR ARMY, THIS IS HOW I WOULD DO IT.
VIGO'S RIGHT.
WE SHOULD TURN BACK, CAPTAIN.
WE HAVE TO GO IN THERE AND ACTIVATE A COMMUNICATIONS BEACON.
WITHOUT IT, WE WILL HAVE A HARD TIME BRINGING OUR ARMY TOGETHER.
IF YOU GO IN THERE, YOU MAY NOT HAVE AN ARMY AT ALL!
VIGO, YOU DON'T UNDERSTAND HOW DIFFICULT IT IS TO GET THE GENERALS TO LISTEN.

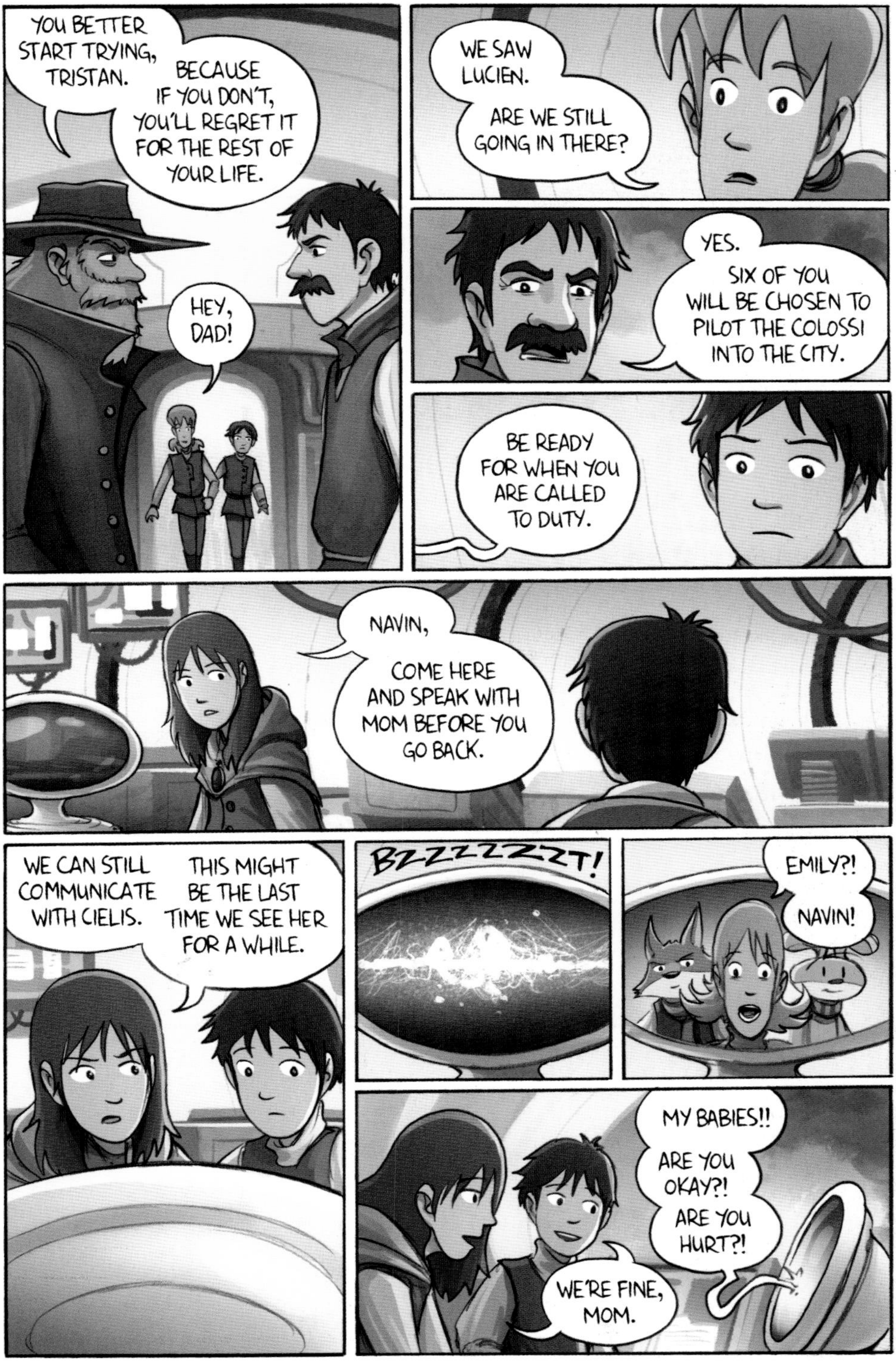
YOU BETTER START TRYING, TRISTAN.
BECAUSE IF YOU DON'T, YOU'LL REGRET IT FOR THE REST OF YOUR LIFE.
HEY, DAD!
WE SAW LUCIEN.
ARE WE STILL GOING IN THERE?
YES.
SIX OF YOU WILL BE CHOSEN TO PILOT THE COLOSSI INTO THE CITY.
BE READY FOR WHEN YOU ARE CALLED TO DUTY.
NAVIN,
COME HERE AND SPEAK WITH MOM BEFORE YOU GO BACK.
WE CAN STILL COMMUNICATE WITH CIELIS.
THIS MIGHT BE THE LAST TIME WE SEE HER FOR A WHILE.
BZZZZZZZT!
EMILY?!
NAVIN!
MY BABIES!!
ARE YOU OKAY?!
ARE YOU HURT?!
WE'RE FINE, MOM.

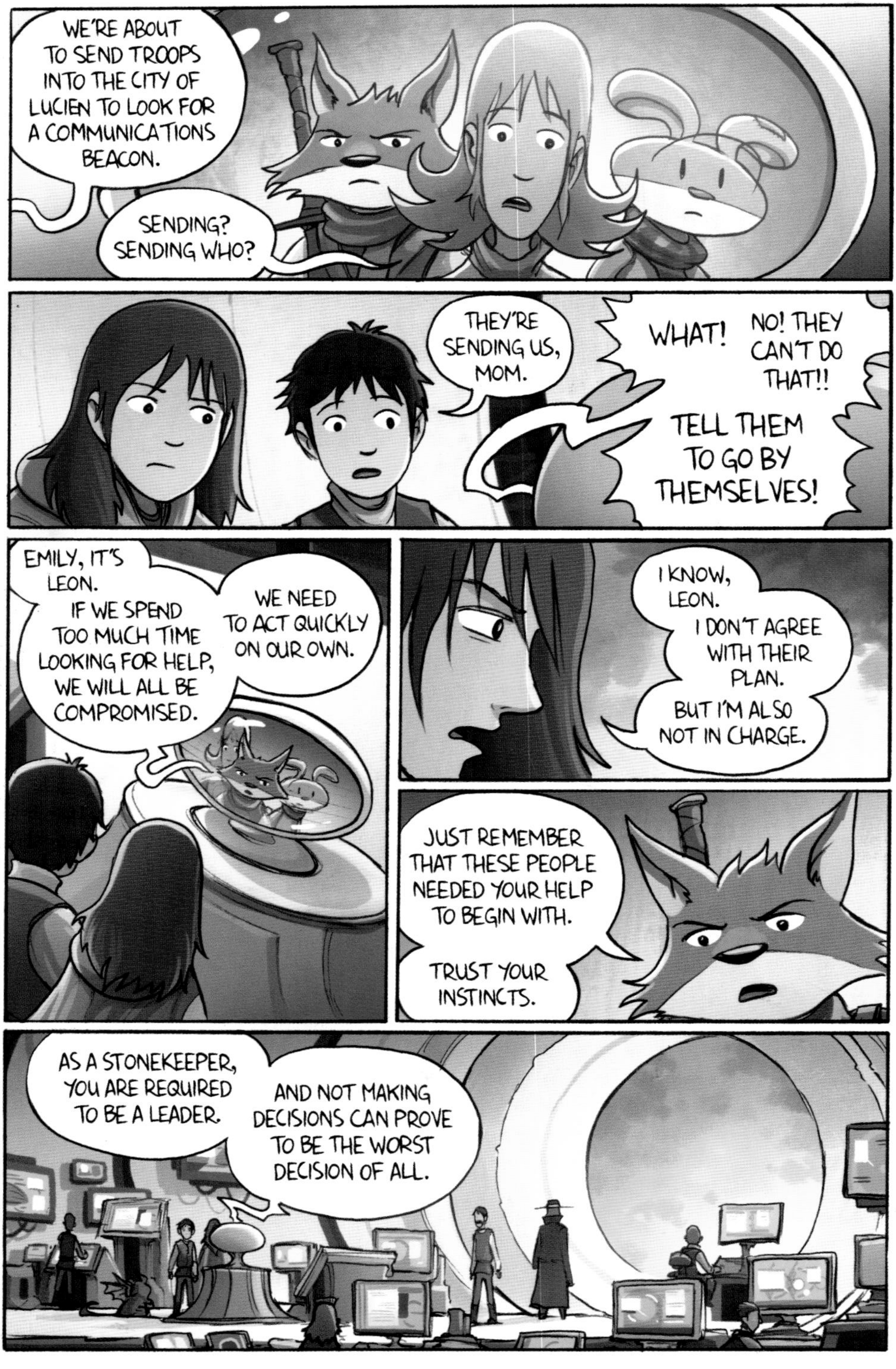
WE'RE ABOUT TO SEND TROOPS INTO THE CITY OF LUCIEN TO LOOK FOR A COMMUNICATIONS BEACON.
SENDING? SENDING WHO?
THEY'RE SENDING US, MOM.
WHAT!
NO! THEY CAN'T DO THAT!!
TELL THEM TO GO BY THEMSELVES!
EMILY, IT'S LEON.
IF WE SPEND TOO MUCH TIME LOOKING FOR HELP, WE WILL ALL BE COMPROMISED.
WE NEED TO ACT QUICKLY ON OUR OWN.
I KNOW, LEON.
I DON'T AGREE WITH THEIR PLAN.
BUT I'M ALSO NOT IN CHARGE.
JUST REMEMBER THAT THESE PEOPLE NEEDED YOUR HELP TO BEGIN WITH.
TRUST YOUR INSTINCTS.
AS A STONEKEEPER, YOU ARE REQUIRED TO BE A LEADER.
AND NOT MAKING DECISIONS CAN PROVE TO BE THE WORST DECISION OF ALL.

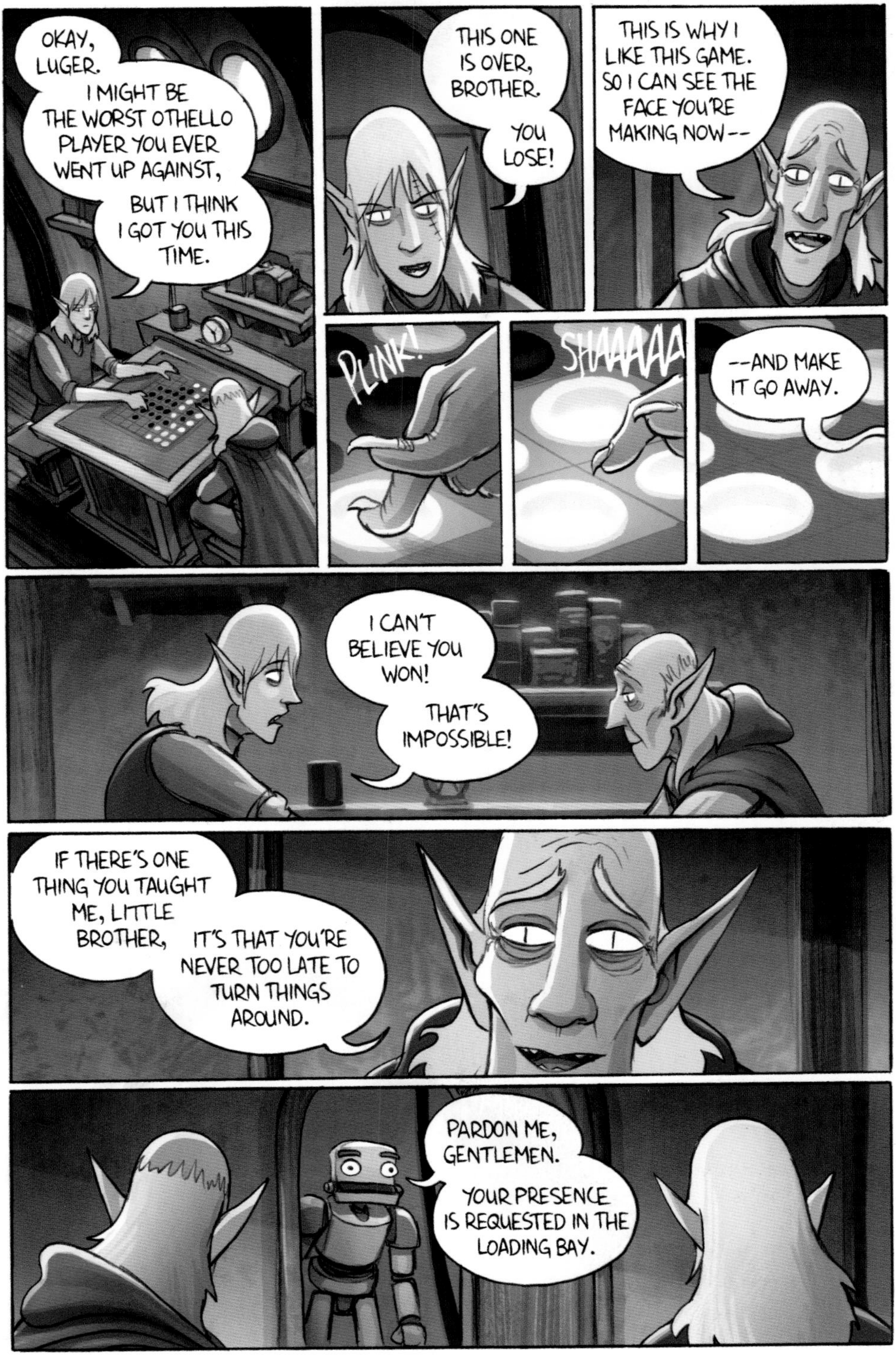

OKAY, LUGER.
I MIGHT BE THE WORST OTHELLO PLAYER YOU EVER WENT UP AGAINST,
BUT I THINK I GOT YOU THIS TIME.
THIS ONE IS OVER, BROTHER.
YOU LOSE!
THIS IS WHY I LIKE THIS GAME. SO I CAN SEE THE FACE YOU'RE MAKING NOW--
PLINK!
SHAAAAAA
--AND MAKE IT GO AWAY.
I CAN'T BELIEVE YOU WON!
THAT'S IMPOSSIBLE!
IF THERE'S ONE THING YOU TAUGHT ME, LITTLE BROTHER,
IT'S THAT YOU'RE NEVER TOO LATE TO TURN THINGS AROUND.
PARDON ME, GENTLEMEN.
YOUR PRESENCE IS REQUESTED IN THE LOADING BAY.

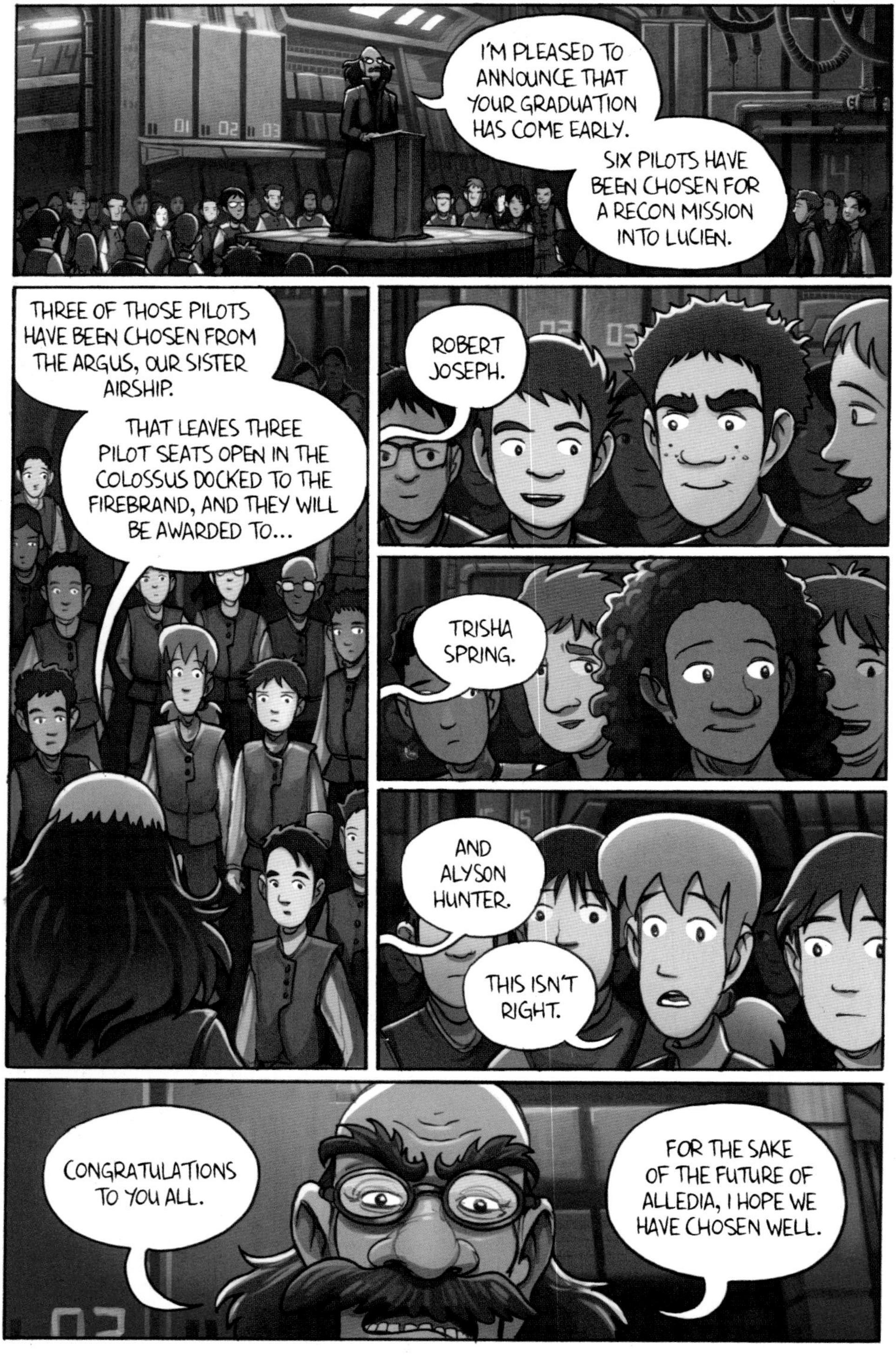
I'M PLEASED TO ANNOUNCE THAT YOUR GRADUATION HAS COME EARLY.
SIX PILOTS HAVE BEEN CHOSEN FOR A RECON MISSION INTO LUCIEN.
THREE OF THOSE PILOTS HAVE BEEN CHOSEN FROM THE ARGUS, OUR SISTER AIRSHIP.
THAT LEAVES THREE PILOT SEATS OPEN IN THE COLOSSUS DOCKED TO THE FIREBRAND, AND THEY WILL BE AWARDED TO...
ROBERT JOSEPH.
TRISHA SPRING.
AND ALYSON HUNTER.
THIS ISN'T RIGHT.
CONGRATULATIONS TO YOU ALL.
FOR THE SAKE OF THE FUTURE OF ALLEDIA, I HOPE WE HAVE CHOSEN WELL.

NAVIN, THEY'RE SUPPOSED TO PICK YOU!

DON'T WORRY.

HE CAN'T STOP ME FROM GETTING OUT THERE.

ONCE I FIND A WAY TO GET RID OF THIS BRACELET, I'LL JOIN YOU ON THE GROUND.

HERE, TAKE THIS.

WHAT IS IT?

IT'S AN OLD TWO-WAY RADIO.

MY DAD AND I USE THEM TO TALK WHEN THE SATLINK GOES DOWN.

CONGRATULATIONS, HUNTER.

STAY IN LINE AND YOU SHOULD BE TAKING YOUR FATHER'S PLACE IN NO TIME.

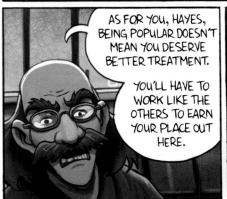

AS FOR YOU, HAYES, BEING POPULAR DOESN'T MEAN YOU DESERVE BETTER TREATMENT.

YOU'LL HAVE TO WORK LIKE THE OTHERS TO EARN YOUR PLACE OUT HERE.

AND I DON'T CARE WHAT THE PROPHECIES SAY.

YOU'RE STILL A SLACKER.

23

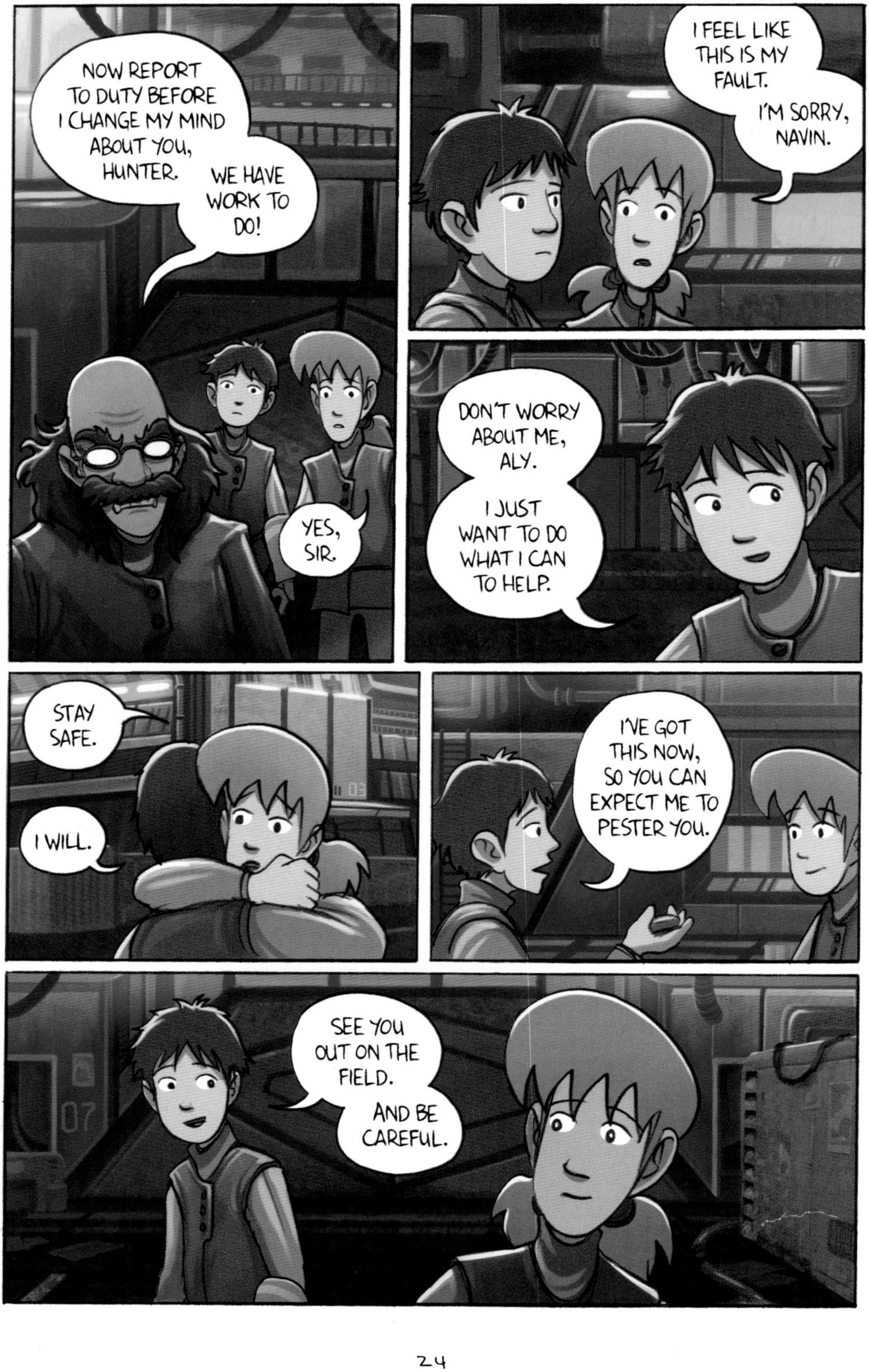
NOW REPORT TO DUTY BEFORE I CHANGE MY MIND ABOUT YOU, HUNTER.
WE HAVE WORK TO DO!
YES, SIR.
I FEEL LIKE THIS IS MY FAULT.
I'M SORRY, NAVIN.
DON'T WORRY ABOUT ME, ALY.
I JUST WANT TO DO WHAT I CAN TO HELP.
STAY SAFE.
I WILL.
I'VE GOT THIS NOW, SO YOU CAN EXPECT ME TO PESTER YOU.
SEE YOU OUT ON THE FIELD.
AND BE CAREFUL.

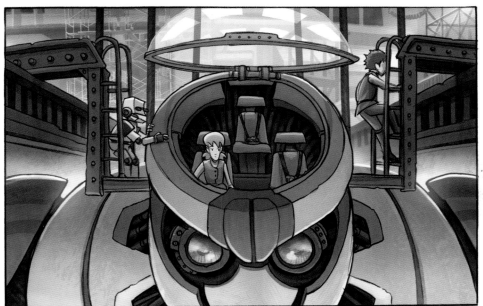

NEED ANY-
THING ELSE?

NO,
THANK
YOU.

HELLO
THERE,
ALY.

SORRY YOUR
BOYFRIEND
DIDN'T MAKE
THE CUT.

LOOKS LIKE
YOU'RE STUCK
HERE WITH
ME.

YOU GOT
IT WRONG,
PORCUPINE.

I'M THE RANKING
OFFICER ON THIS
COLOSSUS.

THAT MEANS
YOU'RE THE ONE
STUCK HERE
WITH ME.

OW!
MY
EAR!

25

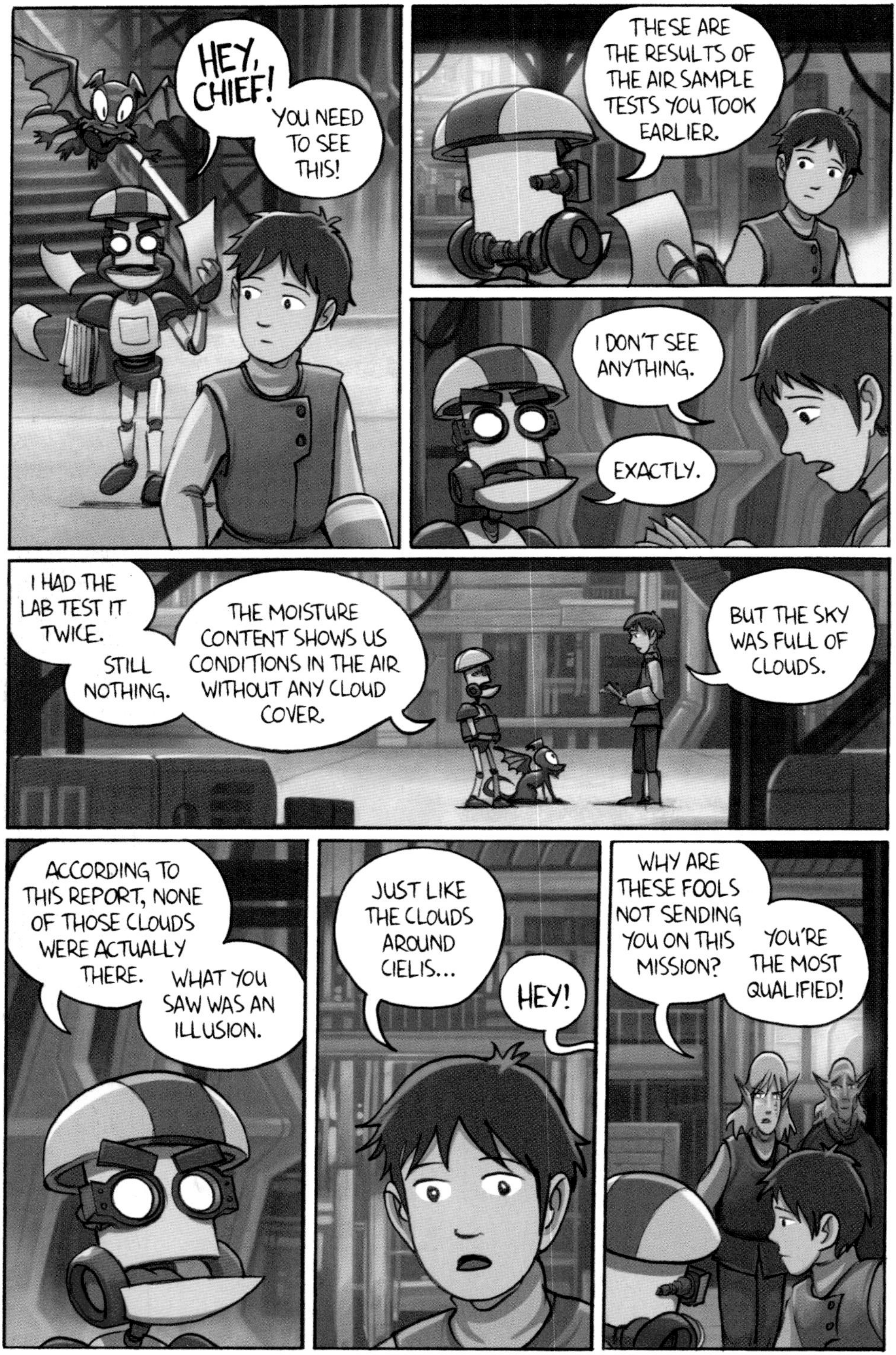
HEY, CHIEF!
YOU NEED TO SEE THIS!
THESE ARE THE RESULTS OF THE AIR SAMPLE TESTS YOU TOOK EARLIER.
I DON'T SEE ANYTHING.
EXACTLY.
I HAD THE LAB TEST IT TWICE.
STILL NOTHING.
THE MOISTURE CONTENT SHOWS US CONDITIONS IN THE AIR WITHOUT ANY CLOUD COVER.
BUT THE SKY WAS FULL OF CLOUDS.
ACCORDING TO THIS REPORT, NONE OF THOSE CLOUDS WERE ACTUALLY THERE.
WHAT YOU SAW WAS AN ILLUSION.
JUST LIKE THE CLOUDS AROUND CIELIS...
HEY!
WHY ARE THESE FOOLS NOT SENDING YOU ON THIS MISSION?
YOU'RE THE MOST QUALIFIED!

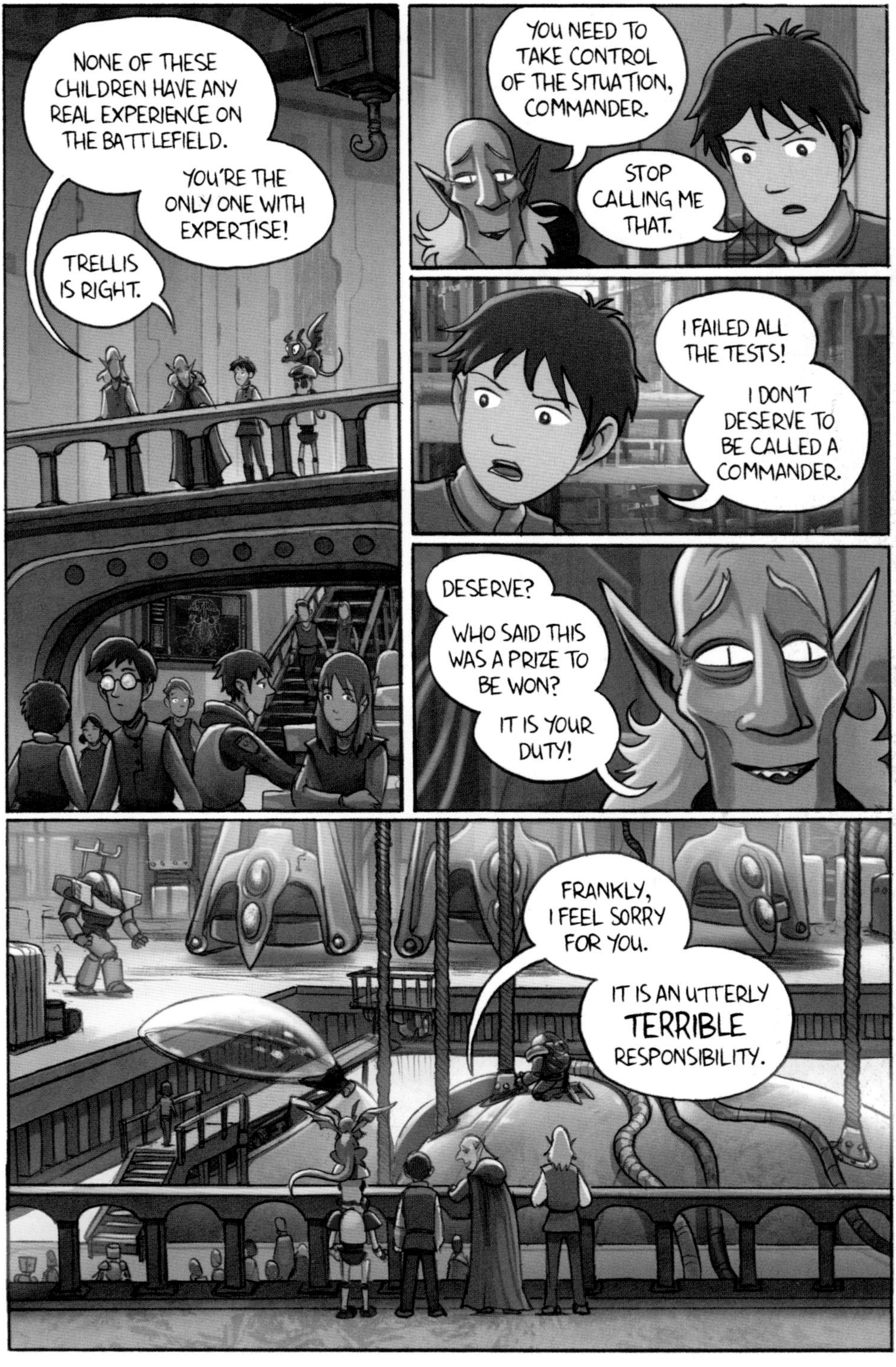
NONE OF THESE CHILDREN HAVE ANY REAL EXPERIENCE ON THE BATTLEFIELD.
YOU'RE THE ONLY ONE WITH EXPERTISE!
TRELLIS IS RIGHT.
YOU NEED TO TAKE CONTROL OF THE SITUATION, COMMANDER.
STOP CALLING ME THAT.
I FAILED ALL THE TESTS!
I DON'T DESERVE TO BE CALLED A COMMANDER.
DESERVE?
WHO SAID THIS WAS A PRIZE TO BE WON?
IT IS YOUR DUTY!
FRANKLY, I FEEL SORRY FOR YOU.
IT IS AN UTTERLY TERRIBLE RESPONSIBILITY.

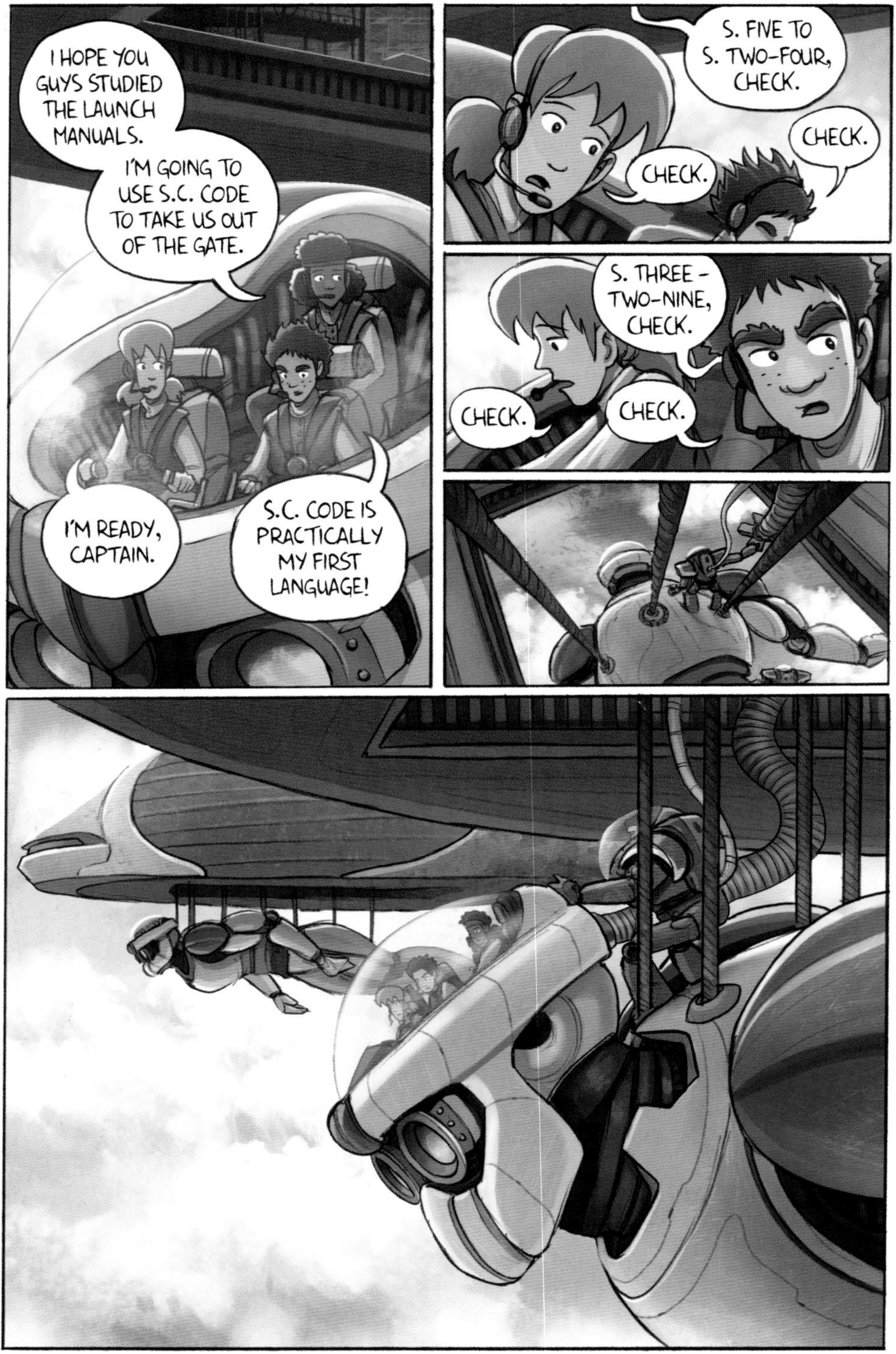
I HOPE YOU GUYS STUDIED THE LAUNCH MANUALS.
I'M GOING TO USE S.C. CODE TO TAKE US OUT OF THE GATE.
I'M READY, CAPTAIN.
S.C. CODE IS PRACTICALLY MY FIRST LANGUAGE!
S. FIVE TO S. TWO-FOUR, CHECK.
CHECK.
CHECK.
S. THREE-TWO-NINE, CHECK.
CHECK.
CHECK.

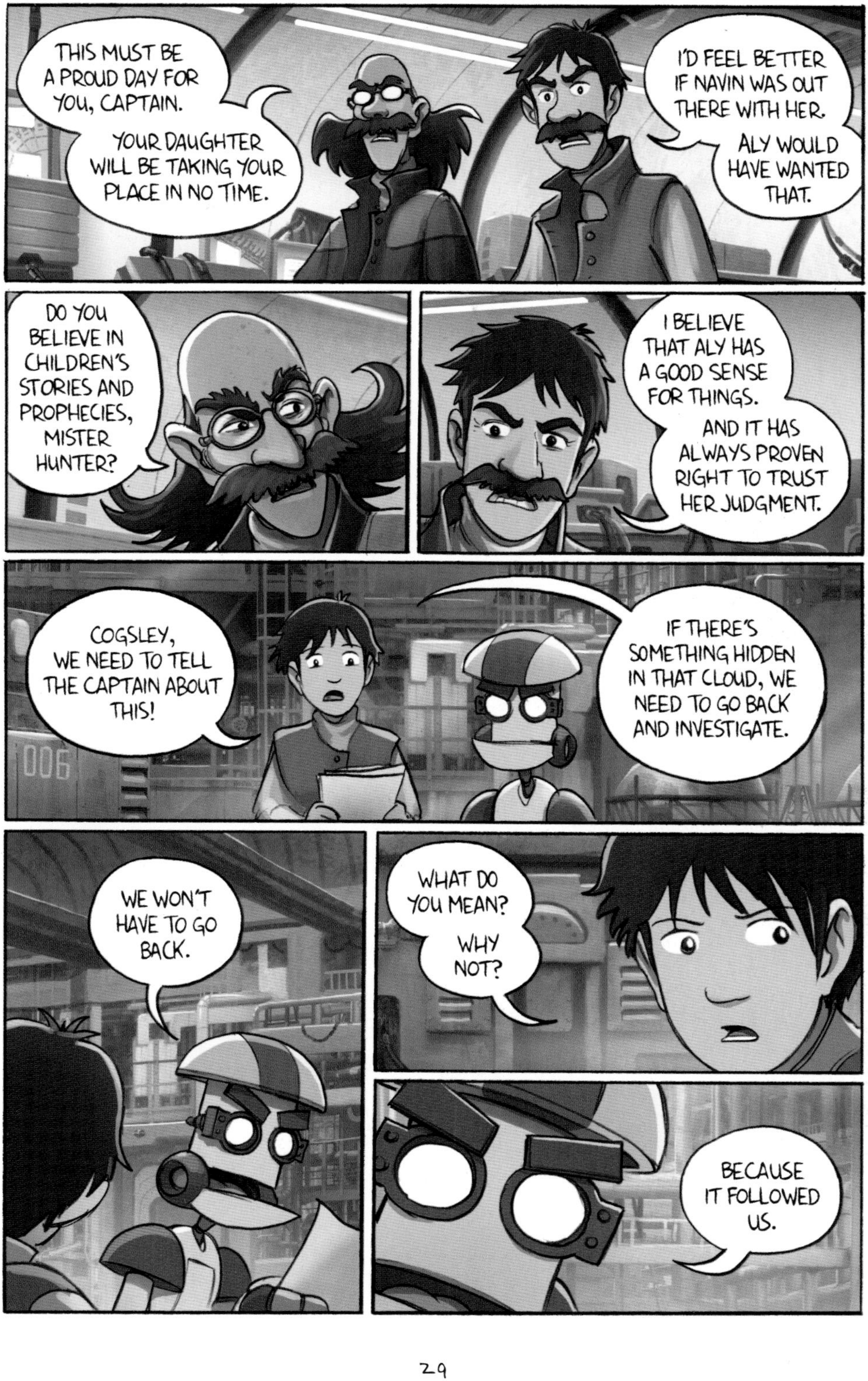
THIS MUST BE A PROUD DAY FOR YOU, CAPTAIN.
YOUR DAUGHTER WILL BE TAKING YOUR PLACE IN NO TIME.
I'D FEEL BETTER IF NAVIN WAS OUT THERE WITH HER.
ALY WOULD HAVE WANTED THAT.
DO YOU BELIEVE IN CHILDREN'S STORIES AND PROPHECIES, MISTER HUNTER?
I BELIEVE THAT ALY HAS A GOOD SENSE FOR THINGS.
AND IT HAS ALWAYS PROVEN RIGHT TO TRUST HER JUDGMENT.
COGSLEY, WE NEED TO TELL THE CAPTAIN ABOUT THIS!
IF THERE'S SOMETHING HIDDEN IN THAT CLOUD, WE NEED TO GO BACK AND INVESTIGATE.
006
WE WON'T HAVE TO GO BACK.
WHAT DO YOU MEAN?
WHY NOT?
BECAUSE IT FOLLOWED US.

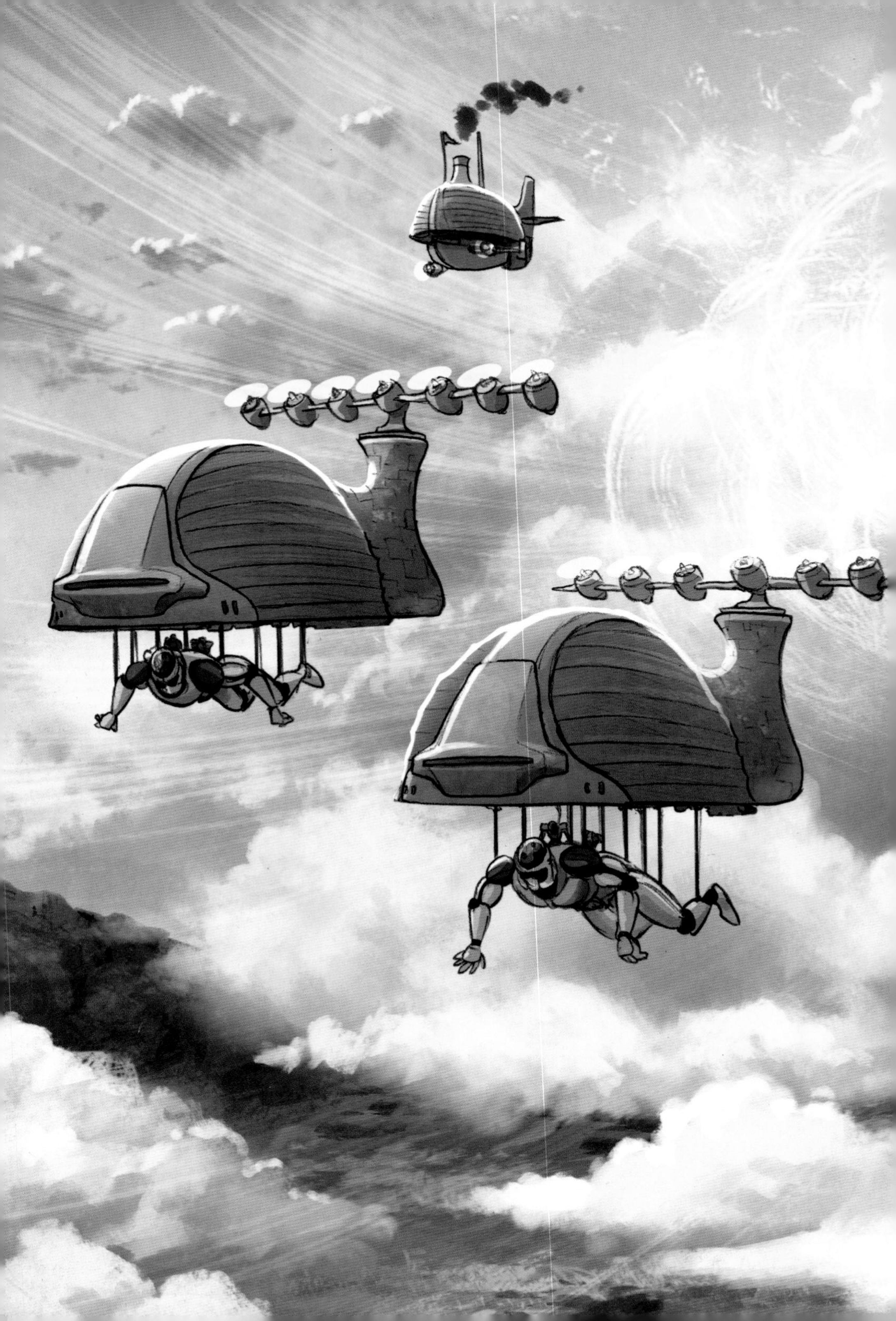

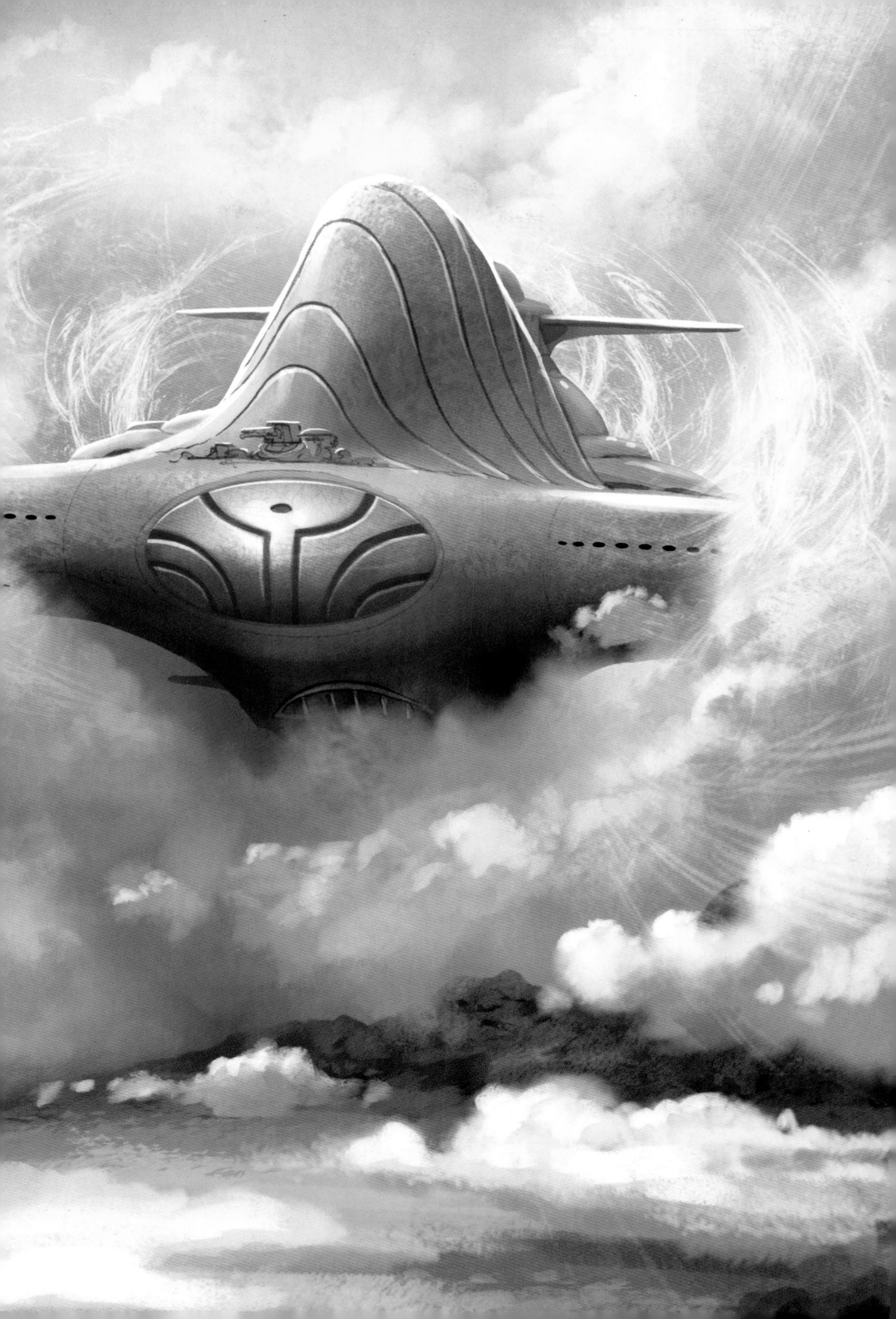

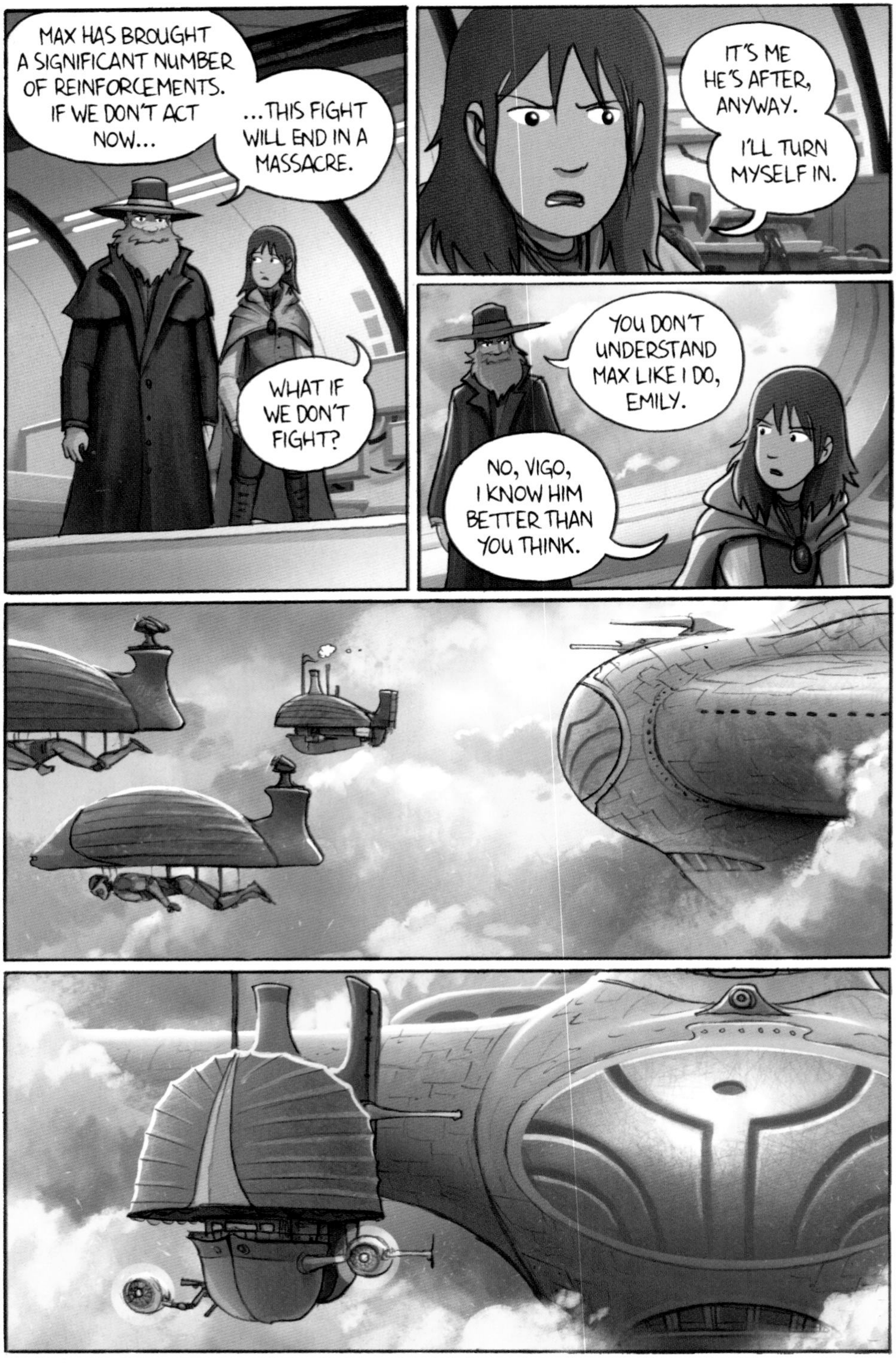
MAX HAS BROUGHT A SIGNIFICANT NUMBER OF REINFORCEMENTS. IF WE DON'T ACT NOW...
...THIS FIGHT WILL END IN A MASSACRE.
WHAT IF WE DON'T FIGHT?
IT'S ME HE'S AFTER, ANYWAY.
I'LL TURN MYSELF IN.
YOU DON'T UNDERSTAND MAX LIKE I DO, EMILY.
NO, VIGO, I KNOW HIM BETTER THAN YOU THINK.

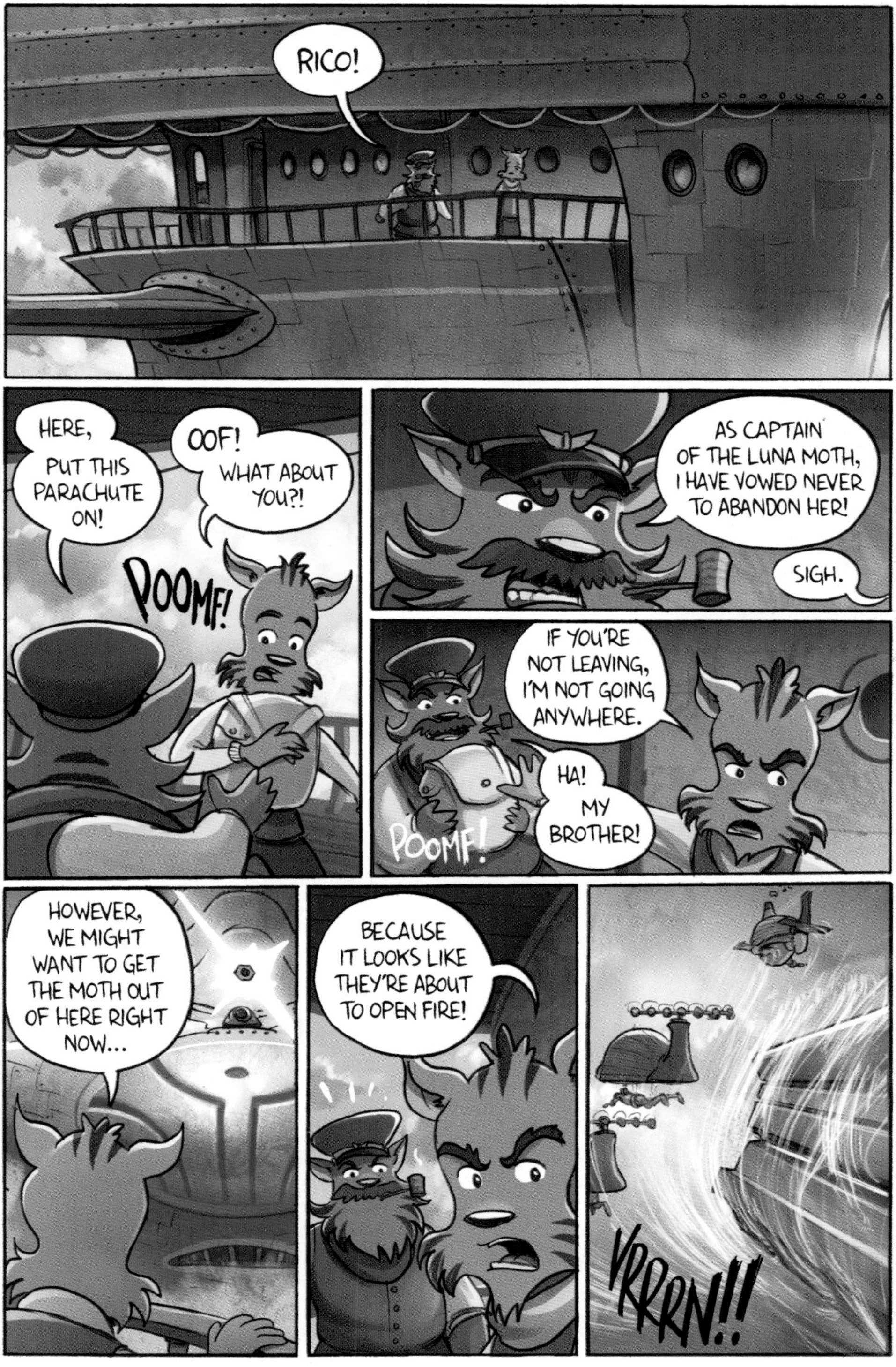
RICO!
HERE, PUT THIS PARACHUTE ON!
OOF!
WHAT ABOUT YOU?!
POOMF!
AS CAPTAIN OF THE LUNA MOTH, I HAVE VOWED NEVER TO ABANDON HER!
SIGH.
IF YOU'RE NOT LEAVING, I'M NOT GOING ANYWHERE.
HA!
MY BROTHER!
POOMF!
HOWEVER, WE MIGHT WANT TO GET THE MOTH OUT OF HERE RIGHT NOW...
BECAUSE IT LOOKS LIKE THEY'RE ABOUT TO OPEN FIRE!
VRRRN!!

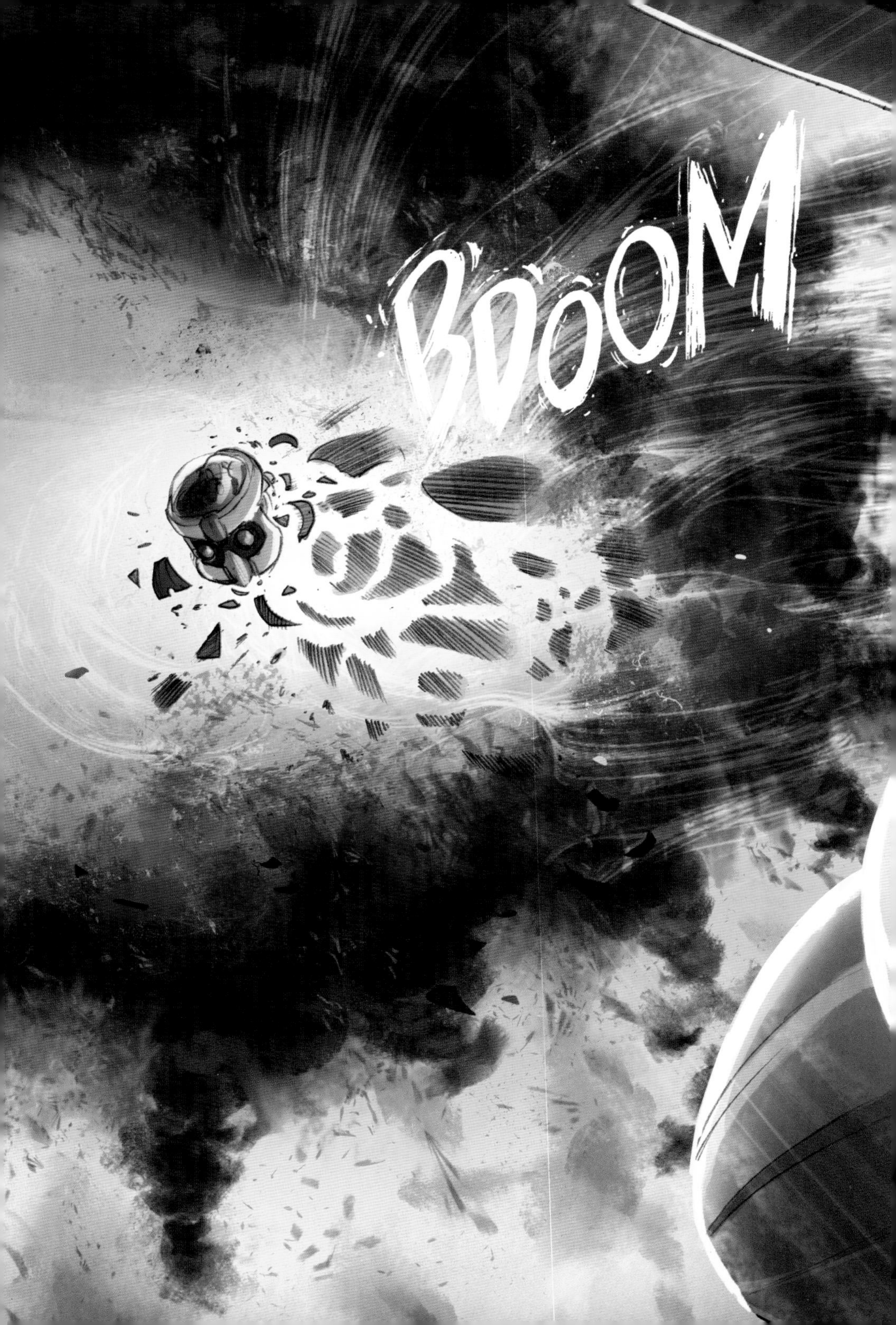
BOOOM

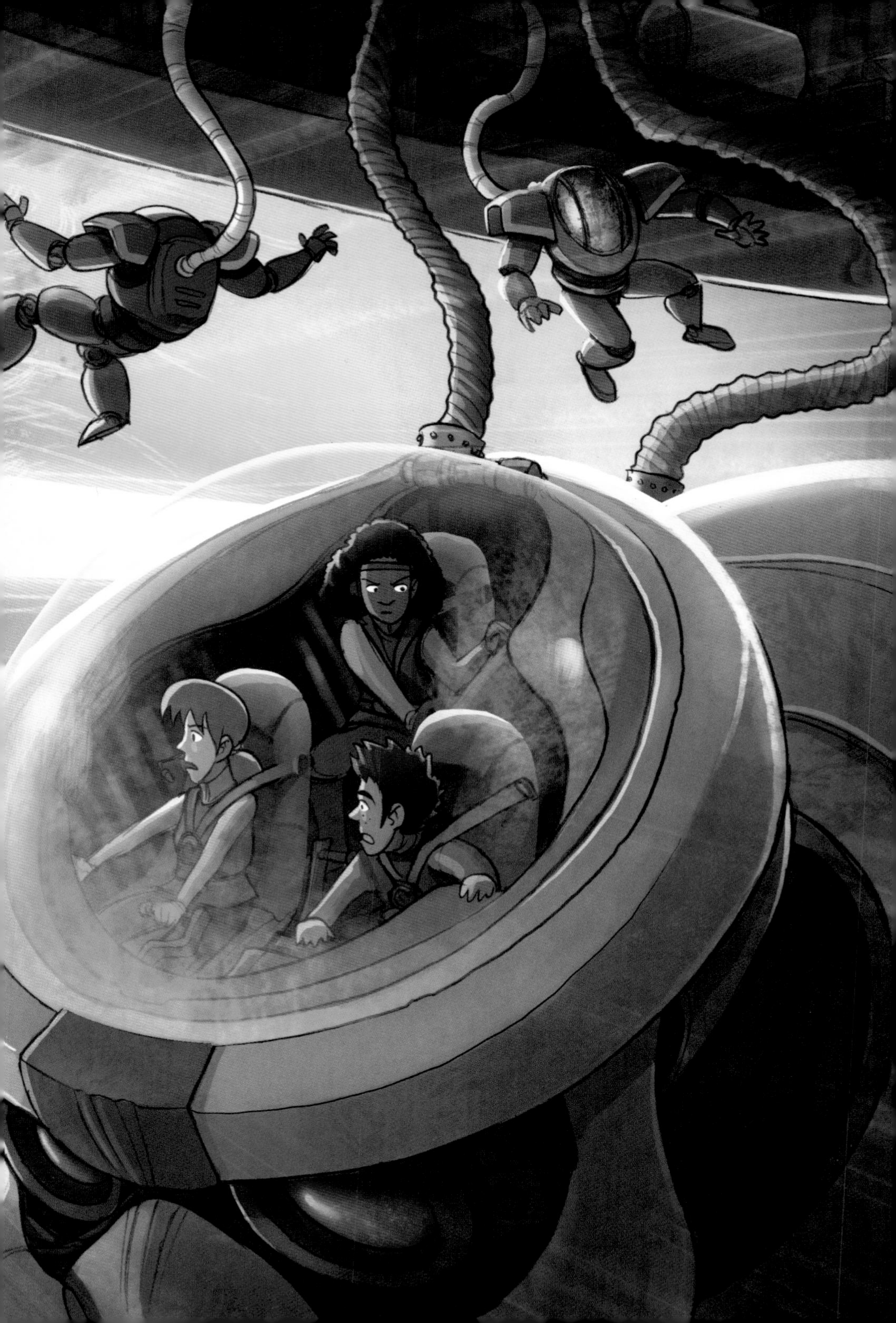

DID YOU SEE THAT?!

THEY'RE-- THEY'RE ALL GONE!!!

STAY FOCUSED!

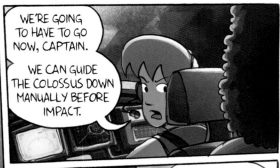

WE'RE GOING TO HAVE TO GO NOW, CAPTAIN.

WE CAN GUIDE THE COLOSSUS DOWN MANUALLY BEFORE IMPACT.

IT SAYS WE'RE STILL TEN MINUTES FROM A SAFE DROP ALTITUDE, HUNTER.

JUST GIVE IT A LITTLE MORE TIME.

MREEEMREEEMRE

EXCUSE ME!

OUT OF MY WAY!

YOU'RE GOING THE WRONG WAY, KID!!

WE NEED TO EVACUATE!!

HEY!

WATCH IT!!

COMING THROUGH!

PROFESSOR!

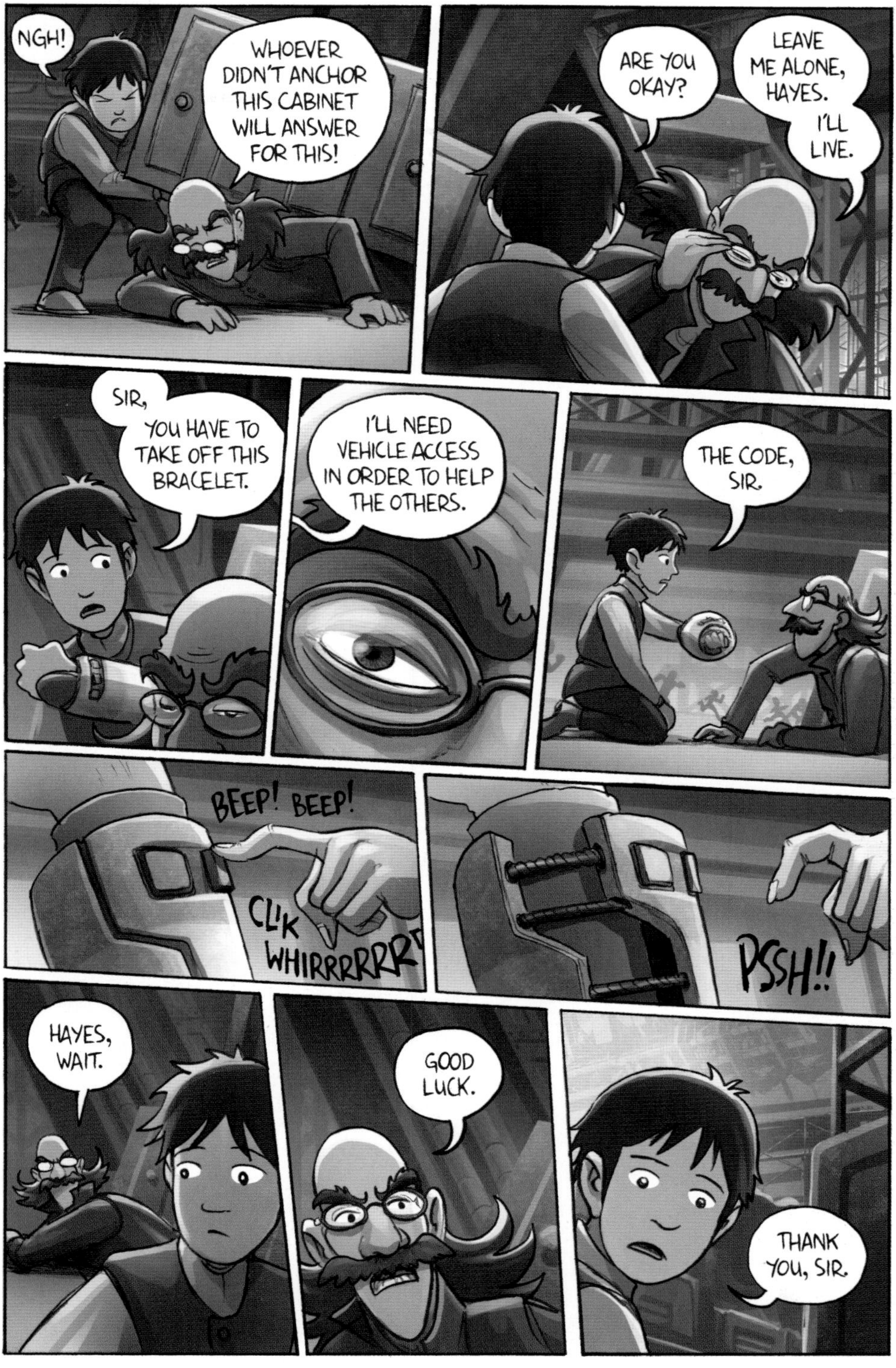
NGH!
WHOEVER DIDN'T ANCHOR THIS CABINET WILL ANSWER FOR THIS!
ARE YOU OKAY?
LEAVE ME ALONE, HAYES.
I'LL LIVE.
SIR,
YOU HAVE TO TAKE OFF THIS BRACELET.
I'LL NEED VEHICLE ACCESS IN ORDER TO HELP THE OTHERS.
THE CODE, SIR.
BEEP! BEEP!
CLIK
WHIRRRRRRT
PSSH!!
HAYES, WAIT.
GOOD LUCK.
THANK YOU, SIR.

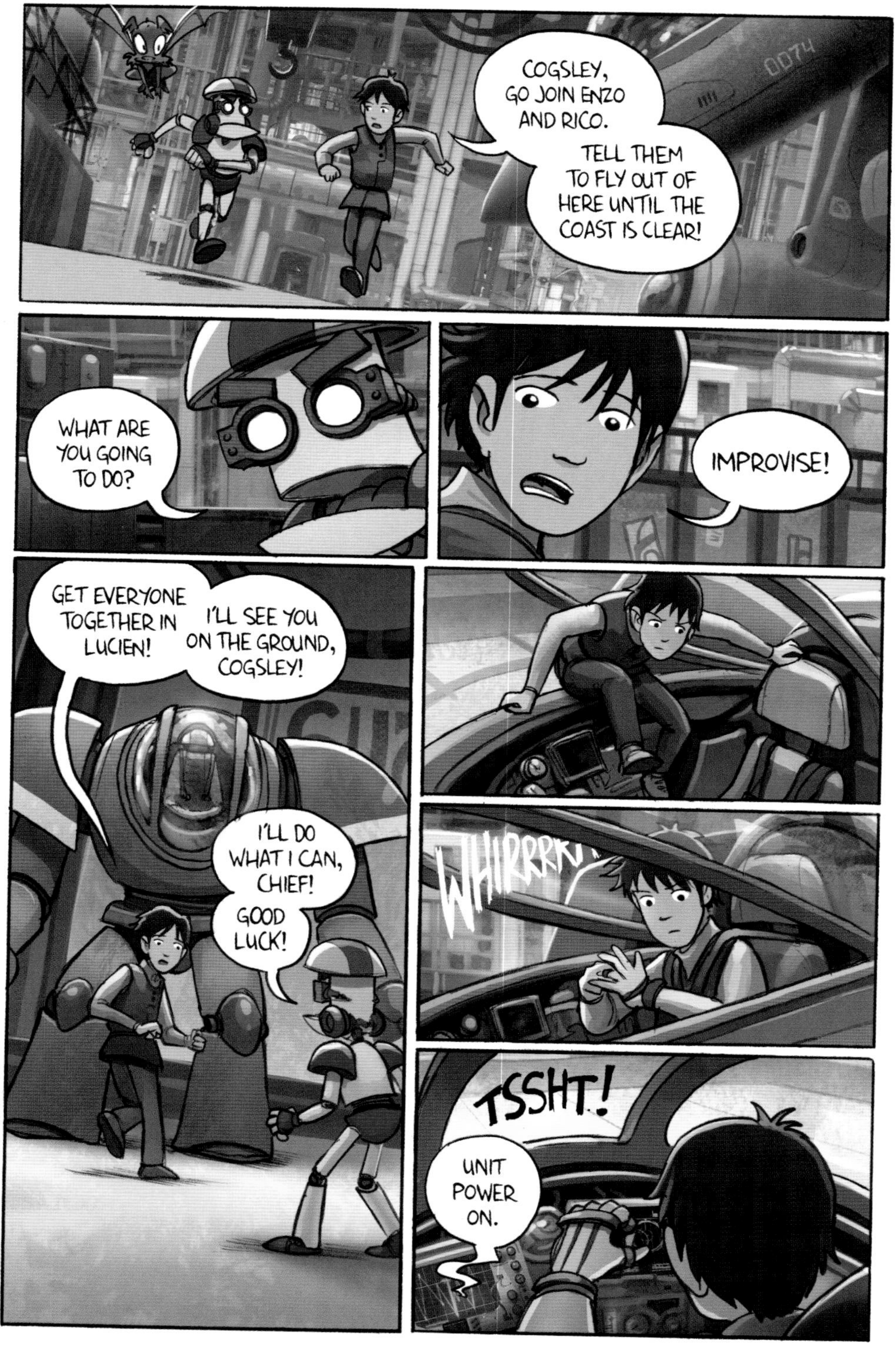
COGSLEY, GO JOIN ENZO AND RICO.
TELL THEM TO FLY OUT OF HERE UNTIL THE COAST IS CLEAR!
WHAT ARE YOU GOING TO DO?
IMPROVISE!
GET EVERYONE TOGETHER IN LUCIEN!
I'LL SEE YOU ON THE GROUND, COGSLEY!
I'LL DO WHAT I CAN, CHIEF!
GOOD LUCK!
WHIRRRK
TSSHT!
UNIT POWER ON.

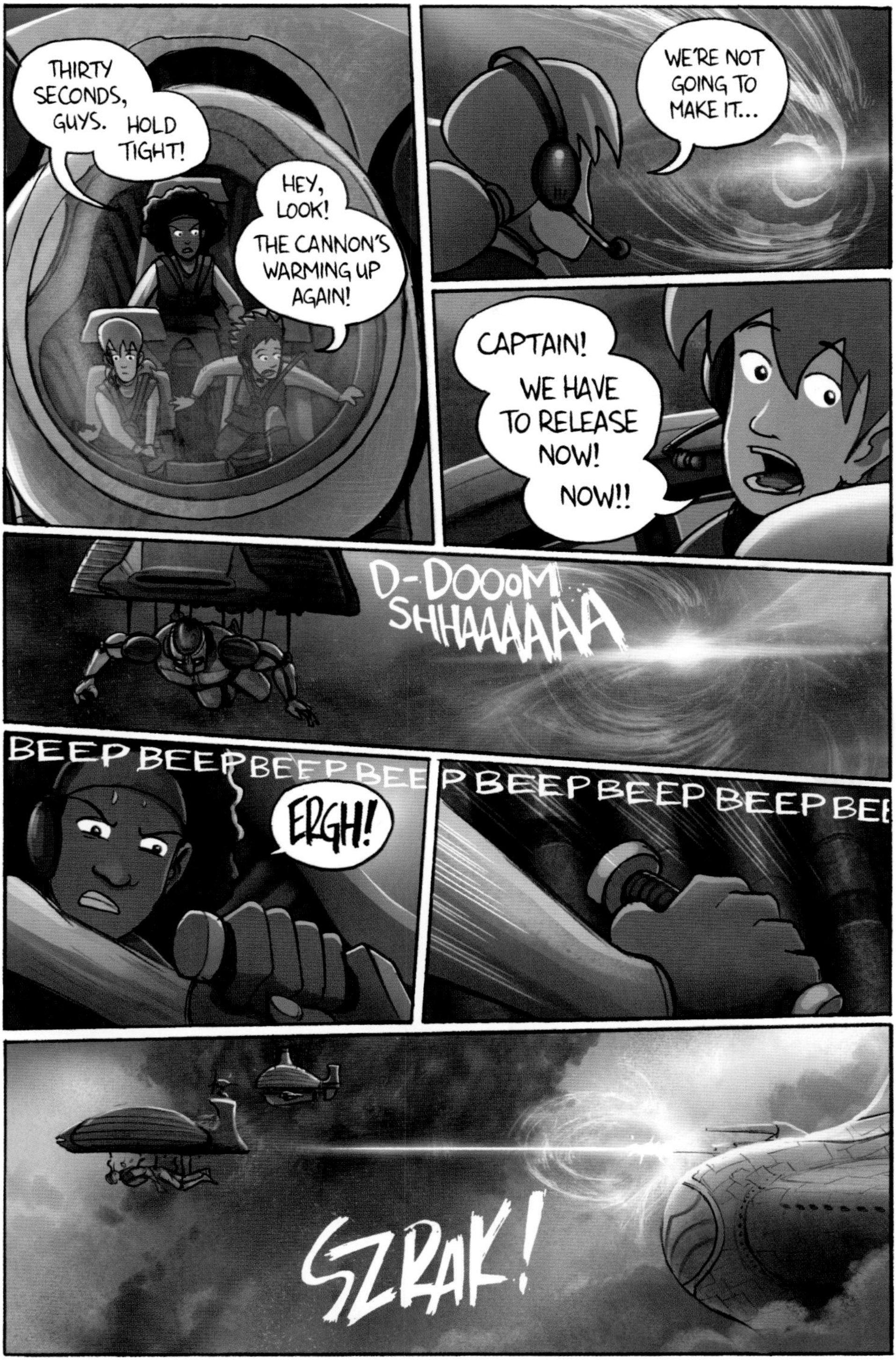

THIRTY SECONDS, GUYS.
HOLD TIGHT!
HEY, LOOK!
THE CANNON'S WARMING UP AGAIN!
WE'RE NOT GOING TO MAKE IT...
CAPTAIN!
WE HAVE TO RELEASE NOW!
NOW!!
D-DOOoM
SHHAAAAAA
BEEP BEEP BEEP BEEP
ERGH!
BEEP BEEP BEEP BEEP
SZRAK!

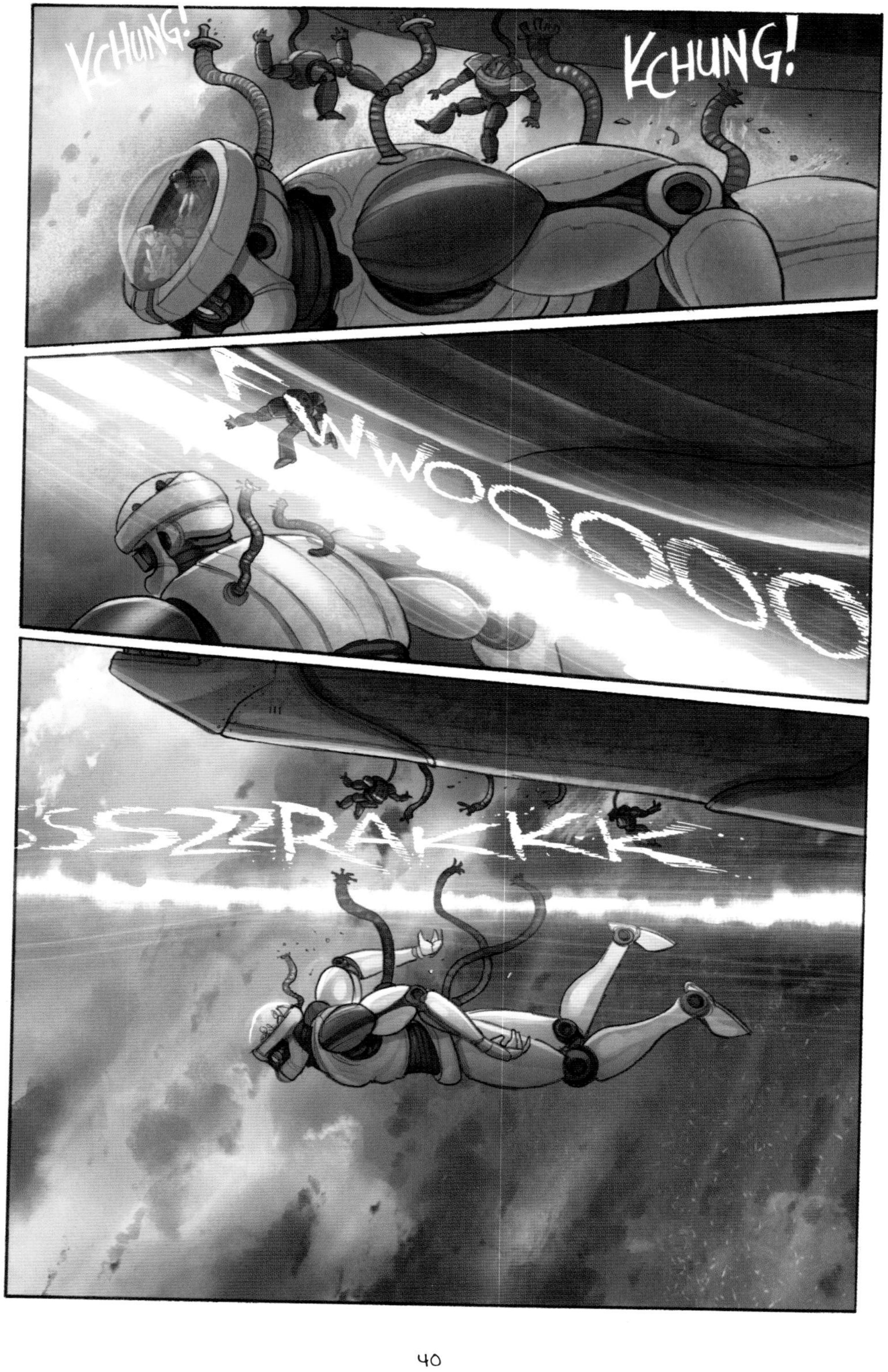
KCHUNG!
KCHUNG!
FWWOOOOOO
SSZZRAKKK

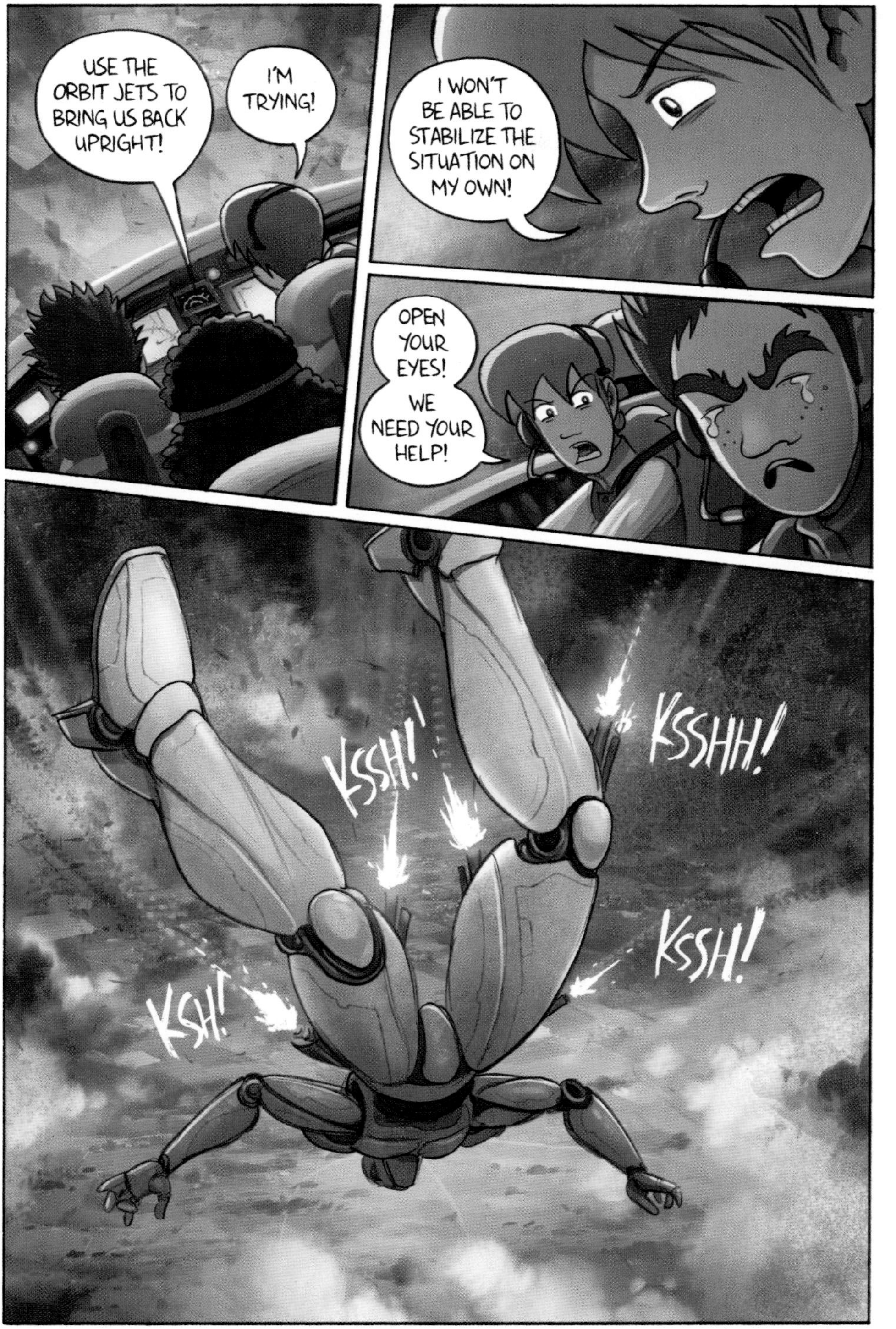
USE THE ORBIT JETS TO BRING US BACK UPRIGHT!
I'M TRYING!
I WON'T BE ABLE TO STABILIZE THE SITUATION ON MY OWN!
OPEN YOUR EYES!
WE NEED YOUR HELP!
KSSH!
KSSHH!
KSH!
KSSH!

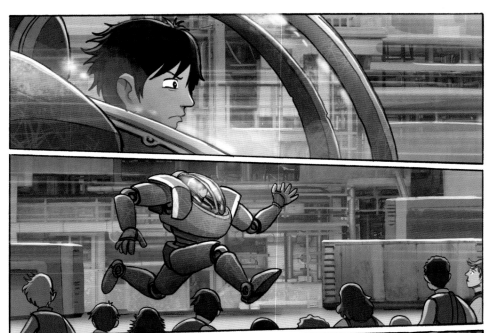

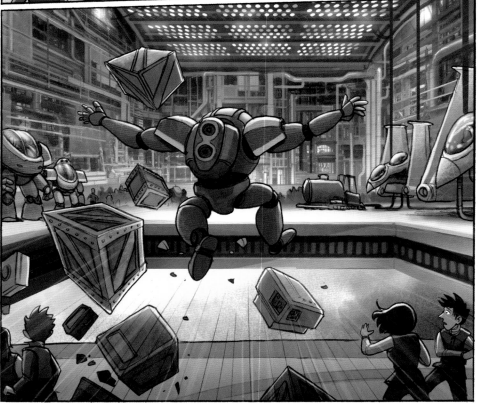

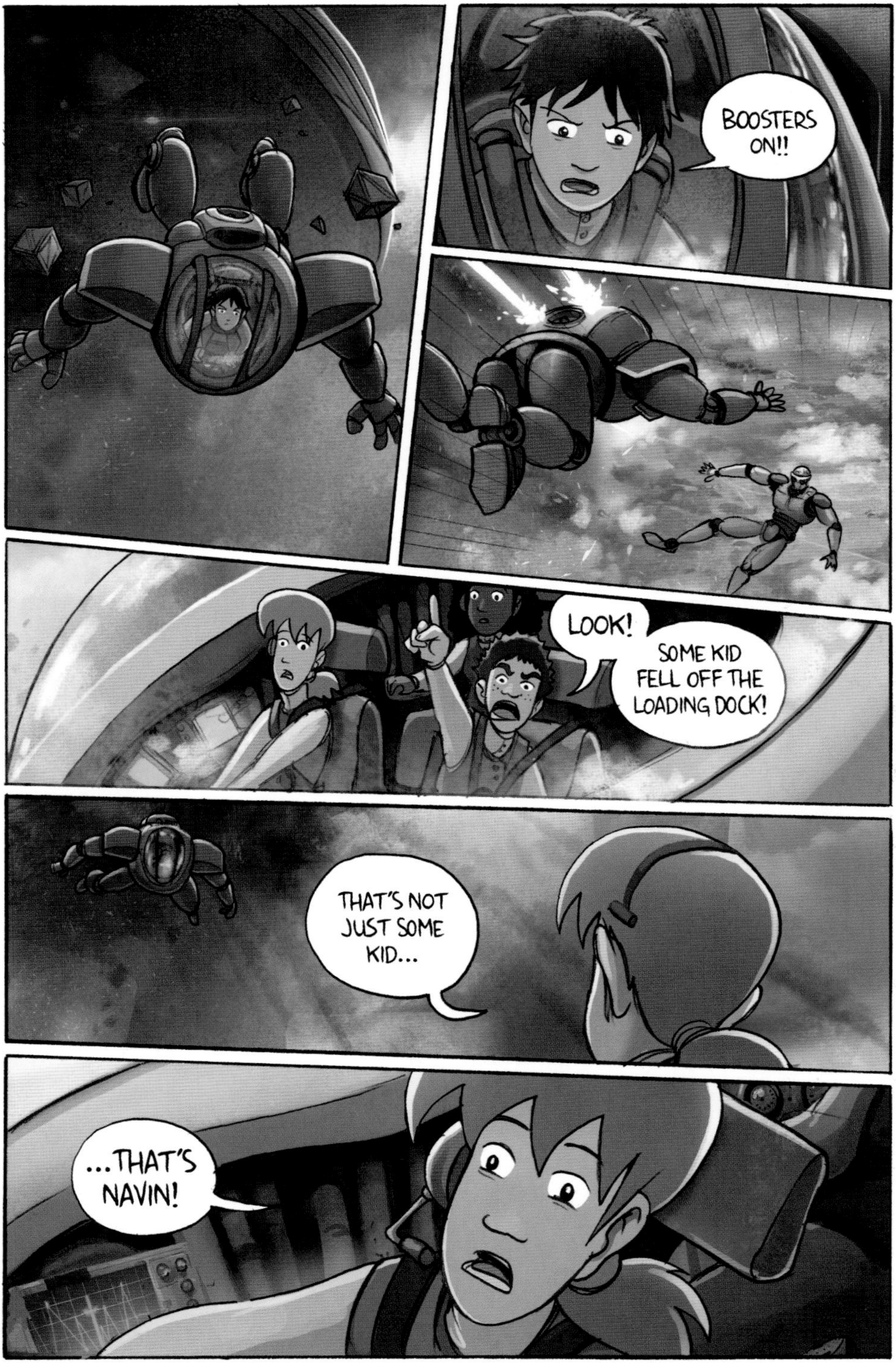
BOOSTERS ON!!
LOOK!
SOME KID FELL OFF THE LOADING DOCK!
THAT'S NOT JUST SOME KID...
...THAT'S NAVIN!

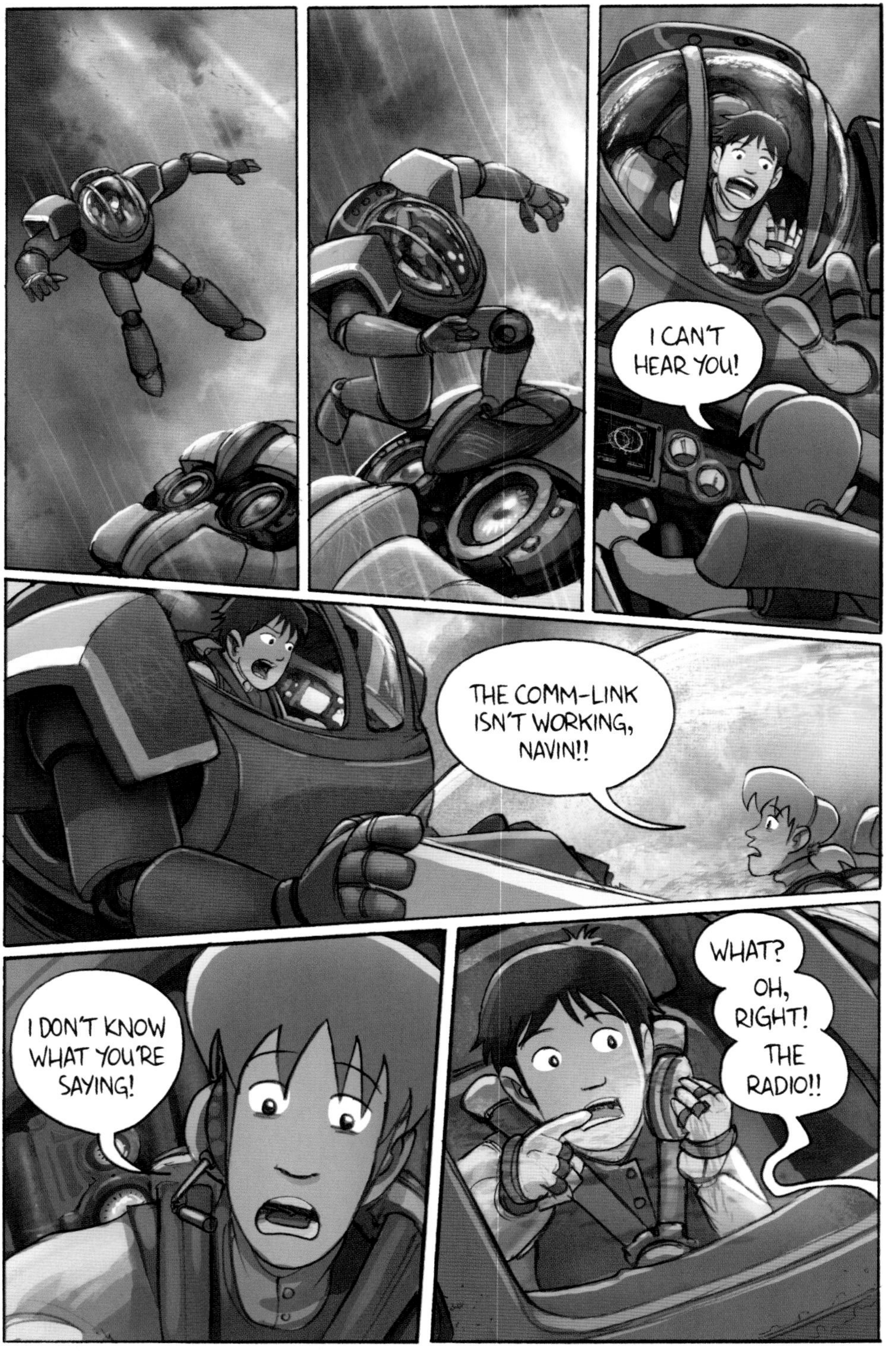
I CAN'T HEAR YOU!
THE COMM-LINK ISN'T WORKING, NAVIN!!
I DON'T KNOW WHAT YOU'RE SAYING!
WHAT?
OH, RIGHT!
THE RADIO!!

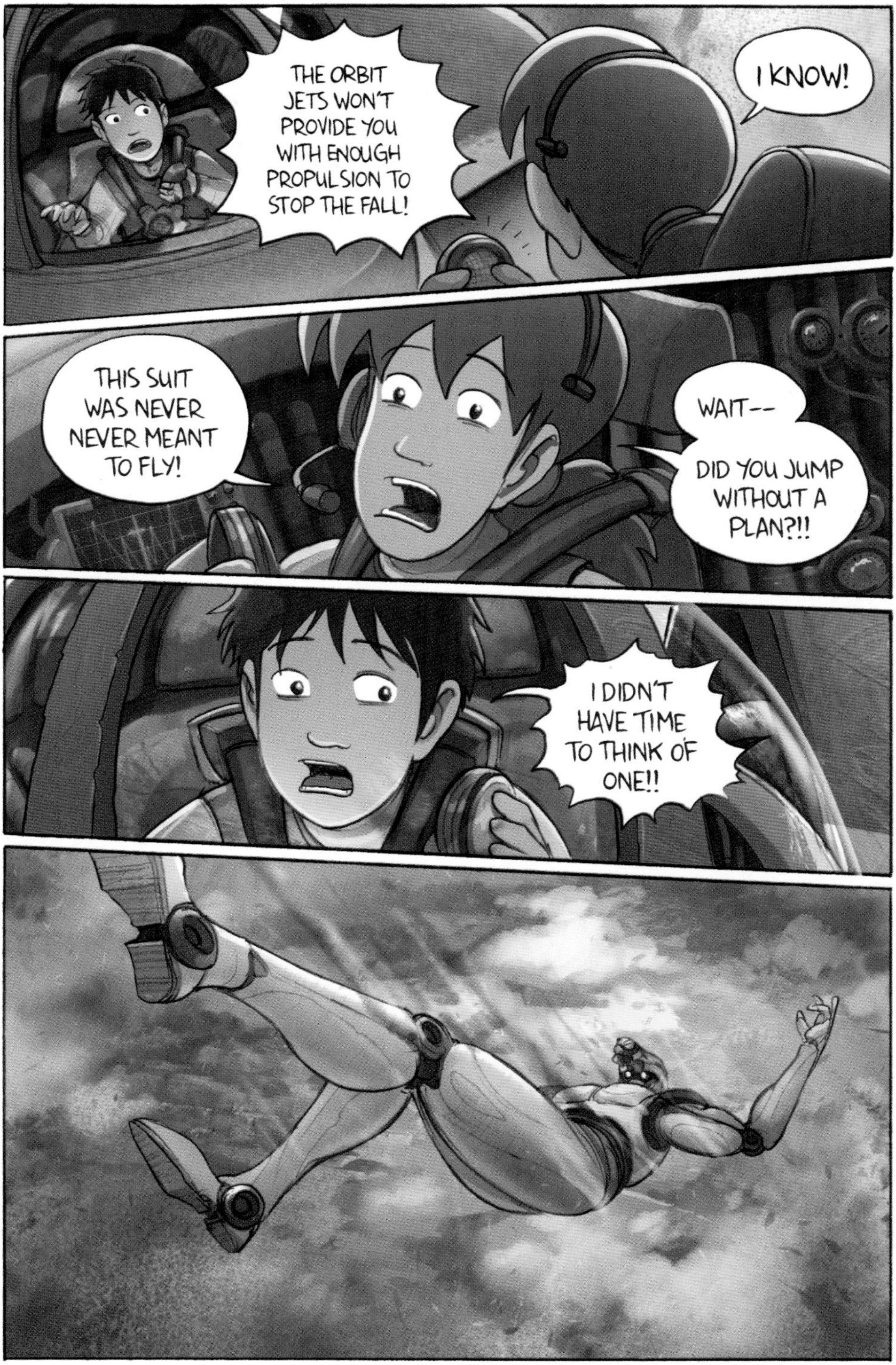
THE ORBIT JETS WON'T PROVIDE YOU WITH ENOUGH PROPULSION TO STOP THE FALL!
I KNOW!
THIS SUIT WAS NEVER NEVER MEANT TO FLY!
WAIT--
DID YOU JUMP WITHOUT A PLAN?!!
I DIDN'T HAVE TIME TO THINK OF ONE!!

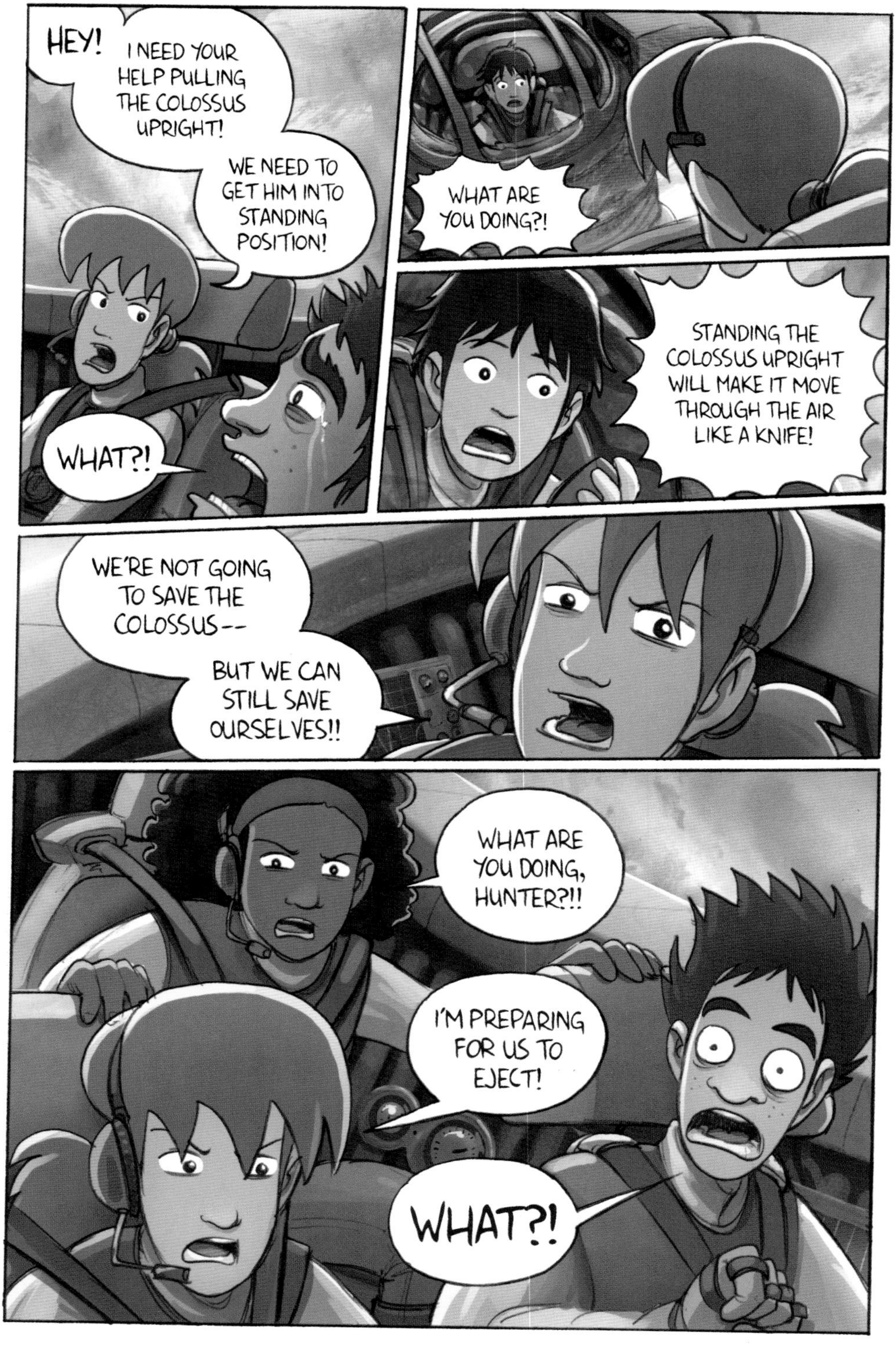
HEY! I NEED YOUR HELP PULLING THE COLOSSUS UPRIGHT!
WE NEED TO GET HIM INTO STANDING POSITION!
WHAT?!
WHAT ARE YOU DOING?!
STANDING THE COLOSSUS UPRIGHT WILL MAKE IT MOVE THROUGH THE AIR LIKE A KNIFE!
WE'RE NOT GOING TO SAVE THE COLOSSUS--
BUT WE CAN STILL SAVE OURSELVES!!
WHAT ARE YOU DOING, HUNTER?!!
I'M PREPARING FOR US TO EJECT!
WHAT?!

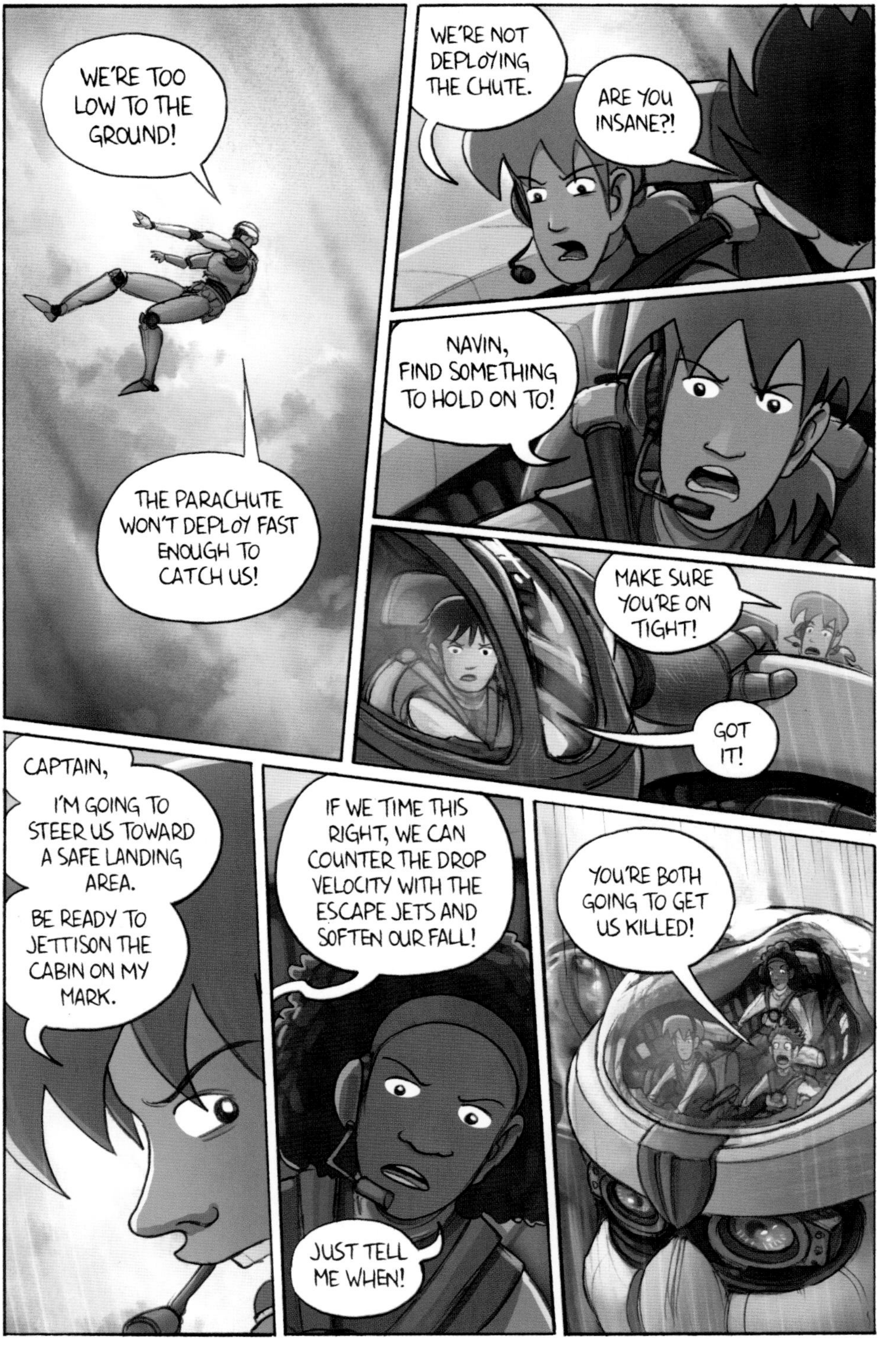
WE'RE TOO LOW TO THE GROUND!
THE PARACHUTE WON'T DEPLOY FAST ENOUGH TO CATCH US!
WE'RE NOT DEPLOYING THE CHUTE.
ARE YOU INSANE?!
NAVIN, FIND SOMETHING TO HOLD ON TO!
MAKE SURE YOU'RE ON TIGHT!
GOT IT!
CAPTAIN,
I'M GOING TO STEER US TOWARD A SAFE LANDING AREA.
BE READY TO JETTISON THE CABIN ON MY MARK.
IF WE TIME THIS RIGHT, WE CAN COUNTER THE DROP VELOCITY WITH THE ESCAPE JETS AND SOFTEN OUR FALL!
JUST TELL ME WHEN!
YOU'RE BOTH GOING TO GET US KILLED!

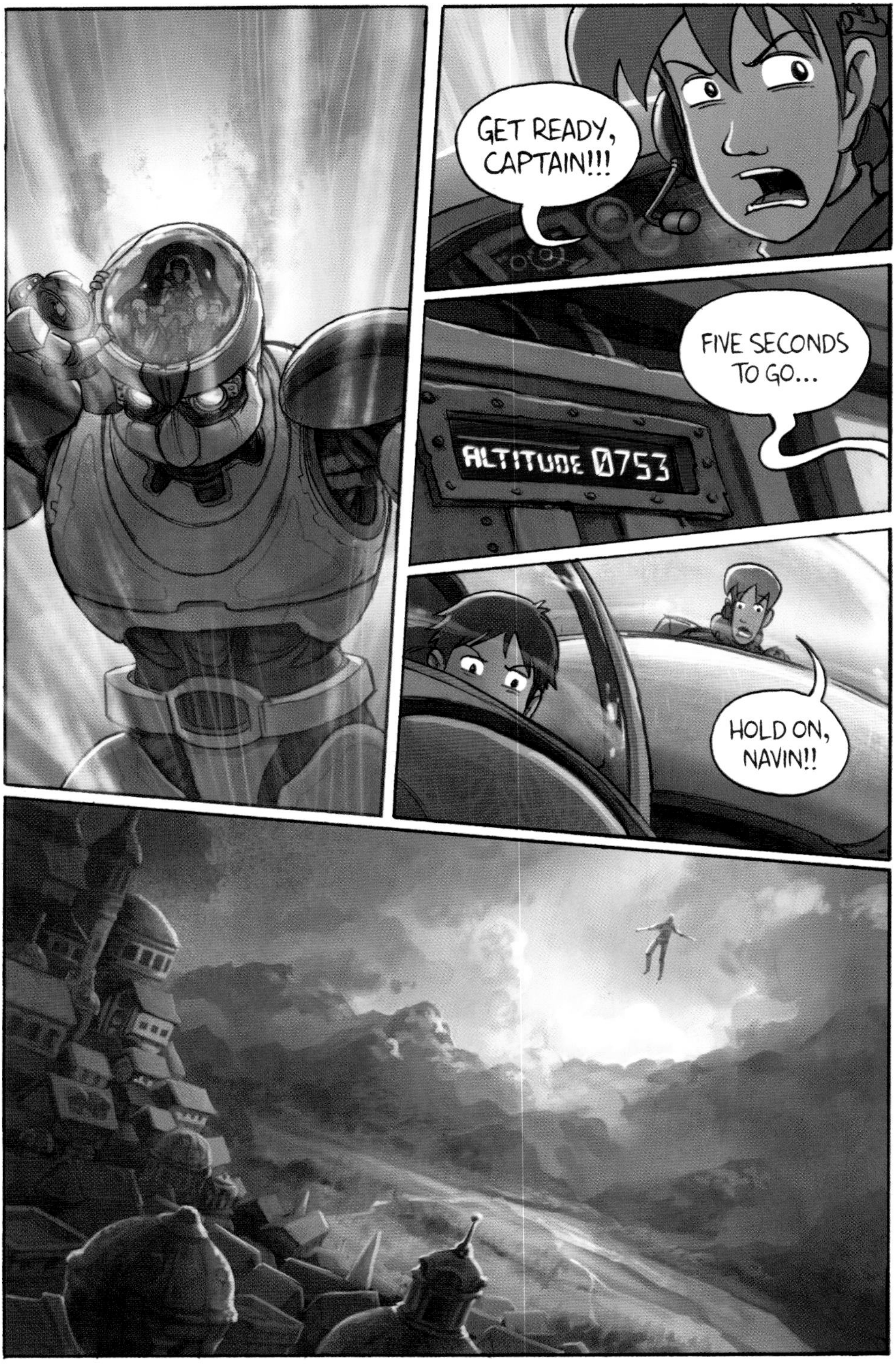
GET READY, CAPTAIN!!!
FIVE SECONDS TO GO...
ALTITUDE 0753
HOLD ON, NAVIN!!

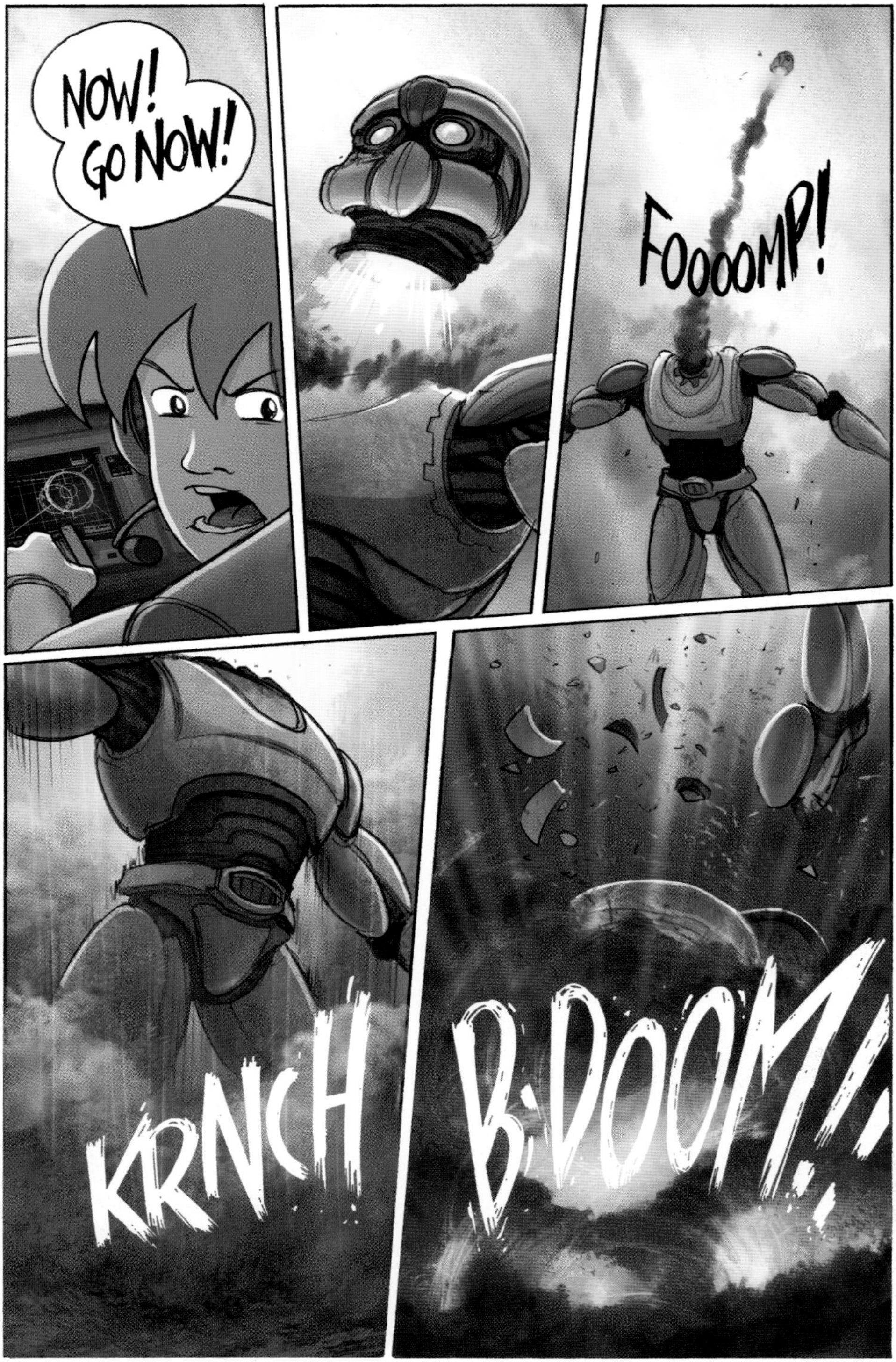
NOW! GO NOW!
FOOOOMP!
KRNCH
B-DOOM!!

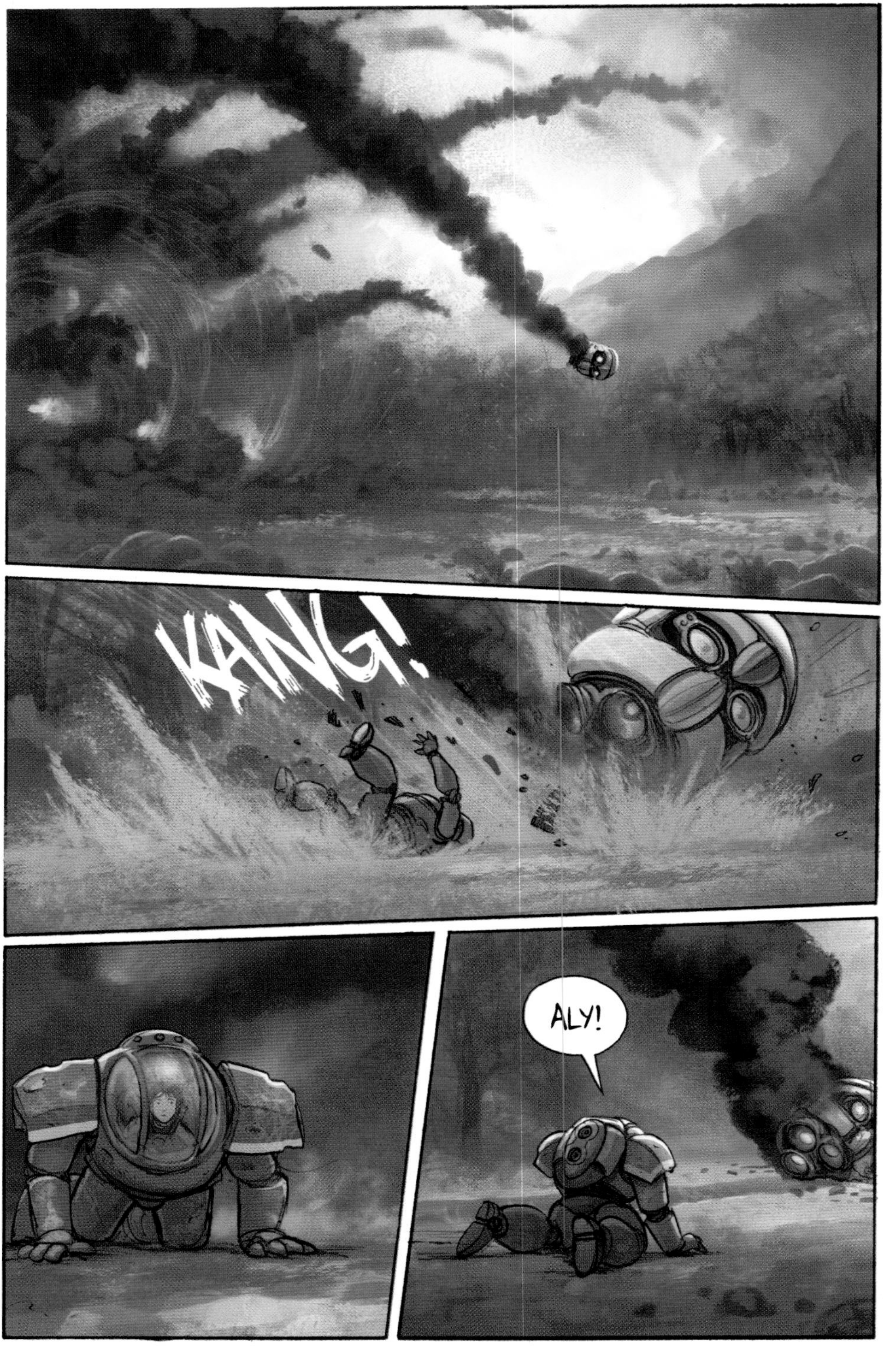
KANG!
ALY!

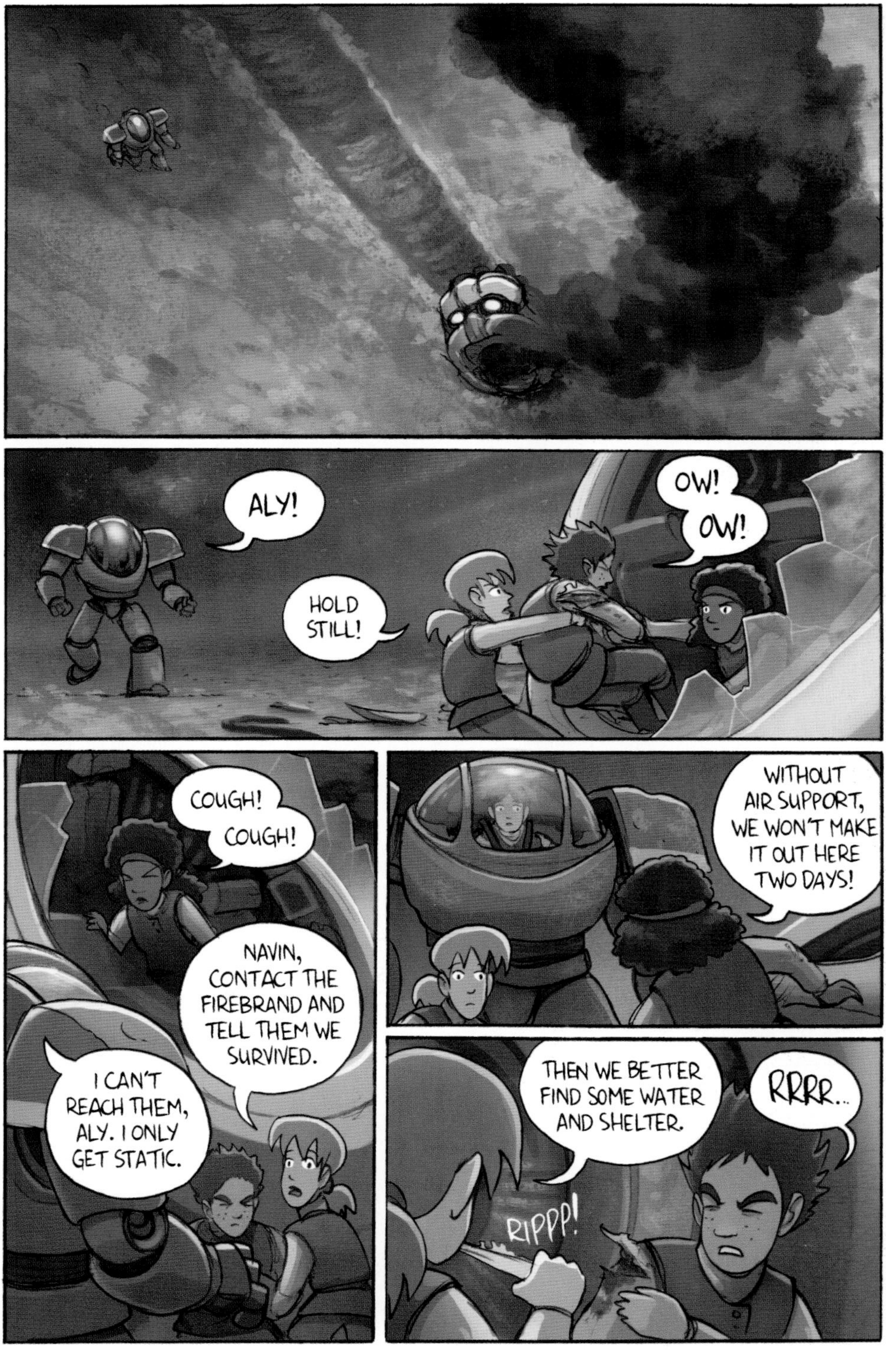
ALY!
OW! OW!
HOLD STILL!
COUGH! COUGH!
NAVIN, CONTACT THE FIREBRAND AND TELL THEM WE SURVIVED.
I CAN'T REACH THEM, ALY. I ONLY GET STATIC.
WITHOUT AIR SUPPORT, WE WON'T MAKE IT OUT HERE TWO DAYS!
THEN WE BETTER FIND SOME WATER AND SHELTER.
RRRR...
RIPPP!

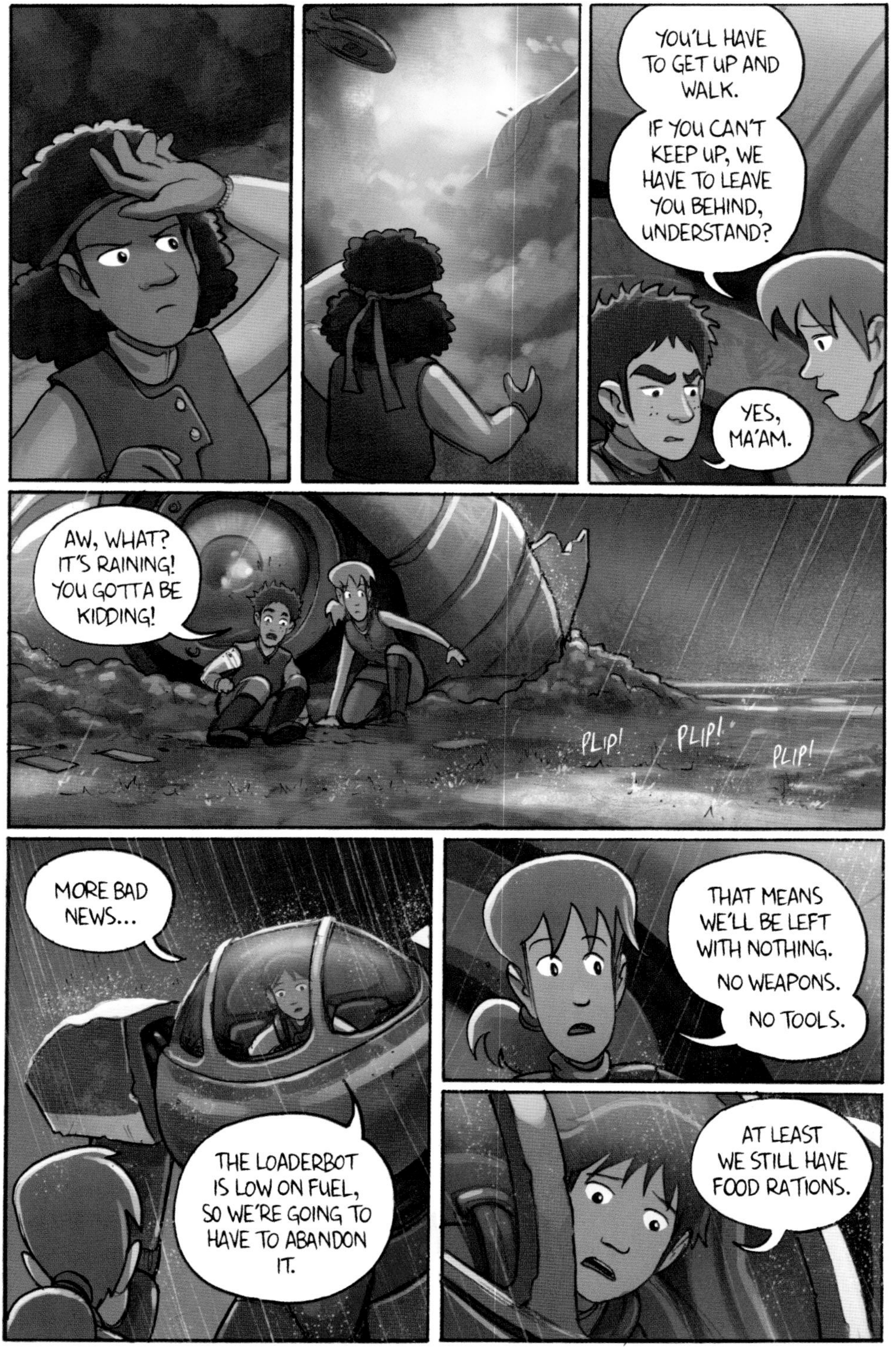
YOU'LL HAVE TO GET UP AND WALK.
IF YOU CAN'T KEEP UP, WE HAVE TO LEAVE YOU BEHIND, UNDERSTAND?
YES, MA'AM.
AW, WHAT? IT'S RAINING! YOU GOTTA BE KIDDING!
PLIP!
PLIP!
PLIP!
MORE BAD NEWS...
THE LOADERBOT IS LOW ON FUEL, SO WE'RE GOING TO HAVE TO ABANDON IT.
THAT MEANS WE'LL BE LEFT WITH NOTHING.
NO WEAPONS.
NO TOOLS.
AT LEAST WE STILL HAVE FOOD RATIONS.

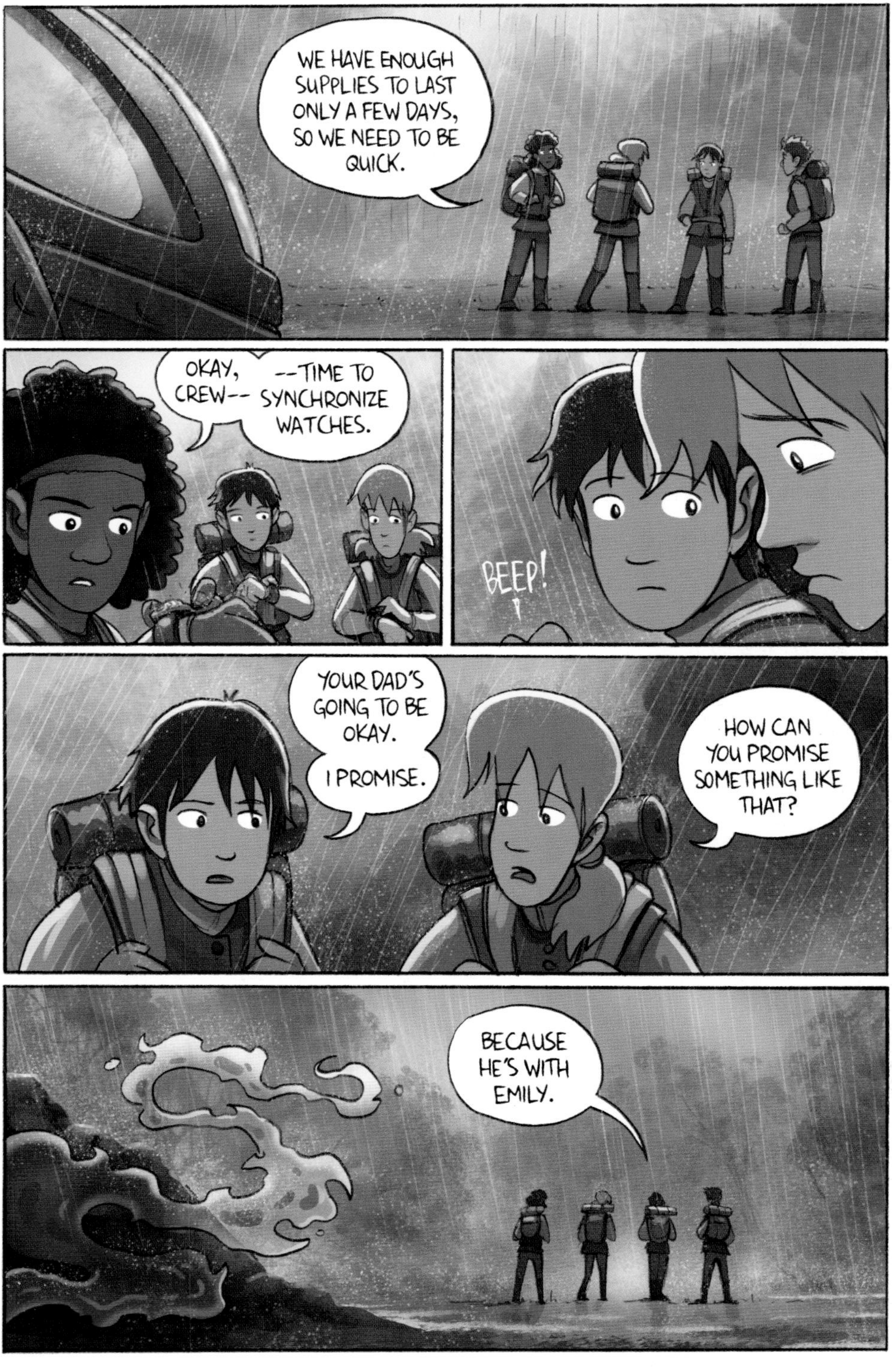
WE HAVE ENOUGH SUPPLIES TO LAST ONLY A FEW DAYS, SO WE NEED TO BE QUICK.
OKAY, CREW--
--TIME TO SYNCHRONIZE WATCHES.
BEEP!
YOUR DAD'S GOING TO BE OKAY.
I PROMISE.
HOW CAN YOU PROMISE SOMETHING LIKE THAT?
BECAUSE HE'S WITH EMILY.

WE CAN'T LET MAX BOARD THIS SHIP, VIGO.

HE WON'T. THAT WOULD LEAVE HIM TOO VULNERABLE.

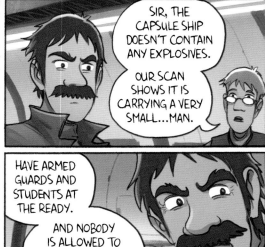

SIR, THE CAPSULE SHIP DOESN'T CONTAIN ANY EXPLOSIVES.

OUR SCAN SHOWS IT IS CARRYING A VERY SMALL...MAN.

HAVE ARMED GUARDS AND STUDENTS AT THE READY.

AND NOBODY IS ALLOWED TO DISCHARGE THEIR WEAPONS WITHOUT MY SAY-SO.

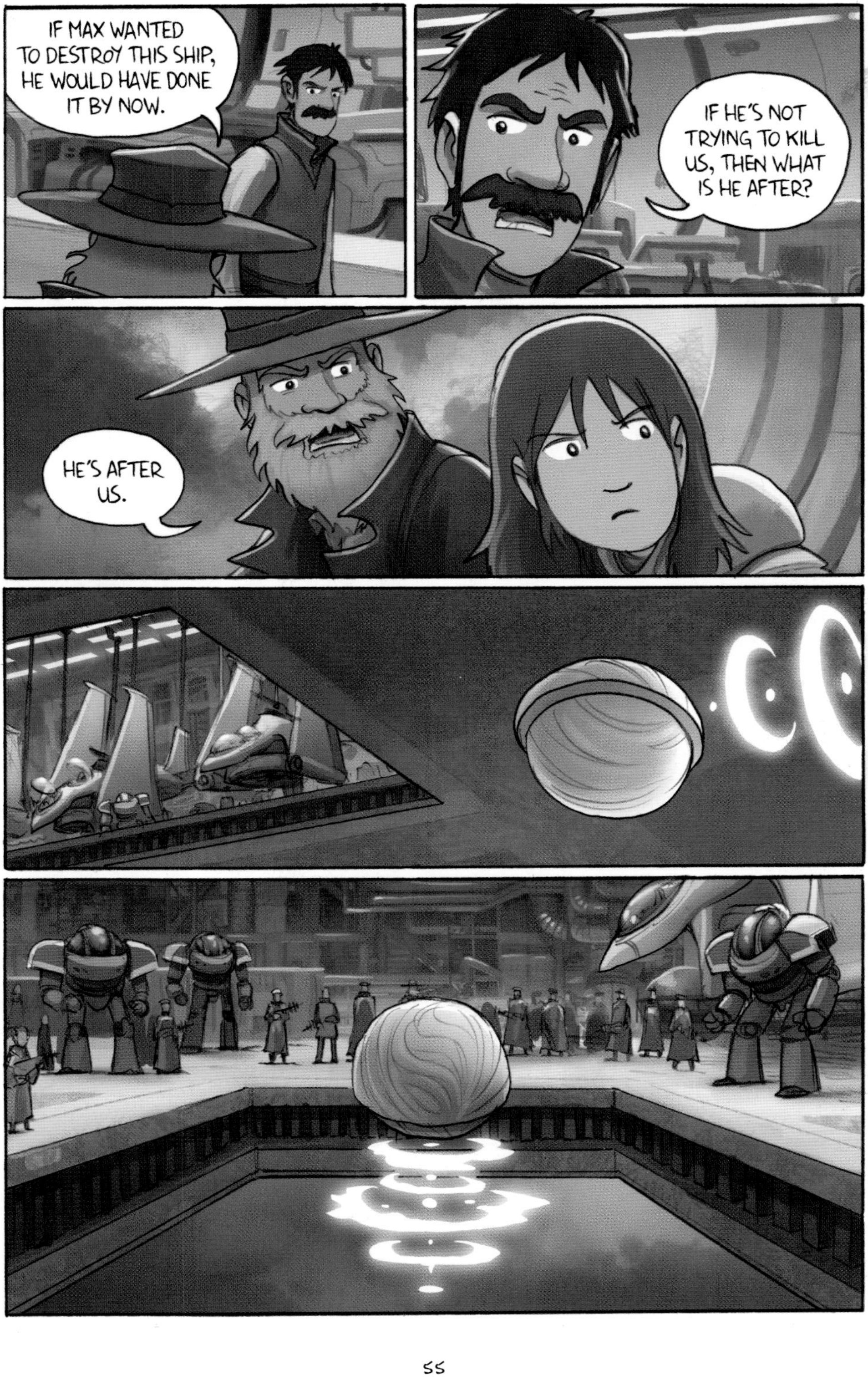
IF MAX WANTED TO DESTROY THIS SHIP, HE WOULD HAVE DONE IT BY NOW.
IF HE'S NOT TRYING TO KILL US, THEN WHAT IS HE AFTER?
HE'S AFTER US.

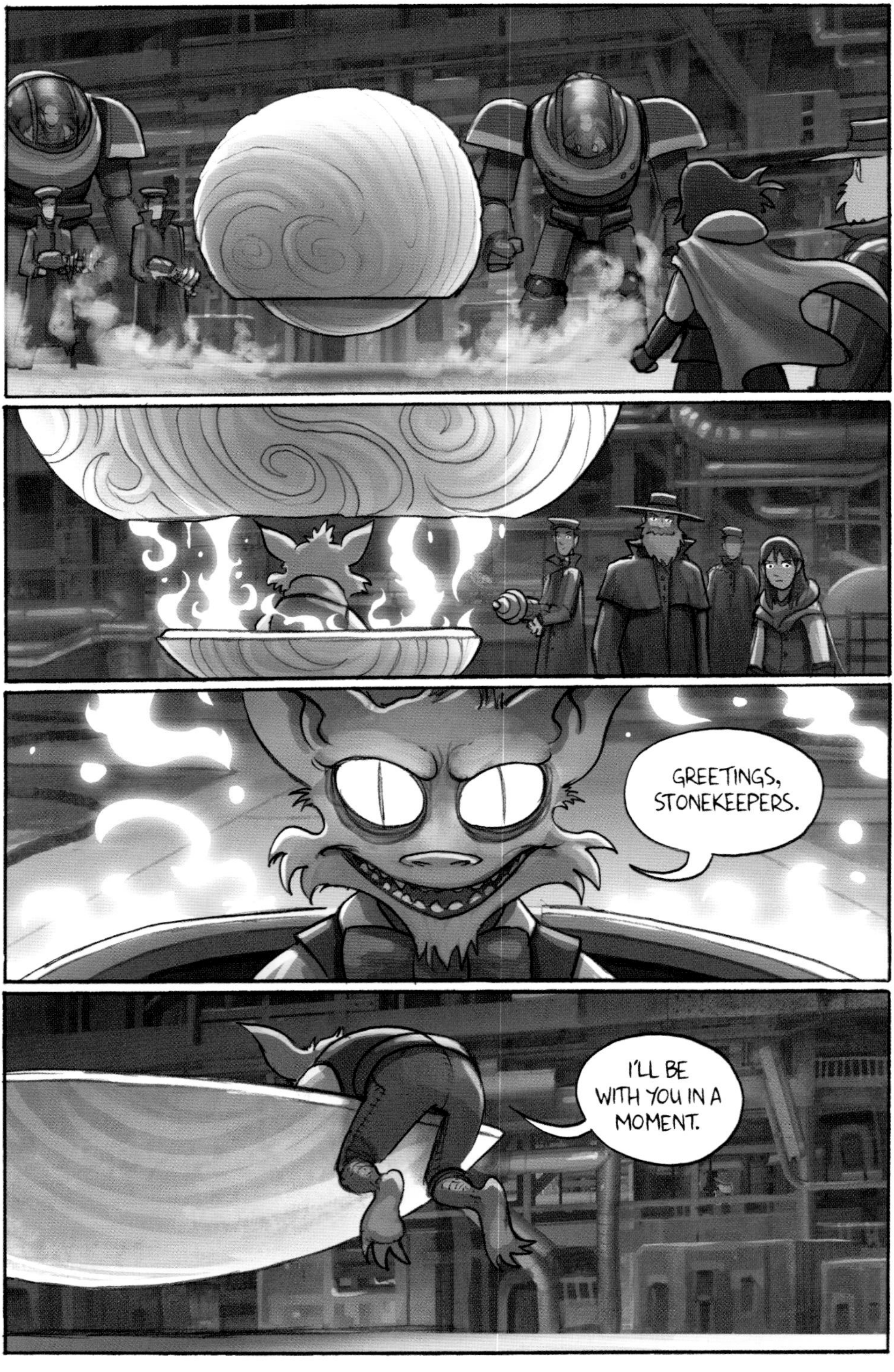
GREETINGS, STONEKEEPERS.
I'LL BE WITH YOU IN A MOMENT.

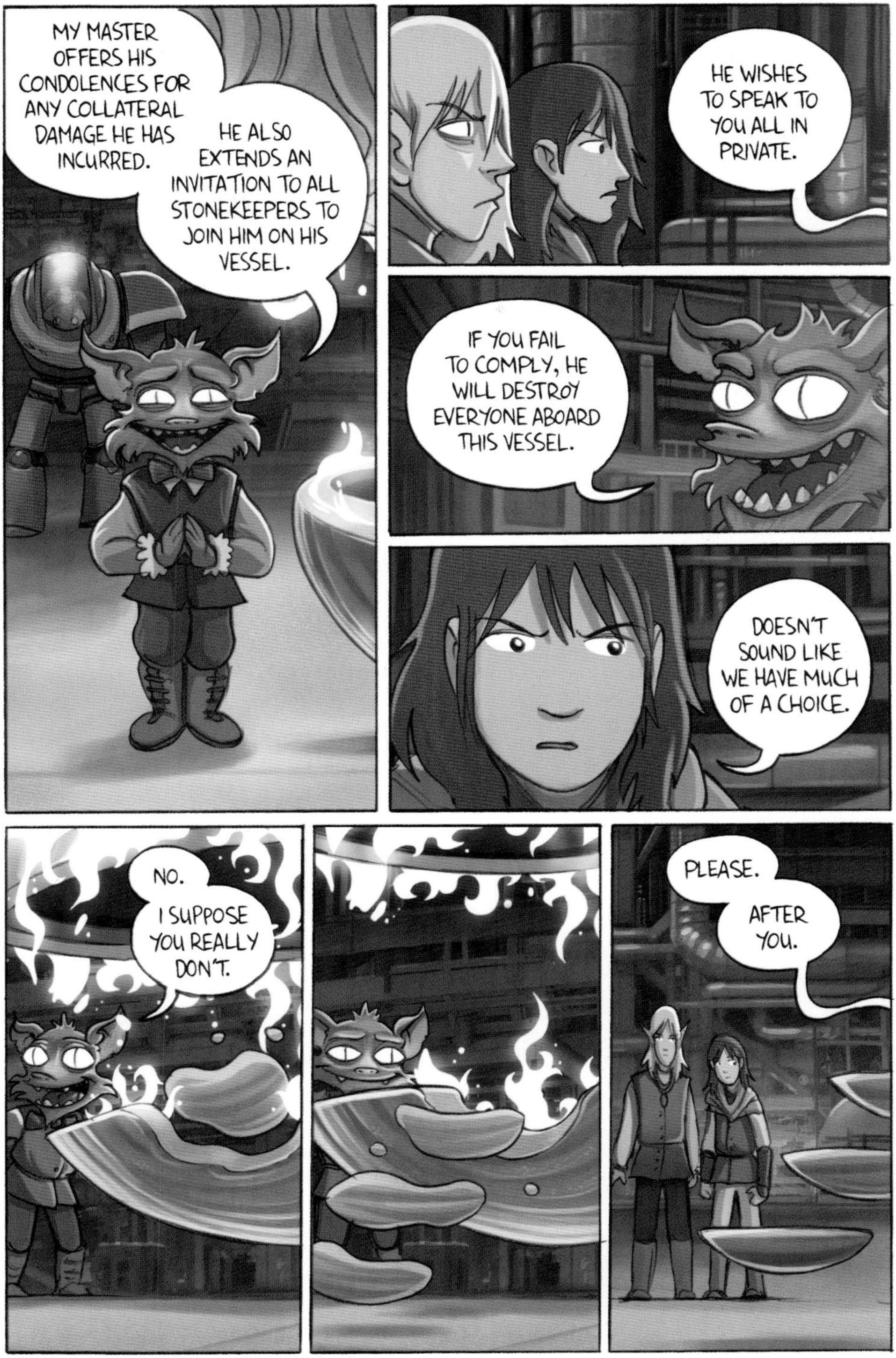
MY MASTER OFFERS HIS CONDOLENCES FOR ANY COLLATERAL DAMAGE HE HAS INCURRED.
HE ALSO EXTENDS AN INVITATION TO ALL STONEKEEPERS TO JOIN HIM ON HIS VESSEL.
HE WISHES TO SPEAK TO YOU ALL IN PRIVATE.
IF YOU FAIL TO COMPLY, HE WILL DESTROY EVERYONE ABOARD THIS VESSEL.
DOESN'T SOUND LIKE WE HAVE MUCH OF A CHOICE.
NO.
I SUPPOSE YOU REALLY DON'T.
PLEASE.
AFTER YOU.

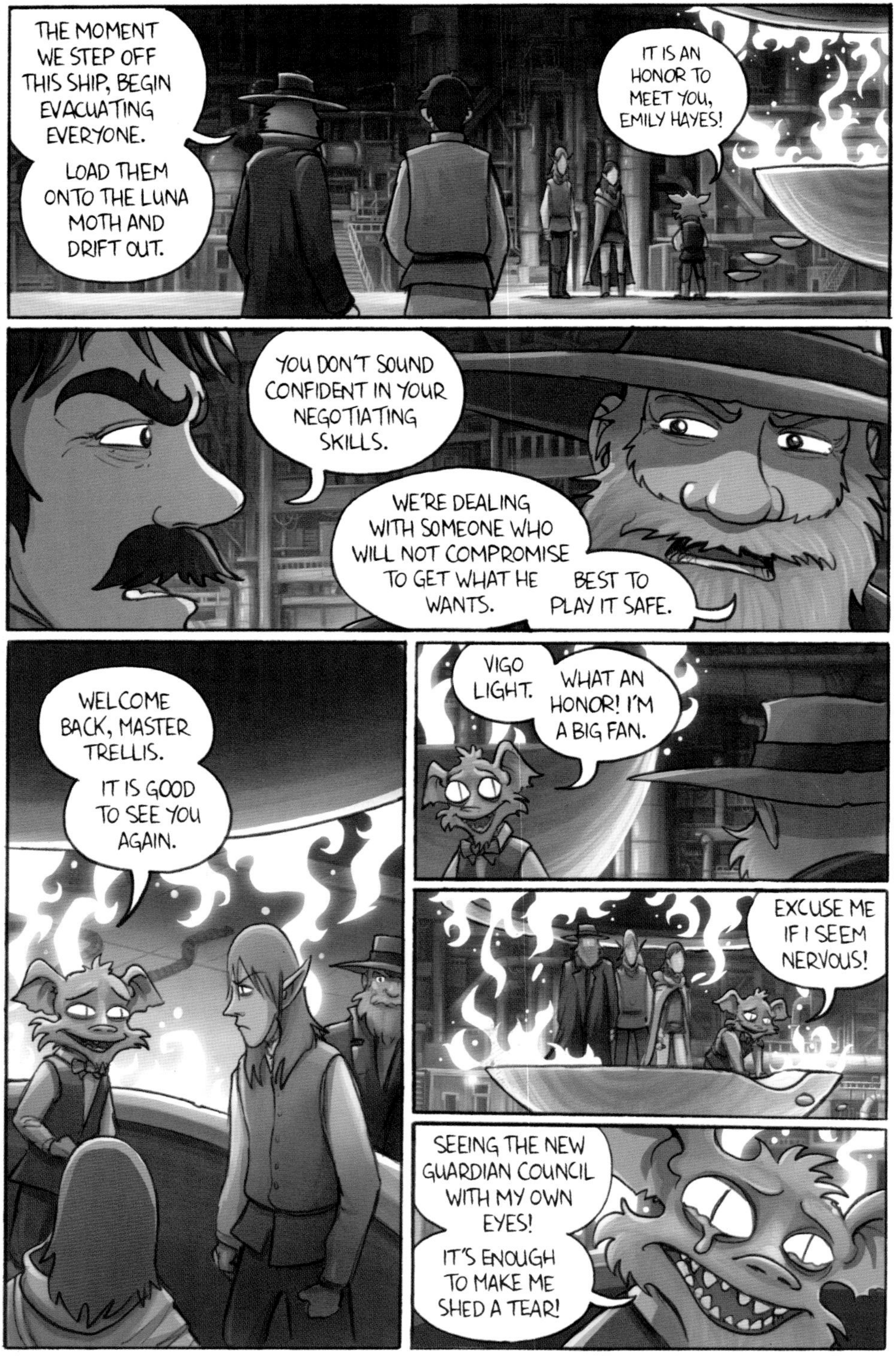
THE MOMENT WE STEP OFF THIS SHIP, BEGIN EVACUATING EVERYONE.
LOAD THEM ONTO THE LUNA MOTH AND DRIFT OUT.
IT IS AN HONOR TO MEET YOU, EMILY HAYES!
YOU DON'T SOUND CONFIDENT IN YOUR NEGOTIATING SKILLS.
WE'RE DEALING WITH SOMEONE WHO WILL NOT COMPROMISE TO GET WHAT HE WANTS.
BEST TO PLAY IT SAFE.
WELCOME BACK, MASTER TRELLIS.
IT IS GOOD TO SEE YOU AGAIN.
VIGO LIGHT.
WHAT AN HONOR! I'M A BIG FAN.
EXCUSE ME IF I SEEM NERVOUS!
SEEING THE NEW GUARDIAN COUNCIL WITH MY OWN EYES!
IT'S ENOUGH TO MAKE ME SHED A TEAR!

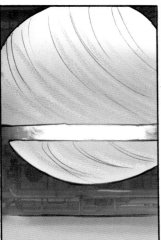

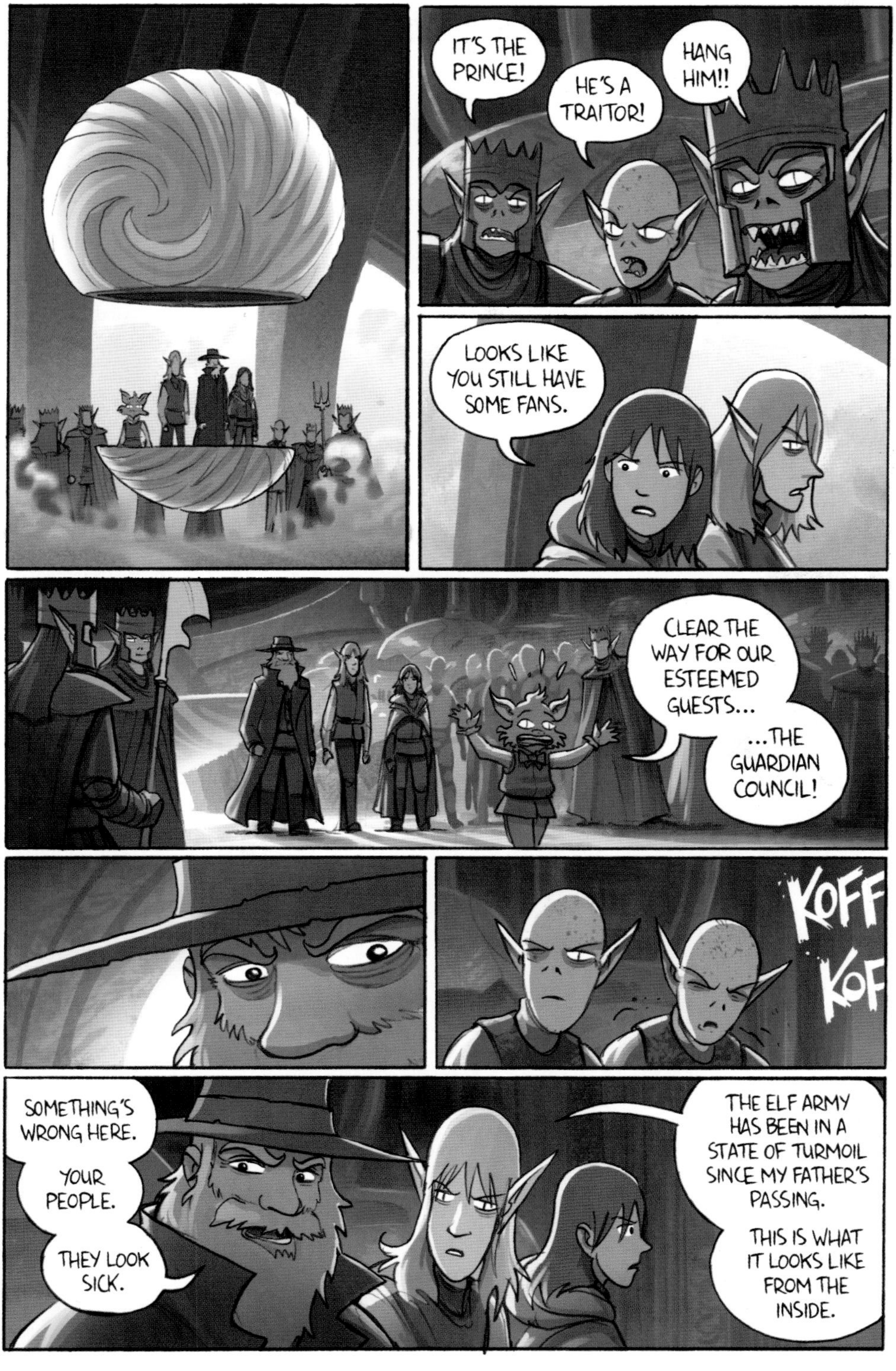
IT'S THE PRINCE!
HE'S A TRAITOR!
HANG HIM!!
LOOKS LIKE YOU STILL HAVE SOME FANS.
CLEAR THE WAY FOR OUR ESTEEMED GUESTS...
...THE GUARDIAN COUNCIL!
KOFF
KOF
SOMETHING'S WRONG HERE.
YOUR PEOPLE.
THEY LOOK SICK.
THE ELF ARMY HAS BEEN IN A STATE OF TURMOIL SINCE MY FATHER'S PASSING.
THIS IS WHAT IT LOOKS LIKE FROM THE INSIDE.

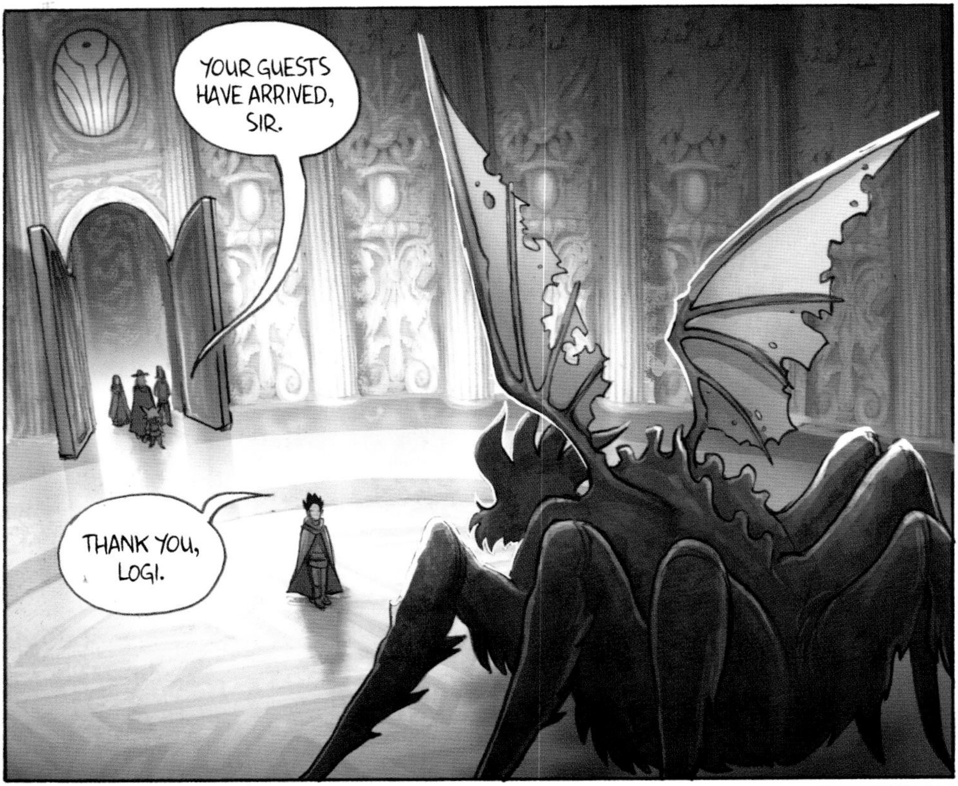
YOUR GUESTS HAVE ARRIVED, SIR.
THANK YOU, LOGI.

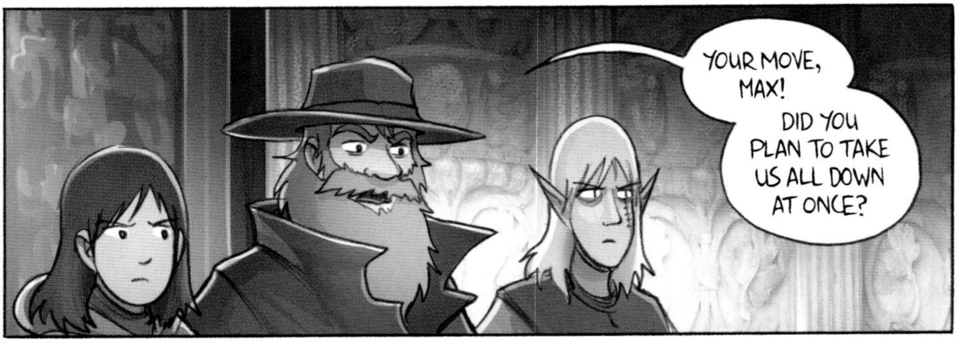
YOUR MOVE, MAX! DID YOU PLAN TO TAKE US ALL DOWN AT ONCE?

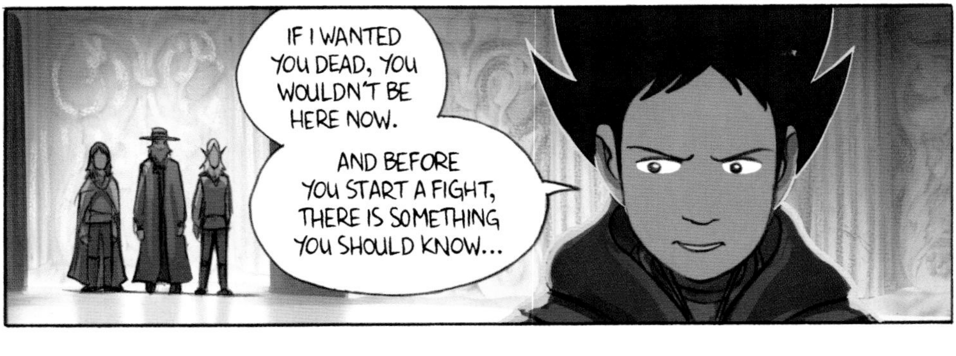
IF I WANTED YOU DEAD, YOU WOULDN'T BE HERE NOW.
AND BEFORE YOU START A FIGHT, THERE IS SOMETHING YOU SHOULD KNOW...

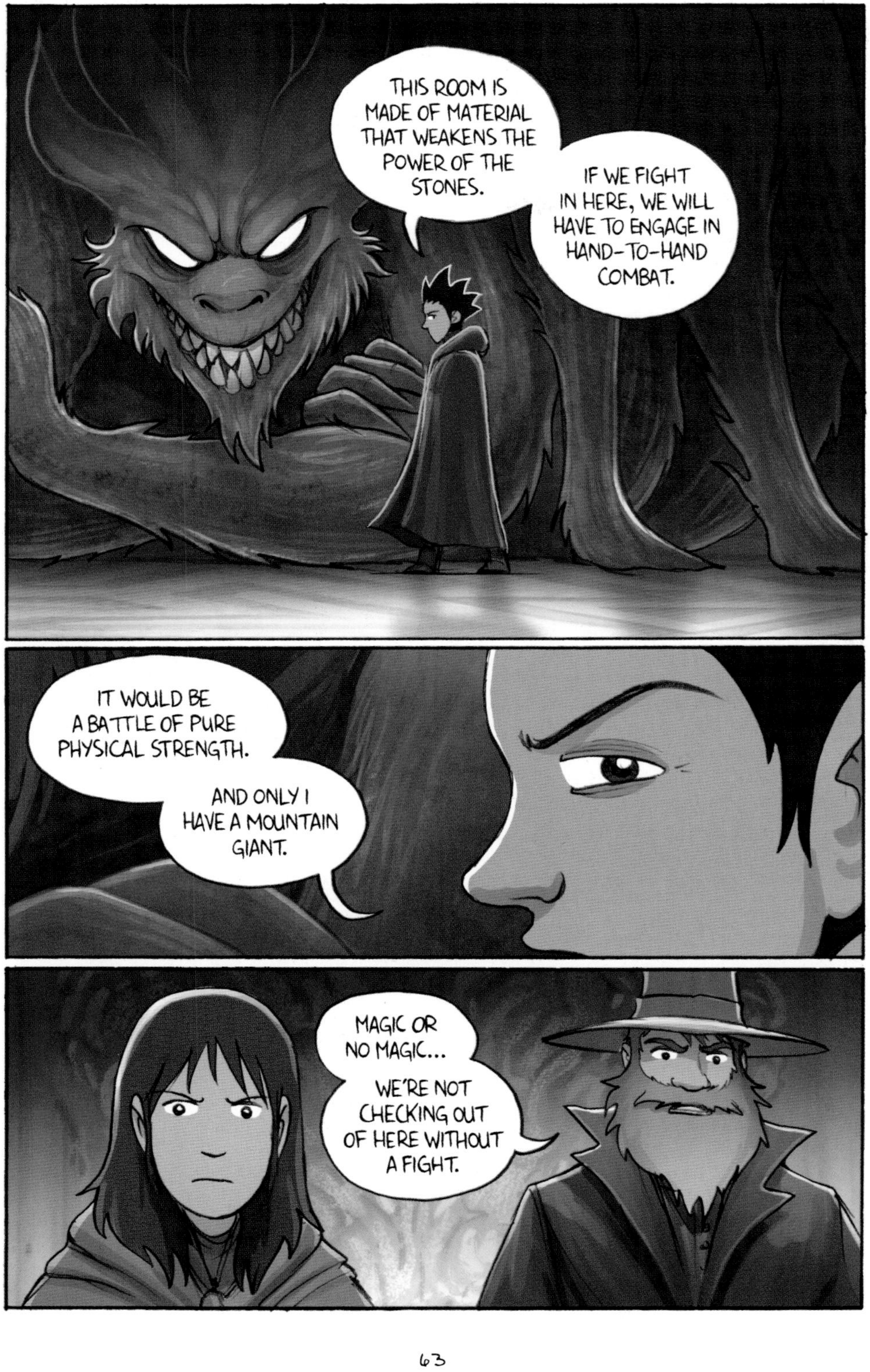
THIS ROOM IS MADE OF MATERIAL THAT WEAKENS THE POWER OF THE STONES.
IF WE FIGHT IN HERE, WE WILL HAVE TO ENGAGE IN HAND-TO-HAND COMBAT.
IT WOULD BE A BATTLE OF PURE PHYSICAL STRENGTH.
AND ONLY I HAVE A MOUNTAIN GIANT.
MAGIC OR NO MAGIC...
WE'RE NOT CHECKING OUT OF HERE WITHOUT A FIGHT.

I DIDN'T BRING YOU HERE TO FIGHT.

I BROUGHT YOU HERE SO WE COULD TALK IN PRIVATE.

KKOOOM!!

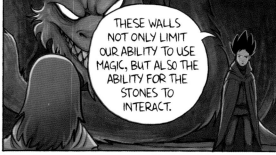

THESE WALLS NOT ONLY LIMIT OUR ABILITY TO USE MAGIC, BUT ALSO THE ABILITY FOR THE STONES TO INTERACT.

THAT MEANS, AS LONG AS WE ARE IN HERE, THE VOICE CANNOT HEAR US SPEAK.

BUT YOU'RE AN AGENT OF THE VOICE.

WHY SHOULD WE LISTEN TO YOU?

64

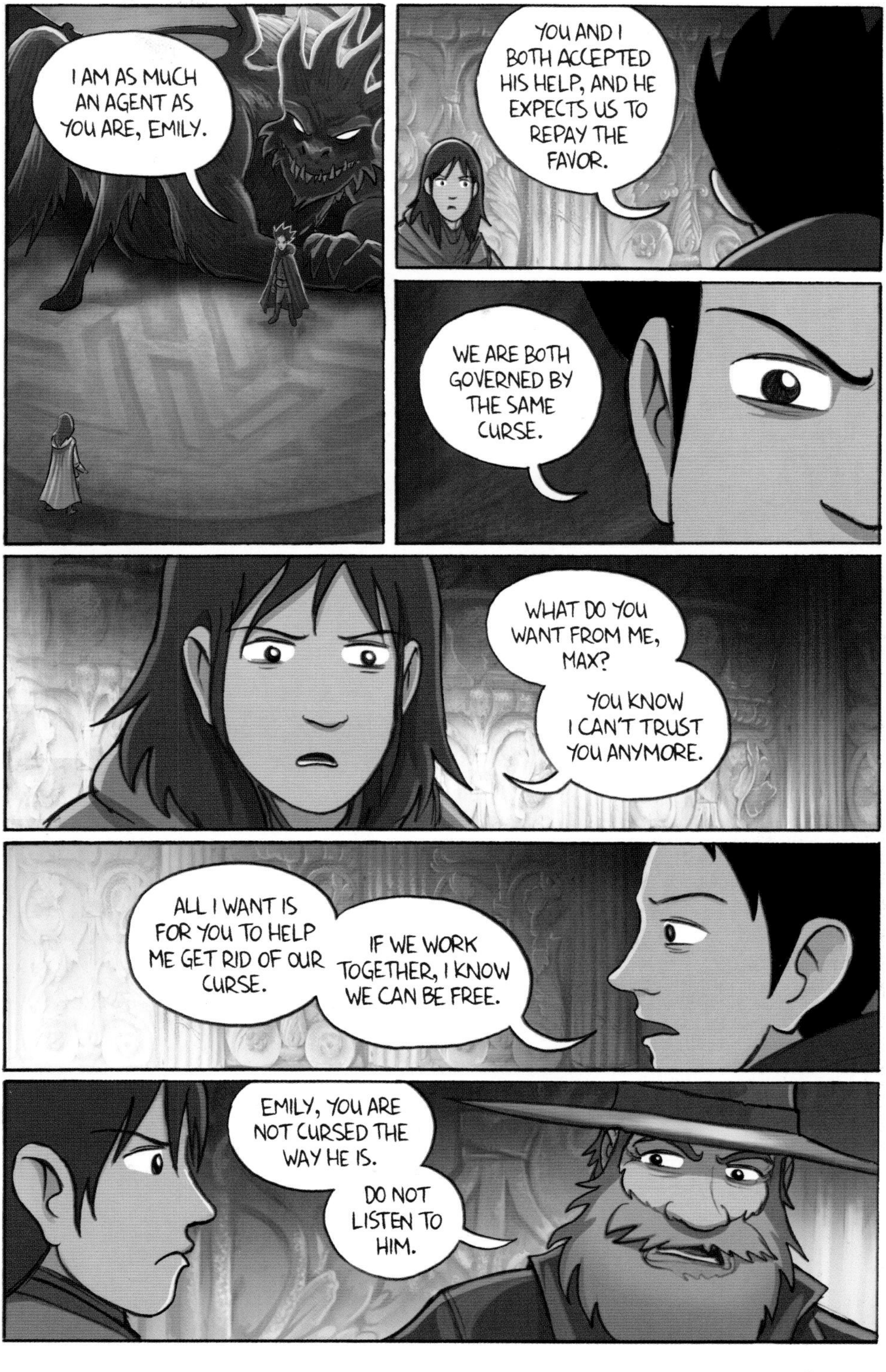
I AM AS MUCH AN AGENT AS YOU ARE, EMILY.
YOU AND I BOTH ACCEPTED HIS HELP, AND HE EXPECTS US TO REPAY THE FAVOR.
WE ARE BOTH GOVERNED BY THE SAME CURSE.
WHAT DO YOU WANT FROM ME, MAX?
YOU KNOW I CAN'T TRUST YOU ANYMORE.
ALL I WANT IS FOR YOU TO HELP ME GET RID OF OUR CURSE.
IF WE WORK TOGETHER, I KNOW WE CAN BE FREE.
EMILY, YOU ARE NOT CURSED THE WAY HE IS.
DO NOT LISTEN TO HIM.

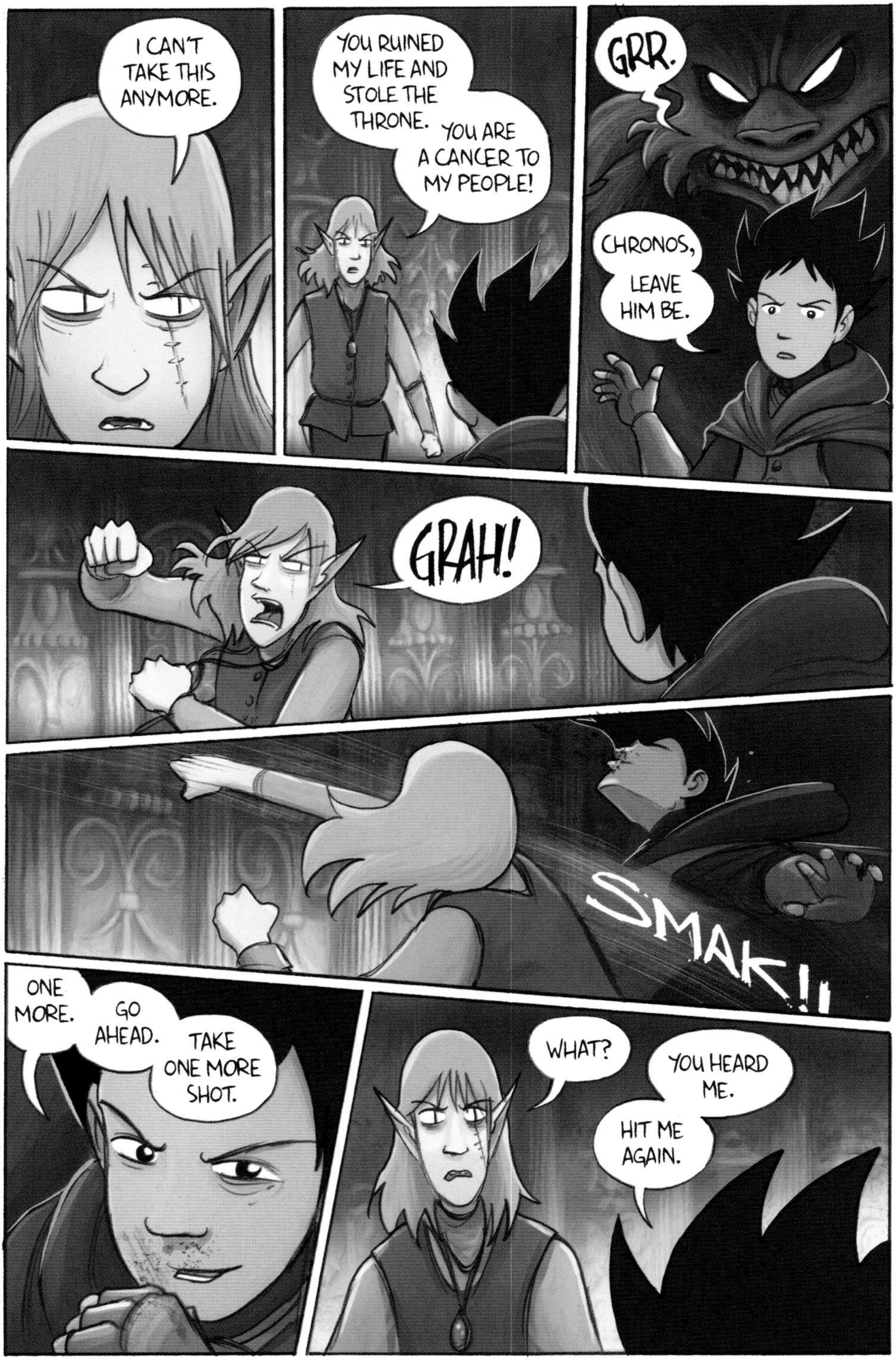
I CAN'T TAKE THIS ANYMORE.
YOU RUINED MY LIFE AND STOLE THE THRONE.
YOU ARE A CANCER TO MY PEOPLE!
GRR.
CHRONOS,
LEAVE HIM BE.
GRAH!
SMAK!!
ONE MORE.
GO AHEAD.
TAKE ONE MORE SHOT.
WHAT?
YOU HEARD ME.
HIT ME AGAIN.

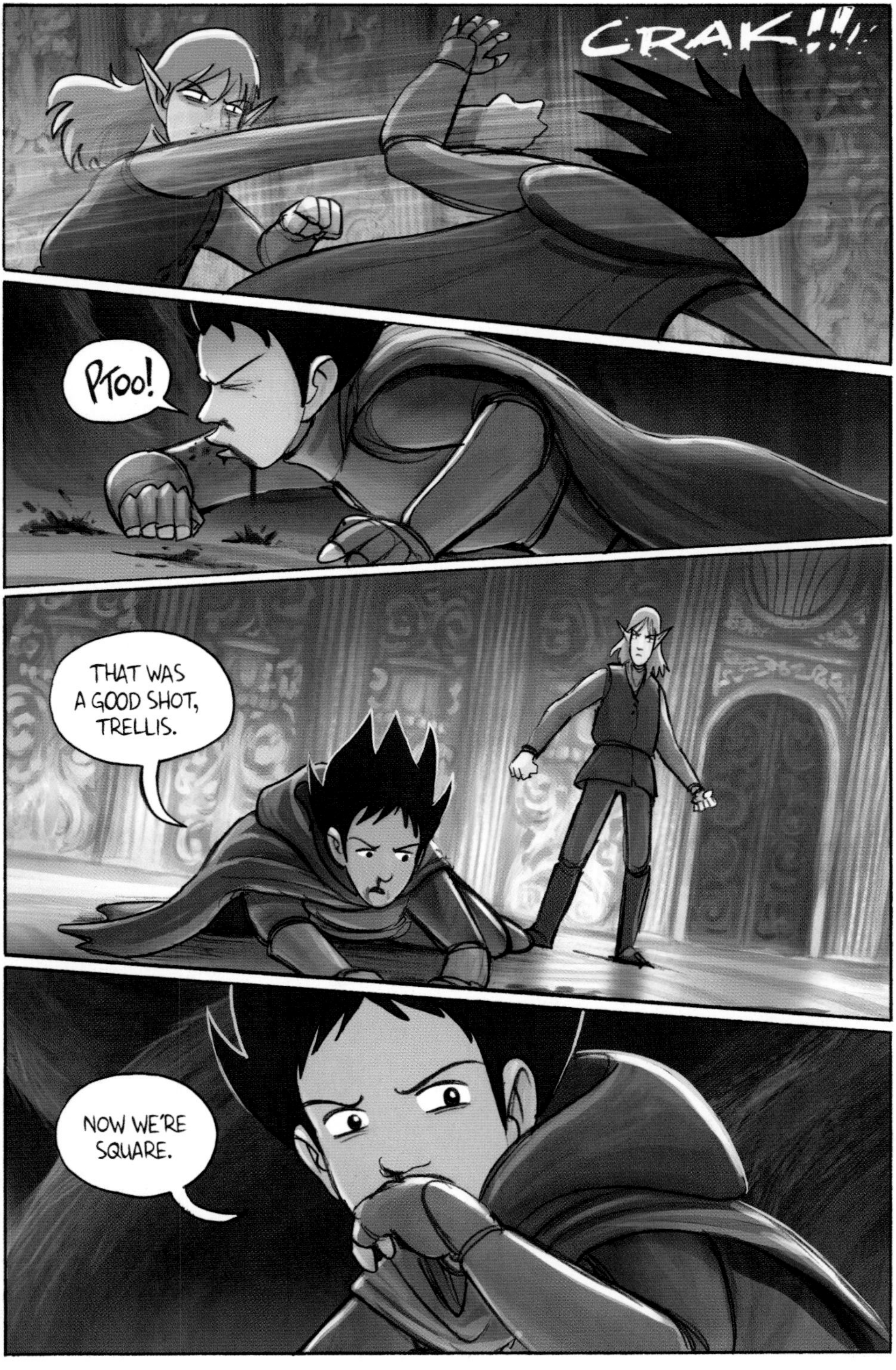
CRAK!!!
PTOO!
THAT WAS A GOOD SHOT, TRELLIS.
NOW WE'RE SQUARE.

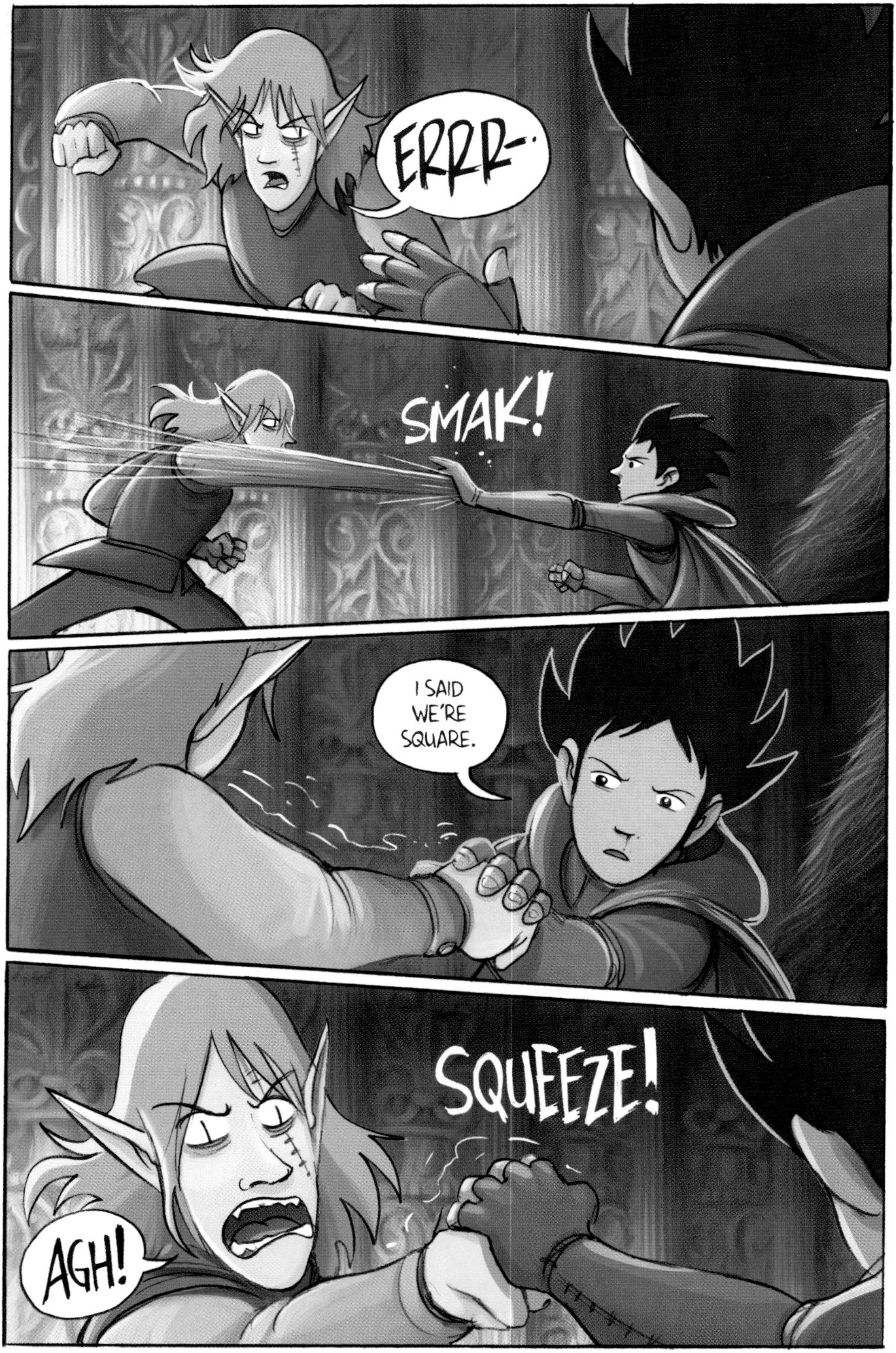
ERRR-
SMAK!
I SAID WE'RE SQUARE.
SQUEEZE!
AGH!

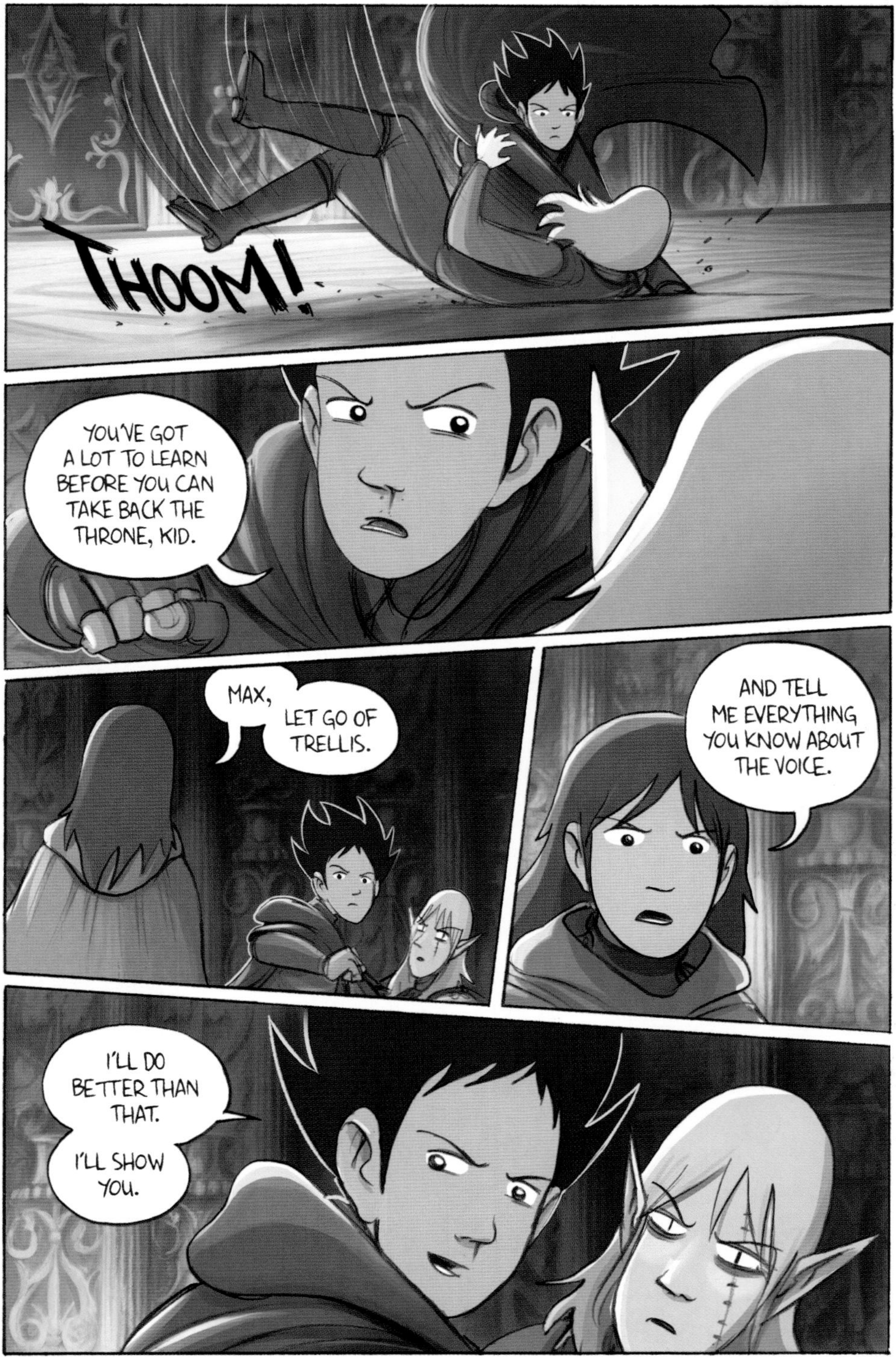
THOOM!
YOU'VE GOT A LOT TO LEARN BEFORE YOU CAN TAKE BACK THE THRONE, KID.
MAX,
LET GO OF TRELLIS.
AND TELL ME EVERYTHING YOU KNOW ABOUT THE VOICE.
I'LL DO BETTER THAN THAT.
I'LL SHOW YOU.

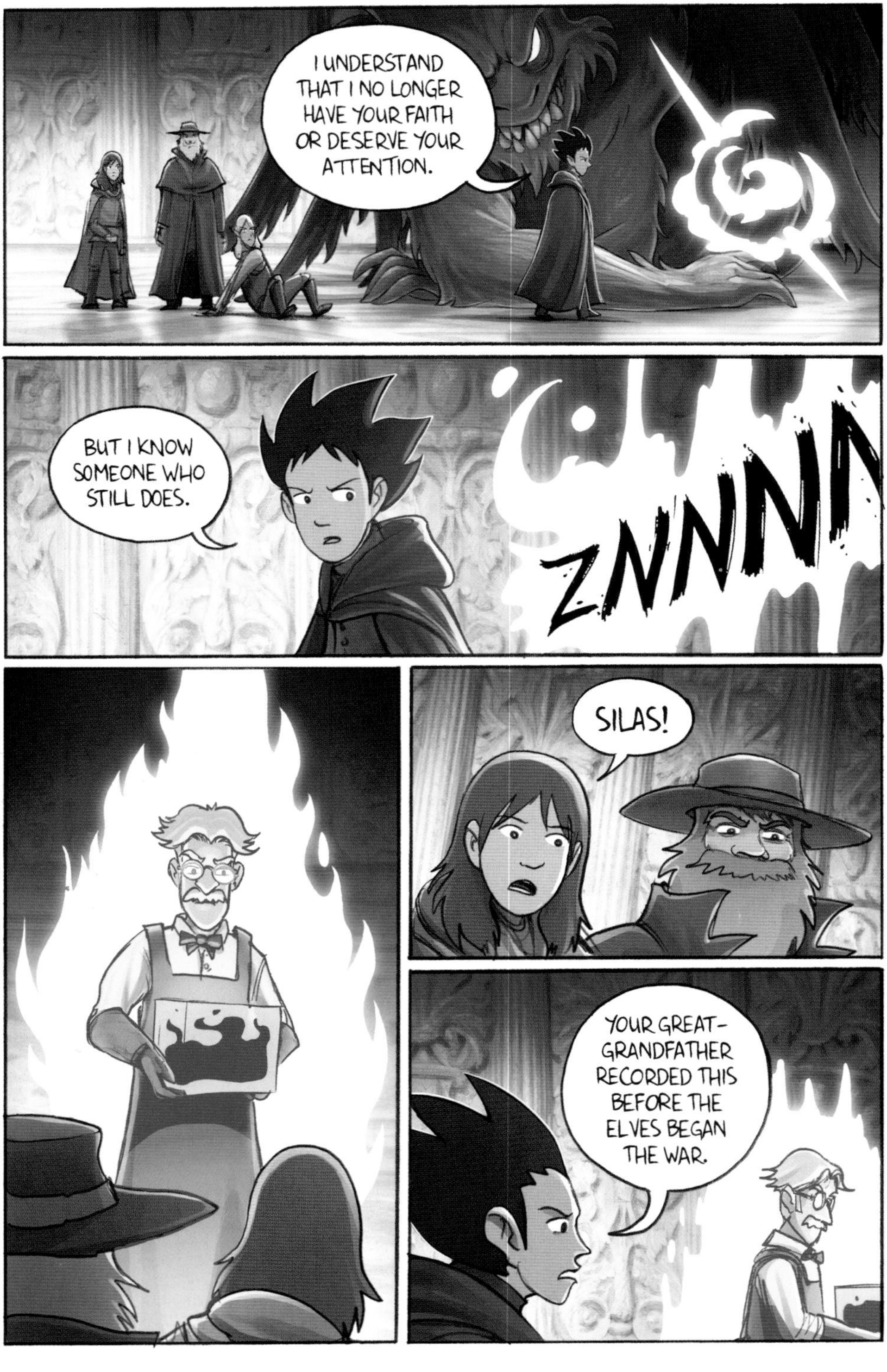
I UNDERSTAND THAT I NO LONGER HAVE YOUR FAITH OR DESERVE YOUR ATTENTION.
BUT I KNOW SOMEONE WHO STILL DOES.
ZNNNN
SILAS!
YOUR GREAT-GRANDFATHER RECORDED THIS BEFORE THE ELVES BEGAN THE WAR.

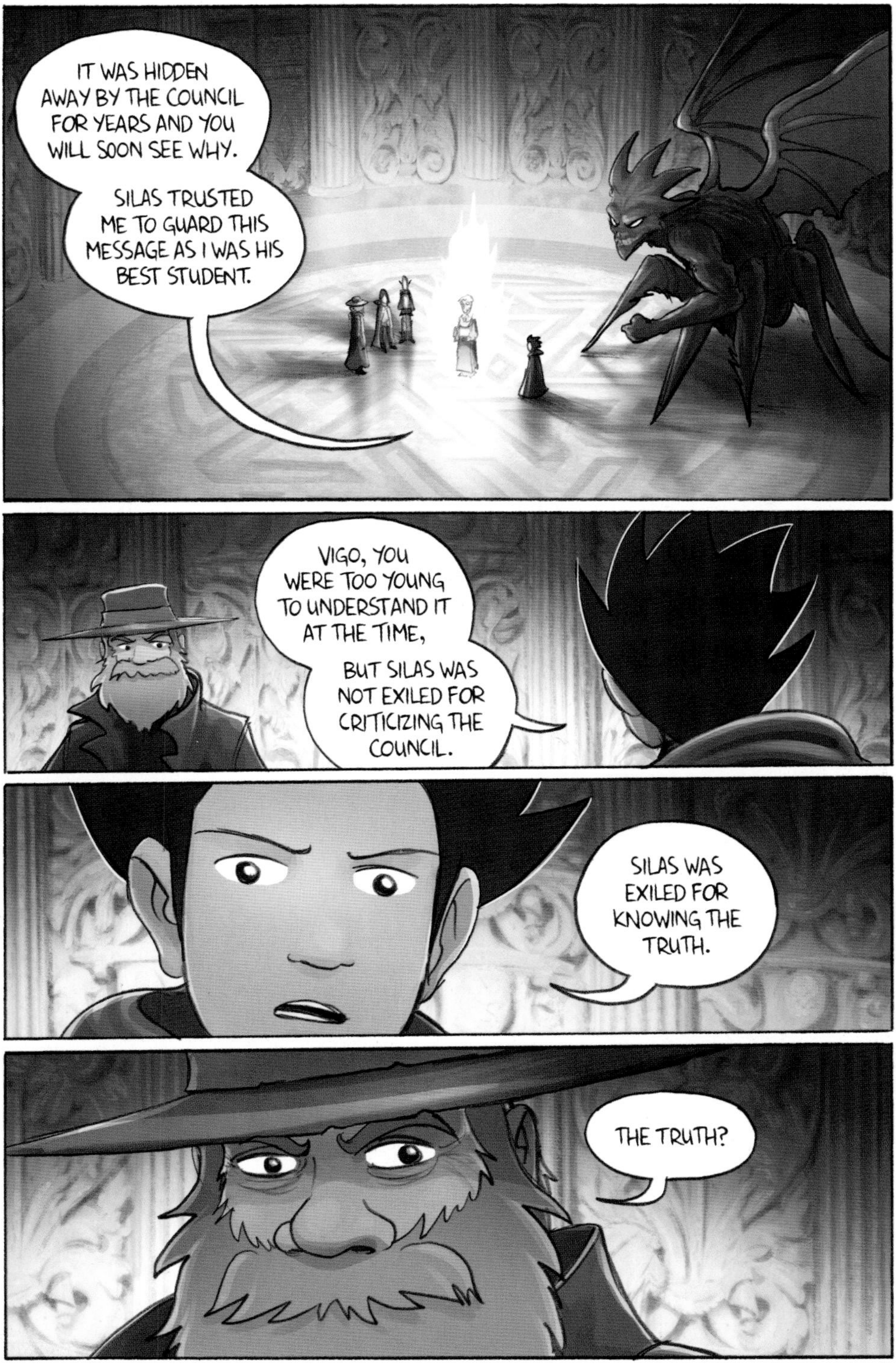
IT WAS HIDDEN AWAY BY THE COUNCIL FOR YEARS AND YOU WILL SOON SEE WHY.
SILAS TRUSTED ME TO GUARD THIS MESSAGE AS I WAS HIS BEST STUDENT.
VIGO, YOU WERE TOO YOUNG TO UNDERSTAND IT AT THE TIME,
BUT SILAS WAS NOT EXILED FOR CRITICIZING THE COUNCIL.
SILAS WAS EXILED FOR KNOWING THE TRUTH.
THE TRUTH?

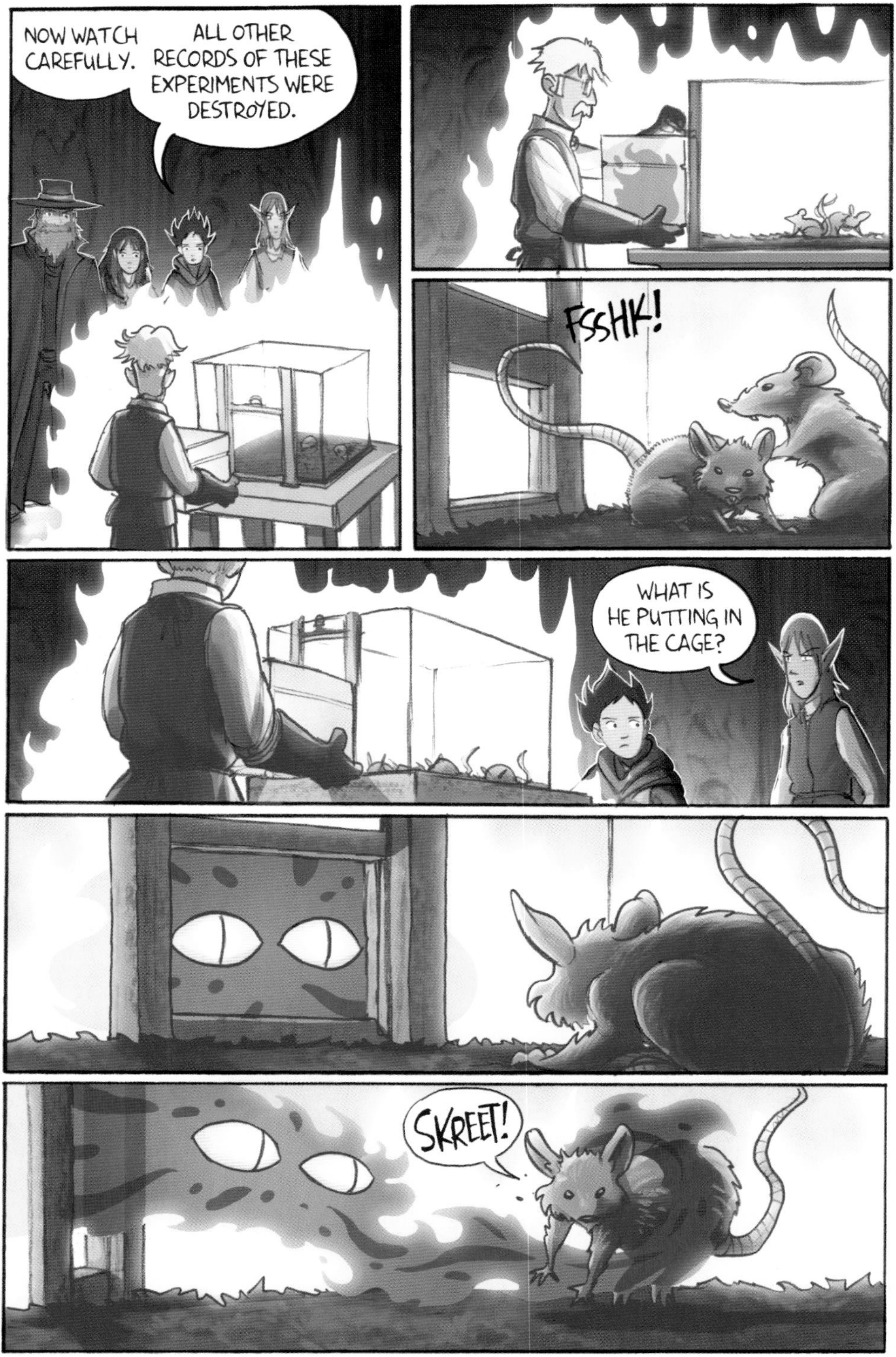
NOW WATCH CAREFULLY.
ALL OTHER RECORDS OF THESE EXPERIMENTS WERE DESTROYED.
FSSHK!
WHAT IS HE PUTTING IN THE CAGE?
SKREET!

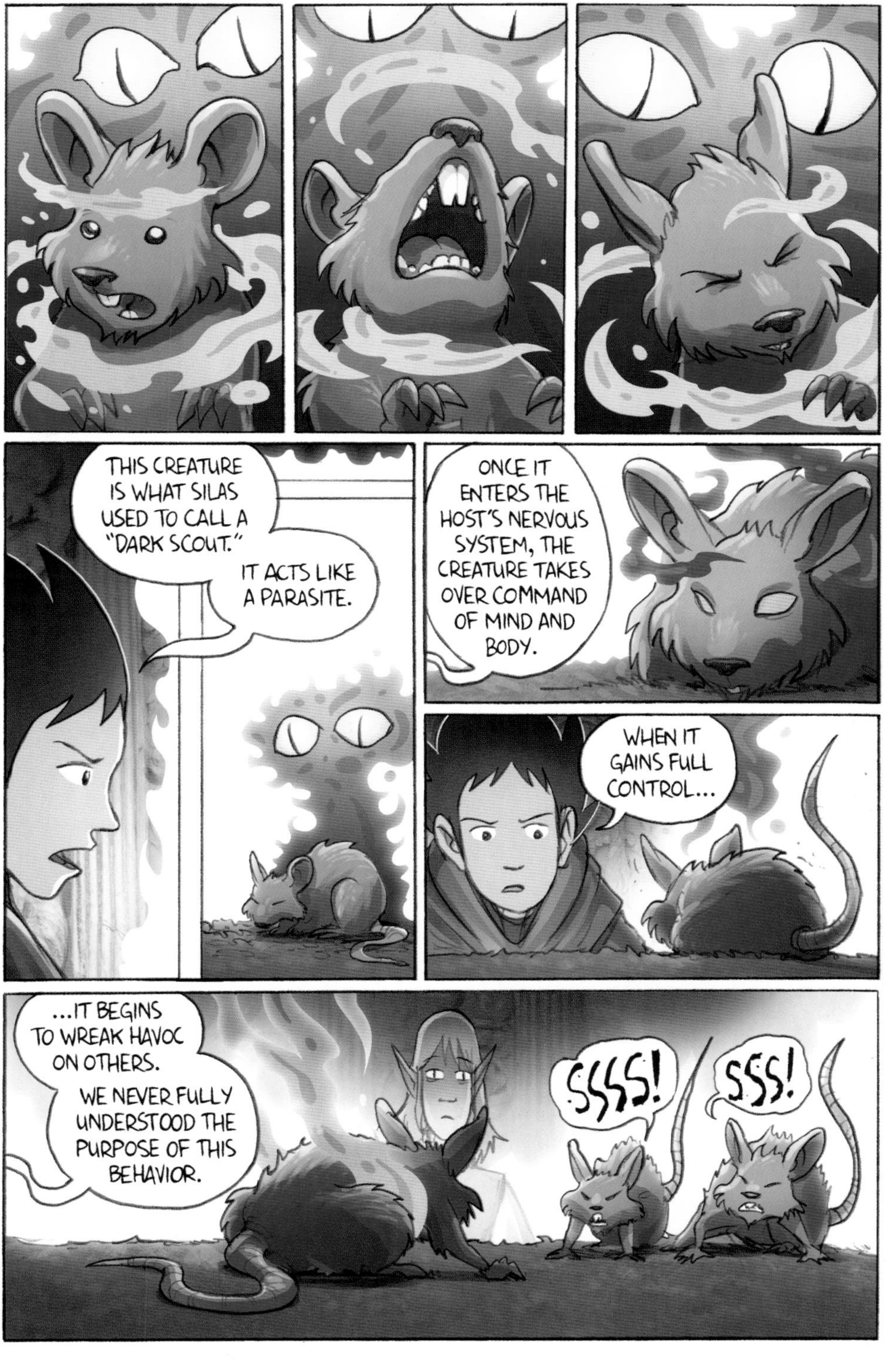
THIS CREATURE IS WHAT SILAS USED TO CALL A "DARK SCOUT."
IT ACTS LIKE A PARASITE.
ONCE IT ENTERS THE HOST'S NERVOUS SYSTEM, THE CREATURE TAKES OVER COMMAND OF MIND AND BODY.
WHEN IT GAINS FULL CONTROL...
...IT BEGINS TO WREAK HAVOC ON OTHERS.
WE NEVER FULLY UNDERSTOOD THE PURPOSE OF THIS BEHAVIOR.
SSSS!
SSS!

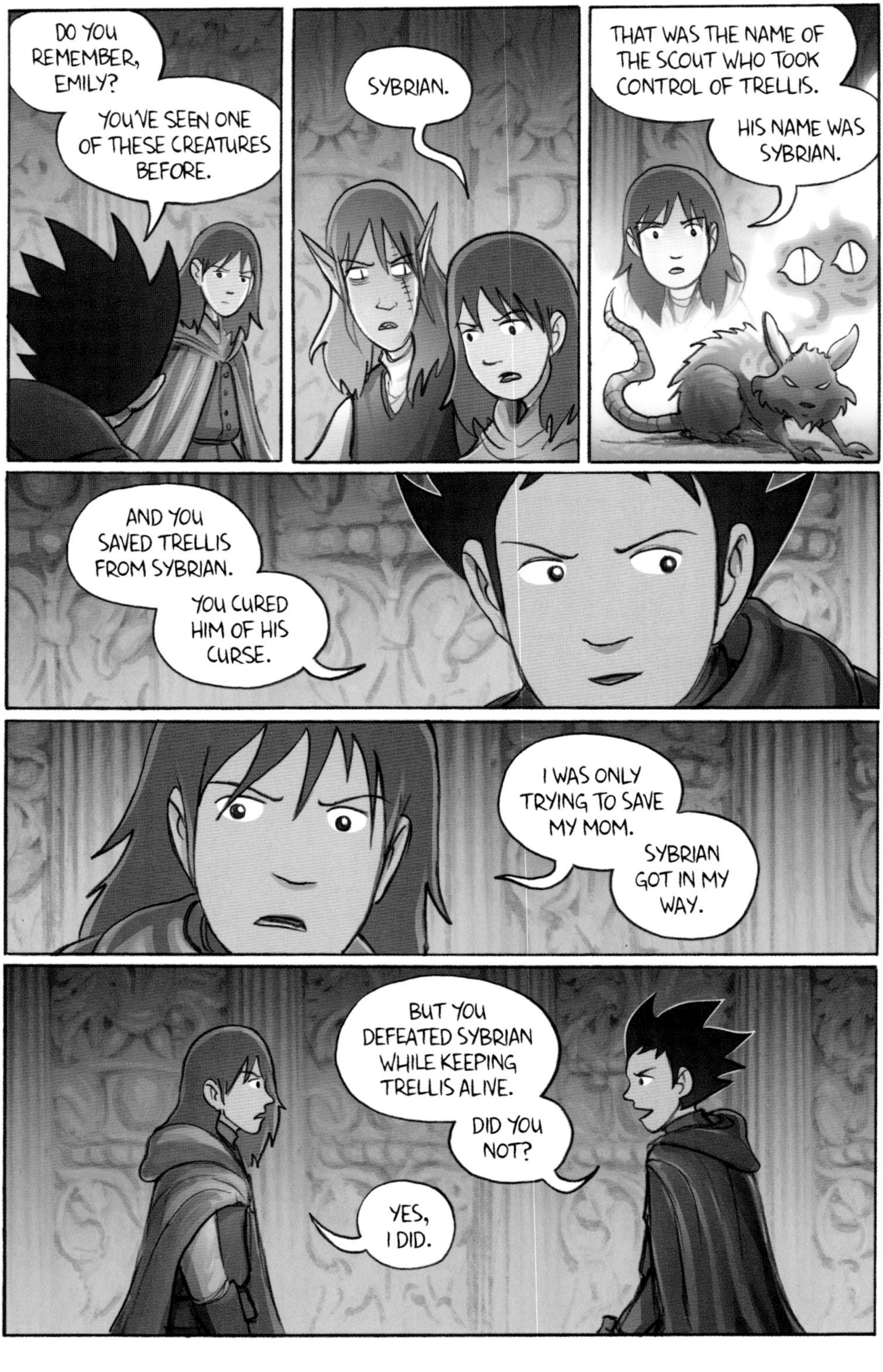
DO YOU REMEMBER, EMILY?
YOU'VE SEEN ONE OF THESE CREATURES BEFORE.
SYBRIAN.
THAT WAS THE NAME OF THE SCOUT WHO TOOK CONTROL OF TRELLIS.
HIS NAME WAS SYBRIAN.
AND YOU SAVED TRELLIS FROM SYBRIAN.
YOU CURED HIM OF HIS CURSE.
I WAS ONLY TRYING TO SAVE MY MOM.
SYBRIAN GOT IN MY WAY.
BUT YOU DEFEATED SYBRIAN WHILE KEEPING TRELLIS ALIVE.
DID YOU NOT?
YES, I DID.

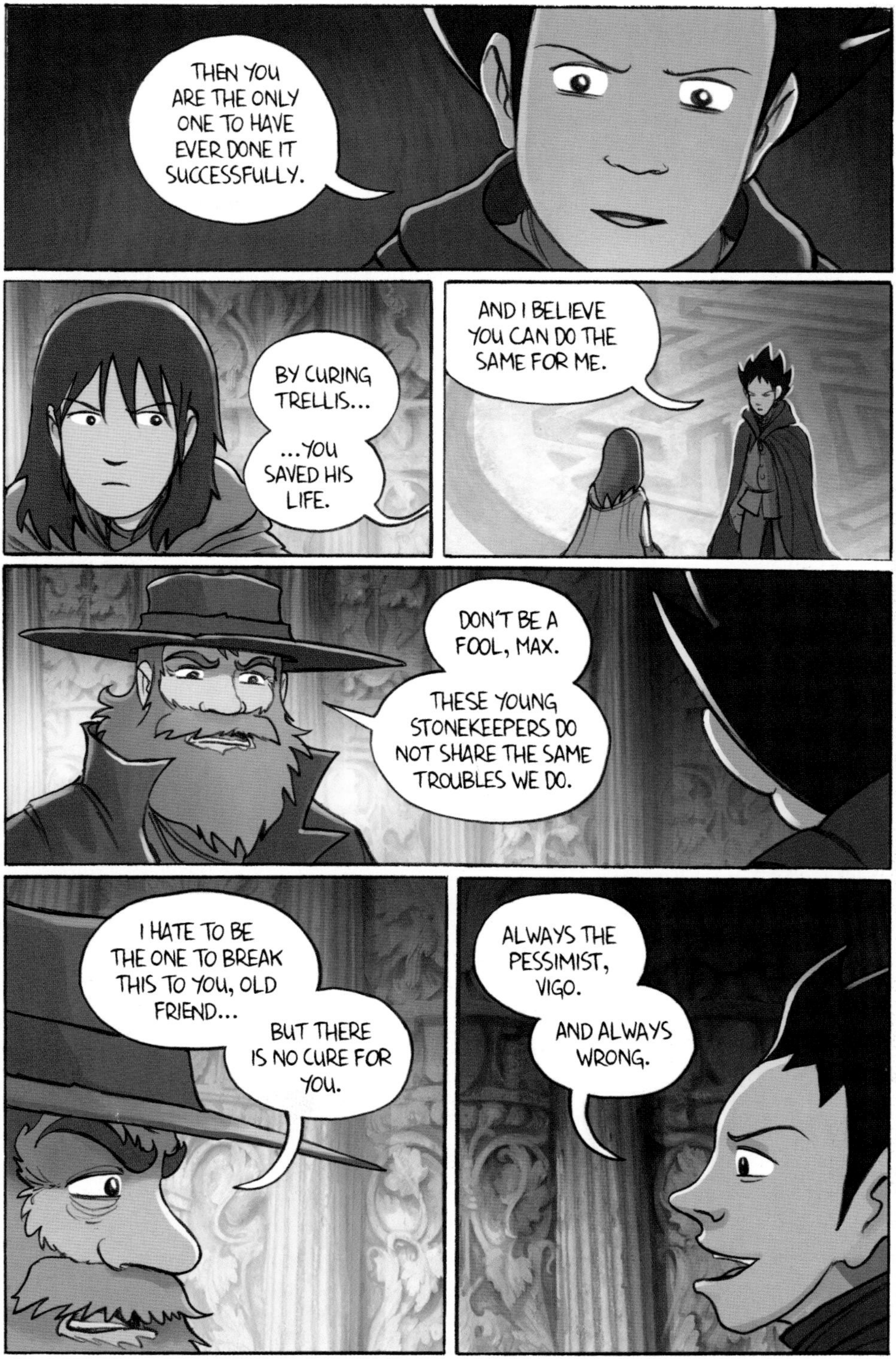
THEN YOU ARE THE ONLY ONE TO HAVE EVER DONE IT SUCCESSFULLY.
BY CURING TRELLIS...
...YOU SAVED HIS LIFE.
AND I BELIEVE YOU CAN DO THE SAME FOR ME.
DON'T BE A FOOL, MAX.
THESE YOUNG STONEKEEPERS DO NOT SHARE THE SAME TROUBLES WE DO.
I HATE TO BE THE ONE TO BREAK THIS TO YOU, OLD FRIEND...
BUT THERE IS NO CURE FOR YOU.
ALWAYS THE PESSIMIST, VIGO.
AND ALWAYS WRONG.

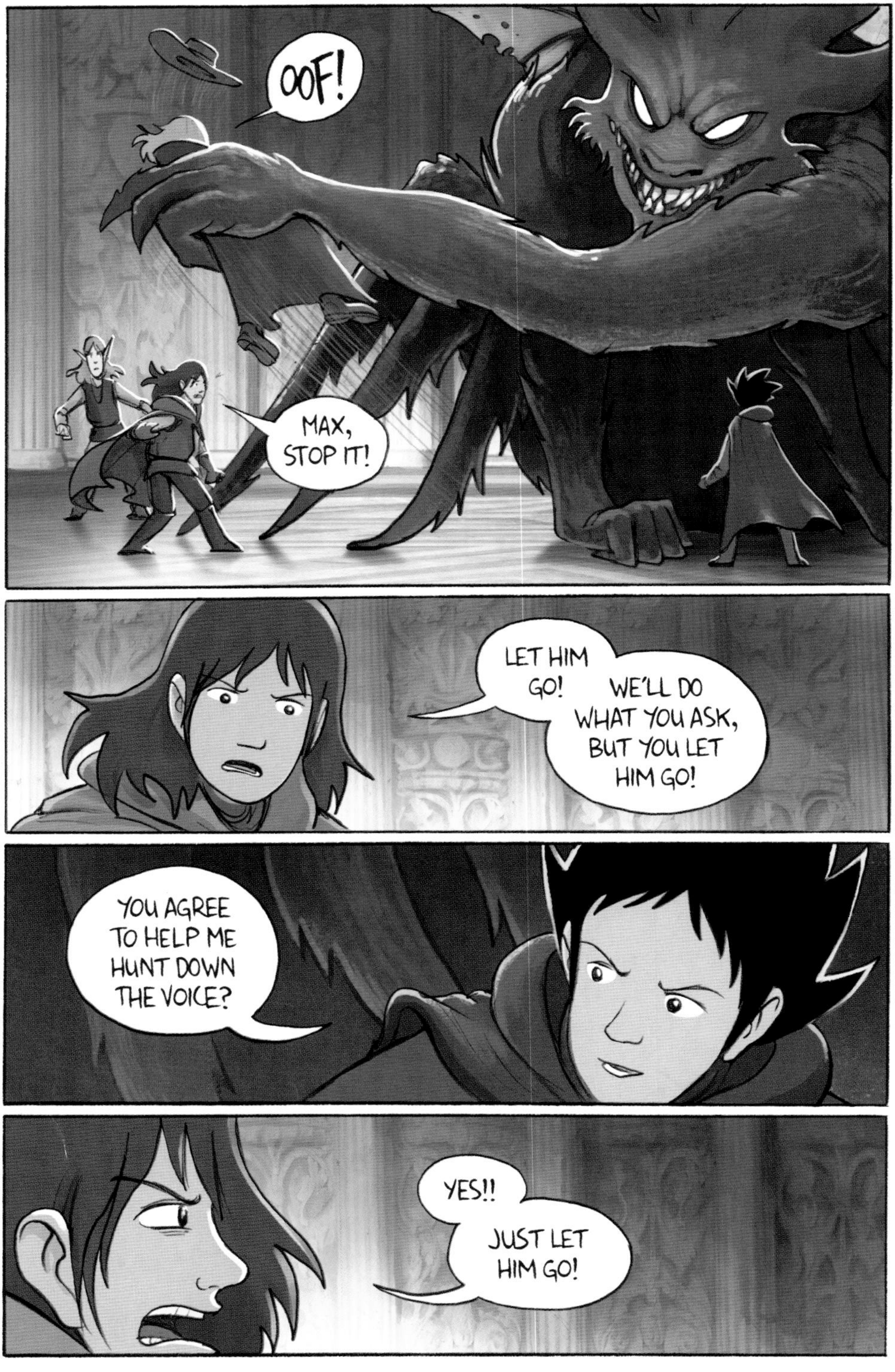
OOF!
MAX, STOP IT!
LET HIM GO!
WE'LL DO WHAT YOU ASK, BUT YOU LET HIM GO!
YOU AGREE TO HELP ME HUNT DOWN THE VOICE?
YES!!
JUST LET HIM GO!

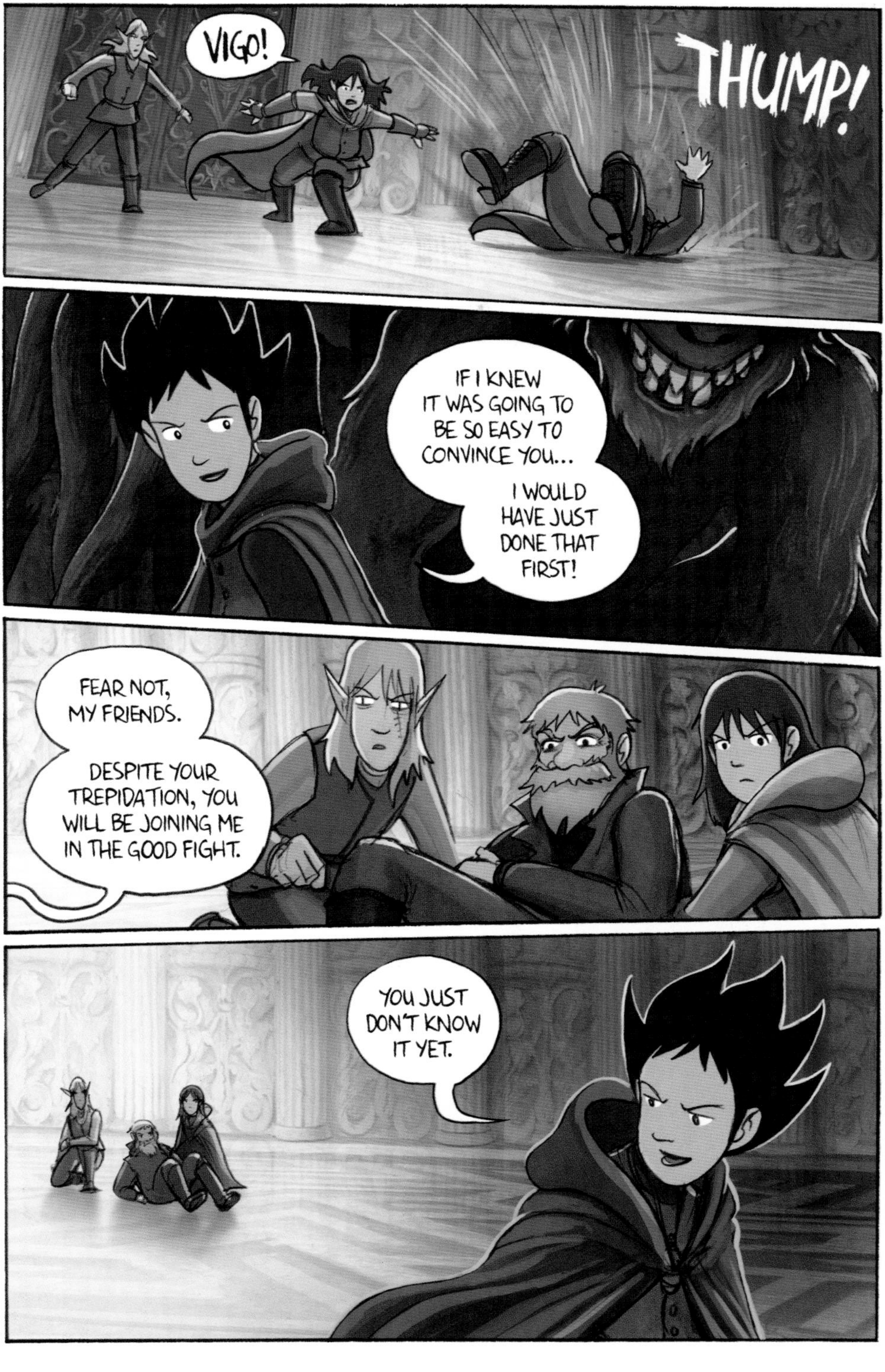
VIGO!
THUMP!
IF I KNEW IT WAS GOING TO BE SO EASY TO CONVINCE YOU...
I WOULD HAVE JUST DONE THAT FIRST!
FEAR NOT, MY FRIENDS.
DESPITE YOUR TREPIDATION, YOU WILL BE JOINING ME IN THE GOOD FIGHT.
YOU JUST DON'T KNOW IT YET.

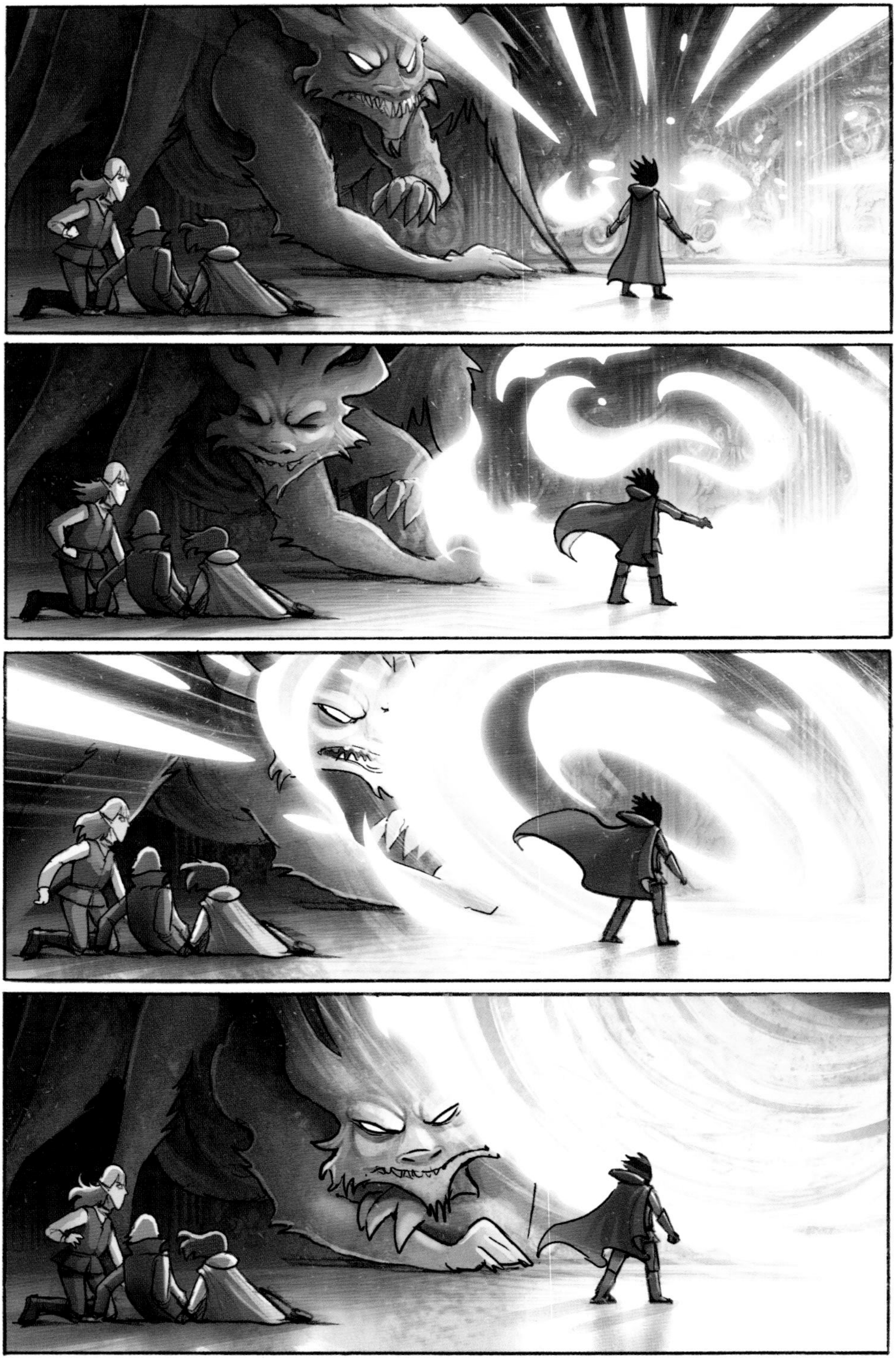

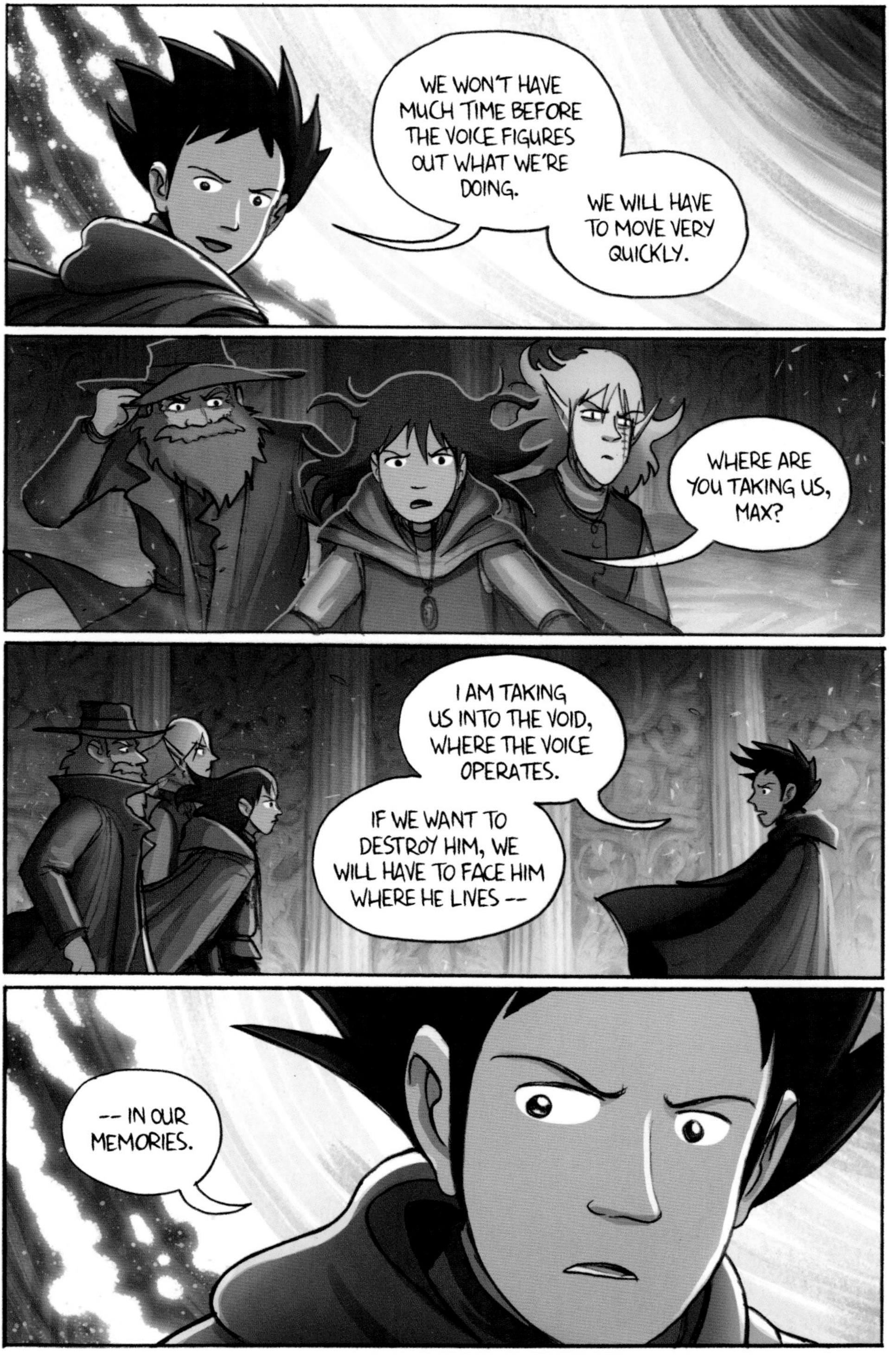
WE WON'T HAVE MUCH TIME BEFORE THE VOICE FIGURES OUT WHAT WE'RE DOING.
WE WILL HAVE TO MOVE VERY QUICKLY.
WHERE ARE YOU TAKING US, MAX?
I AM TAKING US INTO THE VOID, WHERE THE VOICE OPERATES.
IF WE WANT TO DESTROY HIM, WE WILL HAVE TO FACE HIM WHERE HE LIVES --
-- IN OUR MEMORIES.

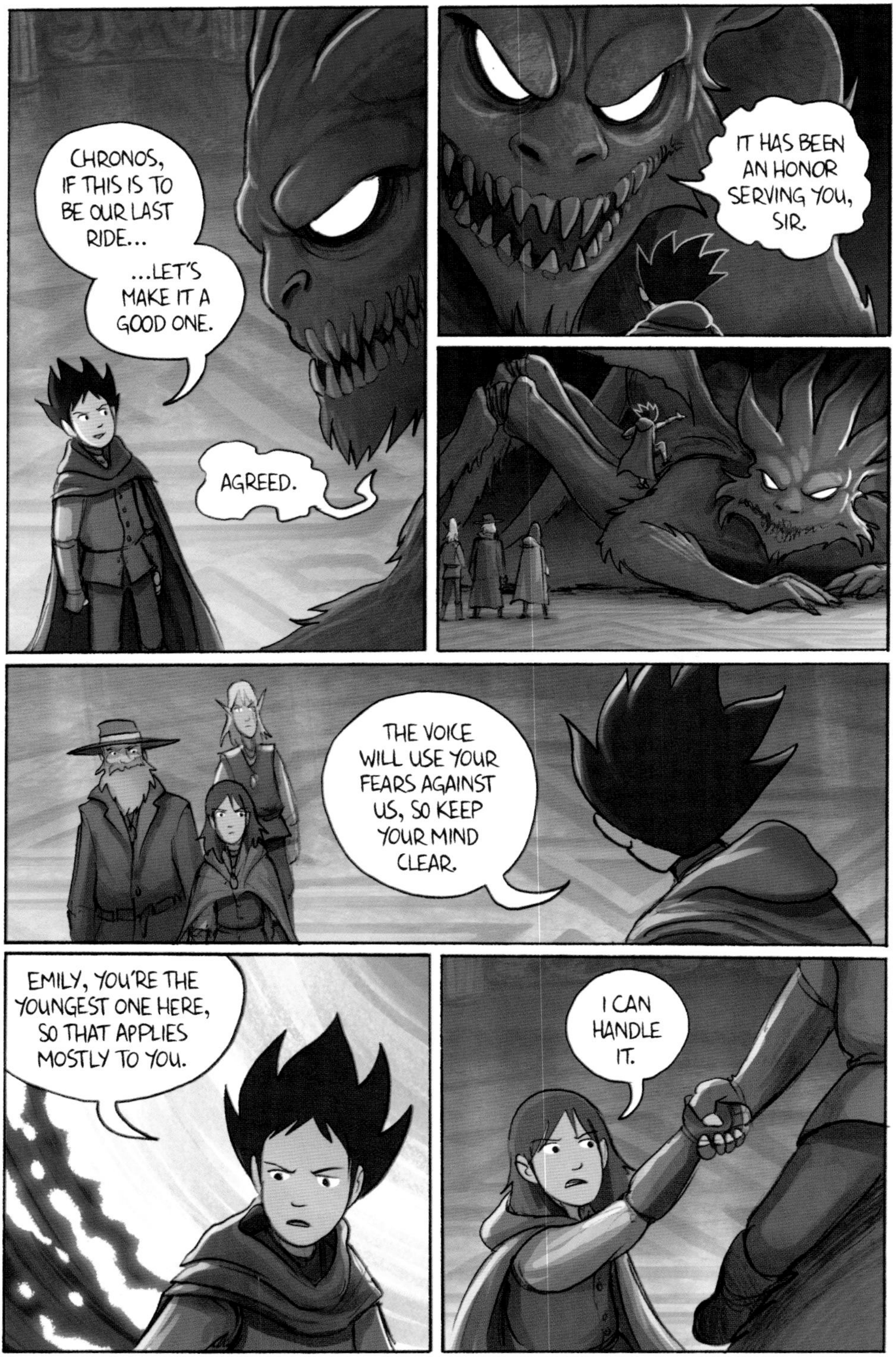
CHRONOS, IF THIS IS TO BE OUR LAST RIDE...
...LET'S MAKE IT A GOOD ONE.
AGREED.
IT HAS BEEN AN HONOR SERVING YOU, SIR.
THE VOICE WILL USE YOUR FEARS AGAINST US, SO KEEP YOUR MIND CLEAR.
EMILY, YOU'RE THE YOUNGEST ONE HERE, SO THAT APPLIES MOSTLY TO YOU.
I CAN HANDLE IT.

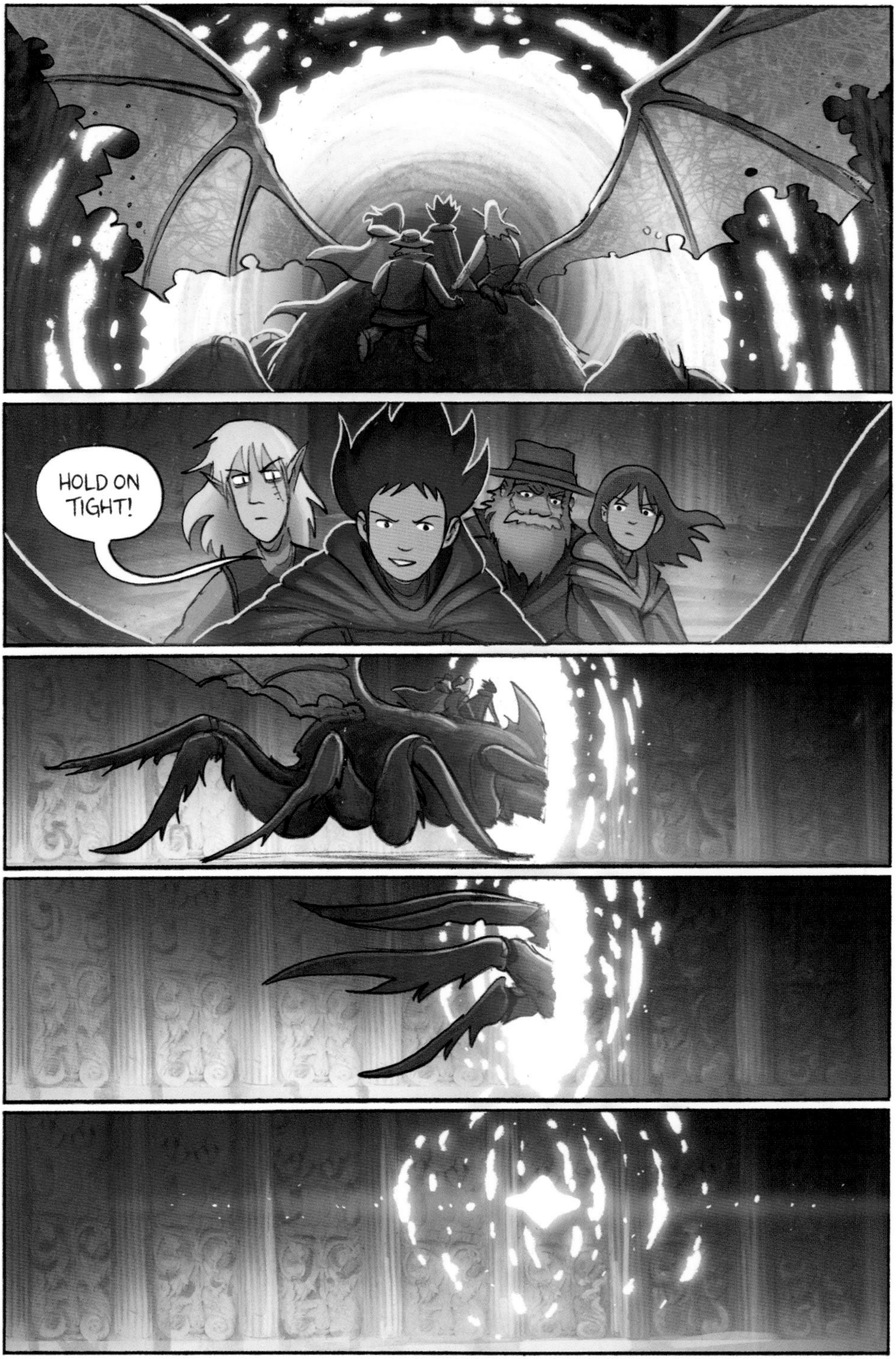
HOLD ON TIGHT!

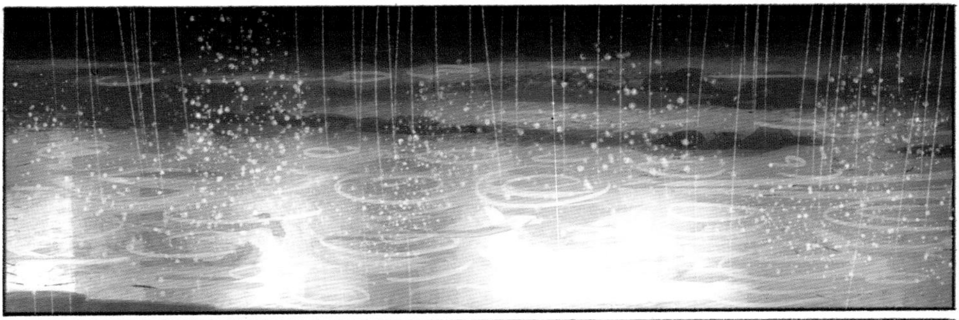

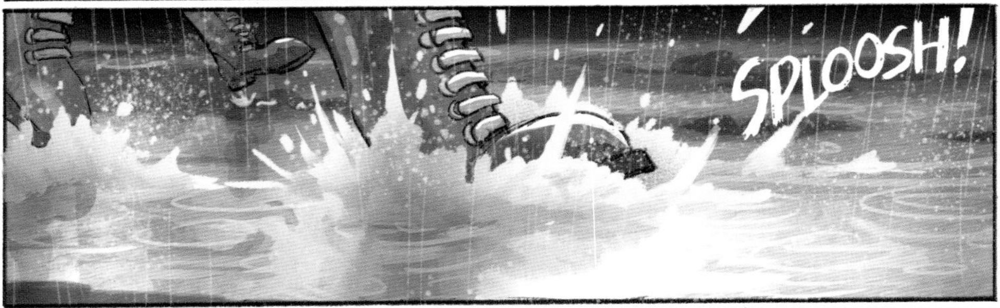
SPLOOSH!

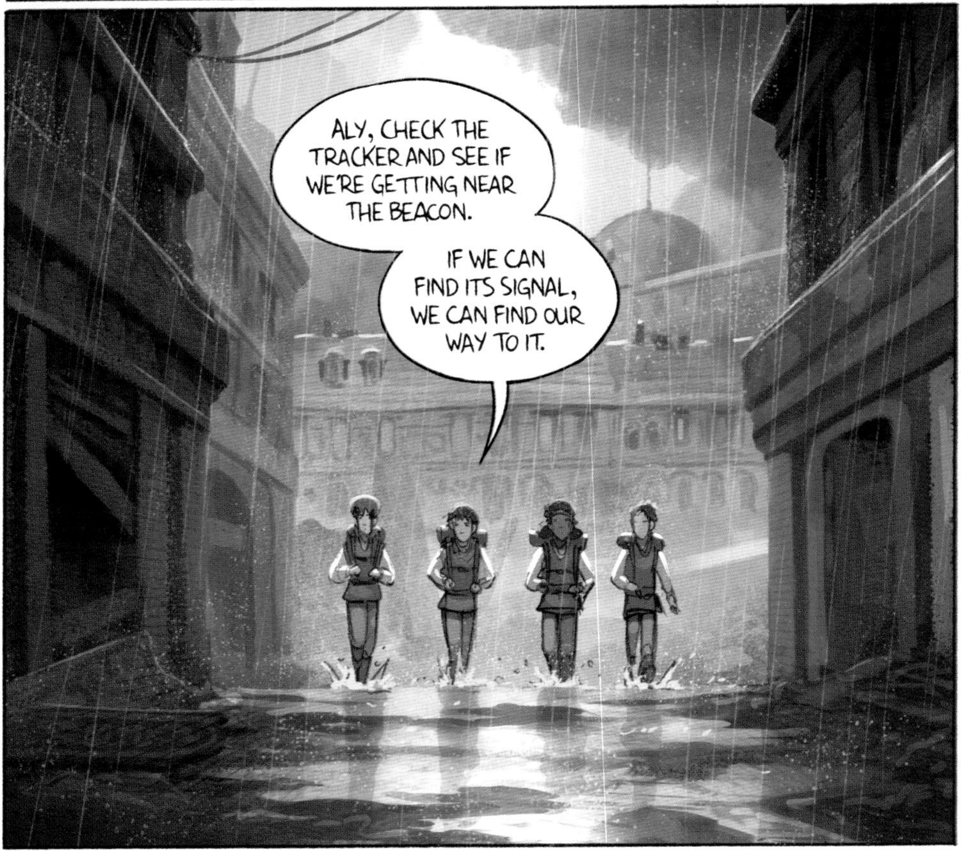
ALY, CHECK THE TRACKER AND SEE IF WE'RE GETTING NEAR THE BEACON.
IF WE CAN FIND ITS SIGNAL, WE CAN FIND OUR WAY TO IT.

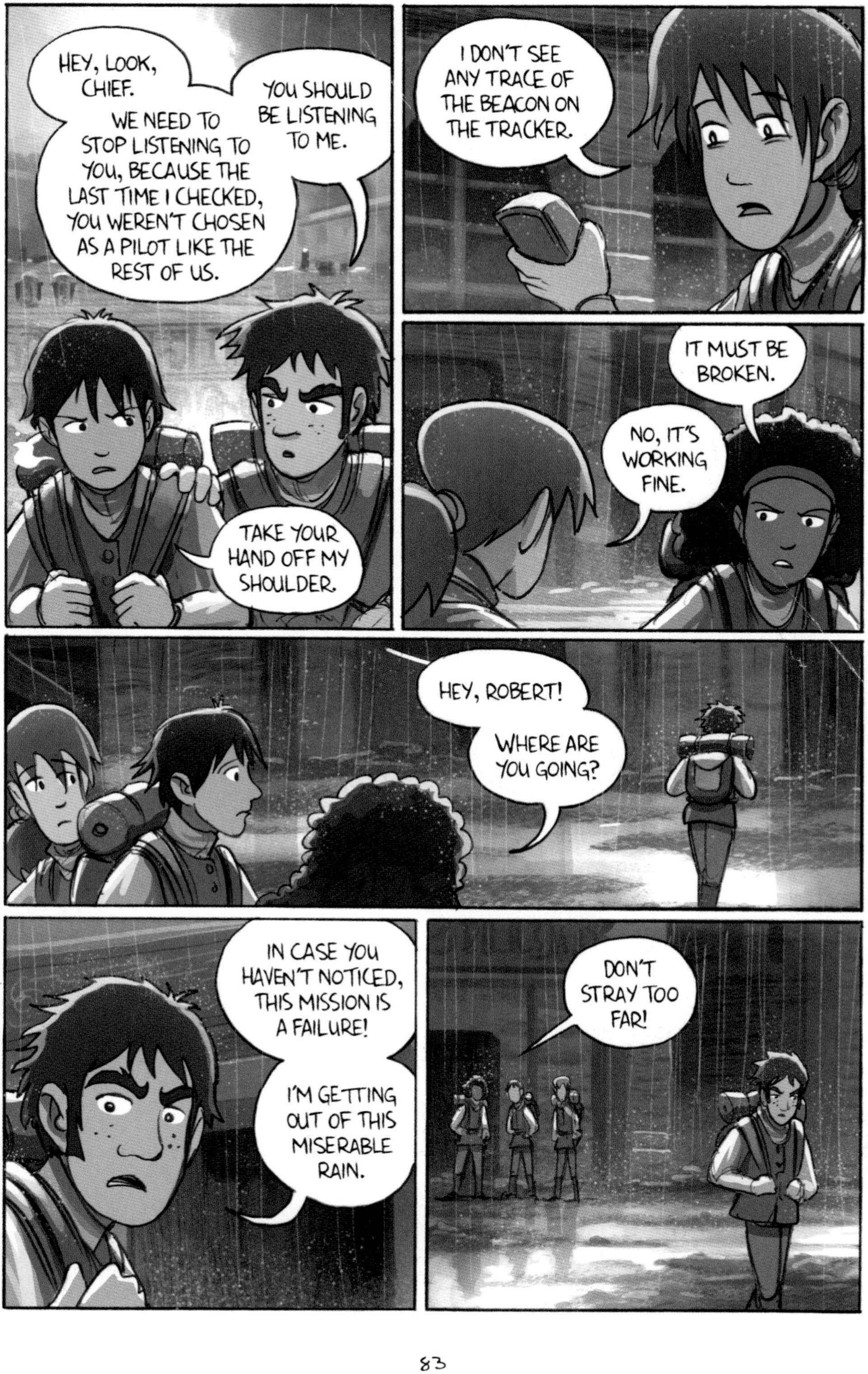
HEY, LOOK, CHIEF.
WE NEED TO STOP LISTENING TO YOU, BECAUSE THE LAST TIME I CHECKED, YOU WEREN'T CHOSEN AS A PILOT LIKE THE REST OF US.
YOU SHOULD BE LISTENING TO ME.
TAKE YOUR HAND OFF MY SHOULDER.
I DON'T SEE ANY TRACE OF THE BEACON ON THE TRACKER.
IT MUST BE BROKEN.
NO, IT'S WORKING FINE.
HEY, ROBERT!
WHERE ARE YOU GOING?
IN CASE YOU HAVEN'T NOTICED, THIS MISSION IS A FAILURE!
I'M GETTING OUT OF THIS MISERABLE RAIN.
DON'T STRAY TOO FAR!

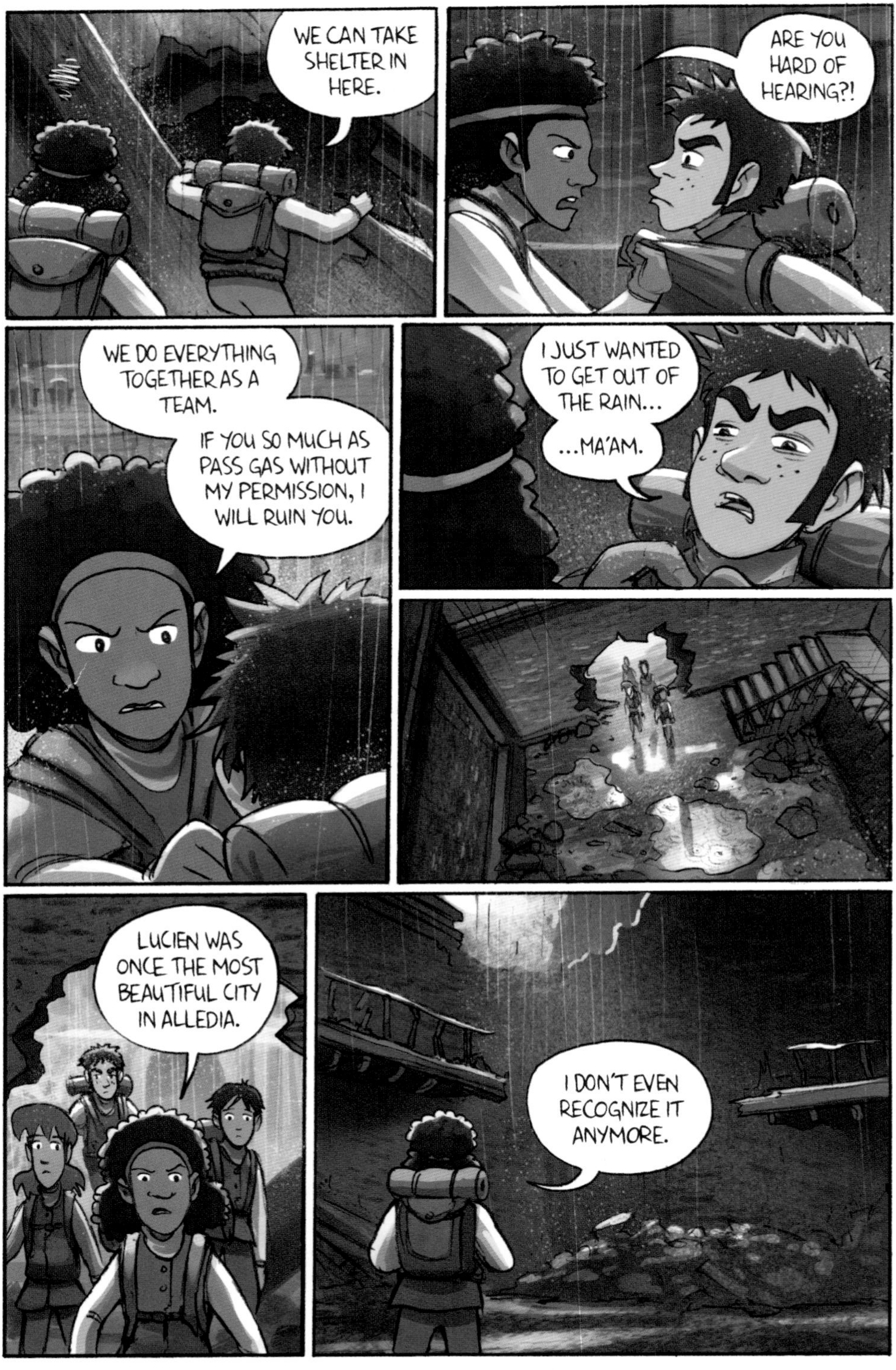
WE CAN TAKE SHELTER IN HERE.
ARE YOU HARD OF HEARING?!
WE DO EVERYTHING TOGETHER AS A TEAM.
IF YOU SO MUCH AS PASS GAS WITHOUT MY PERMISSION, I WILL RUIN YOU.
I JUST WANTED TO GET OUT OF THE RAIN...
...MA'AM.
LUCIEN WAS ONCE THE MOST BEAUTIFUL CITY IN ALLEDIA.
I DON'T EVEN RECOGNIZE IT ANYMORE.

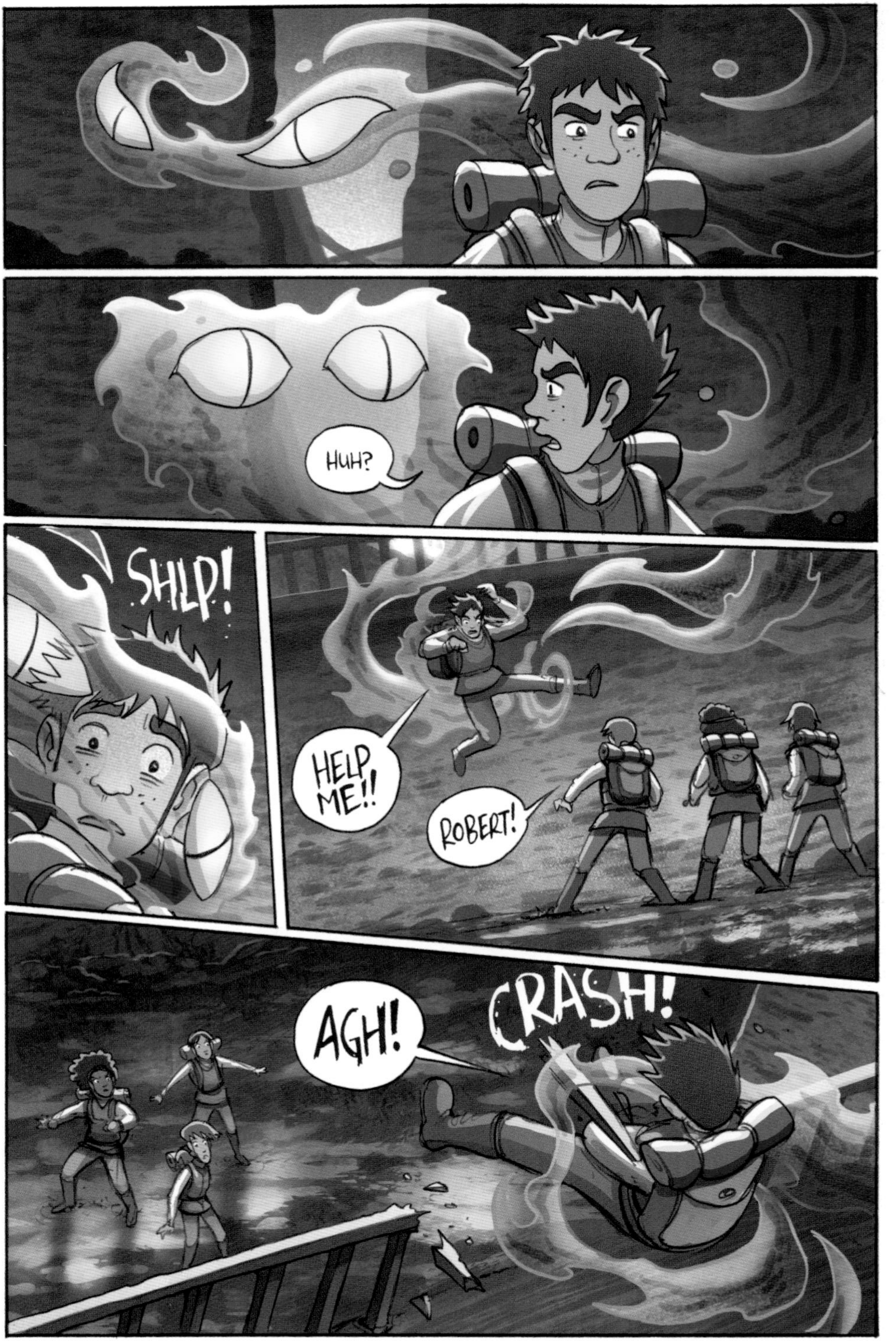
HUH?
SHLP!
HELP ME!!
ROBERT!
AGH!
CRASH!

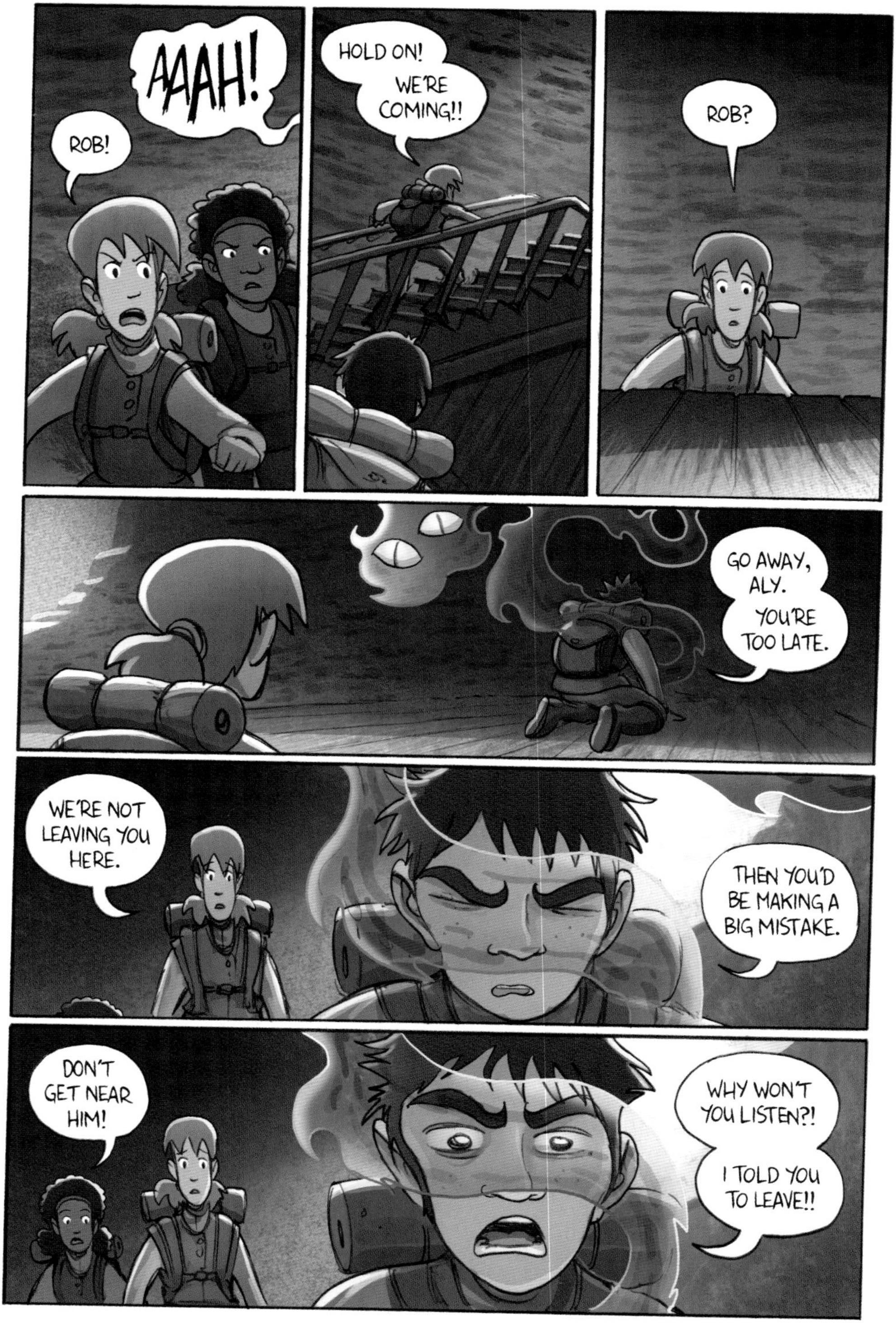
AAAH!
ROB!
HOLD ON!
WE'RE COMING!!
ROB?
GO AWAY, ALY.
YOU'RE TOO LATE.
WE'RE NOT LEAVING YOU HERE.
THEN YOU'D BE MAKING A BIG MISTAKE.
DON'T GET NEAR HIM!
WHY WON'T YOU LISTEN?!
I TOLD YOU TO LEAVE!!

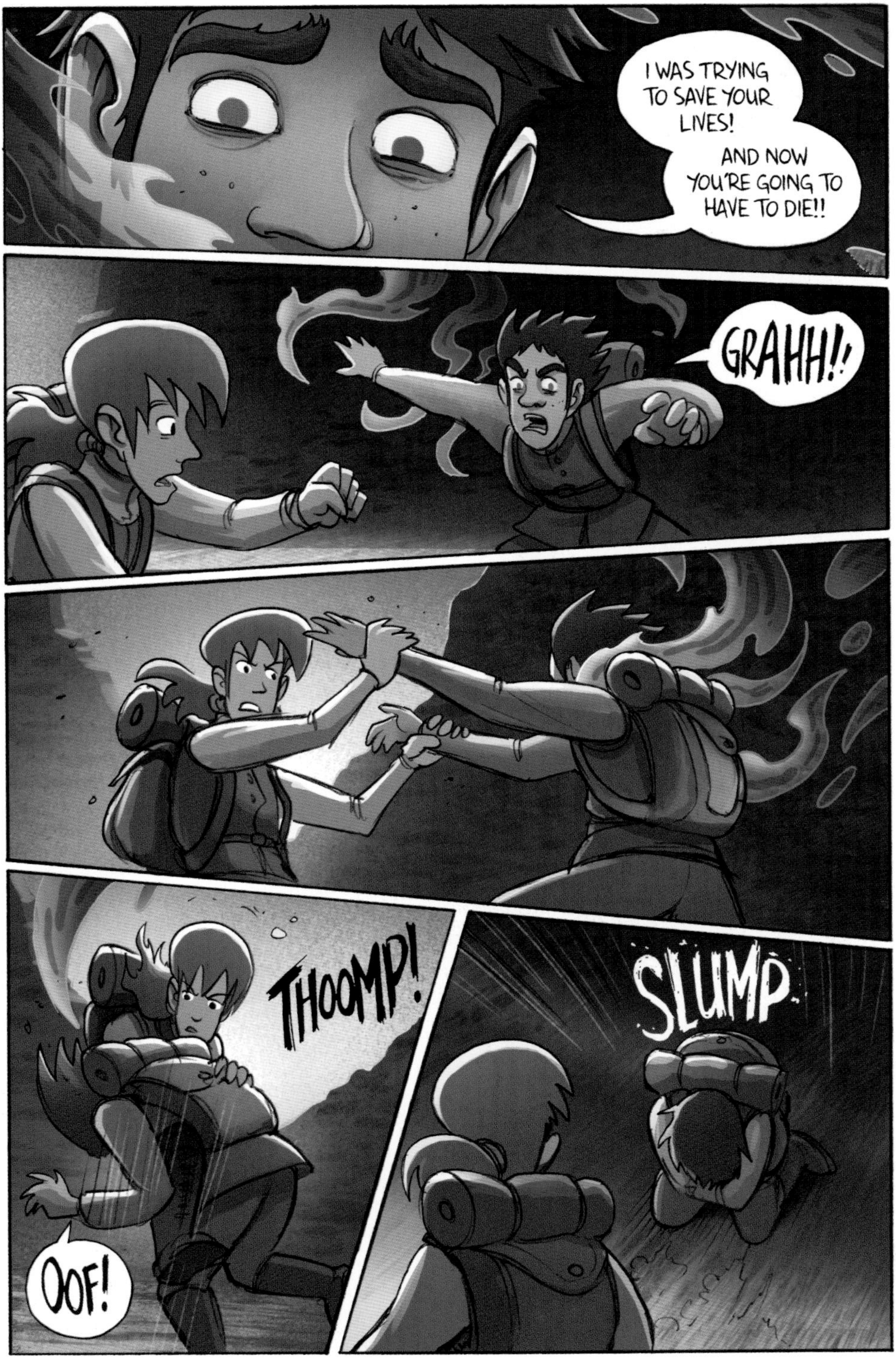
I WAS TRYING TO SAVE YOUR LIVES!
AND NOW YOU'RE GOING TO HAVE TO DIE!!
GRAHH!!
THOOMP!
OOF!
SLUMP

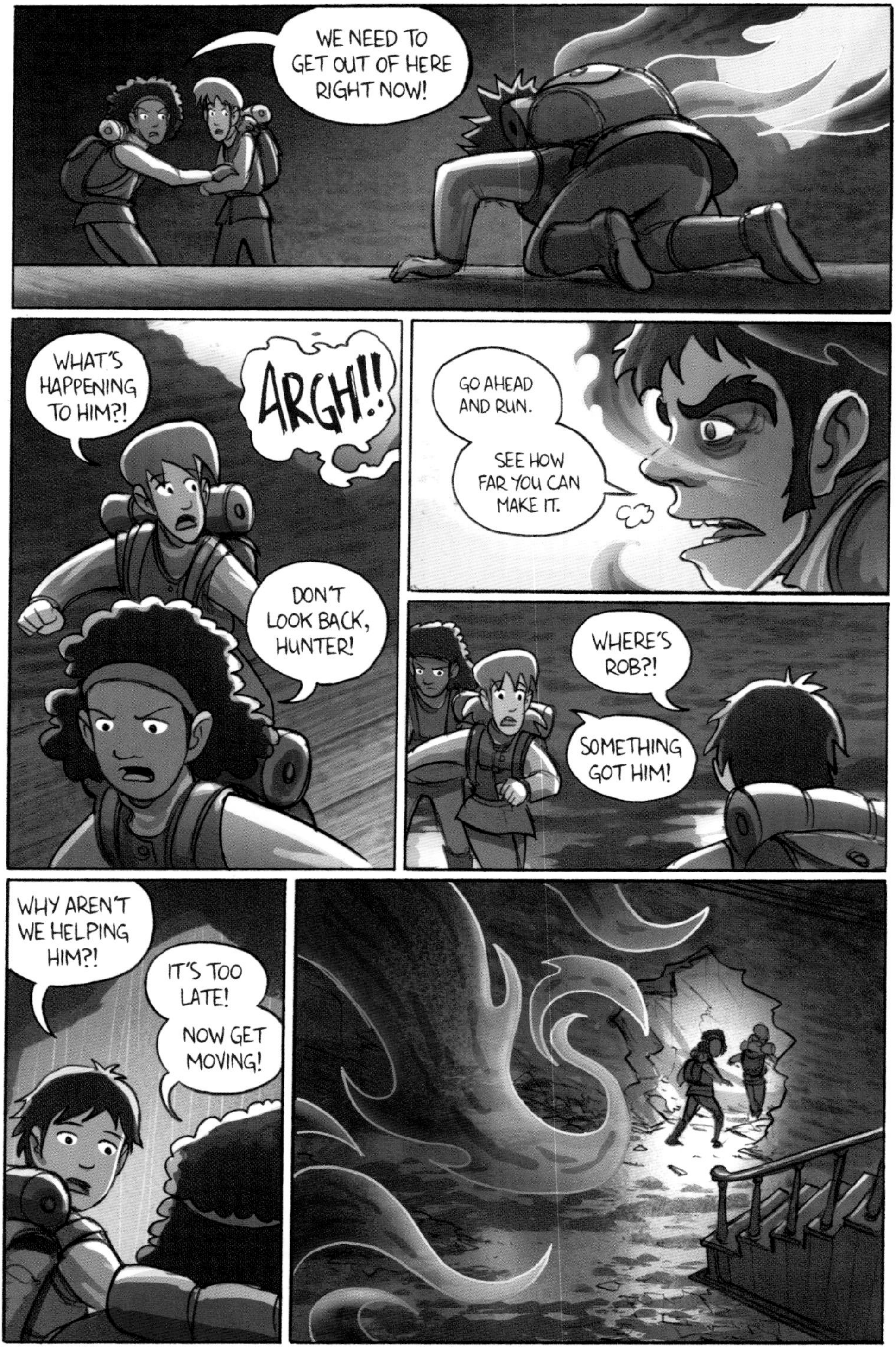
WE NEED TO GET OUT OF HERE RIGHT NOW!
WHAT'S HAPPENING TO HIM?!
ARGH!!
DON'T LOOK BACK, HUNTER!
GO AHEAD AND RUN.
SEE HOW FAR YOU CAN MAKE IT.
WHERE'S ROB?!
SOMETHING GOT HIM!
WHY AREN'T WE HELPING HIM?!
IT'S TOO LATE!
NOW GET MOVING!

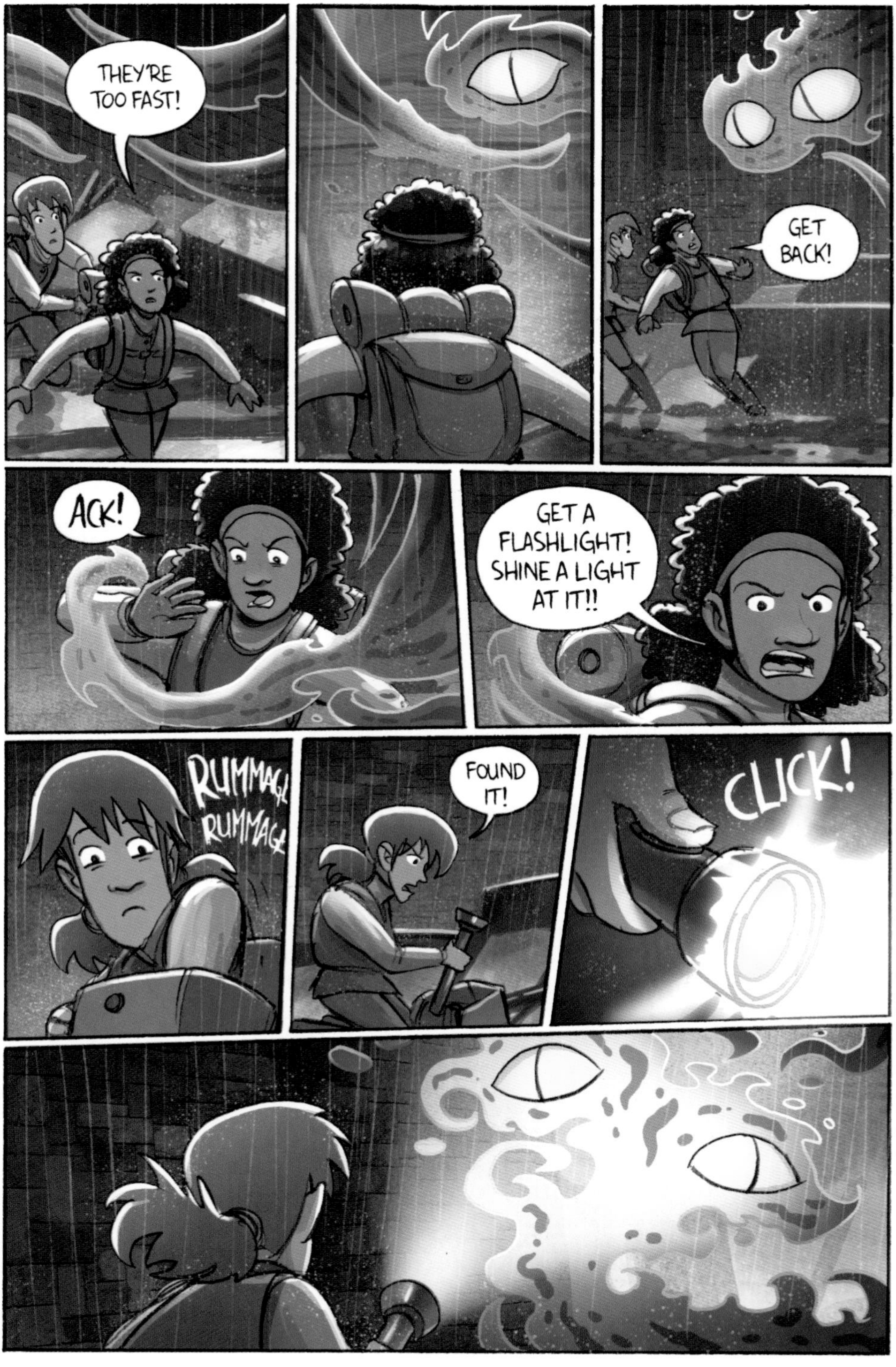
THEY'RE TOO FAST!
GET BACK!
ACK!
GET A FLASHLIGHT! SHINE A LIGHT AT IT!!
RUMMAGE RUMMAGE
FOUND IT!
CLICK!

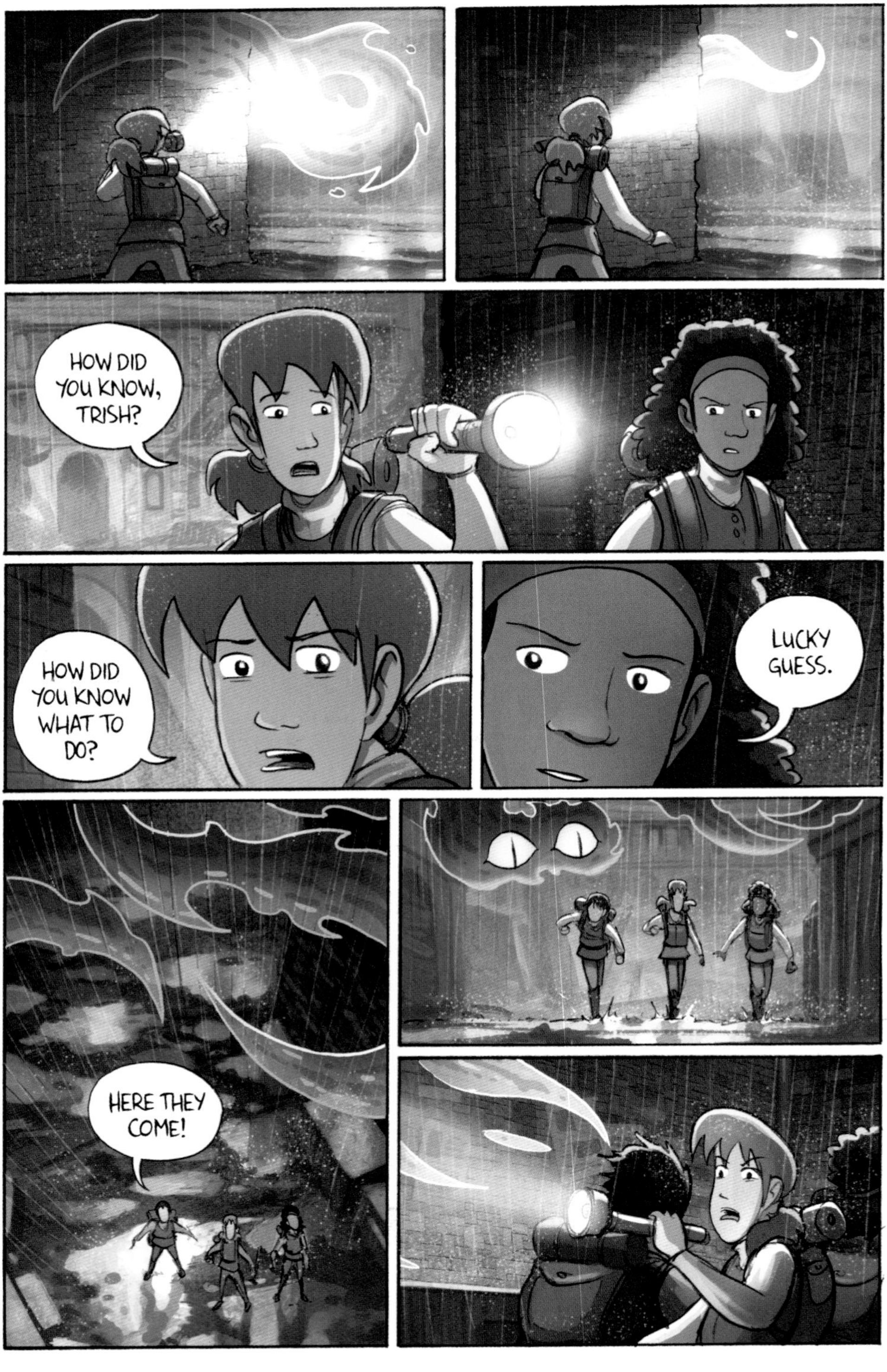
HOW DID YOU KNOW, TRISH?
HOW DID YOU KNOW WHAT TO DO?
LUCKY GUESS.
HERE THEY COME!

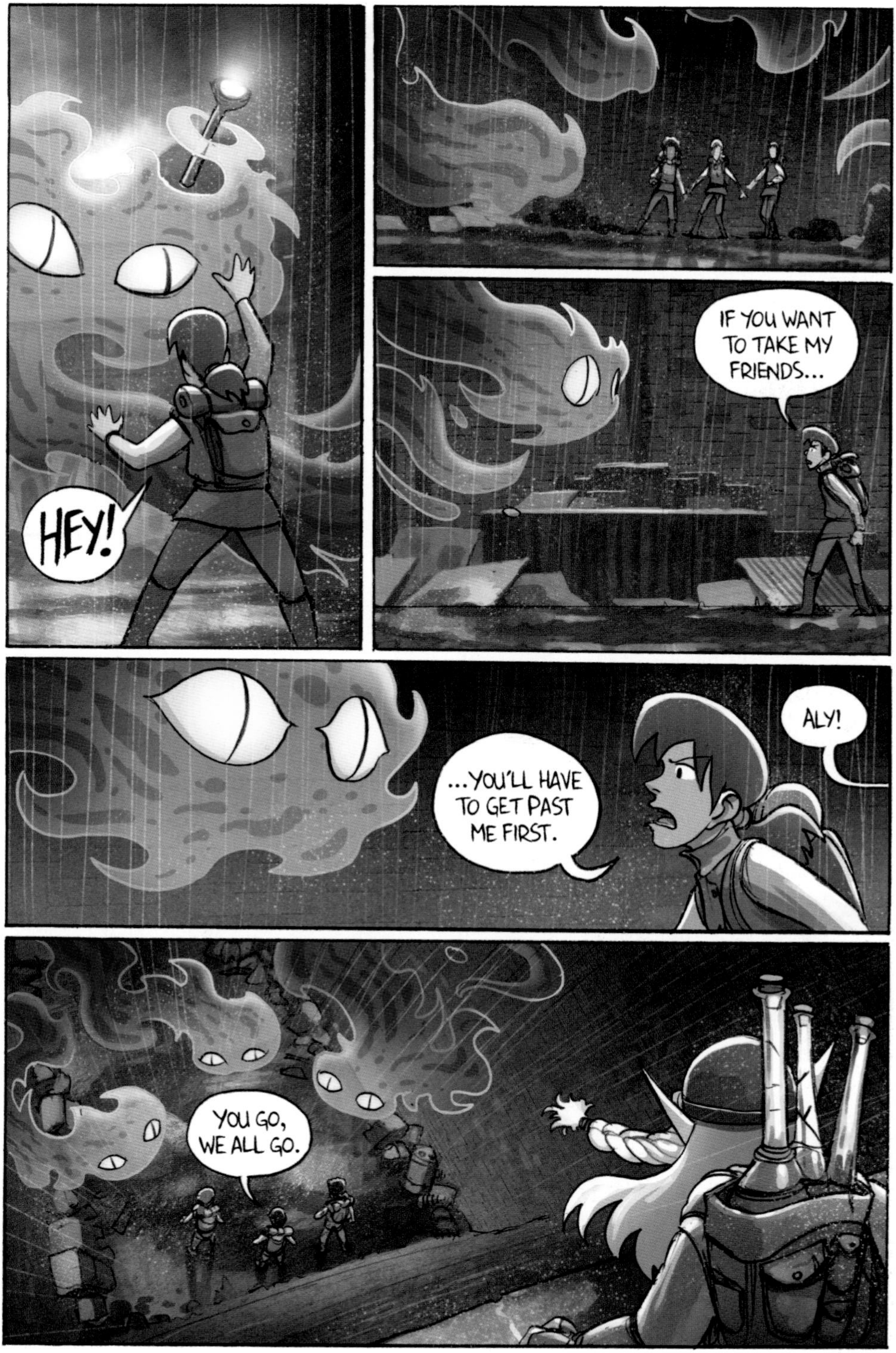
HEY!
IF YOU WANT TO TAKE MY FRIENDS...
...YOU'LL HAVE TO GET PAST ME FIRST.
ALY!
YOU GO, WE ALL GO.

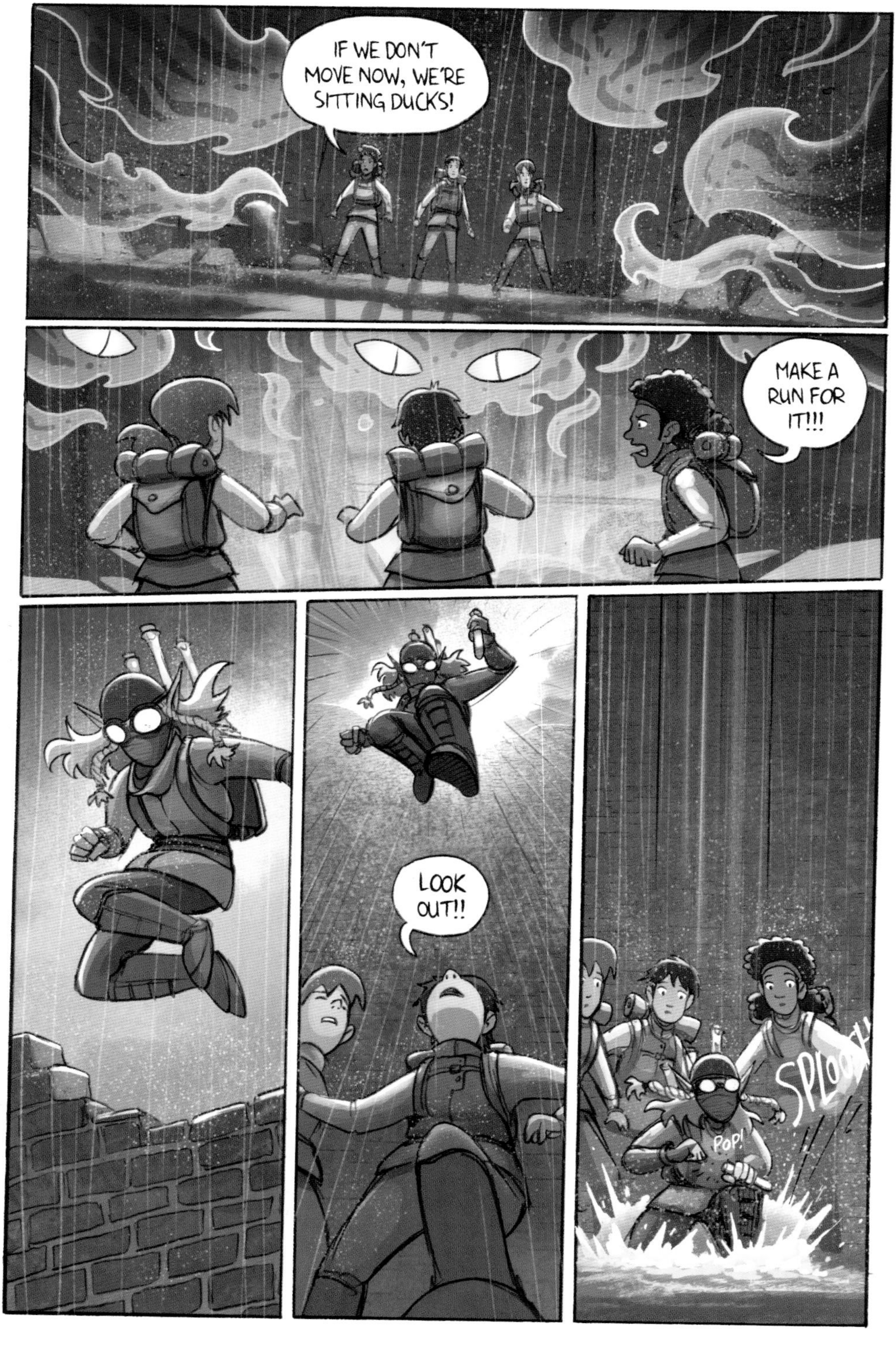
IF WE DON'T MOVE NOW, WE'RE SITTING DUCKS!
MAKE A RUN FOR IT!!!
LOOK OUT!!
POP!
SPLOO

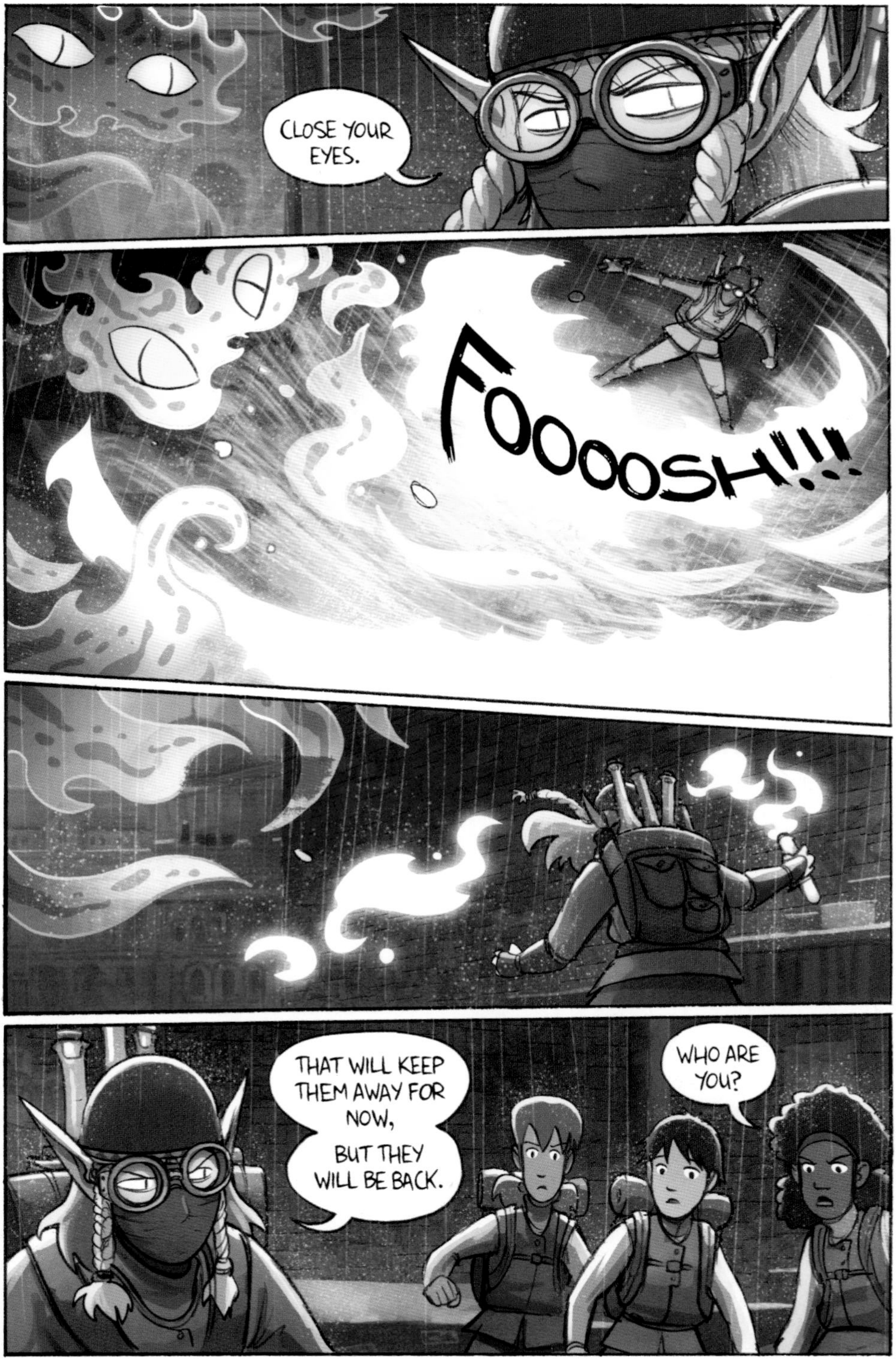

CLOSE YOUR EYES.
FOOOOOSH!!!
THAT WILL KEEP THEM AWAY FOR NOW,
BUT THEY WILL BE BACK.
WHO ARE YOU?

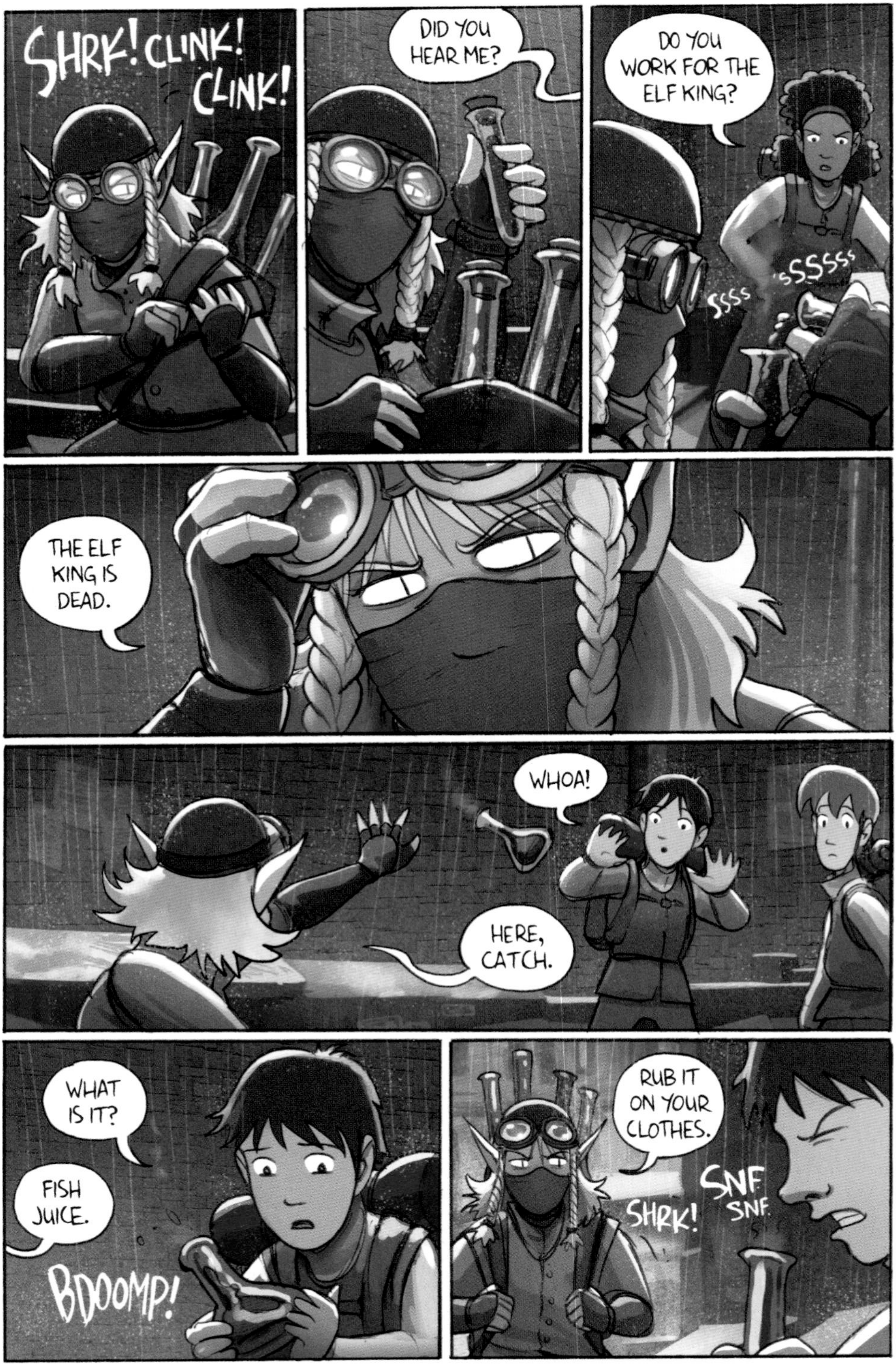
SHRK! CLINK! CLINK!
DID YOU HEAR ME?
DO YOU WORK FOR THE ELF KING?
SSSS SSSSS
THE ELF KING IS DEAD.
WHOA!
HERE, CATCH.
WHAT IS IT?
FISH JUICE.
BDOOMP!
RUB IT ON YOUR CLOTHES.
SHRK!
SNF SNF

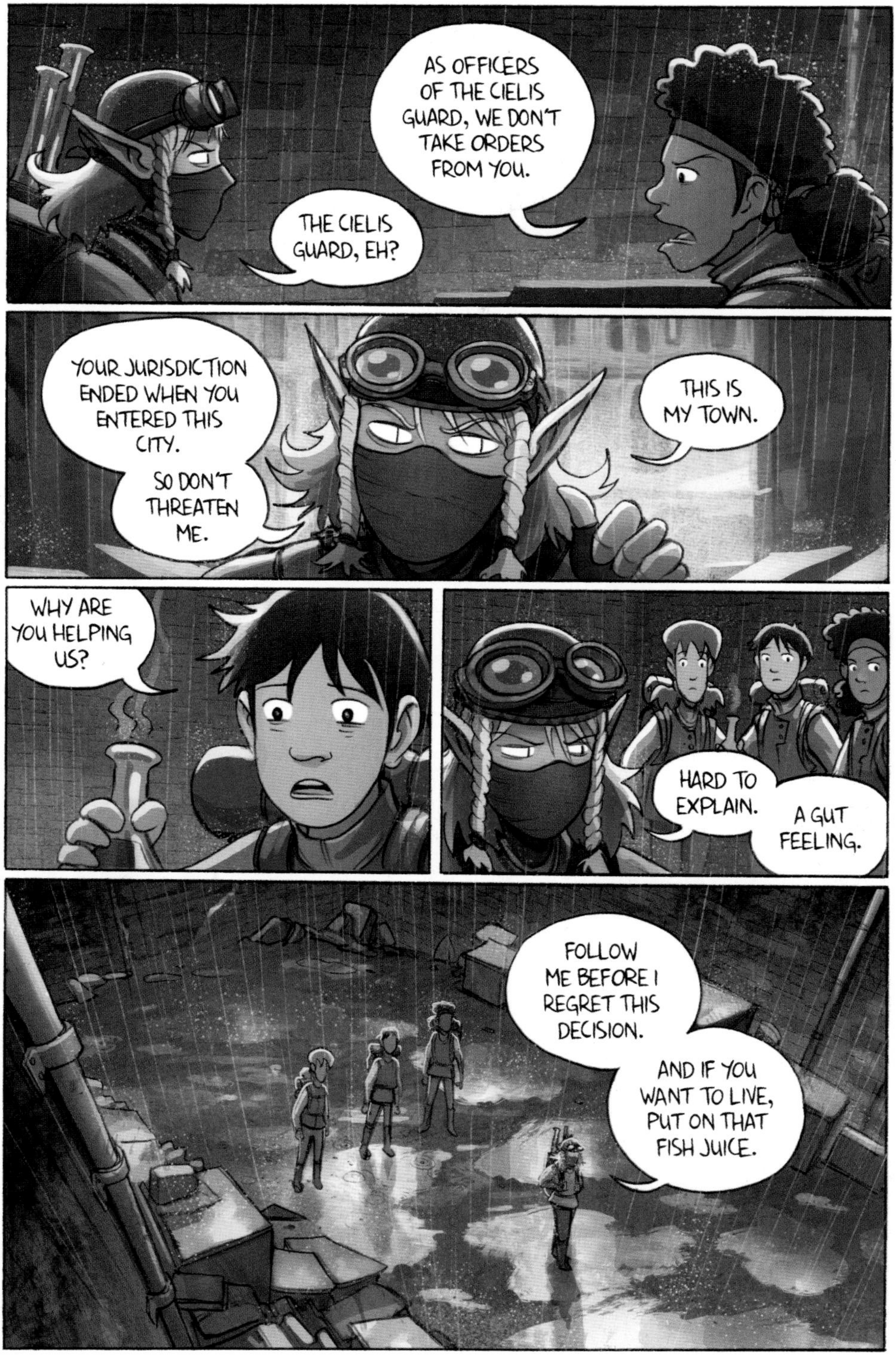
AS OFFICERS OF THE CIELIS GUARD, WE DON'T TAKE ORDERS FROM YOU.
THE CIELIS GUARD, EH?
YOUR JURISDICTION ENDED WHEN YOU ENTERED THIS CITY.
SO DON'T THREATEN ME.
THIS IS MY TOWN.
WHY ARE YOU HELPING US?
HARD TO EXPLAIN.
A GUT FEELING.
FOLLOW ME BEFORE I REGRET THIS DECISION.
AND IF YOU WANT TO LIVE, PUT ON THAT FISH JUICE.

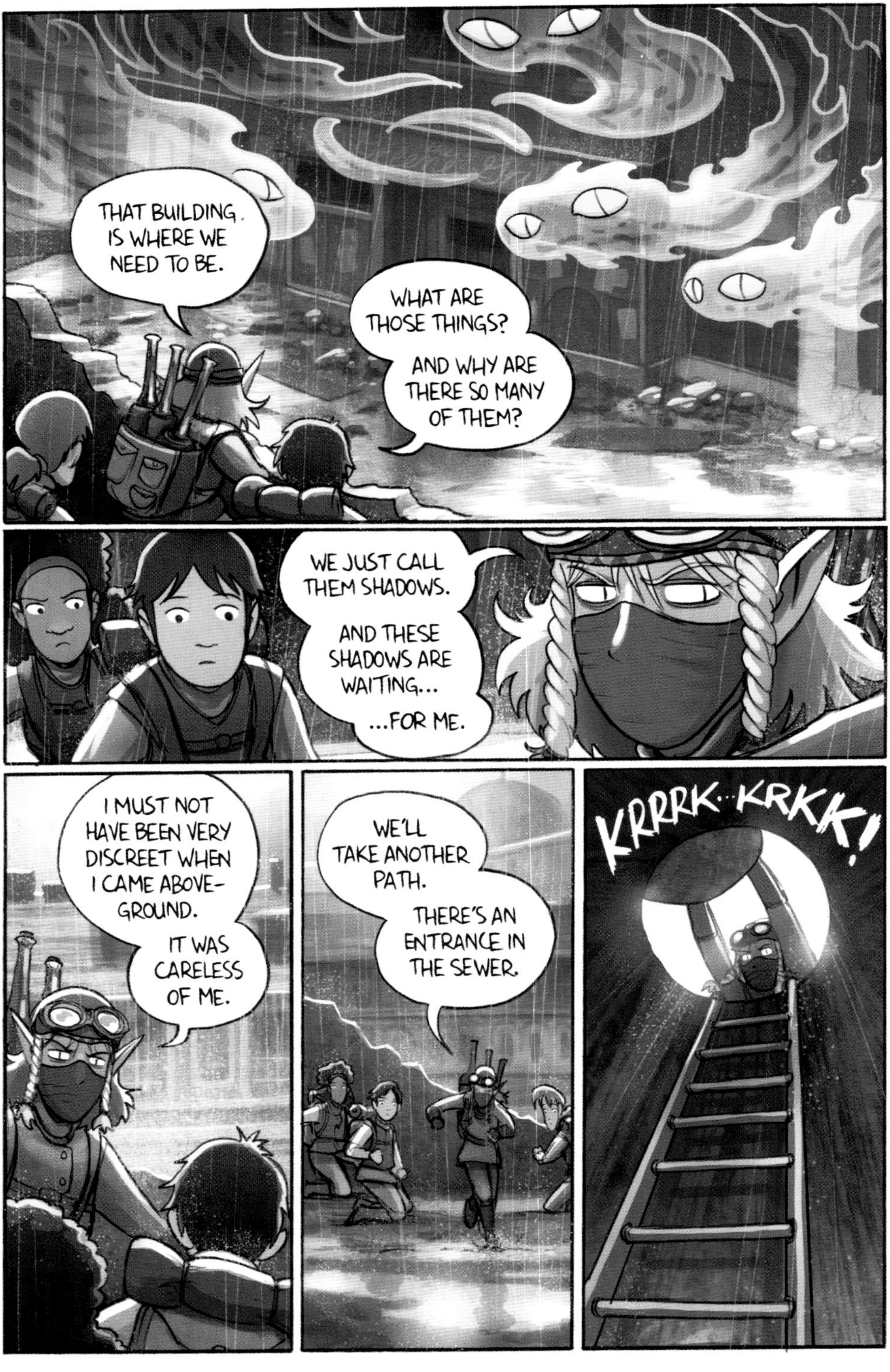
THAT BUILDING IS WHERE WE NEED TO BE.
WHAT ARE THOSE THINGS?
AND WHY ARE THERE SO MANY OF THEM?
WE JUST CALL THEM SHADOWS.
AND THESE SHADOWS ARE WAITING...
...FOR ME.
I MUST NOT HAVE BEEN VERY DISCREET WHEN I CAME ABOVE-GROUND.
IT WAS CARELESS OF ME.
WE'LL TAKE ANOTHER PATH.
THERE'S AN ENTRANCE IN THE SEWER.
KRRRK...KRKK!

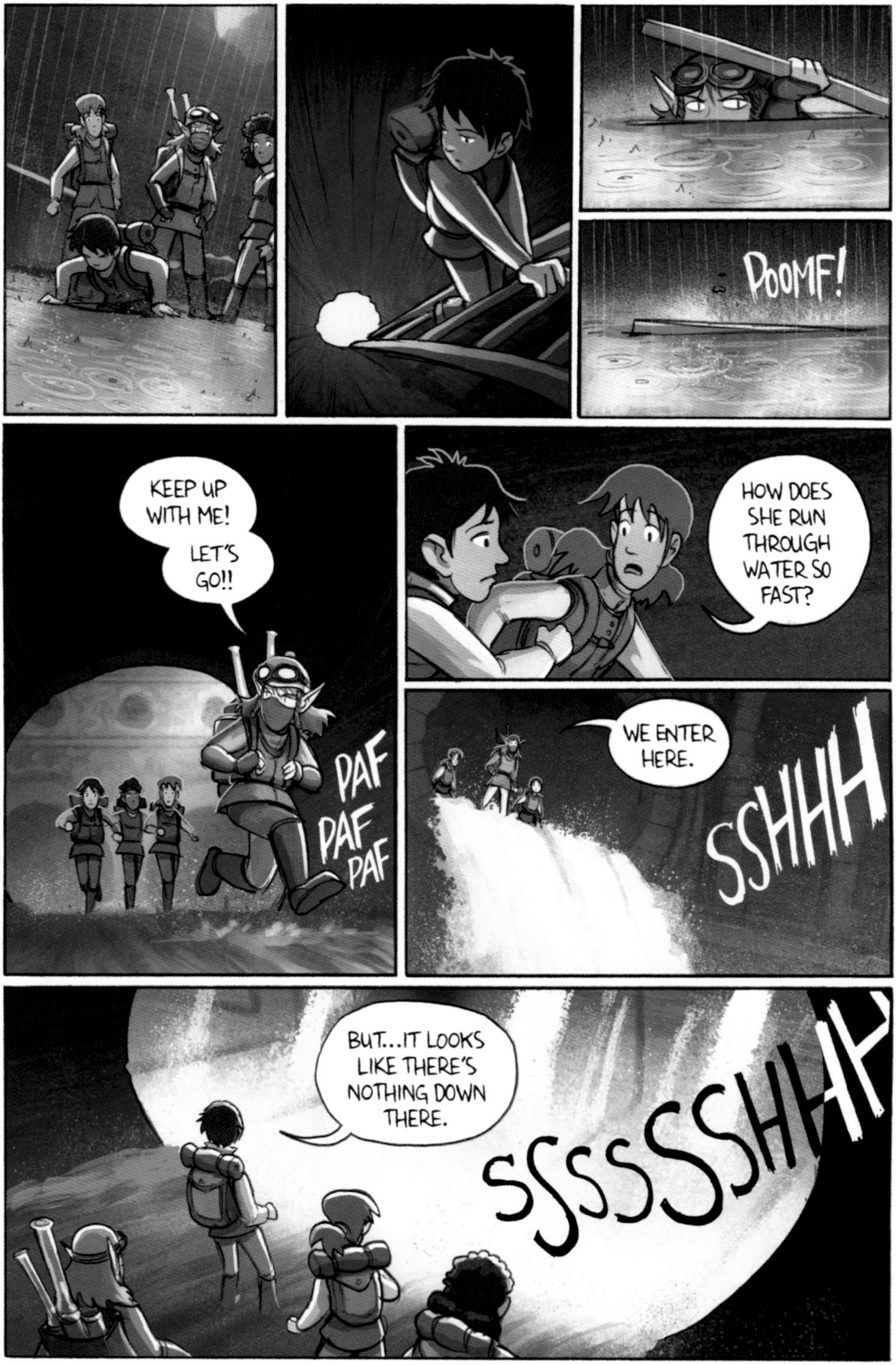
POOMF!
KEEP UP WITH ME!
LET'S GO!!
PAF
PAF
PAF
HOW DOES SHE RUN THROUGH WATER SO FAST?
WE ENTER HERE.
SSHHH
BUT...IT LOOKS LIKE THERE'S NOTHING DOWN THERE.
SSSSSHH

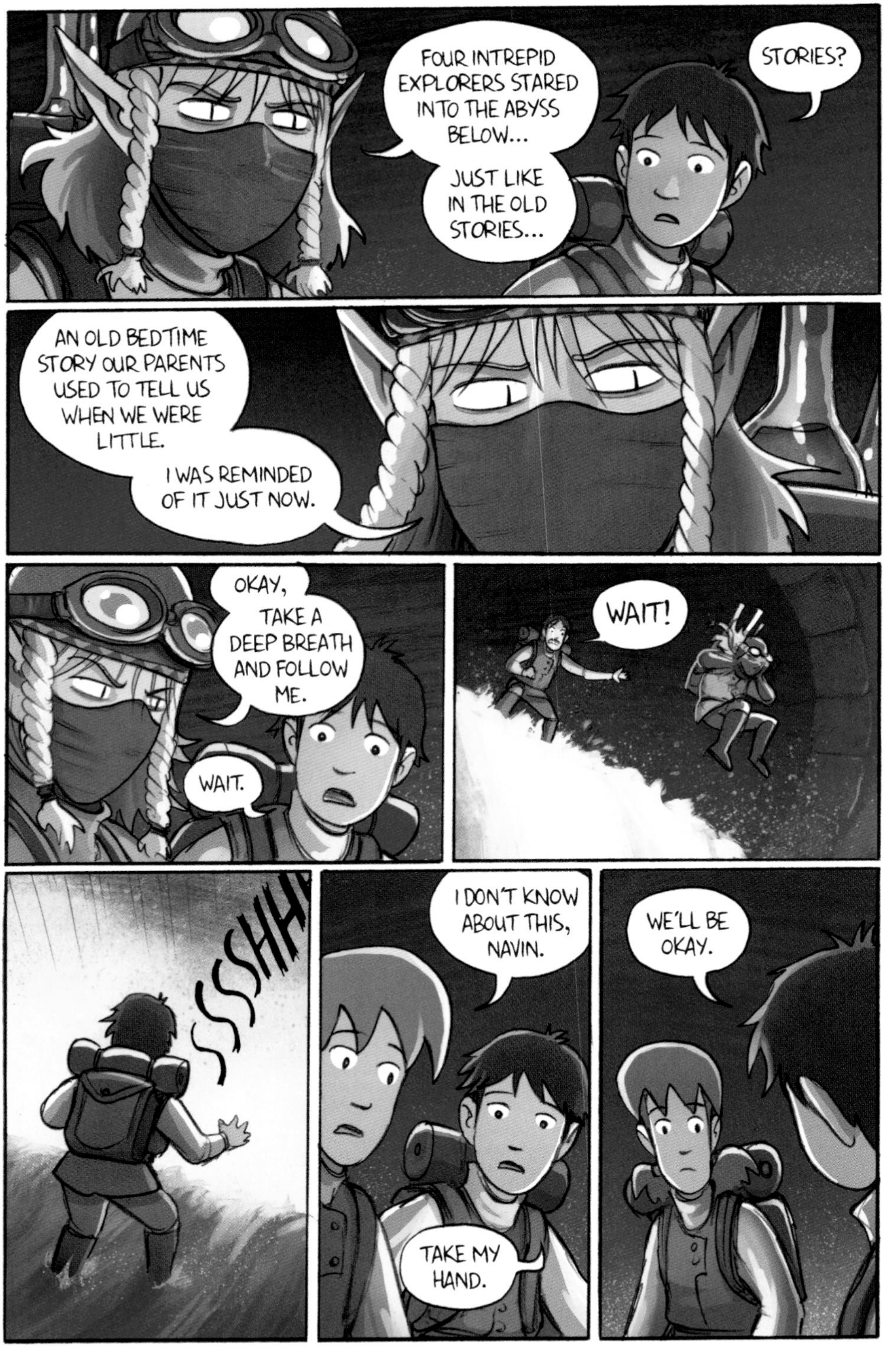
FOUR INTREPID EXPLORERS STARED INTO THE ABYSS BELOW...
JUST LIKE IN THE OLD STORIES...
STORIES?
AN OLD BEDTIME STORY OUR PARENTS USED TO TELL US WHEN WE WERE LITTLE.
I WAS REMINDED OF IT JUST NOW.
OKAY,
TAKE A DEEP BREATH AND FOLLOW ME.
WAIT.
WAIT!
SSSHH
I DON'T KNOW ABOUT THIS, NAVIN.
TAKE MY HAND.
WE'LL BE OKAY.

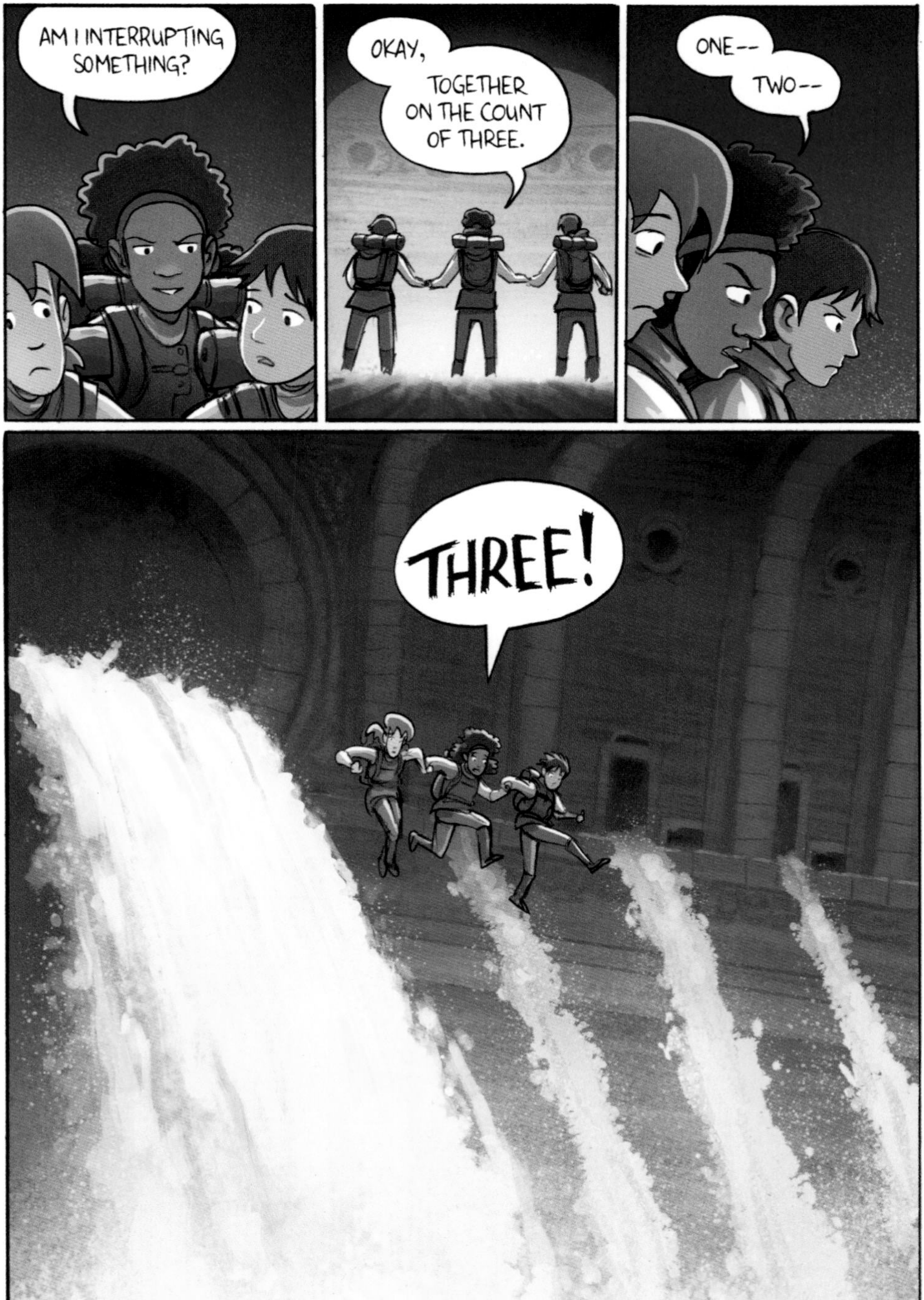
AM I INTERRUPTING SOMETHING?
OKAY,
TOGETHER ON THE COUNT OF THREE.
ONE--
TWO--
THREE!

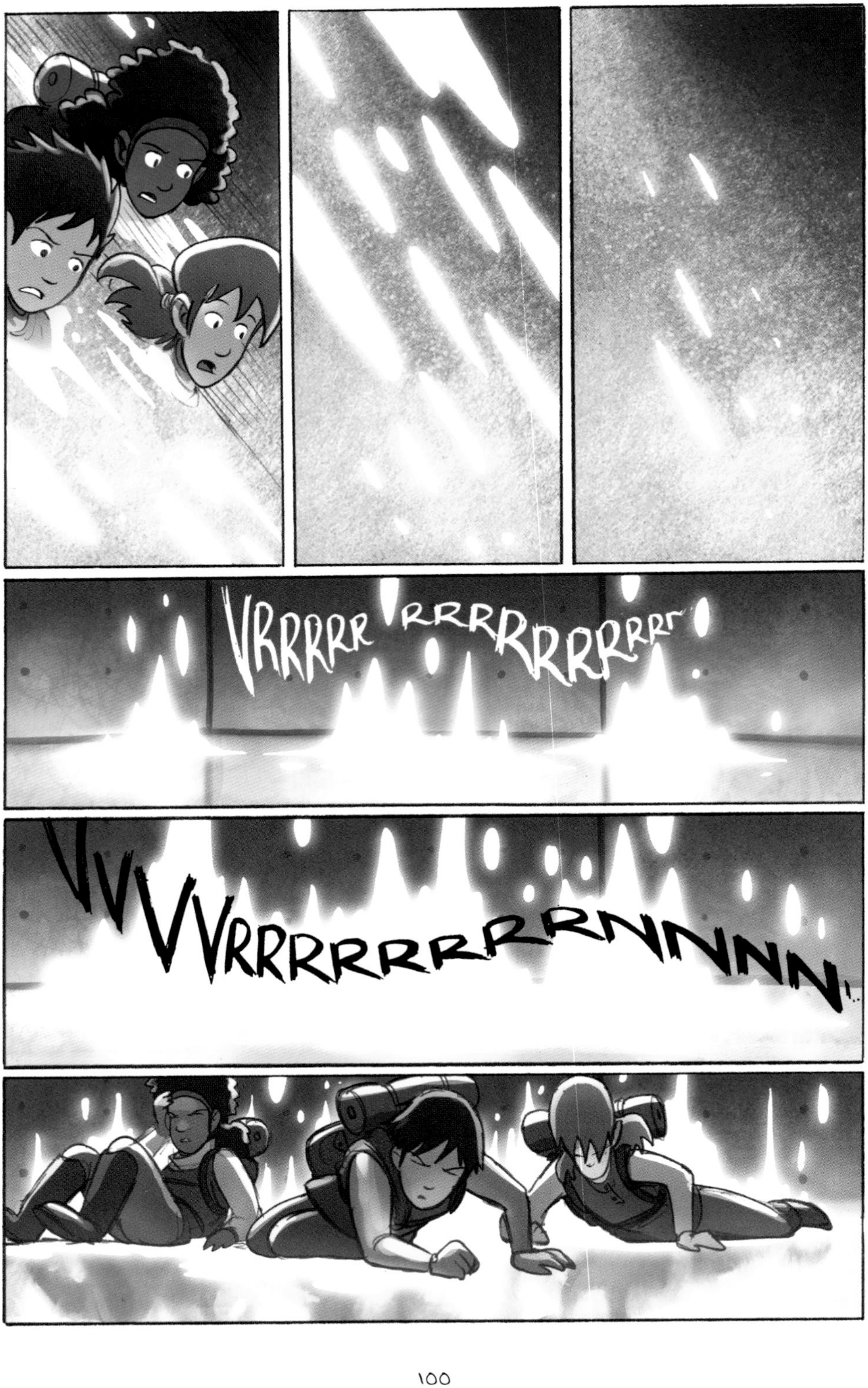
VRRRRR RRRRRRRRRr
VVVVRRRRRRRRNNNNN...

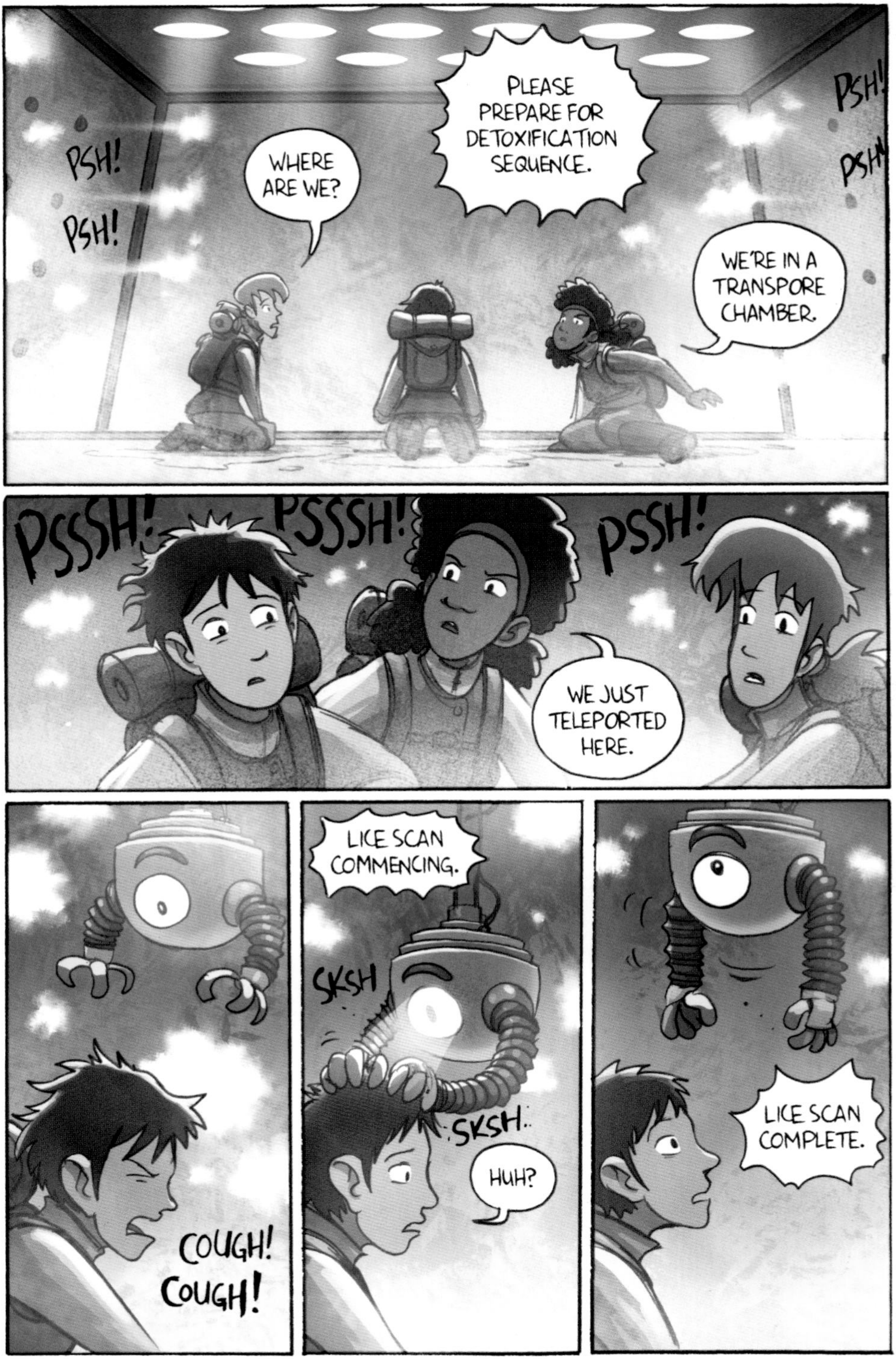
PSH!
PSH!
WHERE ARE WE?
PLEASE PREPARE FOR DETOXIFICATION SEQUENCE.
PSH!
PSH!
WE'RE IN A TRANSPORE CHAMBER.
PSSSH!
PSSSH!
PSSH!
WE JUST TELEPORTED HERE.
COUGH!
COUGH!
LICE SCAN COMMENCING.
SKSH
SKSH..
HUH?
LICE SCAN COMPLETE.

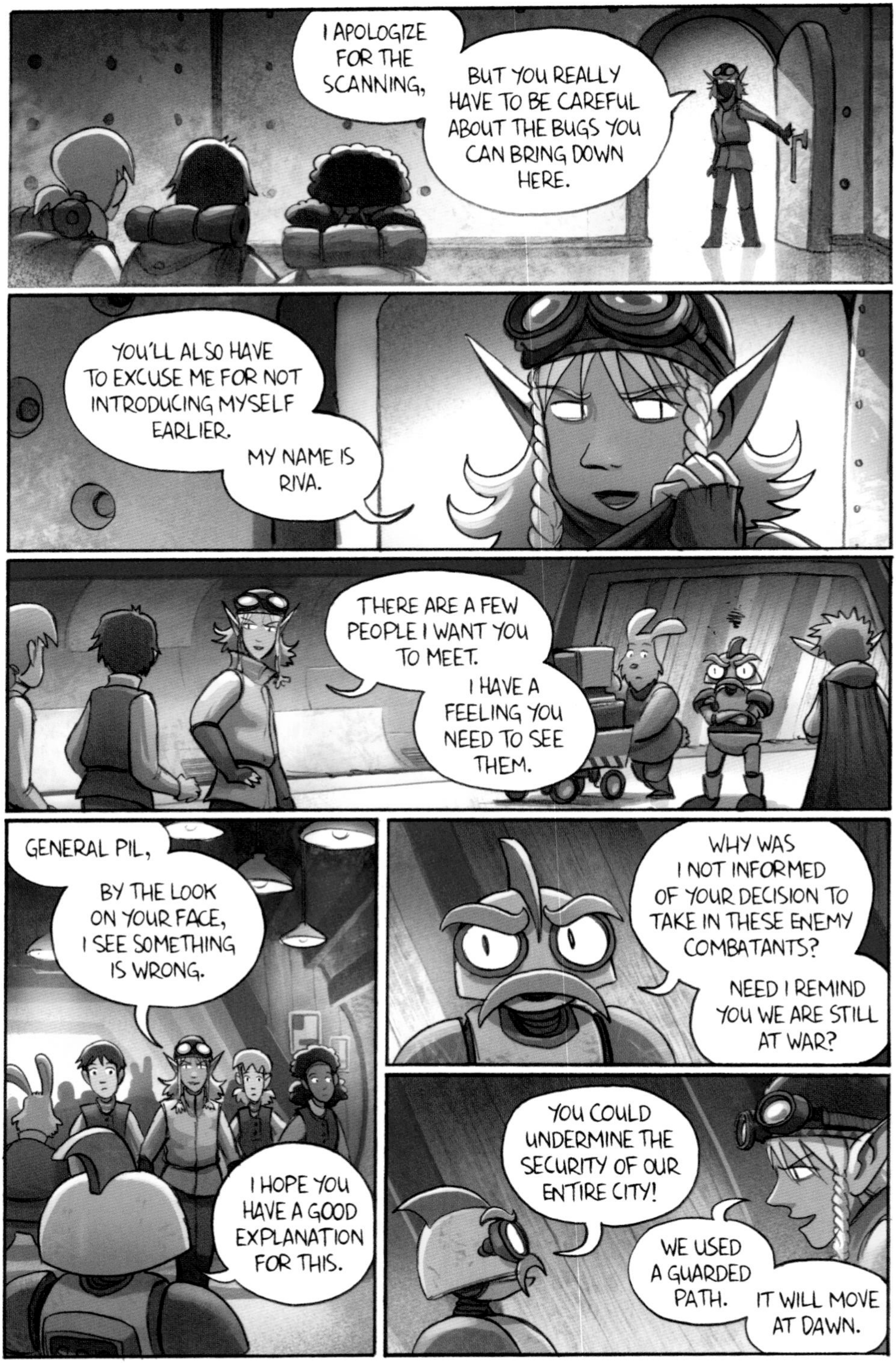
I APOLOGIZE FOR THE SCANNING,
BUT YOU REALLY HAVE TO BE CAREFUL ABOUT THE BUGS YOU CAN BRING DOWN HERE.
YOU'LL ALSO HAVE TO EXCUSE ME FOR NOT INTRODUCING MYSELF EARLIER.
MY NAME IS RIVA.
THERE ARE A FEW PEOPLE I WANT YOU TO MEET.
I HAVE A FEELING YOU NEED TO SEE THEM.
GENERAL PIL,
BY THE LOOK ON YOUR FACE, I SEE SOMETHING IS WRONG.
I HOPE YOU HAVE A GOOD EXPLANATION FOR THIS.
WHY WAS I NOT INFORMED OF YOUR DECISION TO TAKE IN THESE ENEMY COMBATANTS?
NEED I REMIND YOU WE ARE STILL AT WAR?
YOU COULD UNDERMINE THE SECURITY OF OUR ENTIRE CITY!
WE USED A GUARDED PATH.
IT WILL MOVE AT DAWN.

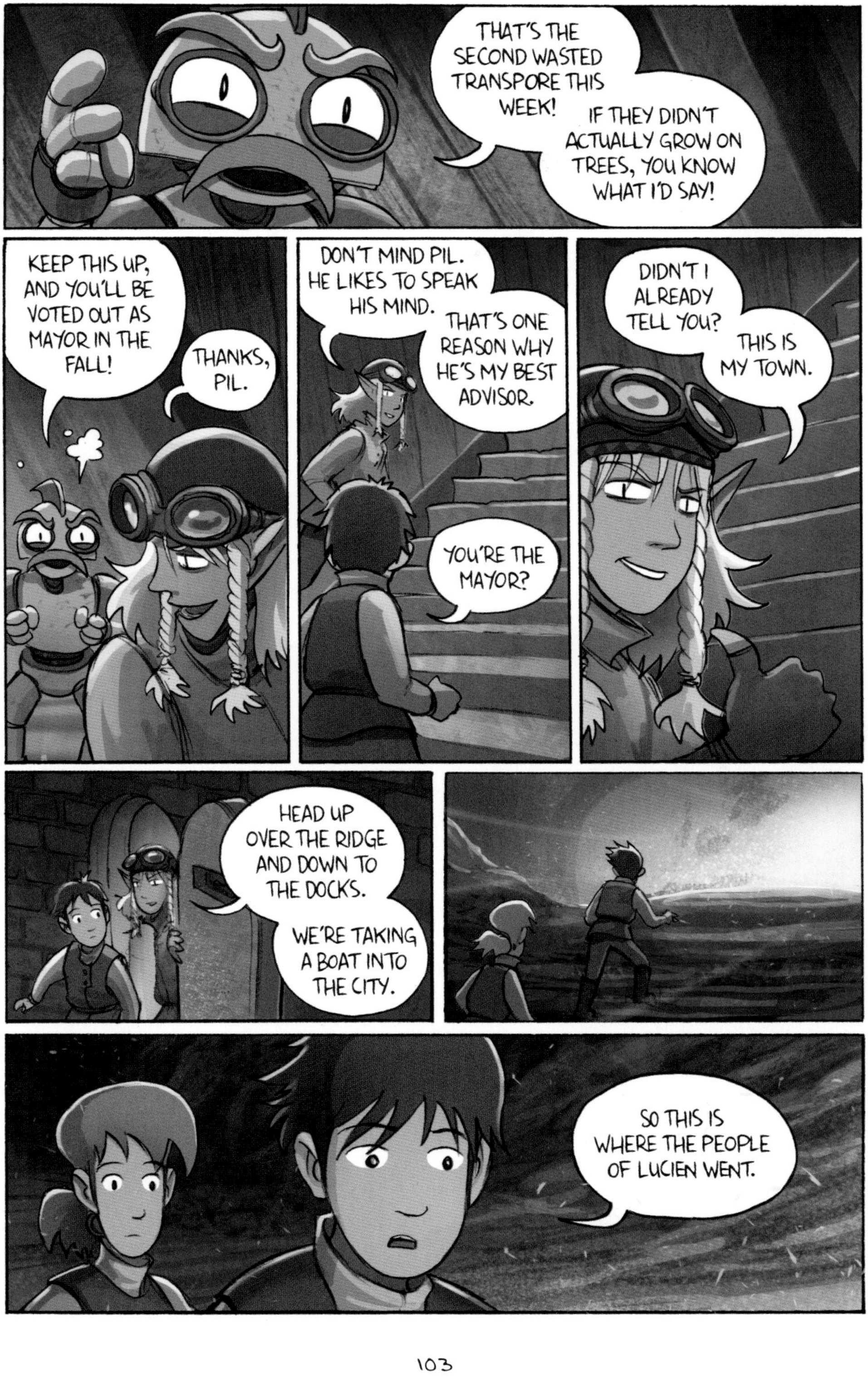
THAT'S THE SECOND WASTED TRANSPORE THIS WEEK!
IF THEY DIDN'T ACTUALLY GROW ON TREES, YOU KNOW WHAT I'D SAY!
KEEP THIS UP, AND YOU'LL BE VOTED OUT AS MAYOR IN THE FALL!
THANKS, PIL.
DON'T MIND PIL. HE LIKES TO SPEAK HIS MIND.
THAT'S ONE REASON WHY HE'S MY BEST ADVISOR.
YOU'RE THE MAYOR?
DIDN'T I ALREADY TELL YOU?
THIS IS MY TOWN.
HEAD UP OVER THE RIDGE AND DOWN TO THE DOCKS.
WE'RE TAKING A BOAT INTO THE CITY.
SO THIS IS WHERE THE PEOPLE OF LUCIEN WENT.

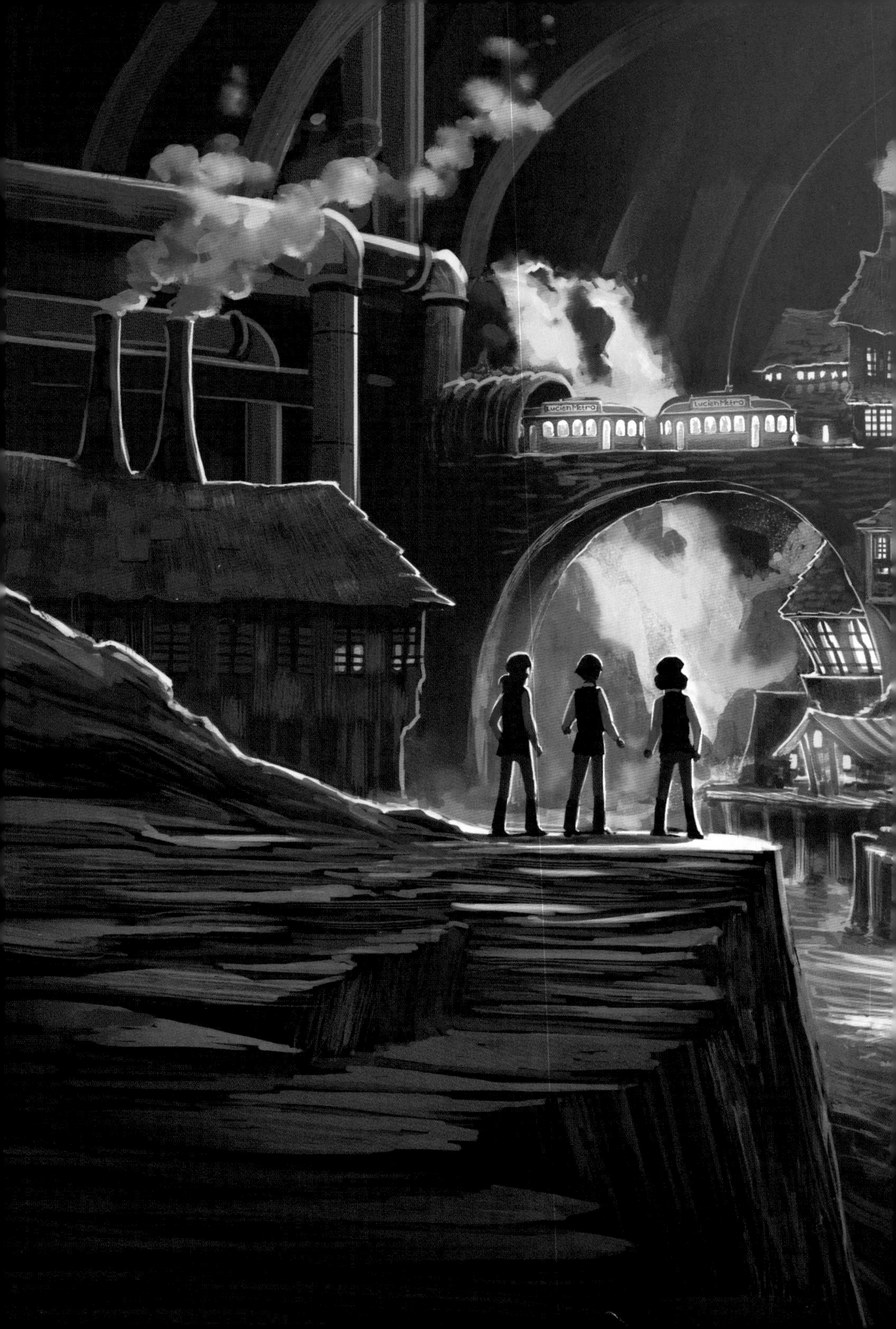
LucienMetro
LucienMetro

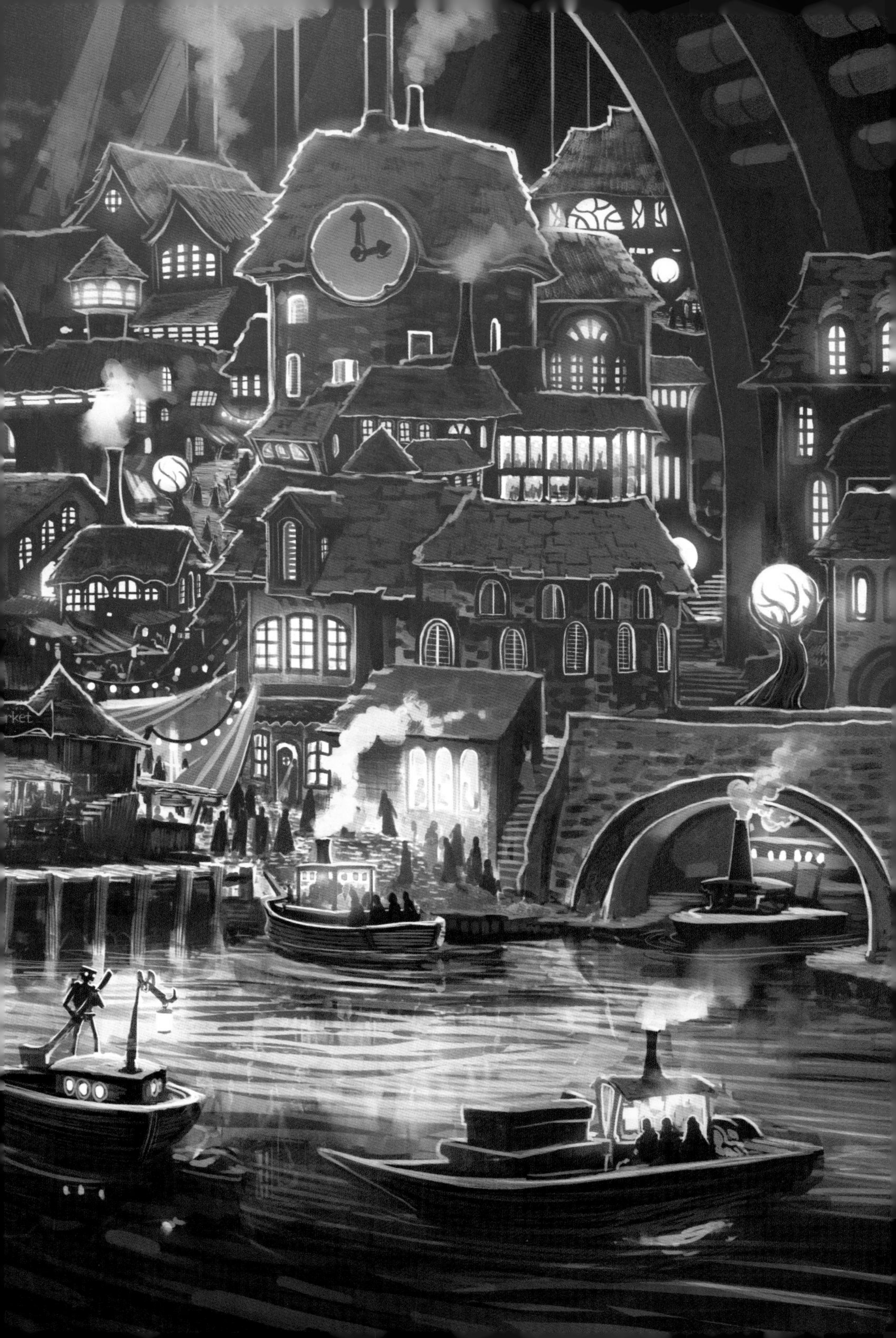

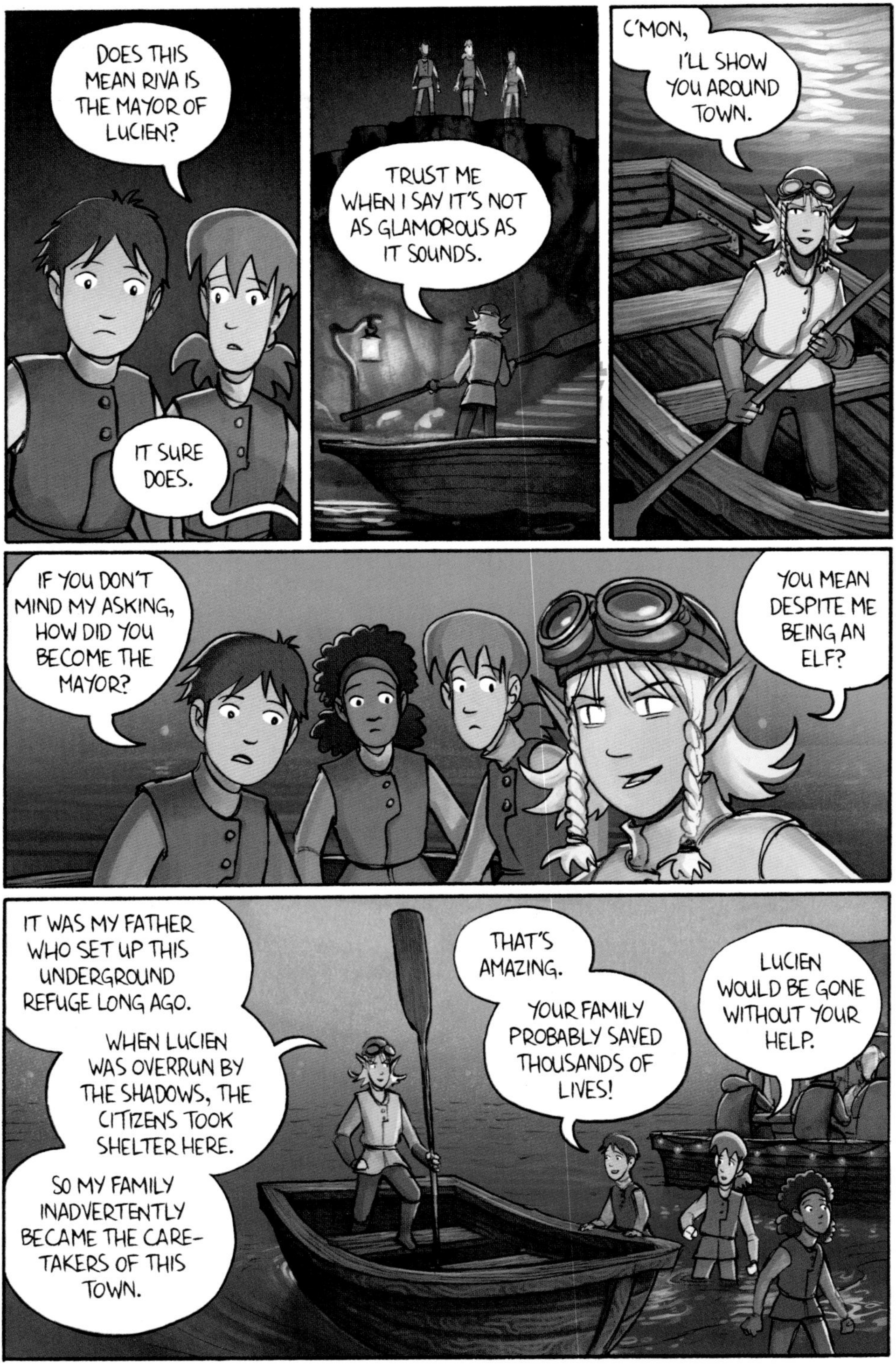
DOES THIS MEAN RIVA IS THE MAYOR OF LUCIEN?
IT SURE DOES.
TRUST ME WHEN I SAY IT'S NOT AS GLAMOROUS AS IT SOUNDS.
C'MON,
I'LL SHOW YOU AROUND TOWN.
IF YOU DON'T MIND MY ASKING, HOW DID YOU BECOME THE MAYOR?
YOU MEAN DESPITE ME BEING AN ELF?
IT WAS MY FATHER WHO SET UP THIS UNDERGROUND REFUGE LONG AGO.
WHEN LUCIEN WAS OVERRUN BY THE SHADOWS, THE CITIZENS TOOK SHELTER HERE.
SO MY FAMILY INADVERTENTLY BECAME THE CARE-TAKERS OF THIS TOWN.
THAT'S AMAZING.
YOUR FAMILY PROBABLY SAVED THOUSANDS OF LIVES!
LUCIEN WOULD BE GONE WITHOUT YOUR HELP.

WHY DID YOUR DAD START BUILDING THIS PLACE TO BEGIN WITH?

OH, HE WAS JUST CRAZY.

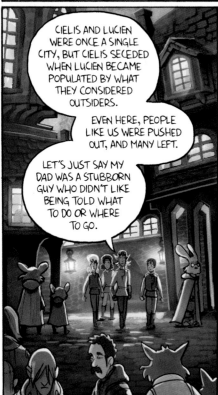

CIELIS AND LUCIEN WERE ONCE A SINGLE CITY, BUT CIELIS SECEDED WHEN LUCIEN BECAME POPULATED BY WHAT THEY CONSIDERED OUTSIDERS.

EVEN HERE, PEOPLE LIKE US WERE PUSHED OUT, AND MANY LEFT.

LET'S JUST SAY MY DAD WAS A STUBBORN GUY WHO DIDN'T LIKE BEING TOLD WHAT TO DO OR WHERE TO GO.

SO THEN HE BUILT THIS.

AMAZING.

EXCUSE ME.

OR INSANE?

MISS RIVA?

WE WANT TO JOIN YOU WHEN YOU FIGHT THE SHADOWS.

I EVEN HAVE MY OWN TROOP.

HOW MANY TIMES HAVE I TOLD YOU, PATRICK?

WE'RE NOT GOING TO FIGHT THE SHADOWS.

BUT MY DAD SAID THAT IF WE DON'T TAKE A STAND, WE'LL ALL BE SORRY.

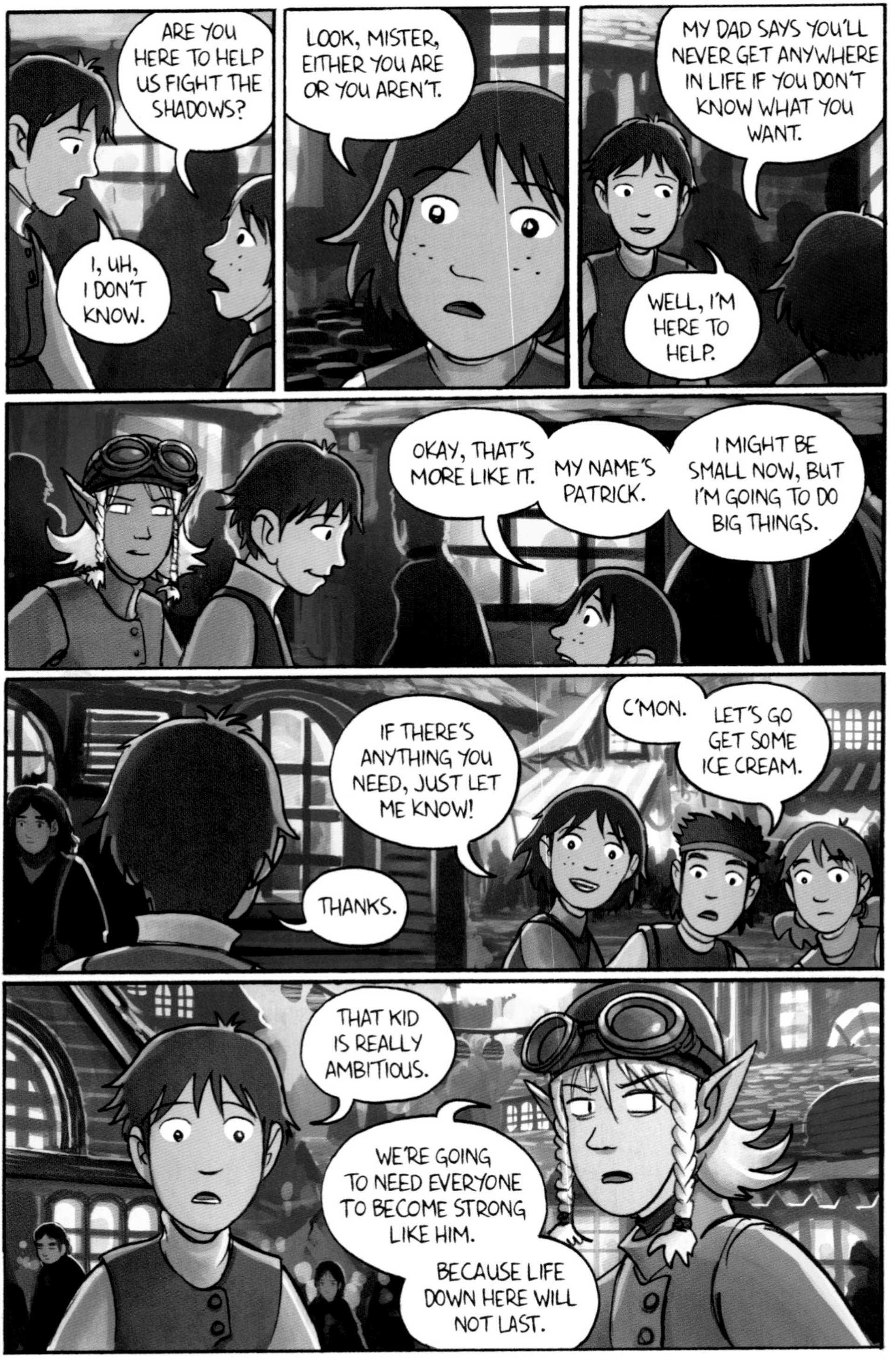
ARE YOU HERE TO HELP US FIGHT THE SHADOWS?
I, UH, I DON'T KNOW.
LOOK, MISTER, EITHER YOU ARE OR YOU AREN'T.
MY DAD SAYS YOU'LL NEVER GET ANYWHERE IN LIFE IF YOU DON'T KNOW WHAT YOU WANT.
WELL, I'M HERE TO HELP.
OKAY, THAT'S MORE LIKE IT.
MY NAME'S PATRICK.
I MIGHT BE SMALL NOW, BUT I'M GOING TO DO BIG THINGS.
IF THERE'S ANYTHING YOU NEED, JUST LET ME KNOW!
THANKS.
C'MON.
LET'S GO GET SOME ICE CREAM.
THAT KID IS REALLY AMBITIOUS.
WE'RE GOING TO NEED EVERYONE TO BECOME STRONG LIKE HIM.
BECAUSE LIFE DOWN HERE WILL NOT LAST.

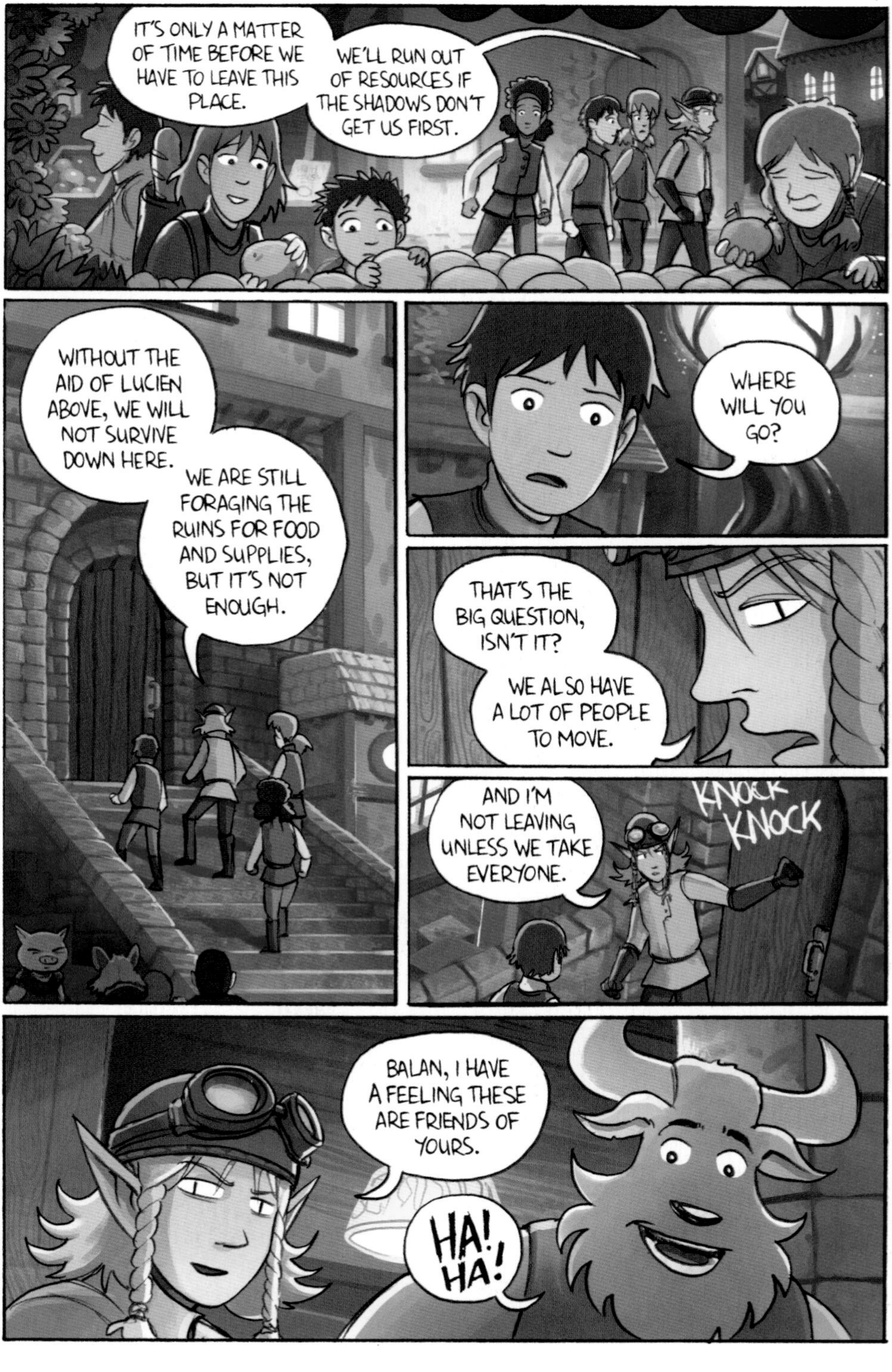
IT'S ONLY A MATTER OF TIME BEFORE WE HAVE TO LEAVE THIS PLACE.
WE'LL RUN OUT OF RESOURCES IF THE SHADOWS DON'T GET US FIRST.
WITHOUT THE AID OF LUCIEN ABOVE, WE WILL NOT SURVIVE DOWN HERE.
WE ARE STILL FORAGING THE RUINS FOR FOOD AND SUPPLIES, BUT IT'S NOT ENOUGH.
WHERE WILL YOU GO?
THAT'S THE BIG QUESTION, ISN'T IT?
WE ALSO HAVE A LOT OF PEOPLE TO MOVE.
AND I'M NOT LEAVING UNLESS WE TAKE EVERYONE.
KNOCK KNOCK
BALAN, I HAVE A FEELING THESE ARE FRIENDS OF YOURS.
HA! HA!

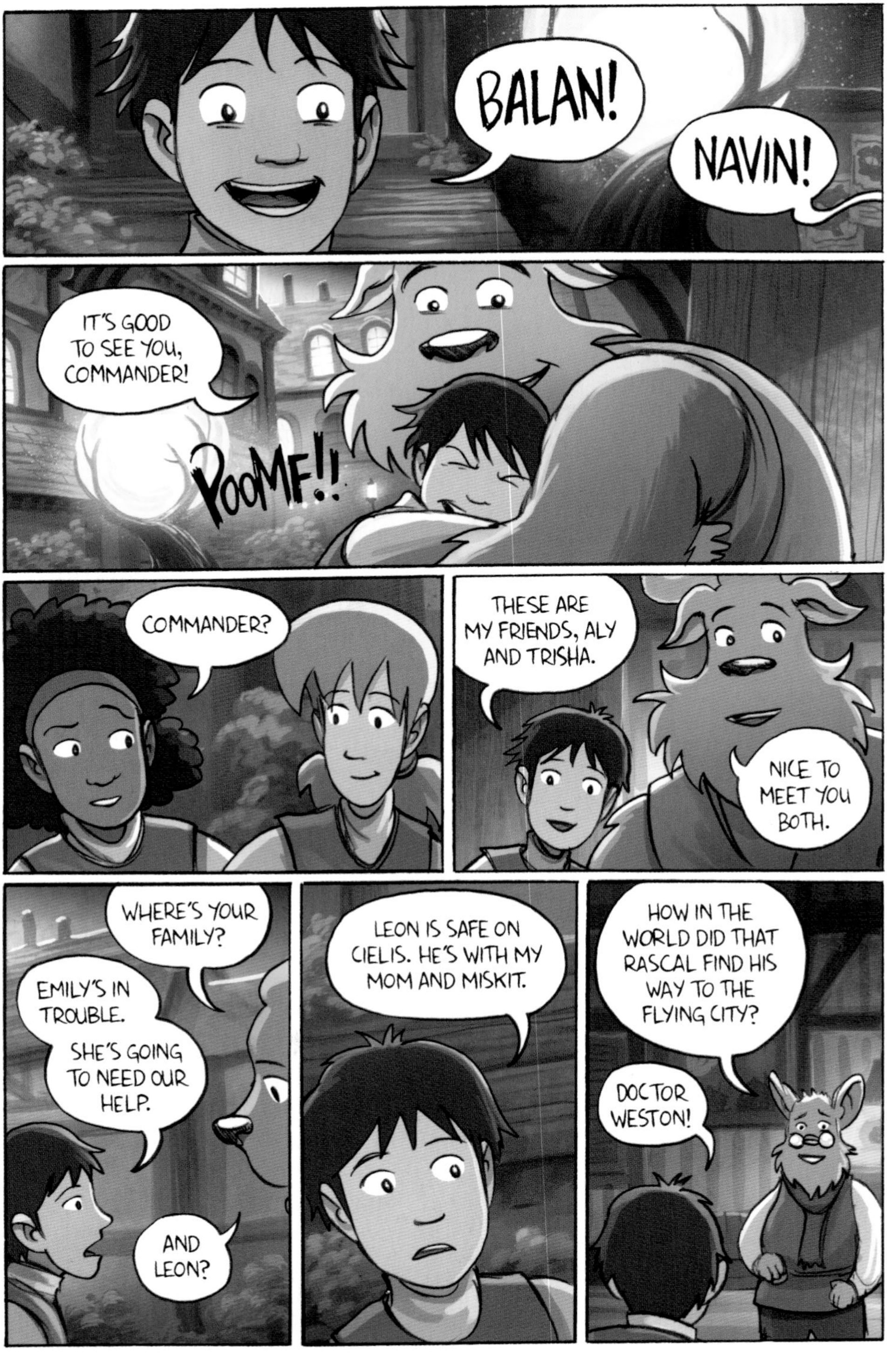
BALAN!
NAVIN!
IT'S GOOD TO SEE YOU, COMMANDER!
POOMF!!
COMMANDER?
THESE ARE MY FRIENDS, ALY AND TRISHA.
NICE TO MEET YOU BOTH.
WHERE'S YOUR FAMILY?
EMILY'S IN TROUBLE.
SHE'S GOING TO NEED OUR HELP.
AND LEON?
LEON IS SAFE ON CIELIS. HE'S WITH MY MOM AND MISKIT.
HOW IN THE WORLD DID THAT RASCAL FIND HIS WAY TO THE FLYING CITY?
DOCTOR WESTON!

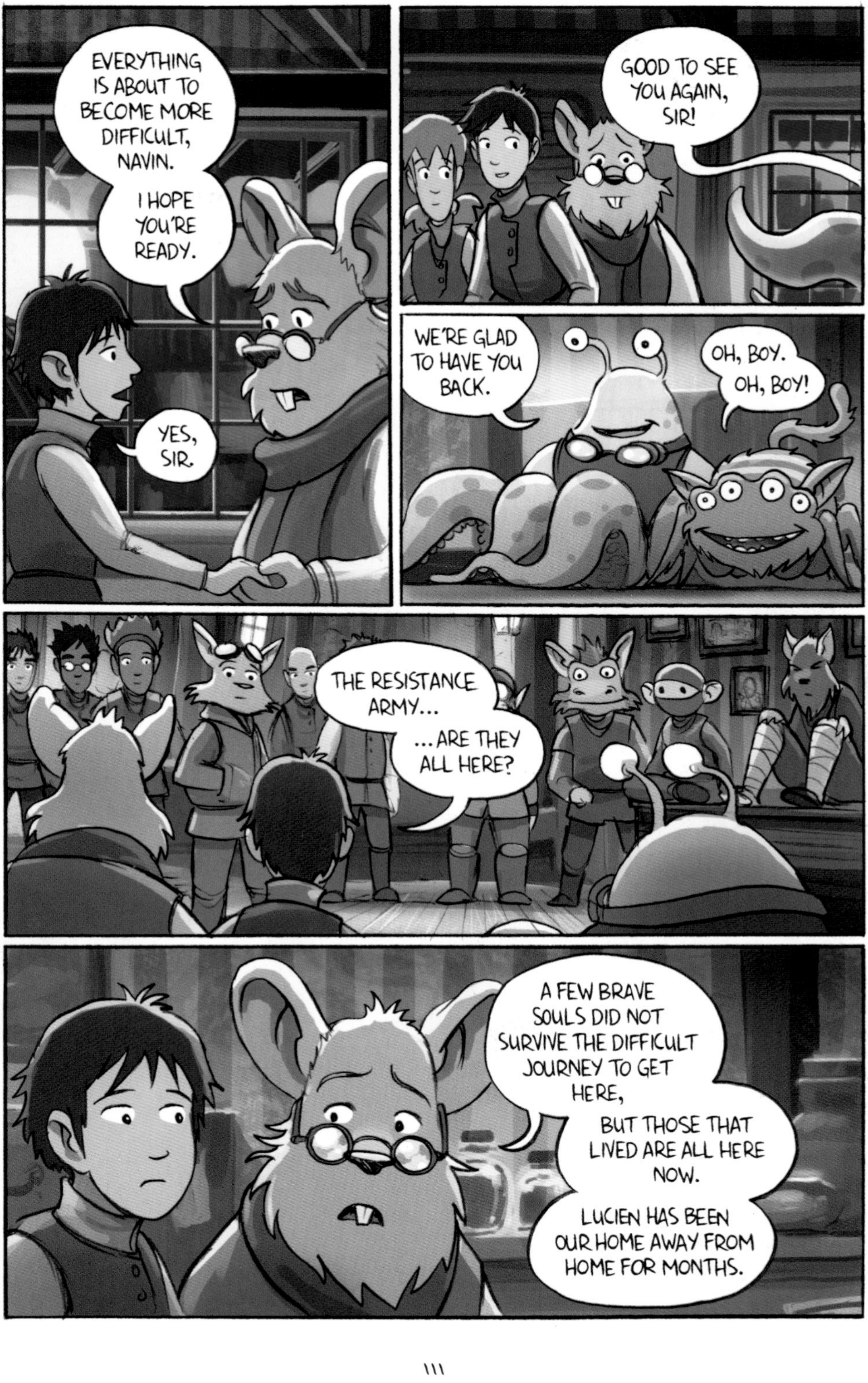
EVERYTHING IS ABOUT TO BECOME MORE DIFFICULT, NAVIN.
I HOPE YOU'RE READY.
YES, SIR.
GOOD TO SEE YOU AGAIN, SIR!
WE'RE GLAD TO HAVE YOU BACK.
OH, BOY. OH, BOY!
THE RESISTANCE ARMY...
...ARE THEY ALL HERE?
A FEW BRAVE SOULS DID NOT SURVIVE THE DIFFICULT JOURNEY TO GET HERE,
BUT THOSE THAT LIVED ARE ALL HERE NOW.
LUCIEN HAS BEEN OUR HOME AWAY FROM HOME FOR MONTHS.

AND SOON, WE WILL ALL HAVE TO FIND A NEW ONE.

WE WILL BE LUCKY TO SURVIVE JUST ONE MORE MONTH DOWN HERE BEFORE WE RUN OUT OF RESOURCES.

WE HAVE NO CHOICE BUT TO LEAVE.

THIS IS A MAP OF THE UNDERGROUND RAILWAY.

AS YOU CAN SEE, THERE'S AN UNFINISHED TUNNEL THAT LEADS TO THE CIELIS CRATER.

CIELIS CRATER

EN

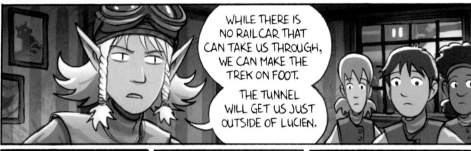

WHILE THERE IS NO RAIL CAR THAT CAN TAKE US THROUGH, WE CAN MAKE THE TREK ON FOOT.

THE TUNNEL WILL GET US JUST OUTSIDE OF LUCIEN.

THE PROBLEM IS THAT WE WON'T BE ABLE TO OUTRUN THE SHADOWS ON OPEN GROUND.

THIS IS WHY I'VE AVOIDED MAKING THE EVACUATION ORDER. I SIMPLY CANNOT ACCEPT THE CASUALTIES THIS WOULD ENTAIL.

BUT IF WE DON'T MAKE THIS SACRIFICE, WE WILL SUFFER EVEN GREATER LOSSES.

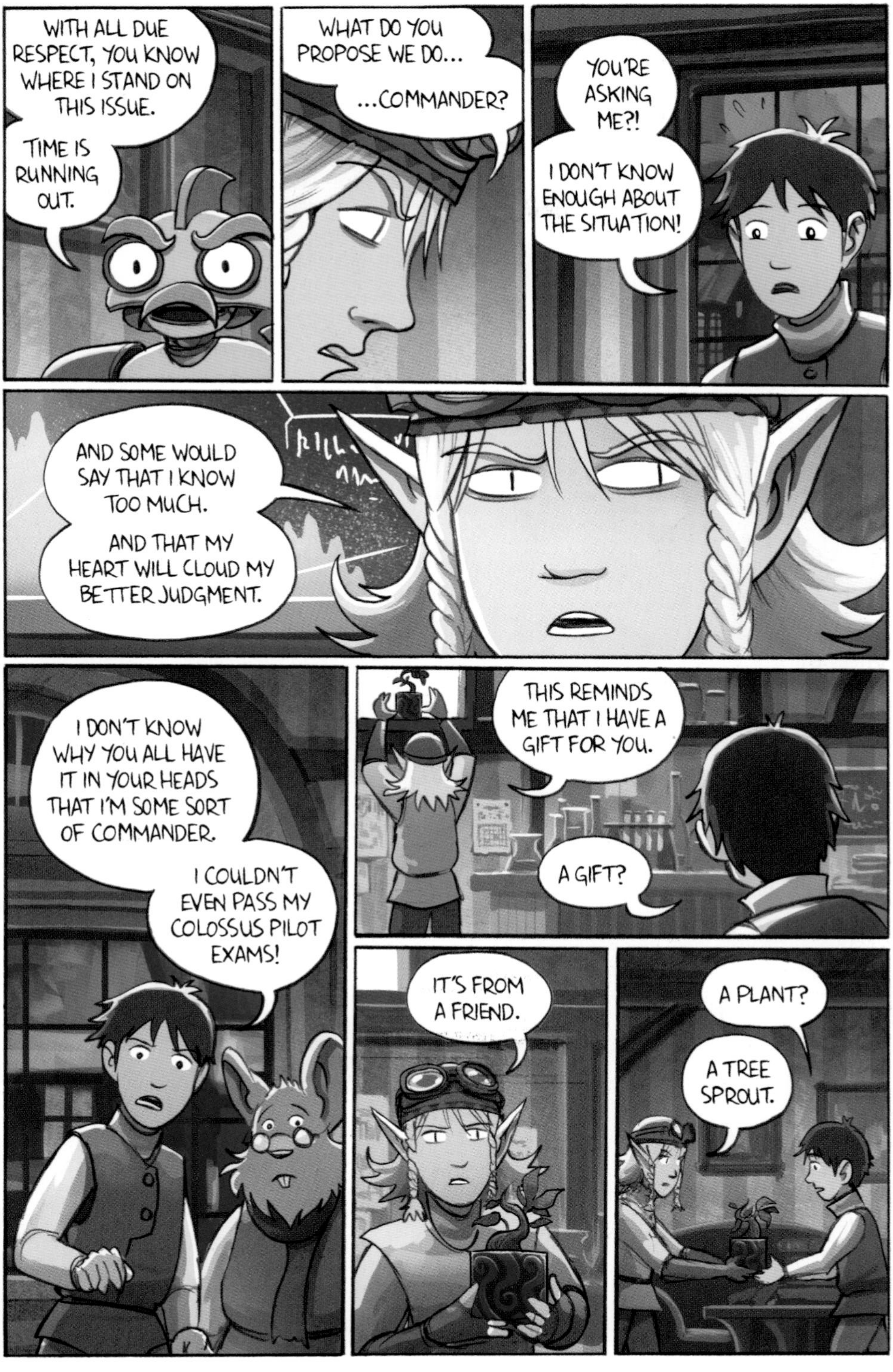
WITH ALL DUE RESPECT, YOU KNOW WHERE I STAND ON THIS ISSUE.
TIME IS RUNNING OUT.
WHAT DO YOU PROPOSE WE DO...
...COMMANDER?
YOU'RE ASKING ME?!
I DON'T KNOW ENOUGH ABOUT THE SITUATION!
AND SOME WOULD SAY THAT I KNOW TOO MUCH.
AND THAT MY HEART WILL CLOUD MY BETTER JUDGMENT.
I DON'T KNOW WHY YOU ALL HAVE IT IN YOUR HEADS THAT I'M SOME SORT OF COMMANDER.
I COULDN'T EVEN PASS MY COLOSSUS PILOT EXAMS!
THIS REMINDS ME THAT I HAVE A GIFT FOR YOU.
A GIFT?
IT'S FROM A FRIEND.
A PLANT?
A TREE SPROUT.

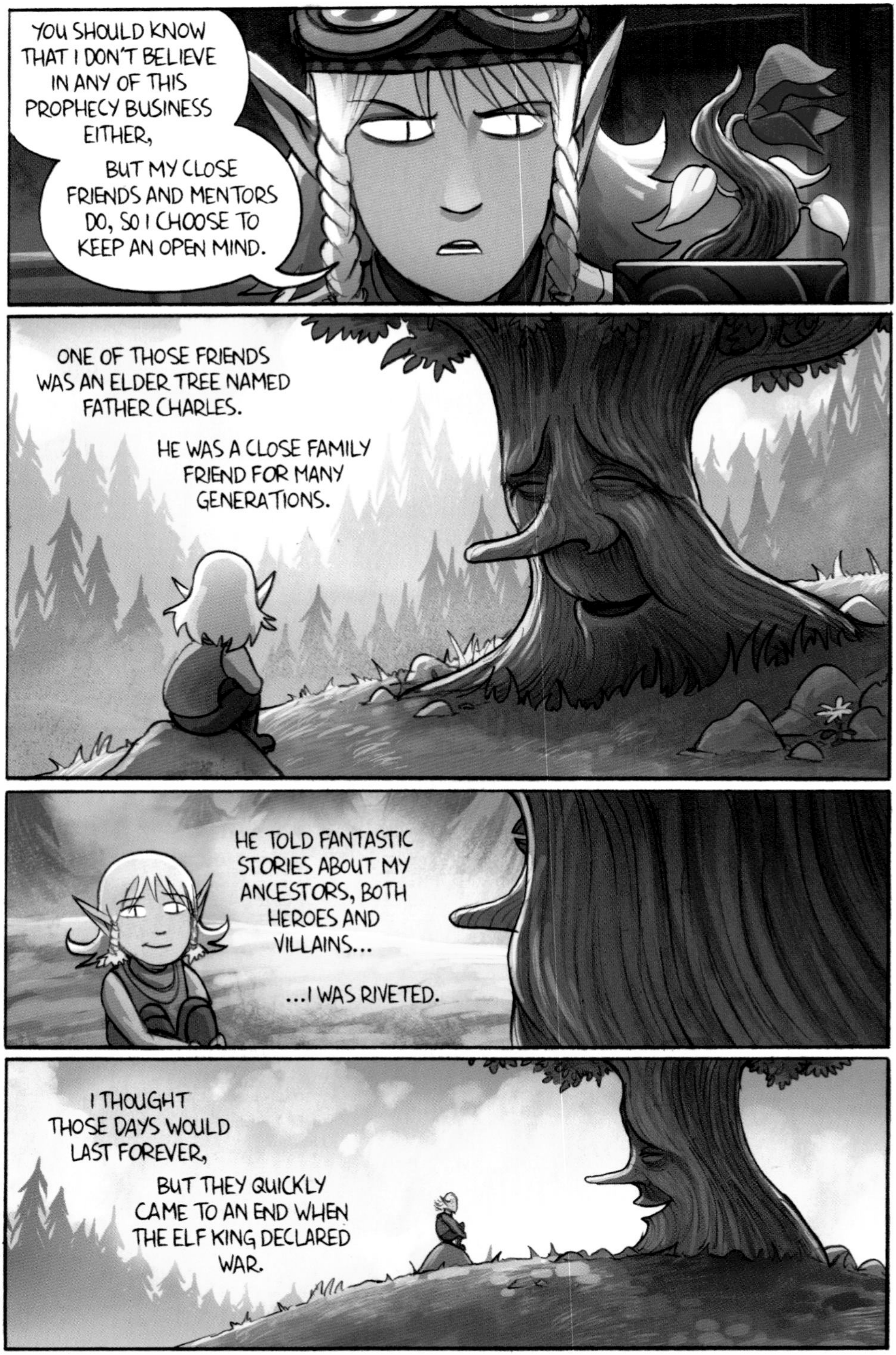
YOU SHOULD KNOW THAT I DON'T BELIEVE IN ANY OF THIS PROPHECY BUSINESS EITHER,
BUT MY CLOSE FRIENDS AND MENTORS DO, SO I CHOOSE TO KEEP AN OPEN MIND.
ONE OF THOSE FRIENDS WAS AN ELDER TREE NAMED FATHER CHARLES.
HE WAS A CLOSE FAMILY FRIEND FOR MANY GENERATIONS.
HE TOLD FANTASTIC STORIES ABOUT MY ANCESTORS, BOTH HEROES AND VILLAINS...
...I WAS RIVETED.
I THOUGHT THOSE DAYS WOULD LAST FOREVER,
BUT THEY QUICKLY CAME TO AN END WHEN THE ELF KING DECLARED WAR.

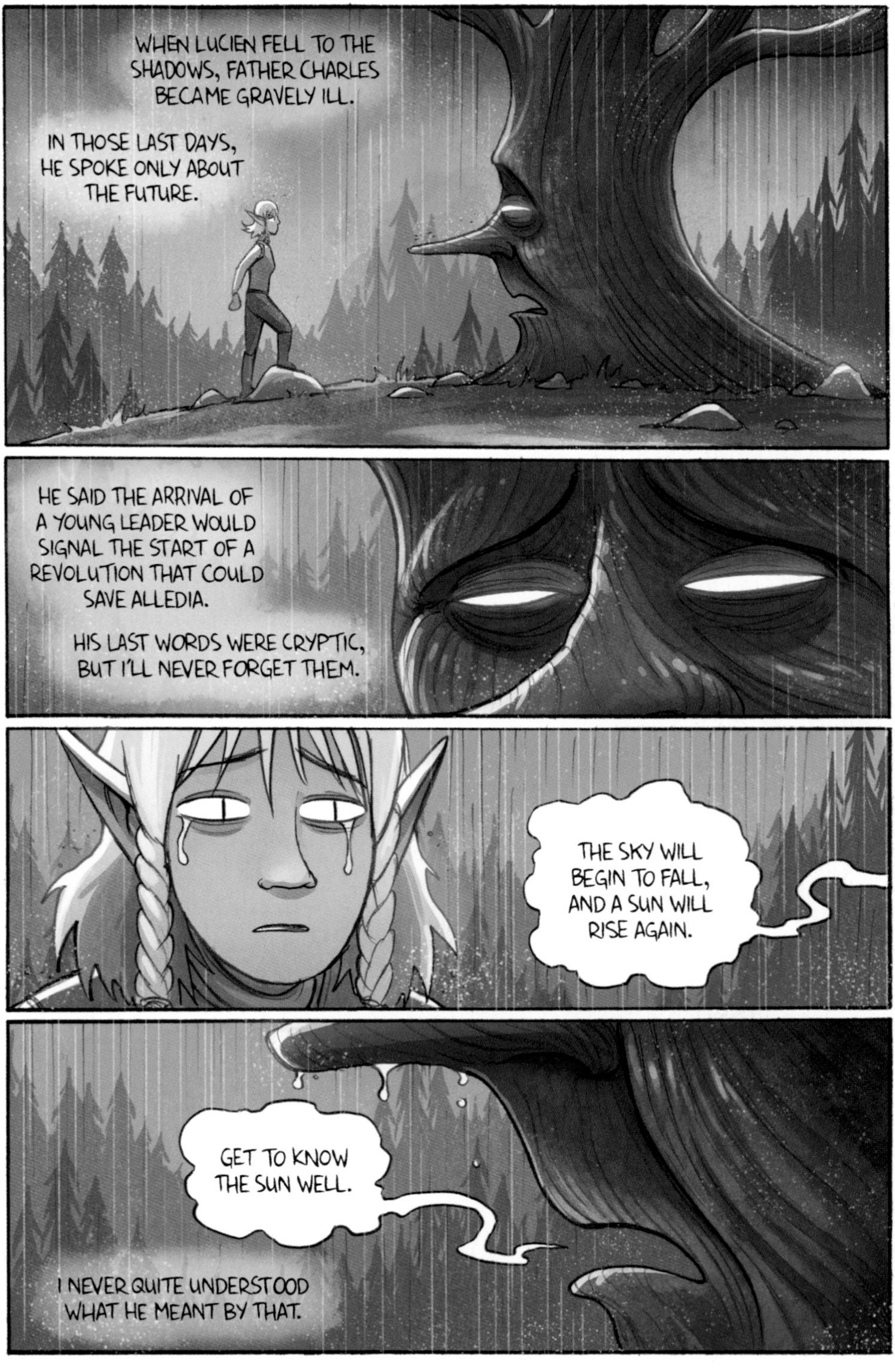
WHEN LUCIEN FELL TO THE SHADOWS, FATHER CHARLES BECAME GRAVELY ILL.
IN THOSE LAST DAYS, HE SPOKE ONLY ABOUT THE FUTURE.
HE SAID THE ARRIVAL OF A YOUNG LEADER WOULD SIGNAL THE START OF A REVOLUTION THAT COULD SAVE ALLEDIA.
HIS LAST WORDS WERE CRYPTIC, BUT I'LL NEVER FORGET THEM.
THE SKY WILL BEGIN TO FALL, AND A SUN WILL RISE AGAIN.
GET TO KNOW THE SUN WELL.
I NEVER QUITE UNDERSTOOD WHAT HE MEANT BY THAT.

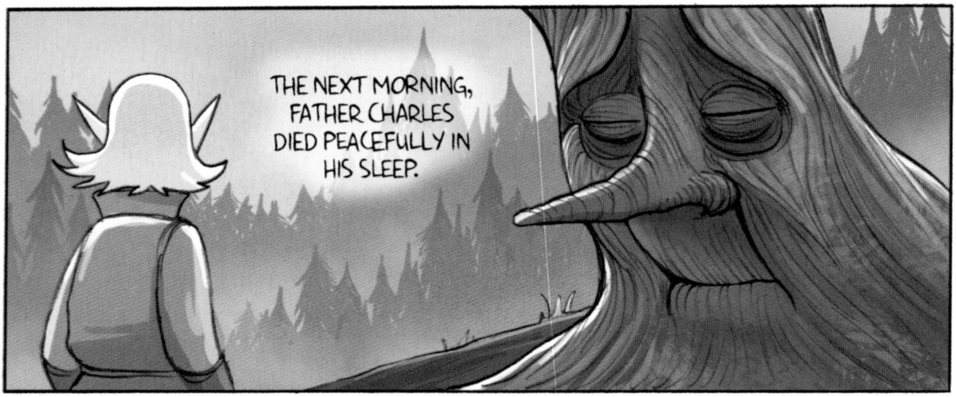
THE NEXT MORNING, FATHER CHARLES DIED PEACEFULLY IN HIS SLEEP.
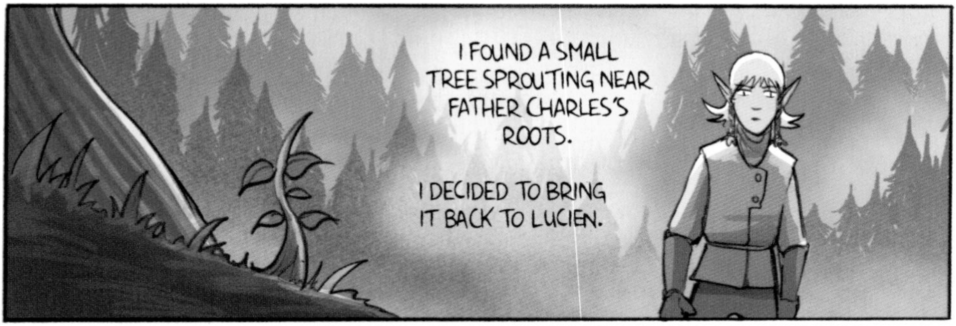
I FOUND A SMALL TREE SPROUTING NEAR FATHER CHARLES'S ROOTS.
I DECIDED TO BRING IT BACK TO LUCIEN.
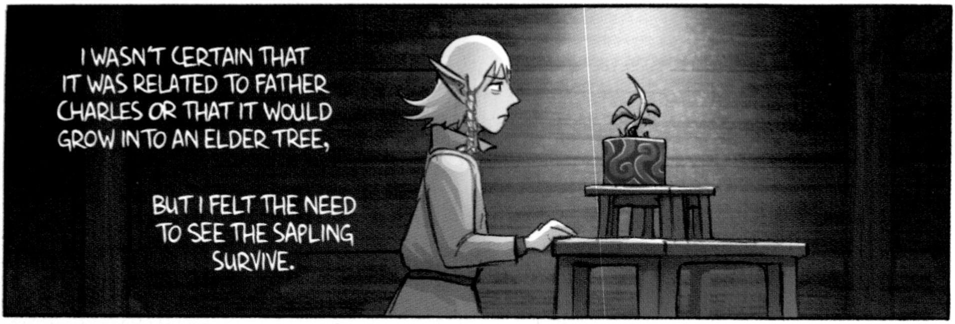
I WASN'T CERTAIN THAT IT WAS RELATED TO FATHER CHARLES OR THAT IT WOULD GROW INTO AN ELDER TREE,
BUT I FELT THE NEED TO SEE THE SAPLING SURVIVE.
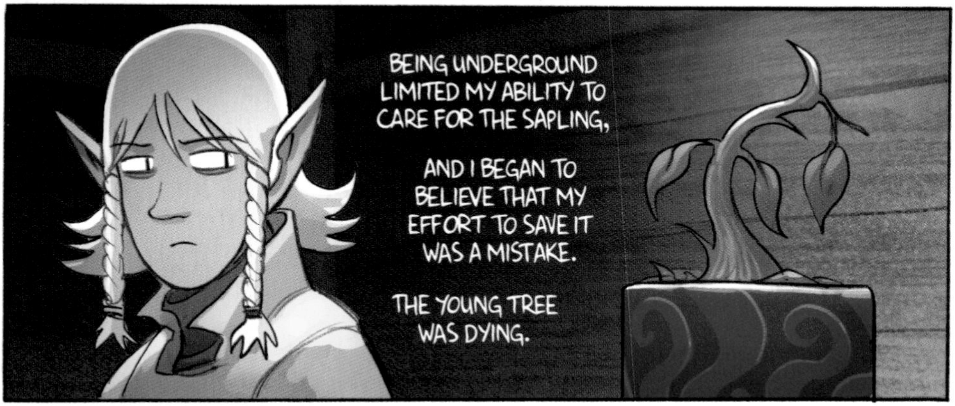
BEING UNDERGROUND LIMITED MY ABILITY TO CARE FOR THE SAPLING,
AND I BEGAN TO BELIEVE THAT MY EFFORT TO SAVE IT WAS A MISTAKE.
THE YOUNG TREE WAS DYING.

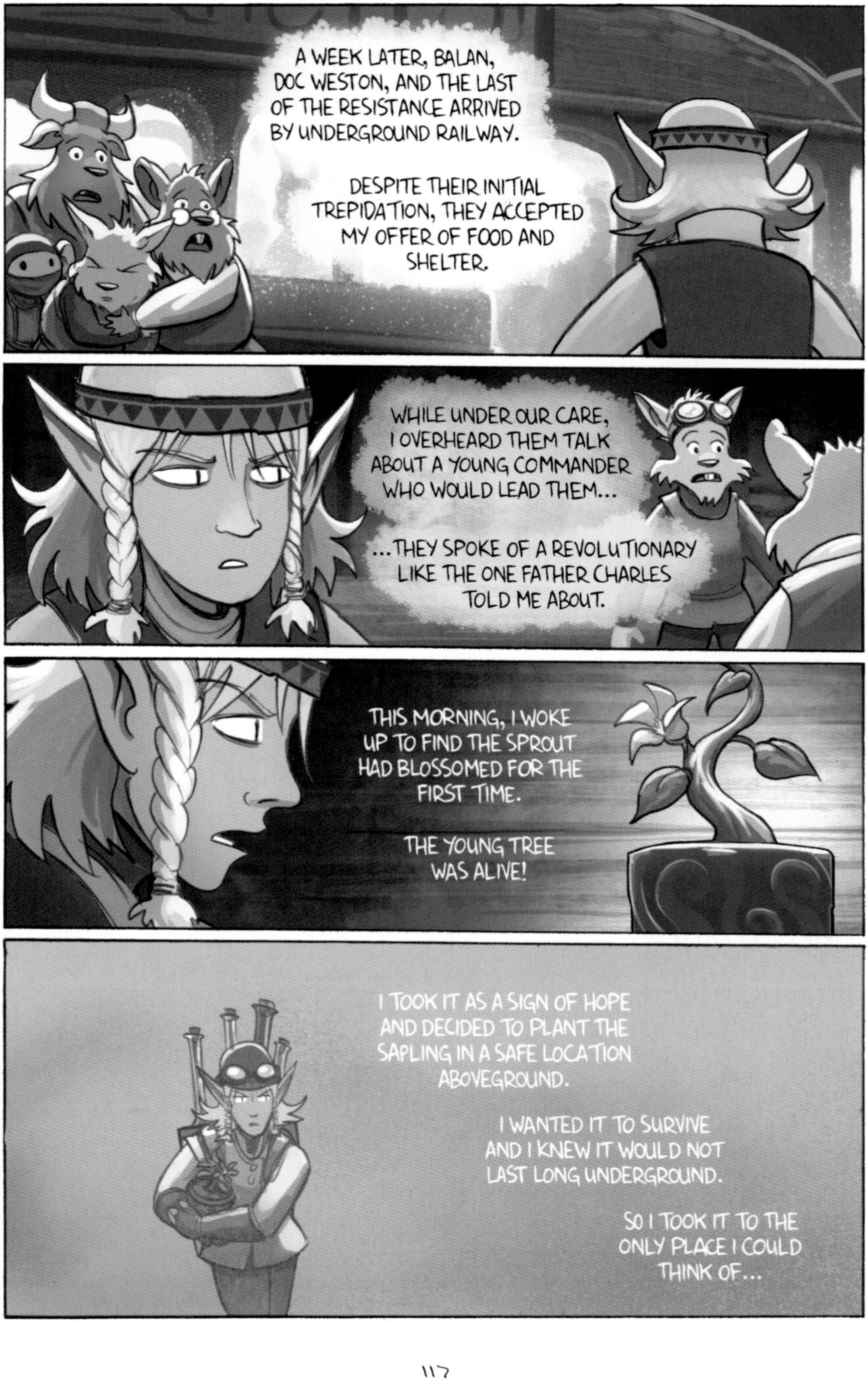
A WEEK LATER, BALAN, DOC WESTON, AND THE LAST OF THE RESISTANCE ARRIVED BY UNDERGROUND RAILWAY.
DESPITE THEIR INITIAL TREPIDATION, THEY ACCEPTED MY OFFER OF FOOD AND SHELTER.
WHILE UNDER OUR CARE, I OVERHEARD THEM TALK ABOUT A YOUNG COMMANDER WHO WOULD LEAD THEM...
...THEY SPOKE OF A REVOLUTIONARY LIKE THE ONE FATHER CHARLES TOLD ME ABOUT.
THIS MORNING, I WOKE UP TO FIND THE SPROUT HAD BLOSSOMED FOR THE FIRST TIME.
THE YOUNG TREE WAS ALIVE!
I TOOK IT AS A SIGN OF HOPE AND DECIDED TO PLANT THE SAPLING IN A SAFE LOCATION ABOVEGROUND.
I WANTED IT TO SURVIVE AND I KNEW IT WOULD NOT LAST LONG UNDERGROUND.
SO I TOOK IT TO THE ONLY PLACE I COULD THINK OF...

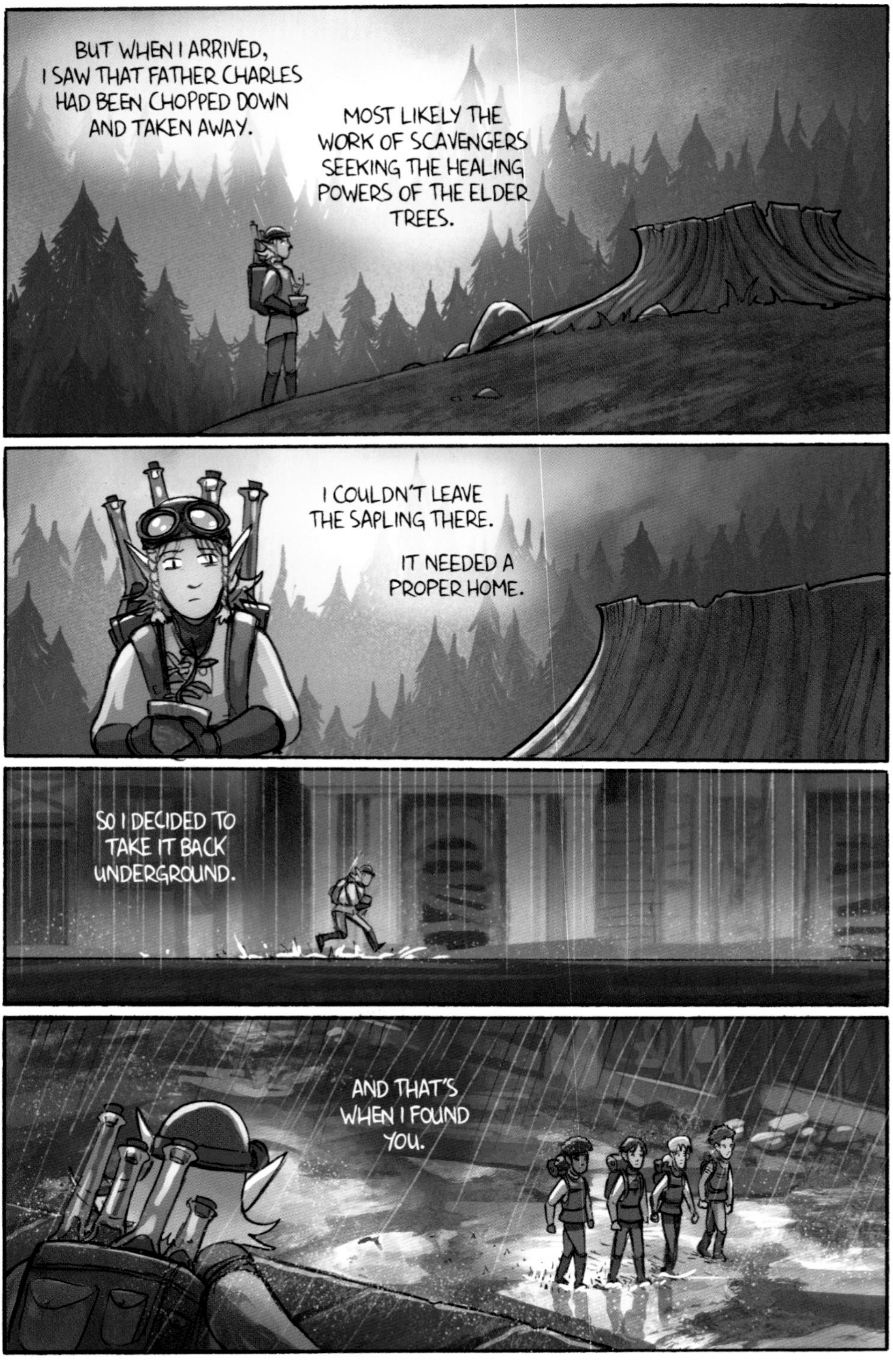
BUT WHEN I ARRIVED, I SAW THAT FATHER CHARLES HAD BEEN CHOPPED DOWN AND TAKEN AWAY.
MOST LIKELY THE WORK OF SCAVENGERS SEEKING THE HEALING POWERS OF THE ELDER TREES.
I COULDN'T LEAVE THE SAPLING THERE.
IT NEEDED A PROPER HOME.
SO I DECIDED TO TAKE IT BACK UNDERGROUND.
AND THAT'S WHEN I FOUND YOU.

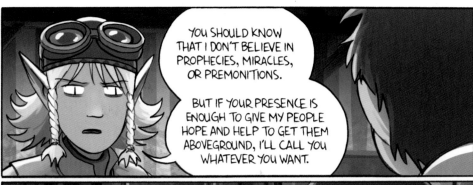

YOU SHOULD KNOW THAT I DON'T BELIEVE IN PROPHECIES, MIRACLES, OR PREMONITIONS.

BUT IF YOUR PRESENCE IS ENOUGH TO GIVE MY PEOPLE HOPE AND HELP TO GET THEM ABOVEGROUND, I'LL CALL YOU WHATEVER YOU WANT.

YOU CAN JUST CALL ME NAVIN.

AND IF IT'S ANY CONSOLATION, I DON'T BELIEVE IN THAT STUFF EITHER.

HEH.

WELL THEN, NAVIN, I THINK WE'RE GOING TO GET ALONG JUST FINE.

RIVA!

COME TAKE A LOOK AT THIS!

SHADOWS BREACHED THE EAST GATE.

HOW LONG AGO?

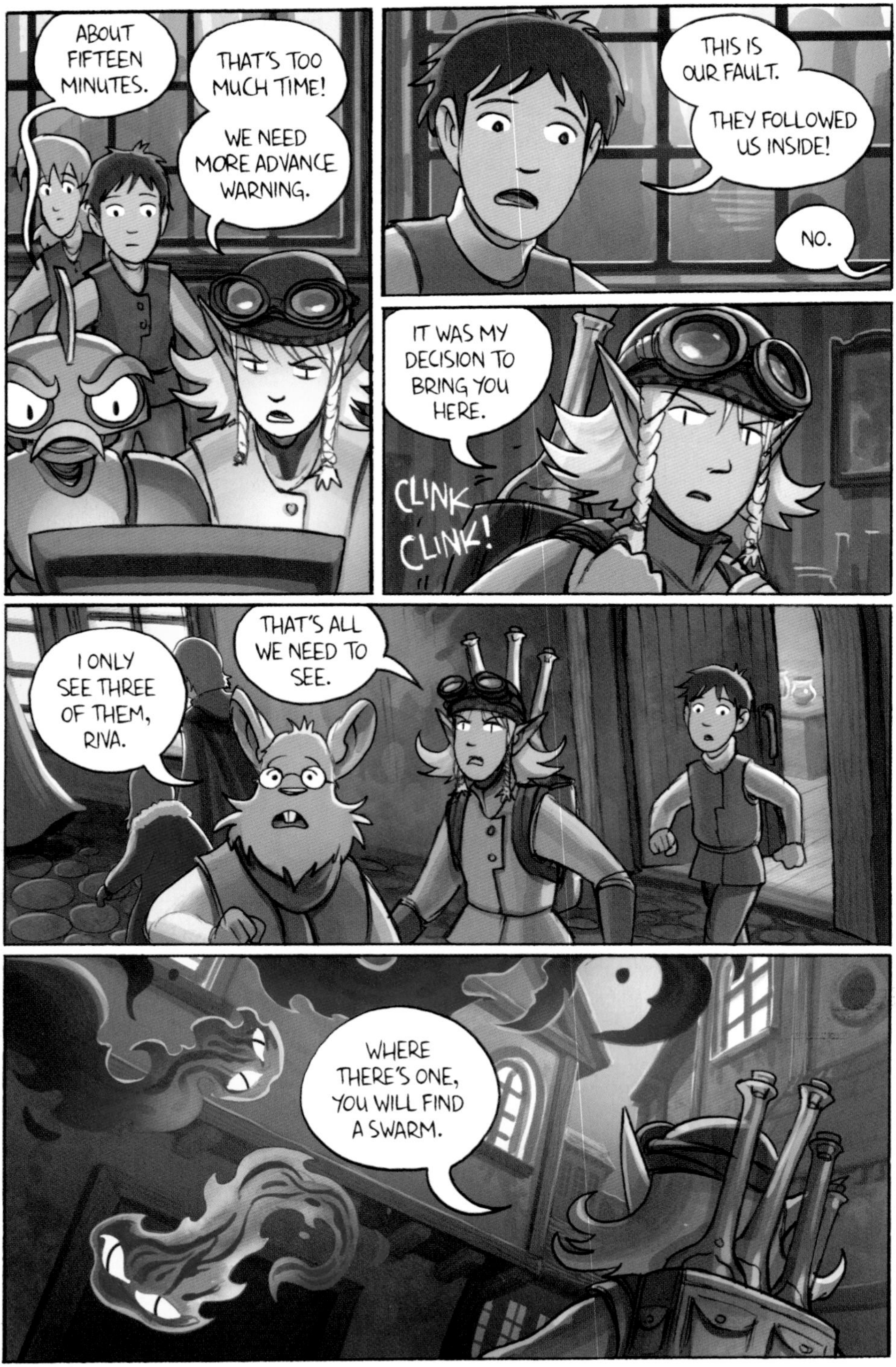
ABOUT FIFTEEN MINUTES.
THAT'S TOO MUCH TIME!
WE NEED MORE ADVANCE WARNING.
THIS IS OUR FAULT.
THEY FOLLOWED US INSIDE!
NO.
IT WAS MY DECISION TO BRING YOU HERE.
CLINK CLINK!
I ONLY SEE THREE OF THEM, RIVA.
THAT'S ALL WE NEED TO SEE.
WHERE THERE'S ONE, YOU WILL FIND A SWARM.

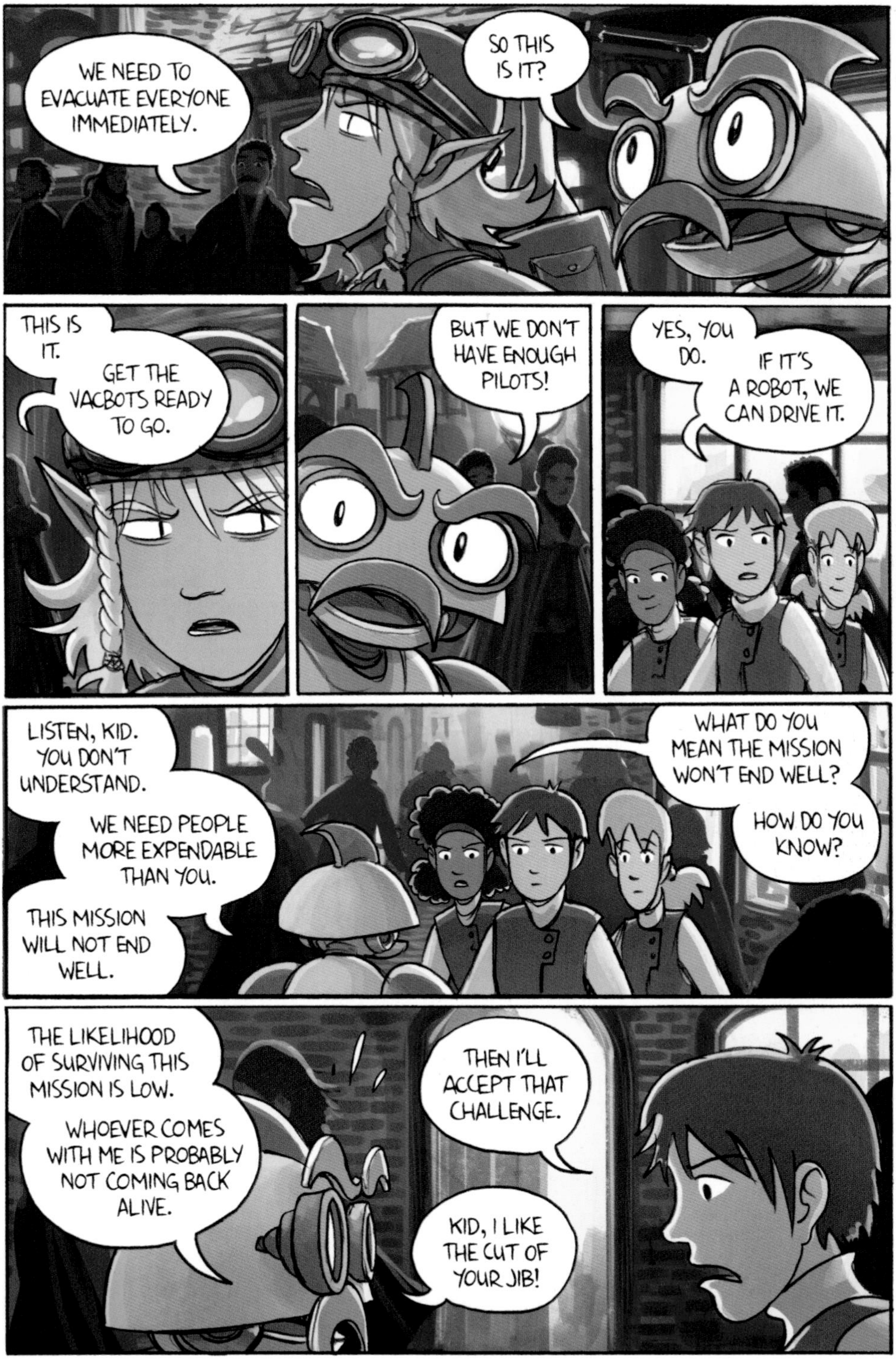
WE NEED TO EVACUATE EVERYONE IMMEDIATELY.
SO THIS IS IT?
THIS IS IT.
GET THE VACBOTS READY TO GO.
BUT WE DON'T HAVE ENOUGH PILOTS!
YES, YOU DO.
IF IT'S A ROBOT, WE CAN DRIVE IT.
LISTEN, KID. YOU DON'T UNDERSTAND.
WE NEED PEOPLE MORE EXPENDABLE THAN YOU.
THIS MISSION WILL NOT END WELL.
WHAT DO YOU MEAN THE MISSION WON'T END WELL?
HOW DO YOU KNOW?
THE LIKELIHOOD OF SURVIVING THIS MISSION IS LOW.
WHOEVER COMES WITH ME IS PROBABLY NOT COMING BACK ALIVE.
!
THEN I'LL ACCEPT THAT CHALLENGE.
KID, I LIKE THE CUT OF YOUR JIB!

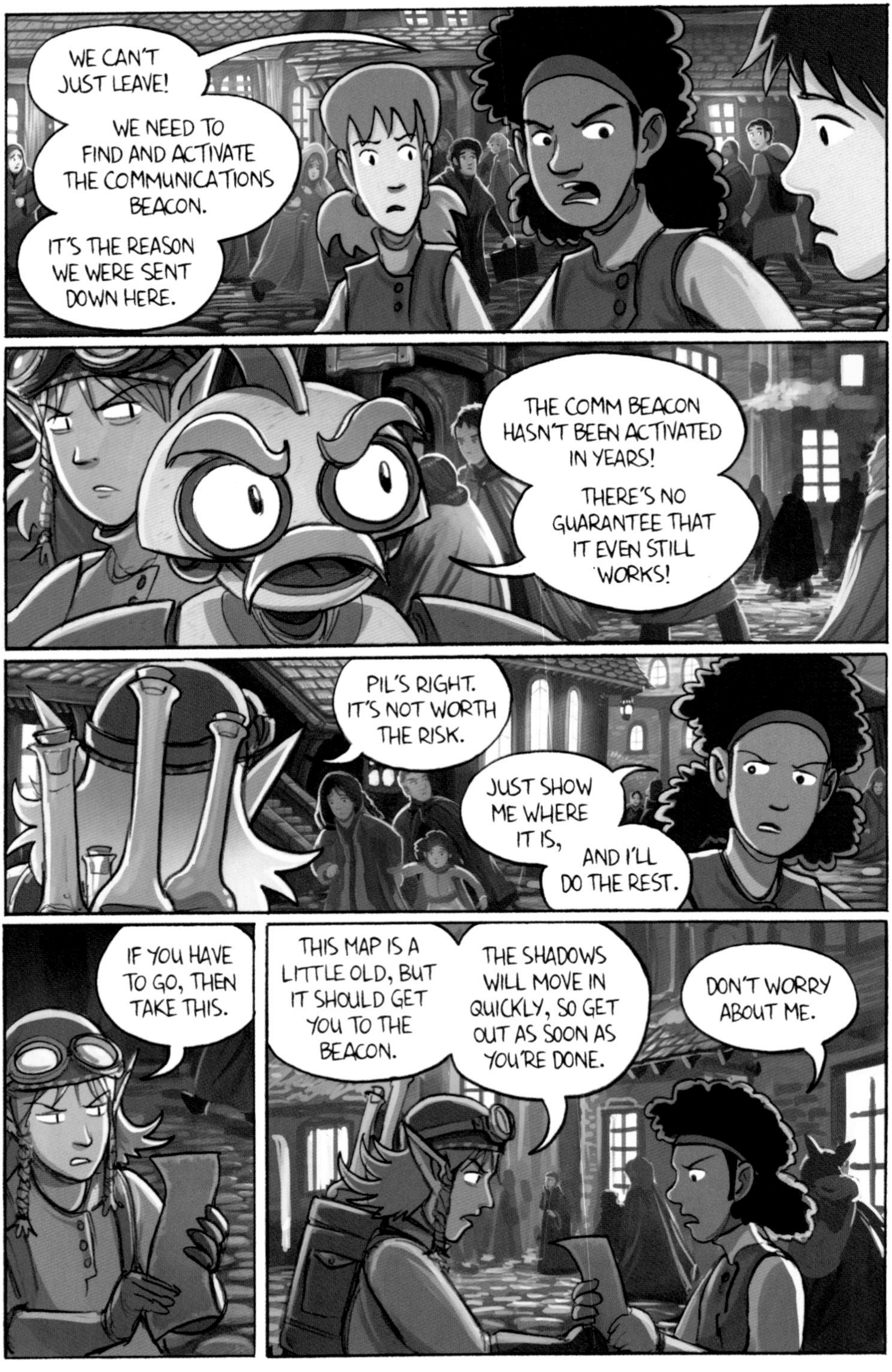
WE CAN'T JUST LEAVE!
WE NEED TO FIND AND ACTIVATE THE COMMUNICATIONS BEACON.
IT'S THE REASON WE WERE SENT DOWN HERE.
THE COMM BEACON HASN'T BEEN ACTIVATED IN YEARS!
THERE'S NO GUARANTEE THAT IT EVEN STILL WORKS!
PIL'S RIGHT. IT'S NOT WORTH THE RISK.
JUST SHOW ME WHERE IT IS,
AND I'LL DO THE REST.
IF YOU HAVE TO GO, THEN TAKE THIS.
THIS MAP IS A LITTLE OLD, BUT IT SHOULD GET YOU TO THE BEACON.
THE SHADOWS WILL MOVE IN QUICKLY, SO GET OUT AS SOON AS YOU'RE DONE.
DON'T WORRY ABOUT ME.

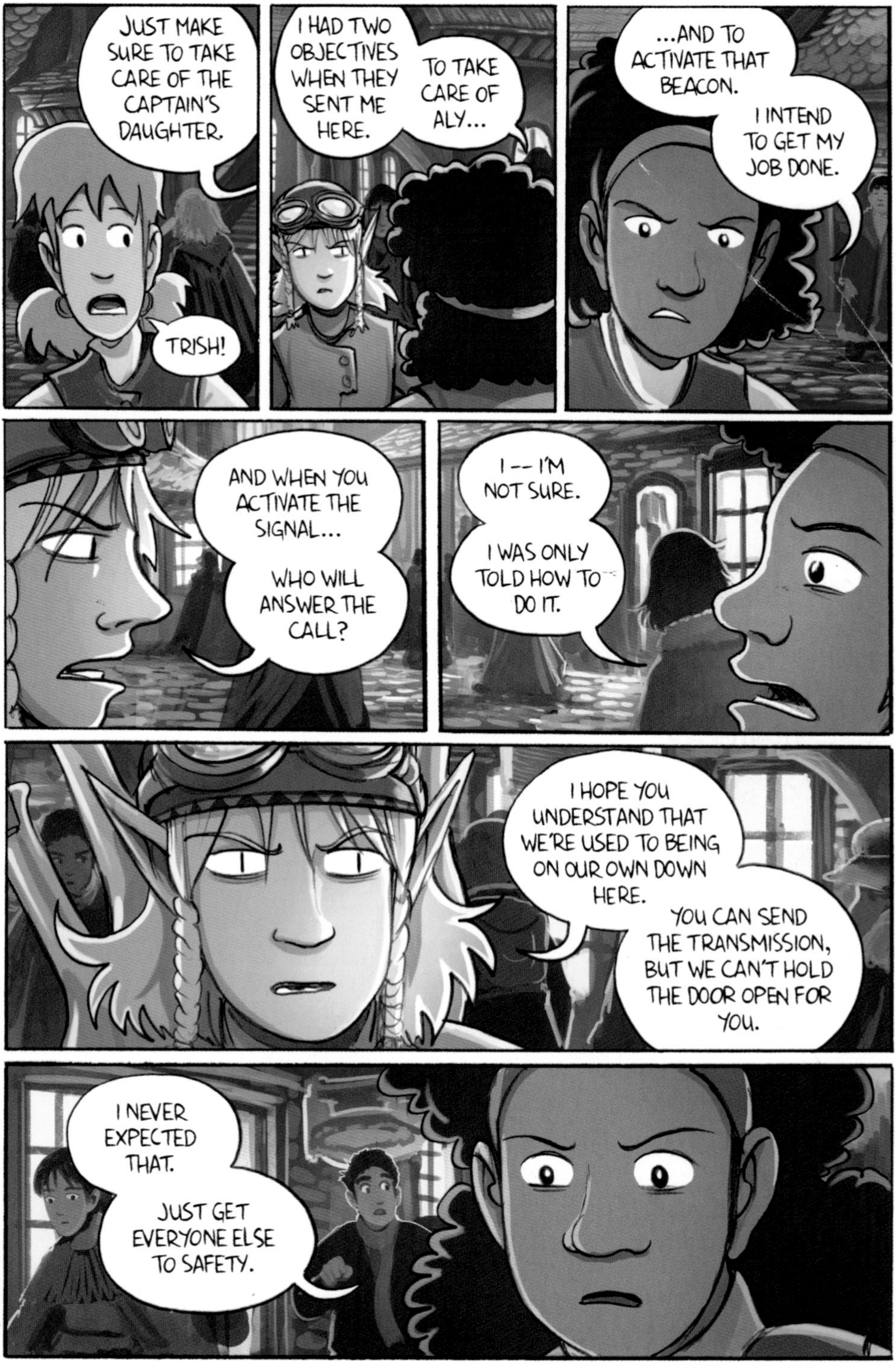

JUST MAKE SURE TO TAKE CARE OF THE CAPTAIN'S DAUGHTER.
TRISH!
I HAD TWO OBJECTIVES WHEN THEY SENT ME HERE.
TO TAKE CARE OF ALY...
...AND TO ACTIVATE THAT BEACON.
I INTEND TO GET MY JOB DONE.
AND WHEN YOU ACTIVATE THE SIGNAL...
WHO WILL ANSWER THE CALL?
I -- I'M NOT SURE.
I WAS ONLY TOLD HOW TO DO IT.
I HOPE YOU UNDERSTAND THAT WE'RE USED TO BEING ON OUR OWN DOWN HERE.
YOU CAN SEND THE TRANSMISSION, BUT WE CAN'T HOLD THE DOOR OPEN FOR YOU.
I NEVER EXPECTED THAT.
JUST GET EVERYONE ELSE TO SAFETY.

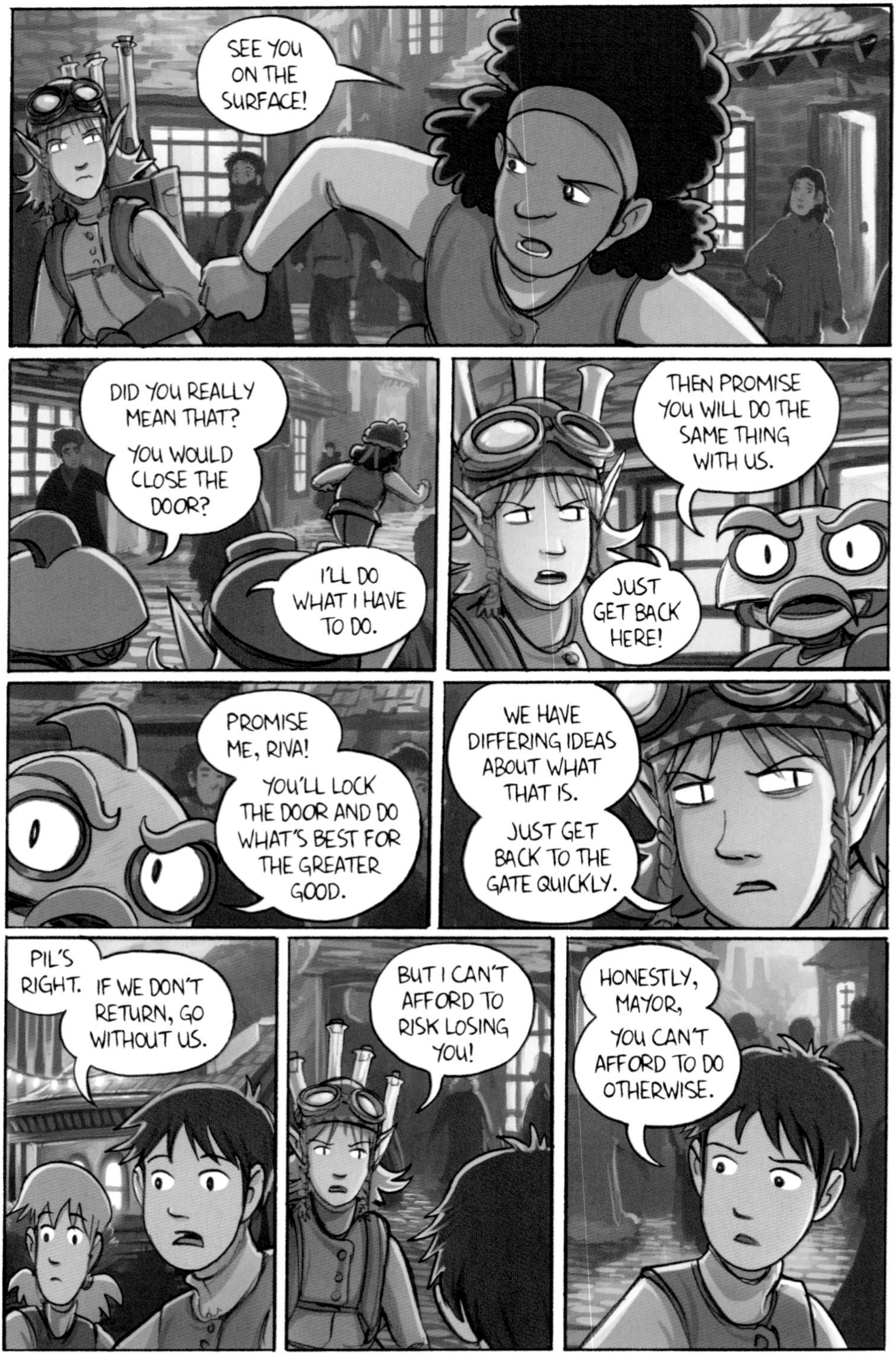
SEE YOU ON THE SURFACE!
DID YOU REALLY MEAN THAT?
YOU WOULD CLOSE THE DOOR?
I'LL DO WHAT I HAVE TO DO.
THEN PROMISE YOU WILL DO THE SAME THING WITH US.
JUST GET BACK HERE!
PROMISE ME, RIVA!
YOU'LL LOCK THE DOOR AND DO WHAT'S BEST FOR THE GREATER GOOD.
WE HAVE DIFFERING IDEAS ABOUT WHAT THAT IS.
JUST GET BACK TO THE GATE QUICKLY.
PIL'S RIGHT.
IF WE DON'T RETURN, GO WITHOUT US.
BUT I CAN'T AFFORD TO RISK LOSING YOU!
HONESTLY, MAYOR,
YOU CAN'T AFFORD TO DO OTHERWISE.

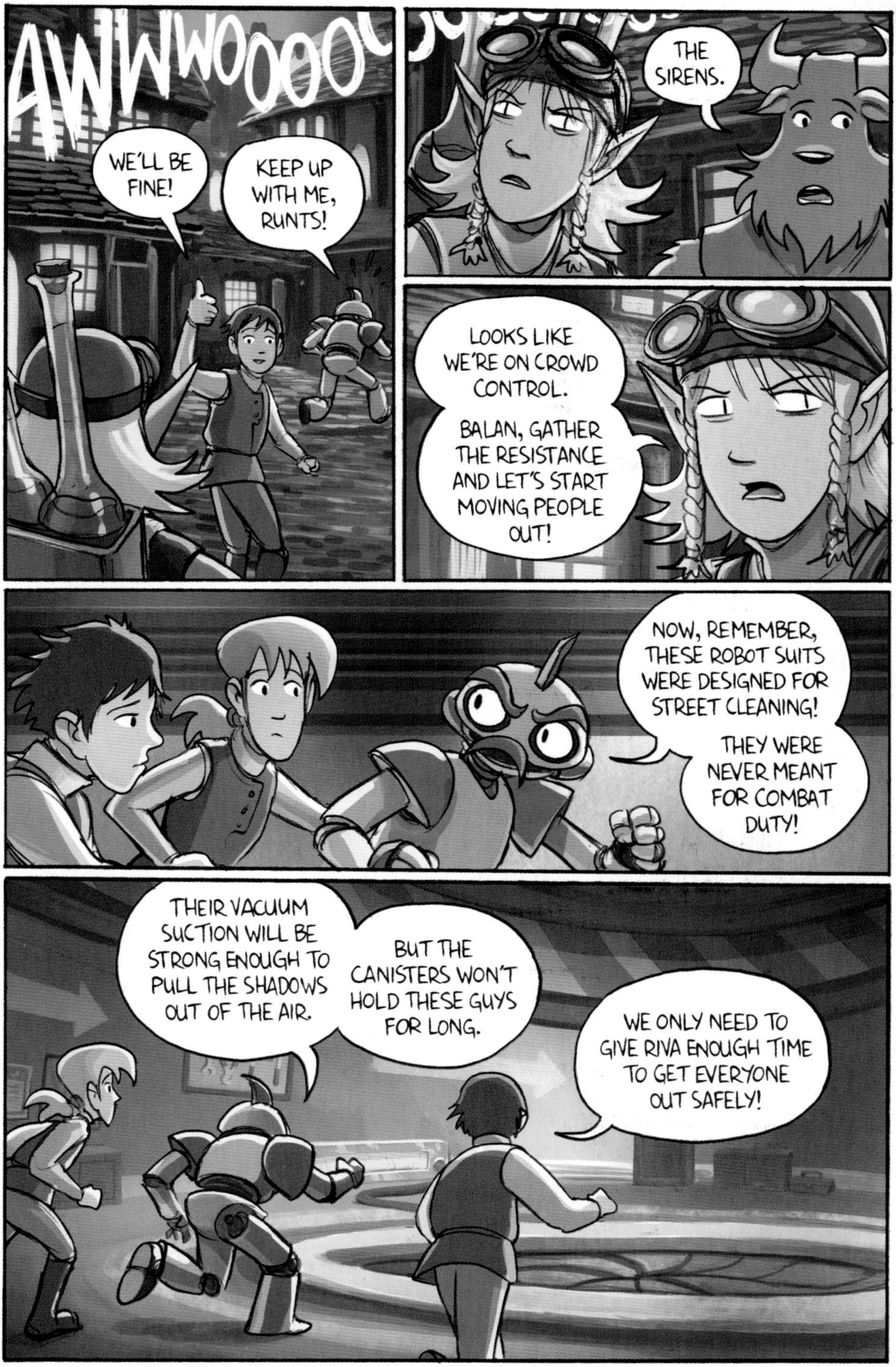
AWWOOOOOOOOO
WE'LL BE FINE!
KEEP UP WITH ME, RUNTS!
THE SIRENS.
LOOKS LIKE WE'RE ON CROWD CONTROL.
BALAN, GATHER THE RESISTANCE AND LET'S START MOVING PEOPLE OUT!
NOW, REMEMBER, THESE ROBOT SUITS WERE DESIGNED FOR STREET CLEANING!
THEY WERE NEVER MEANT FOR COMBAT DUTY!
THEIR VACUUM SUCTION WILL BE STRONG ENOUGH TO PULL THE SHADOWS OUT OF THE AIR.
BUT THE CANISTERS WON'T HOLD THESE GUYS FOR LONG.
WE ONLY NEED TO GIVE RIVA ENOUGH TIME TO GET EVERYONE OUT SAFELY!

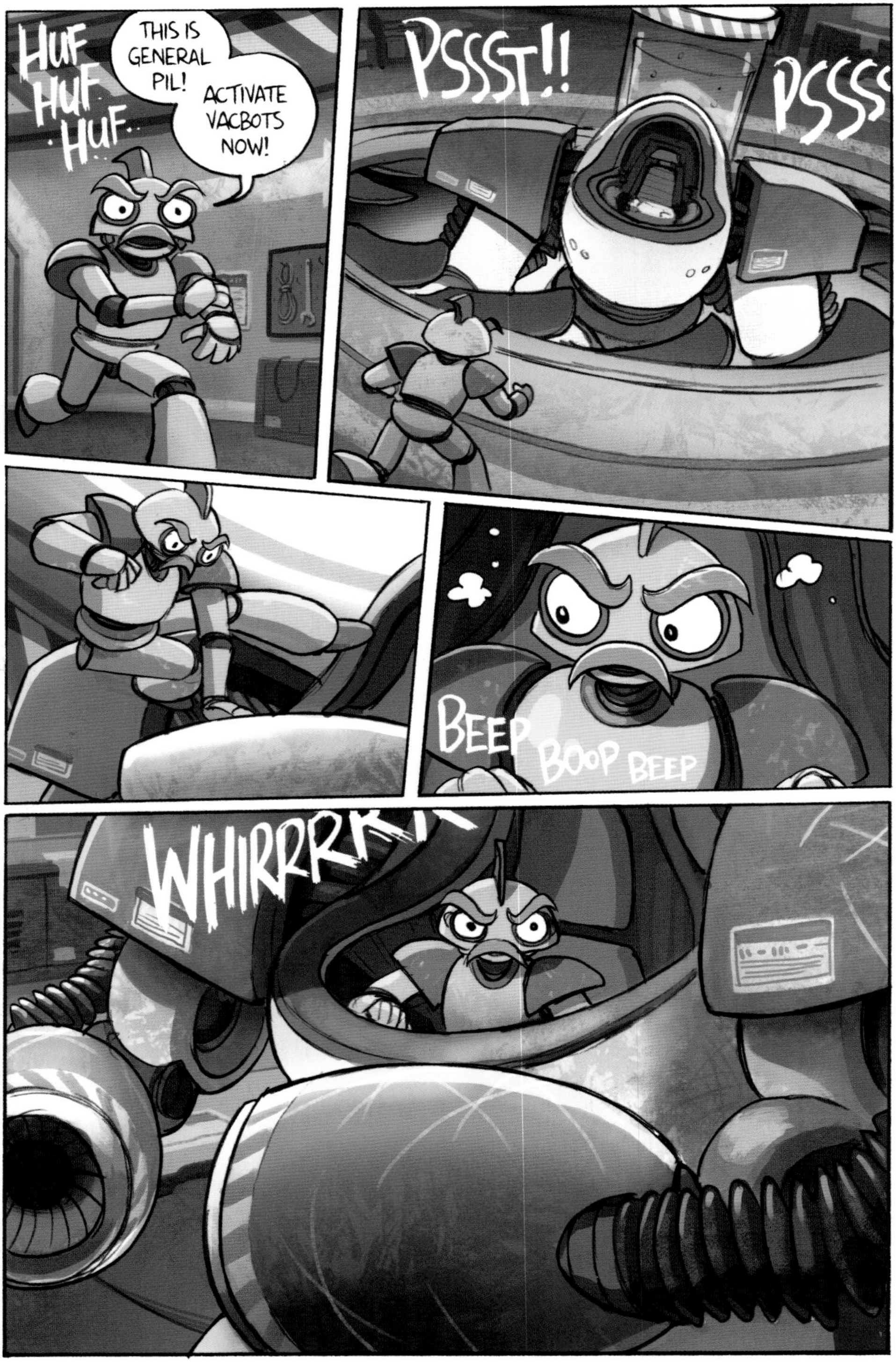
HUF HUF HUF
THIS IS GENERAL PIL!
ACTIVATE VACBOTS NOW!
PSSST!!
PSSSS
BEEP BOOP BEEP
WHIRRRRR

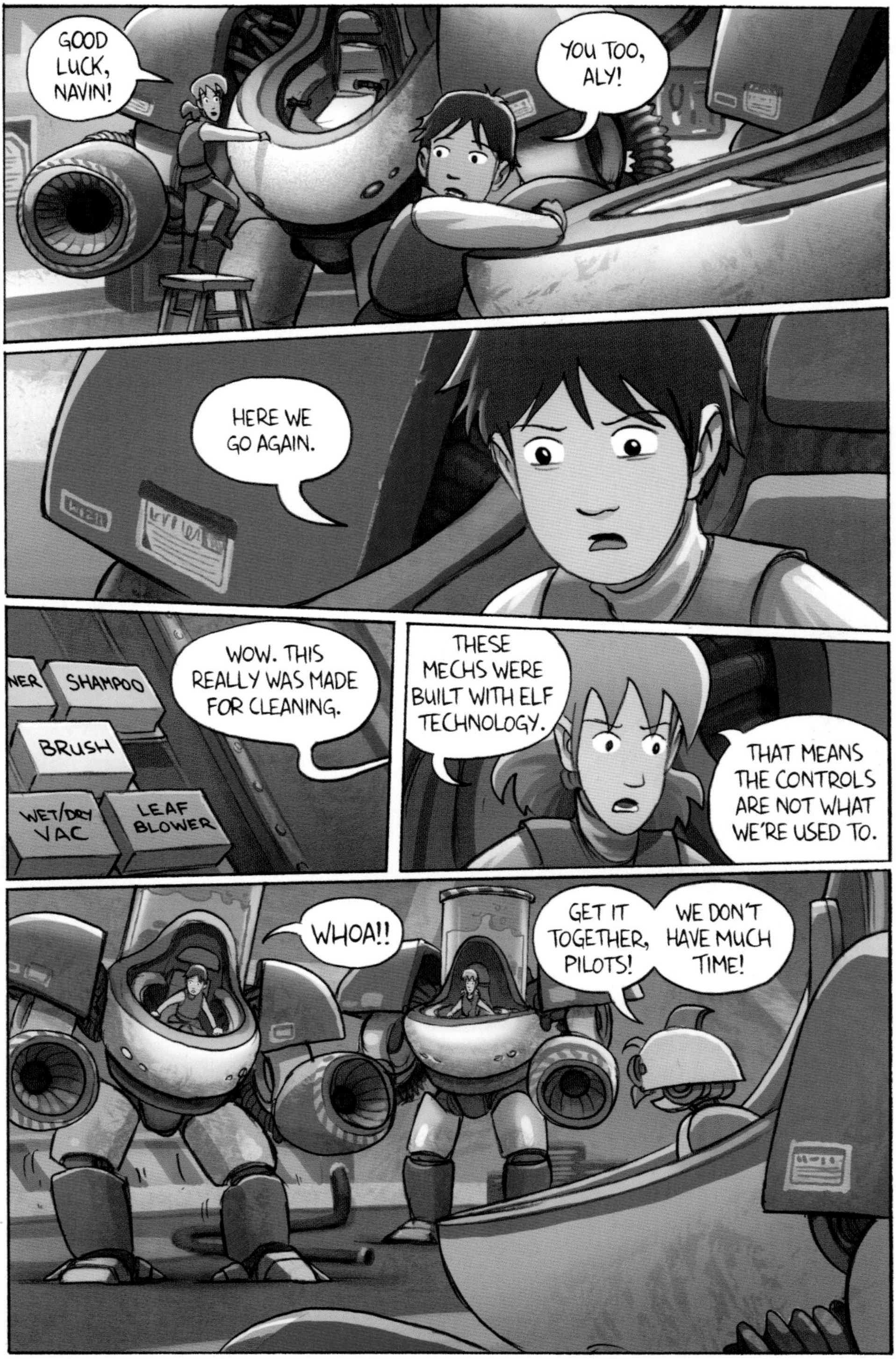
GOOD LUCK, NAVIN!
YOU TOO, ALY!
HERE WE GO AGAIN.
NER
SHAMPOO
BRUSH
WET/DRY VAC
LEAF BLOWER
WOW. THIS REALLY WAS MADE FOR CLEANING.
THESE MECHS WERE BUILT WITH ELF TECHNOLOGY.
THAT MEANS THE CONTROLS ARE NOT WHAT WE'RE USED TO.
WHOA!!
GET IT TOGETHER, PILOTS!
WE DON'T HAVE MUCH TIME!

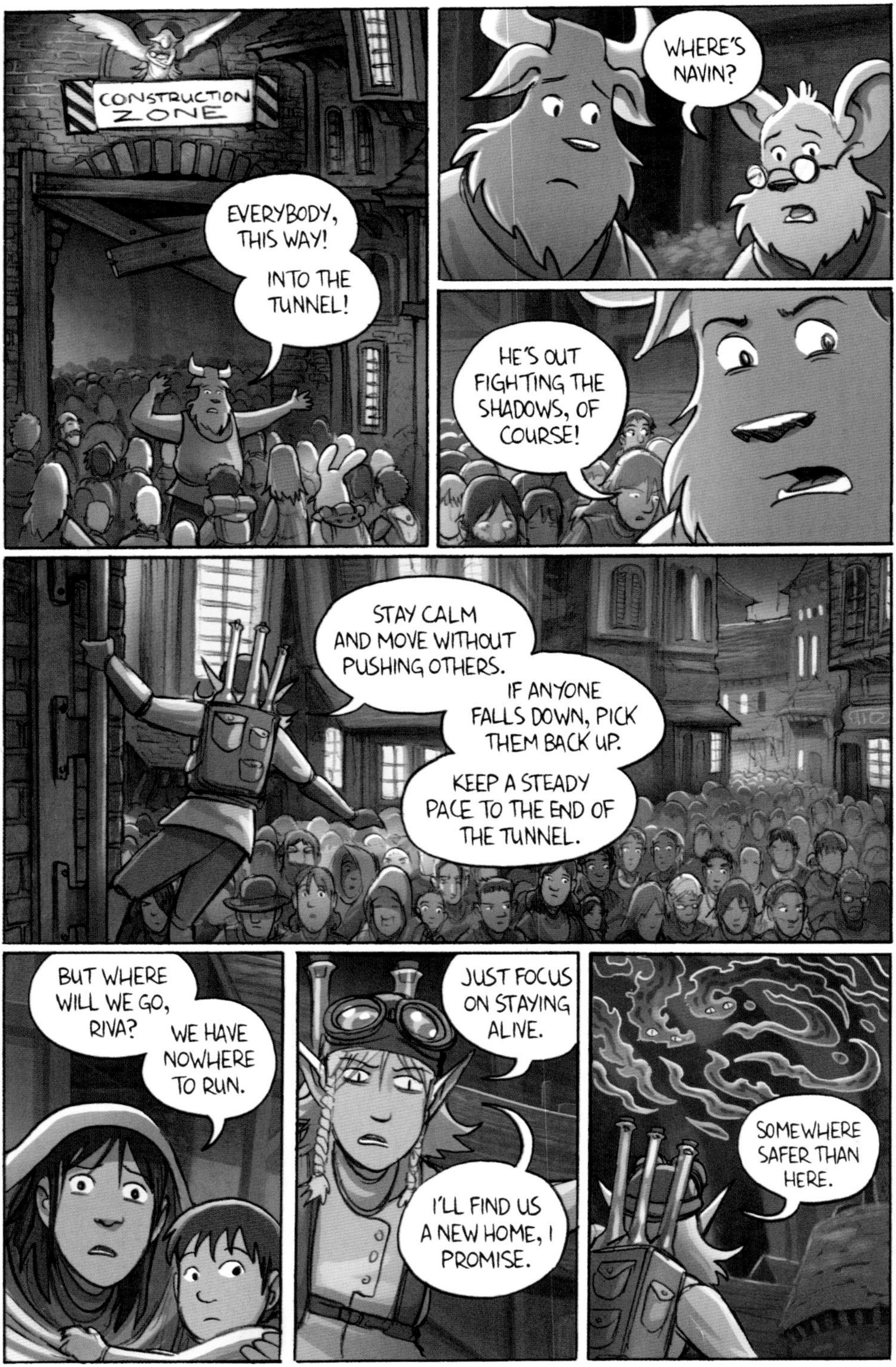
CONSTRUCTION ZONE
EVERYBODY, THIS WAY!
INTO THE TUNNEL!
WHERE'S NAVIN?
HE'S OUT FIGHTING THE SHADOWS, OF COURSE!
STAY CALM AND MOVE WITHOUT PUSHING OTHERS.
IF ANYONE FALLS DOWN, PICK THEM BACK UP.
KEEP A STEADY PACE TO THE END OF THE TUNNEL.
BUT WHERE WILL WE GO, RIVA?
WE HAVE NOWHERE TO RUN.
JUST FOCUS ON STAYING ALIVE.
I'LL FIND US A NEW HOME, I PROMISE.
SOMEWHERE SAFER THAN HERE.

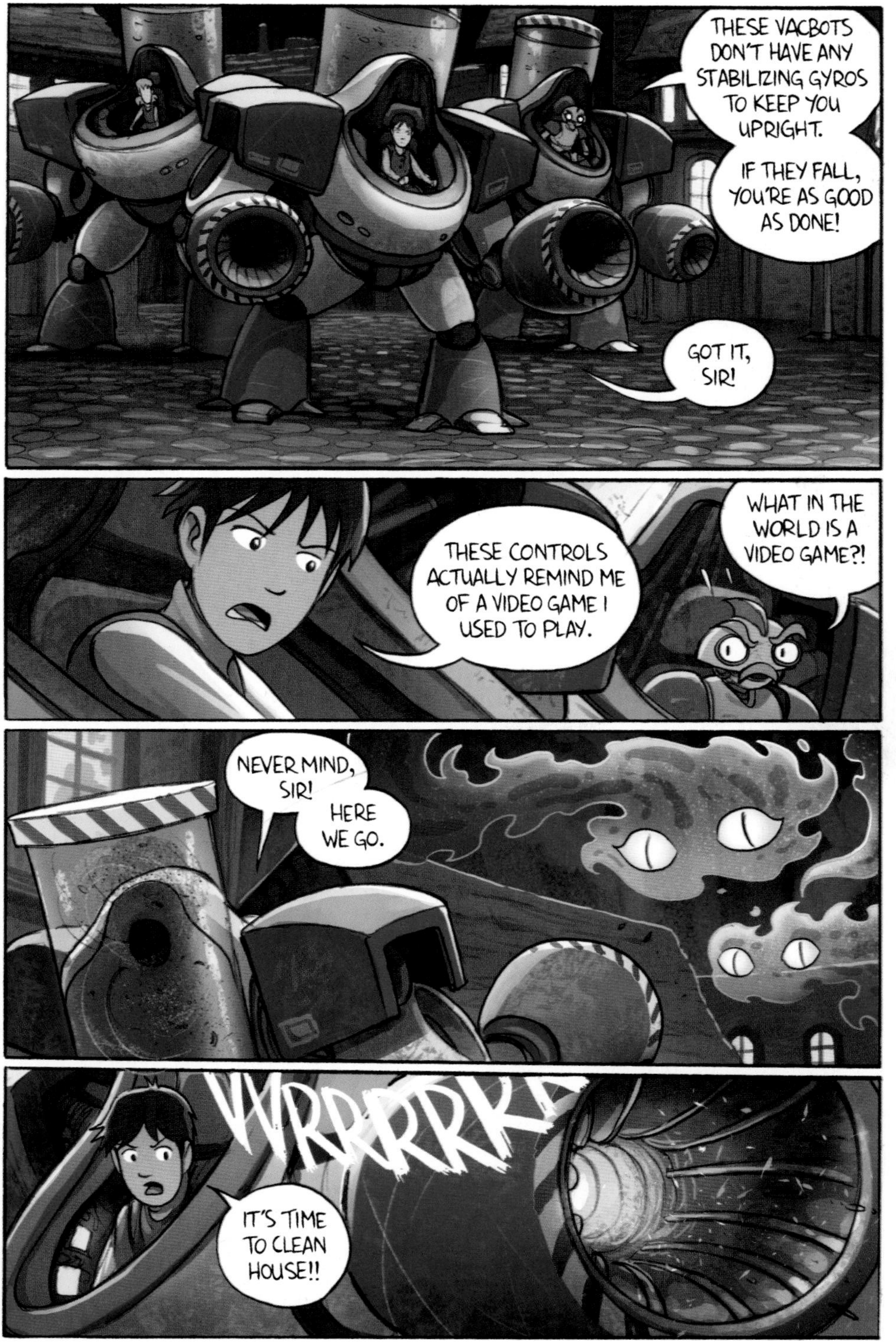
THESE VACBOTS DON'T HAVE ANY STABILIZING GYROS TO KEEP YOU UPRIGHT.
IF THEY FALL, YOU'RE AS GOOD AS DONE!
GOT IT, SIR!
THESE CONTROLS ACTUALLY REMIND ME OF A VIDEO GAME I USED TO PLAY.
WHAT IN THE WORLD IS A VIDEO GAME?!
NEVER MIND, SIR!
HERE WE GO.
WRRRRRR
IT'S TIME TO CLEAN HOUSE!!

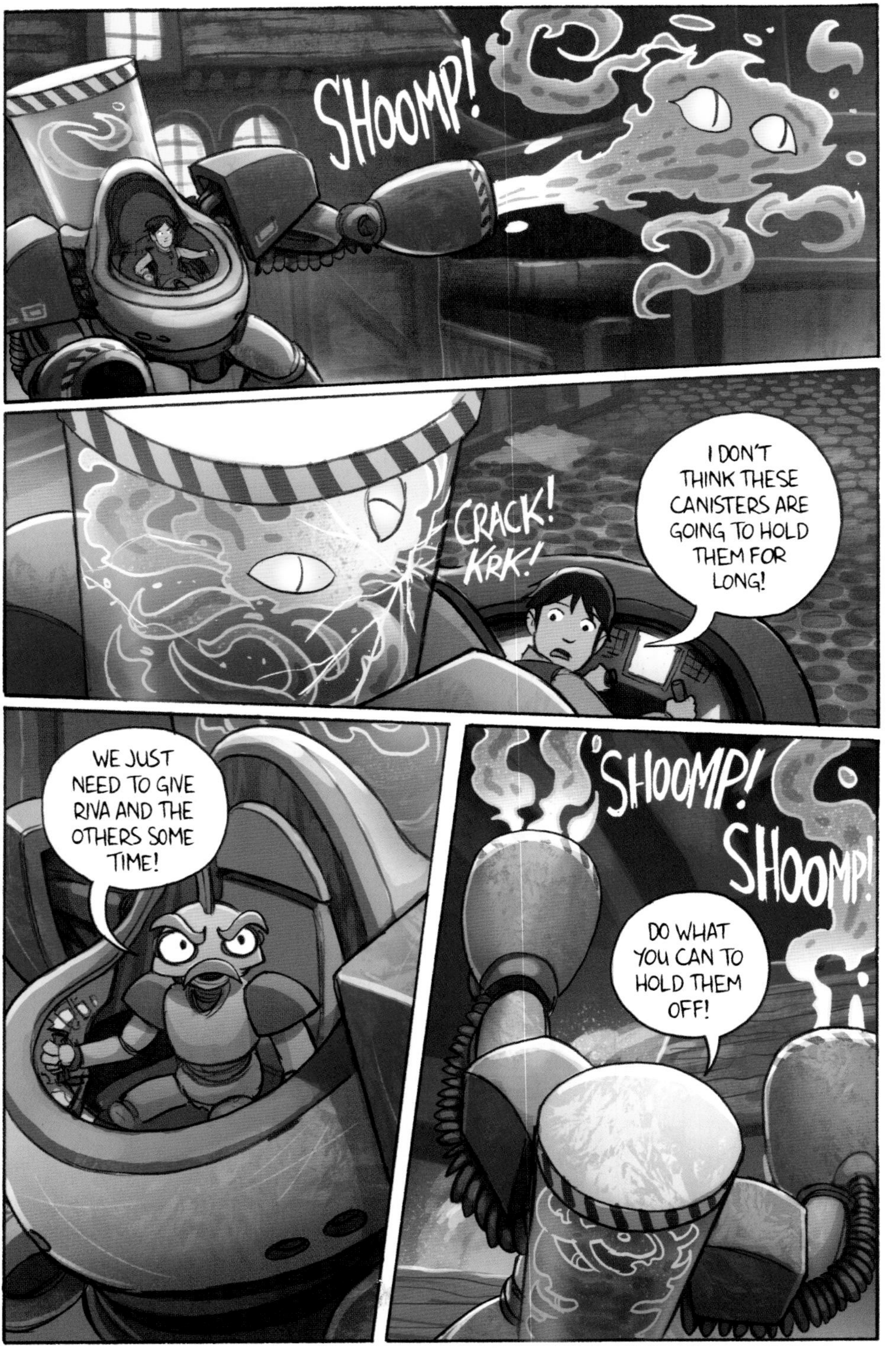
SHOOMP!
CRACK!
KRK!
I DON'T THINK THESE CANISTERS ARE GOING TO HOLD THEM FOR LONG!
WE JUST NEED TO GIVE RIVA AND THE OTHERS SOME TIME!
SHOOMP!
SHOOMP!
DO WHAT YOU CAN TO HOLD THEM OFF!

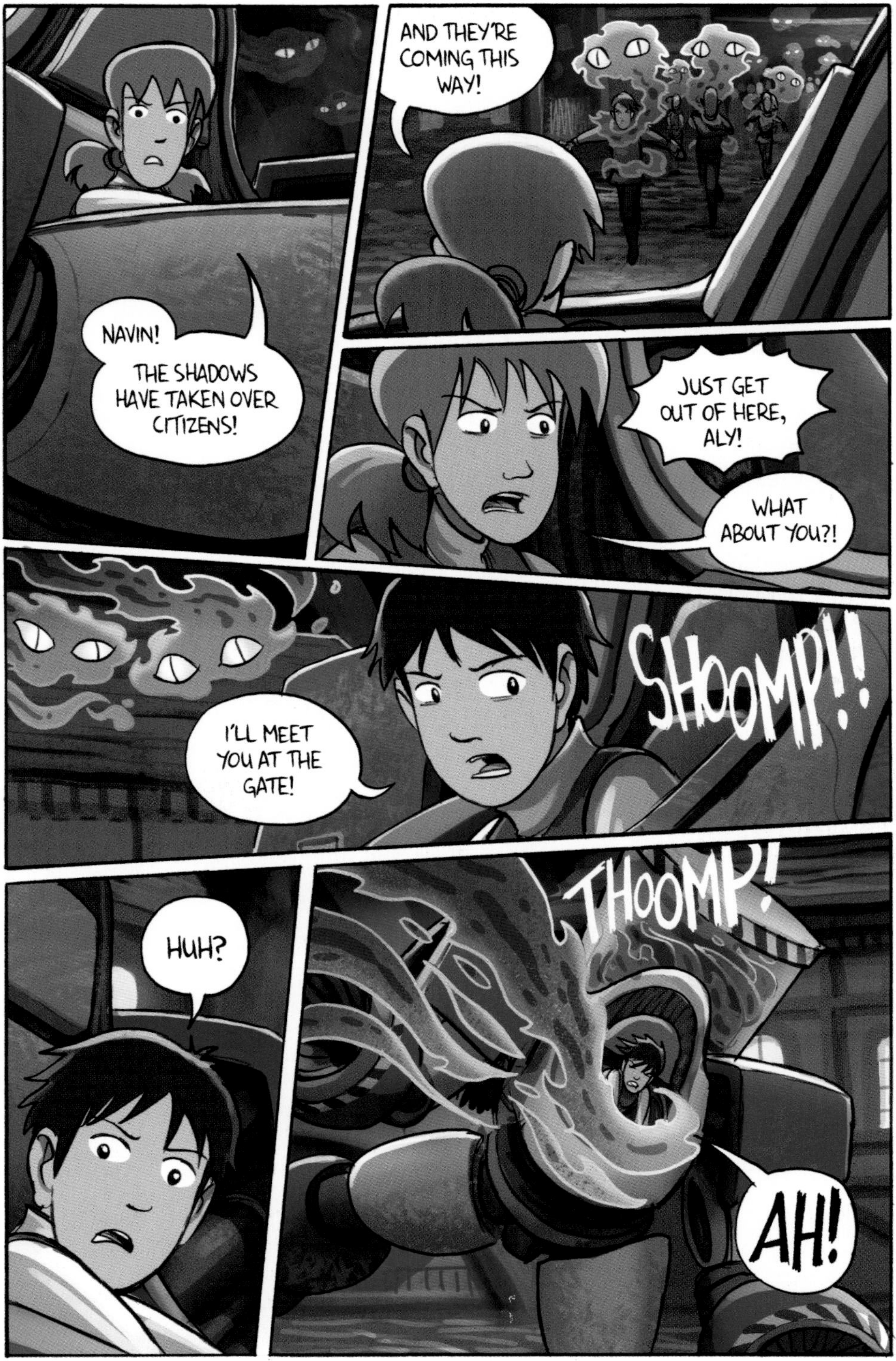
NAVIN!
THE SHADOWS HAVE TAKEN OVER CITIZENS!
AND THEY'RE COMING THIS WAY!
JUST GET OUT OF HERE, ALY!
WHAT ABOUT YOU?!
I'LL MEET YOU AT THE GATE!
SHOOMP!!
HUH?
THOOMP!
AH!

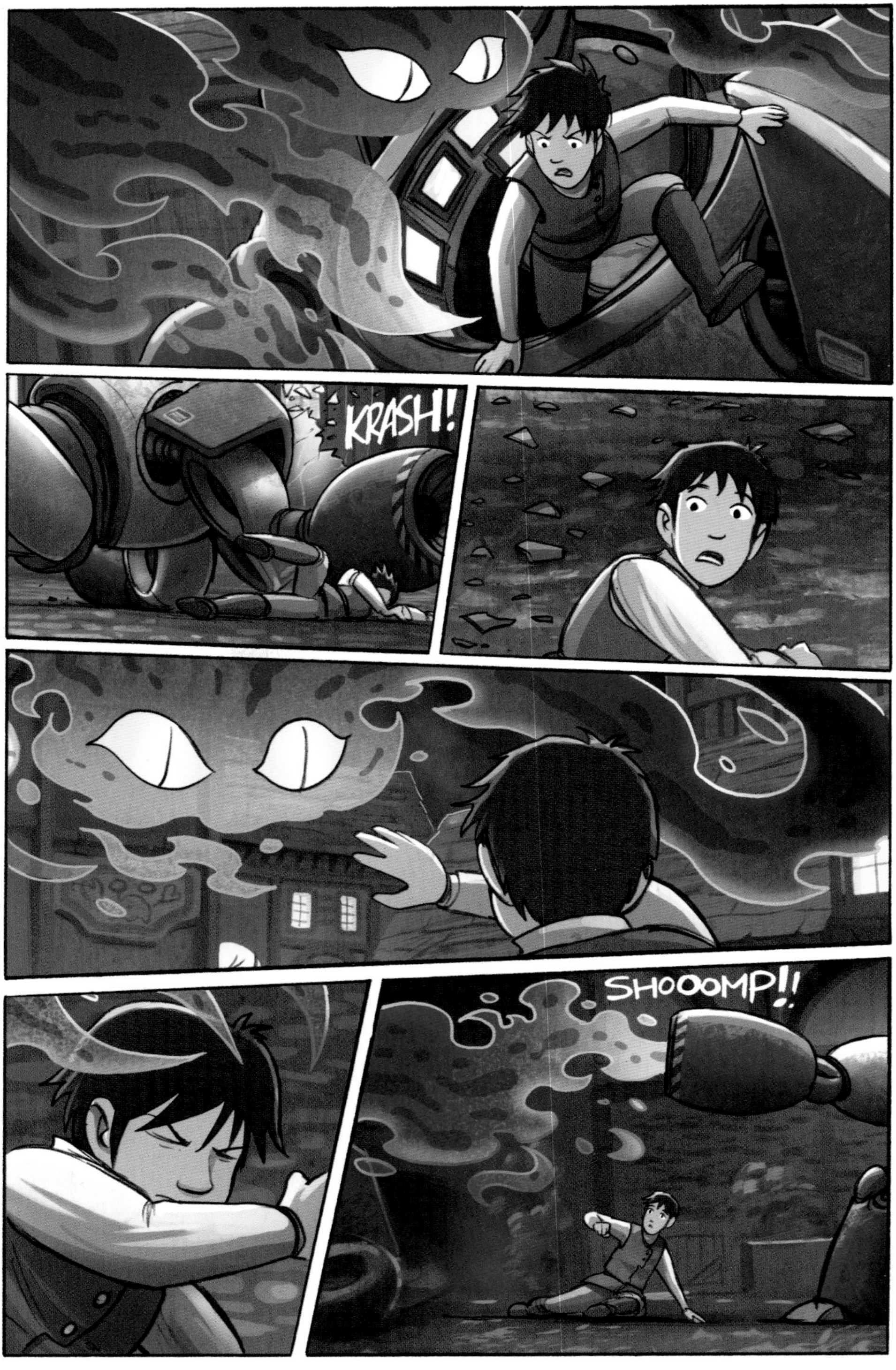
KRASH!
SHOOOMP!!

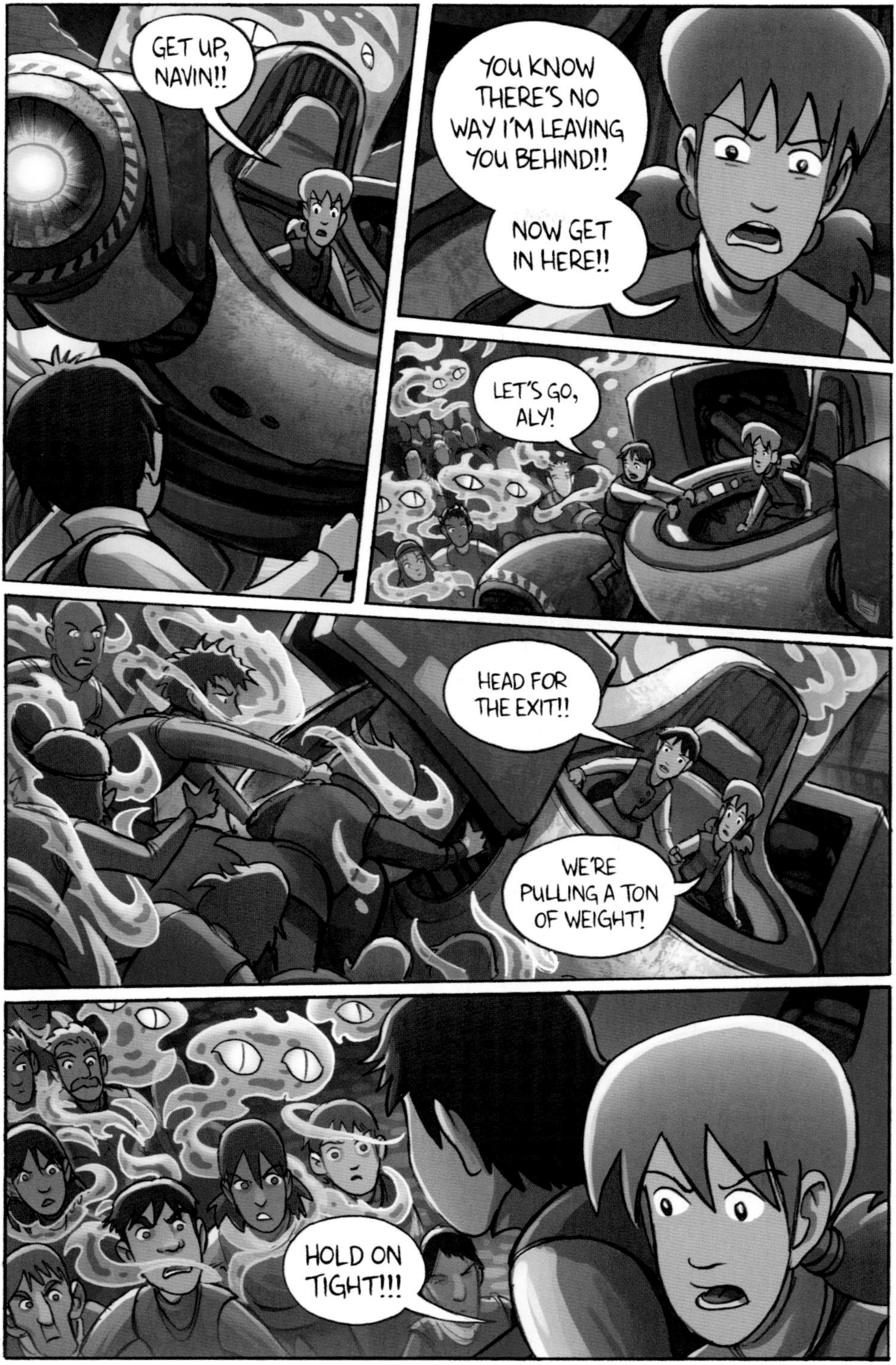
GET UP, NAVIN!!
YOU KNOW THERE'S NO WAY I'M LEAVING YOU BEHIND!!
NOW GET IN HERE!!
LET'S GO, ALY!
HEAD FOR THE EXIT!!
WE'RE PULLING A TON OF WEIGHT!
HOLD ON TIGHT!!!

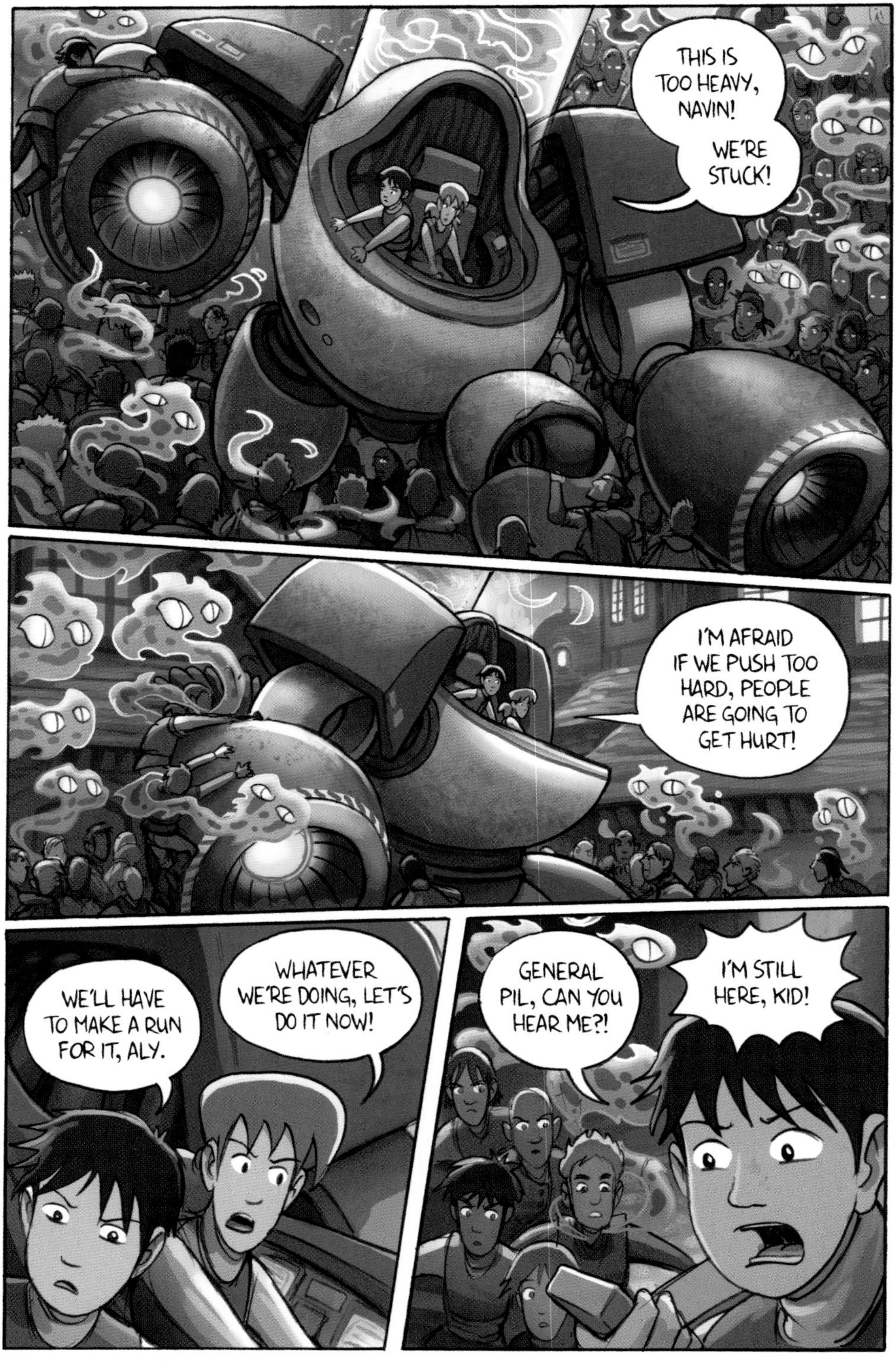
THIS IS TOO HEAVY, NAVIN!
WE'RE STUCK!
I'M AFRAID IF WE PUSH TOO HARD, PEOPLE ARE GOING TO GET HURT!
WE'LL HAVE TO MAKE A RUN FOR IT, ALY.
WHATEVER WE'RE DOING, LET'S DO IT NOW!
GENERAL PIL, CAN YOU HEAR ME?!
I'M STILL HERE, KID!

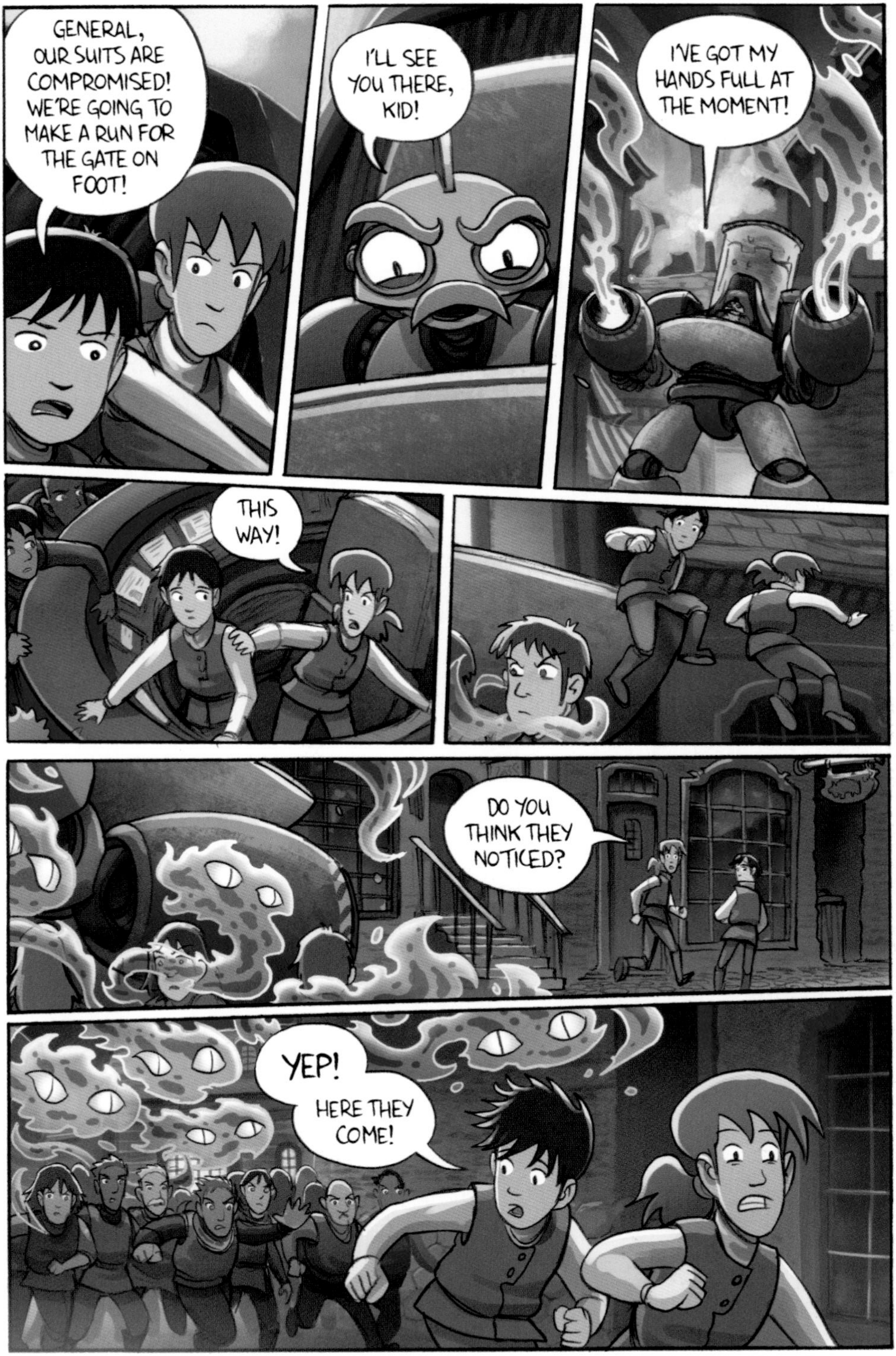
GENERAL, OUR SUITS ARE COMPROMISED! WE'RE GOING TO MAKE A RUN FOR THE GATE ON FOOT!
I'LL SEE YOU THERE, KID!
I'VE GOT MY HANDS FULL AT THE MOMENT!
THIS WAY!
DO YOU THINK THEY NOTICED?
YEP!
HERE THEY COME!

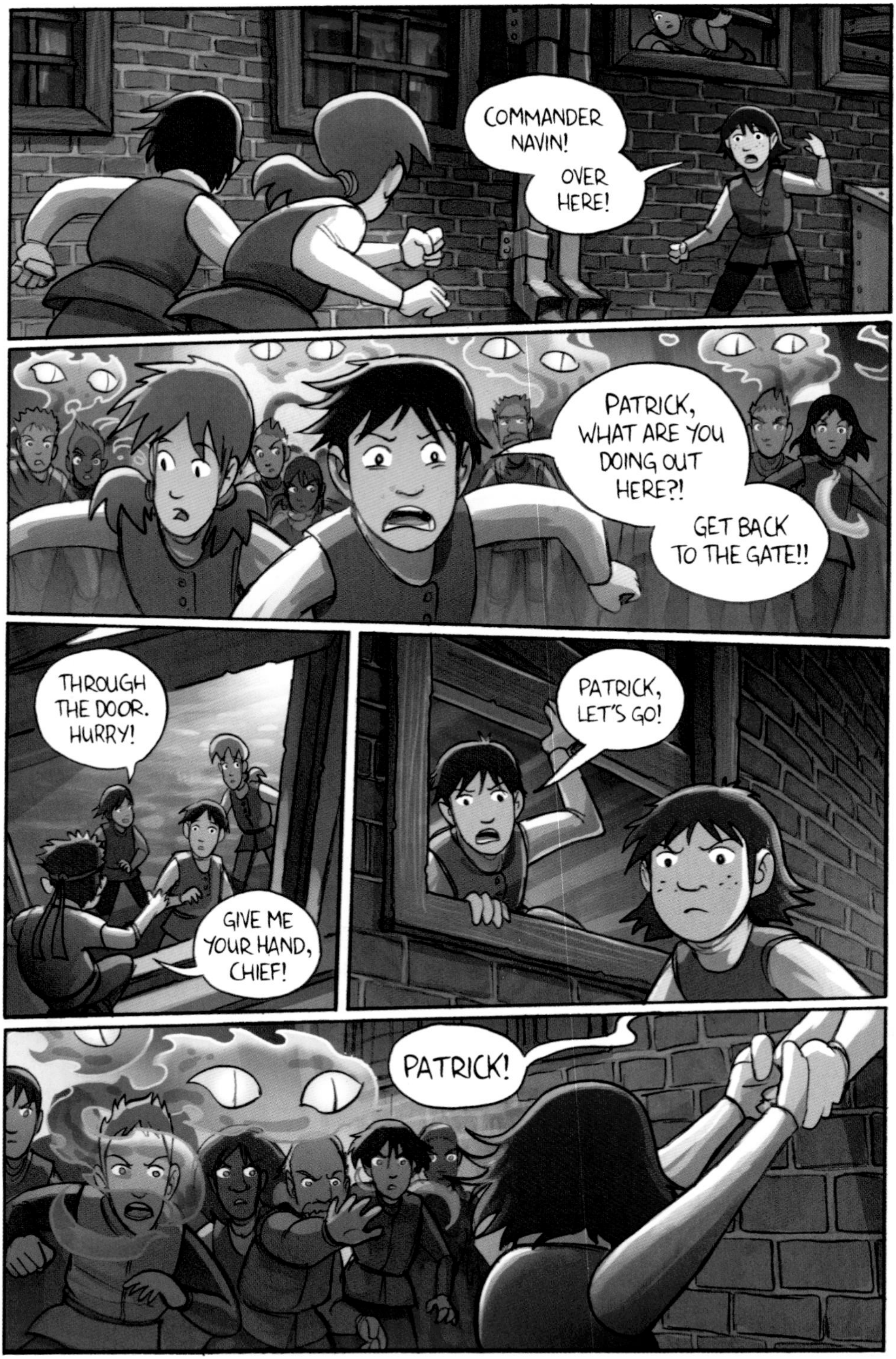
COMMANDER NAVIN!
OVER HERE!
PATRICK, WHAT ARE YOU DOING OUT HERE?!
GET BACK TO THE GATE!!
THROUGH THE DOOR. HURRY!
GIVE ME YOUR HAND, CHIEF!
PATRICK, LET'S GO!
PATRICK!

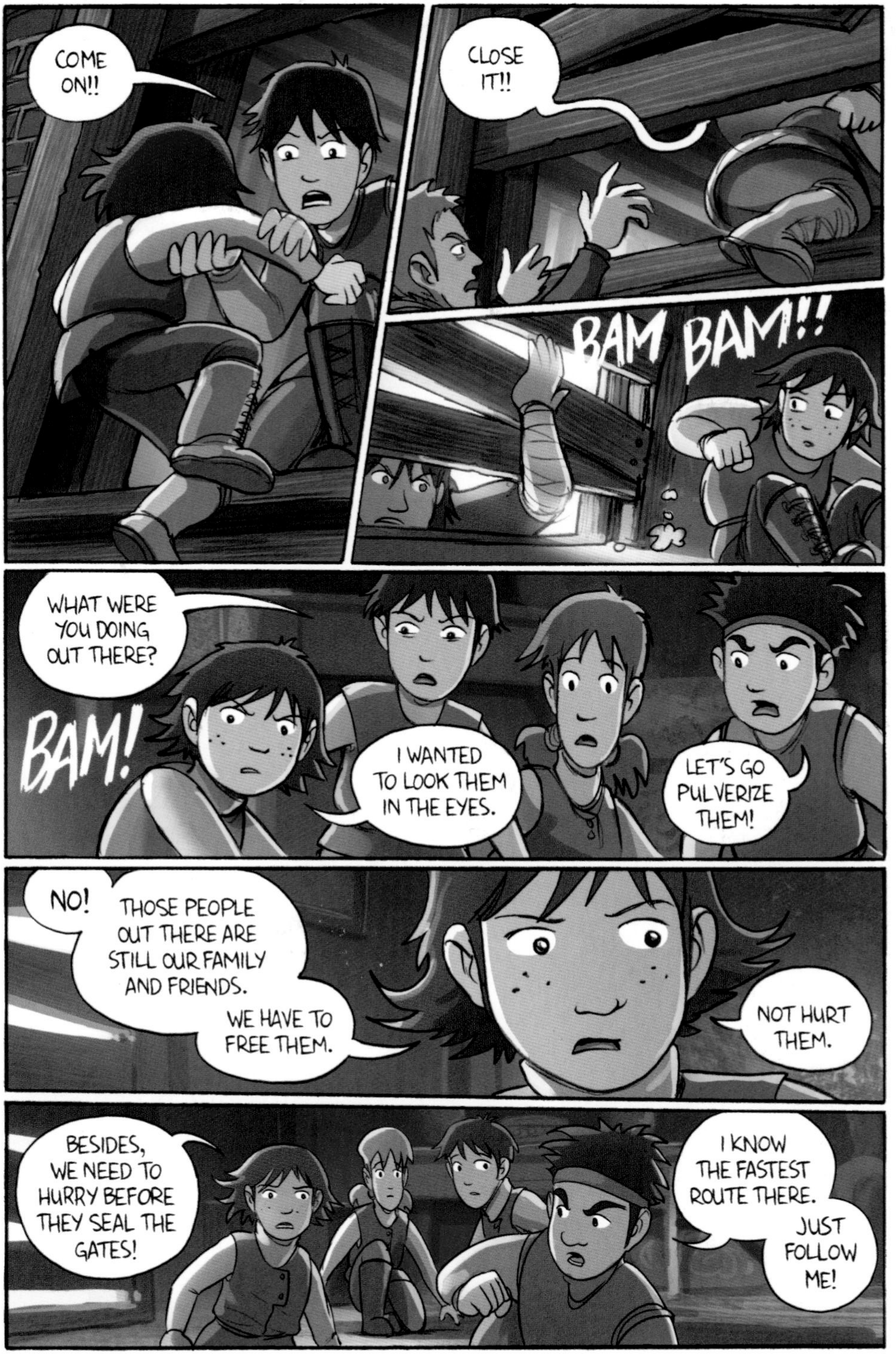
COME ON!!
CLOSE IT!!
BAM BAM!!
WHAT WERE YOU DOING OUT THERE?
BAM!
I WANTED TO LOOK THEM IN THE EYES.
LET'S GO PULVERIZE THEM!
NO!
THOSE PEOPLE OUT THERE ARE STILL OUR FAMILY AND FRIENDS.
WE HAVE TO FREE THEM.
NOT HURT THEM.
BESIDES, WE NEED TO HURRY BEFORE THEY SEAL THE GATES!
I KNOW THE FASTEST ROUTE THERE.
JUST FOLLOW ME!

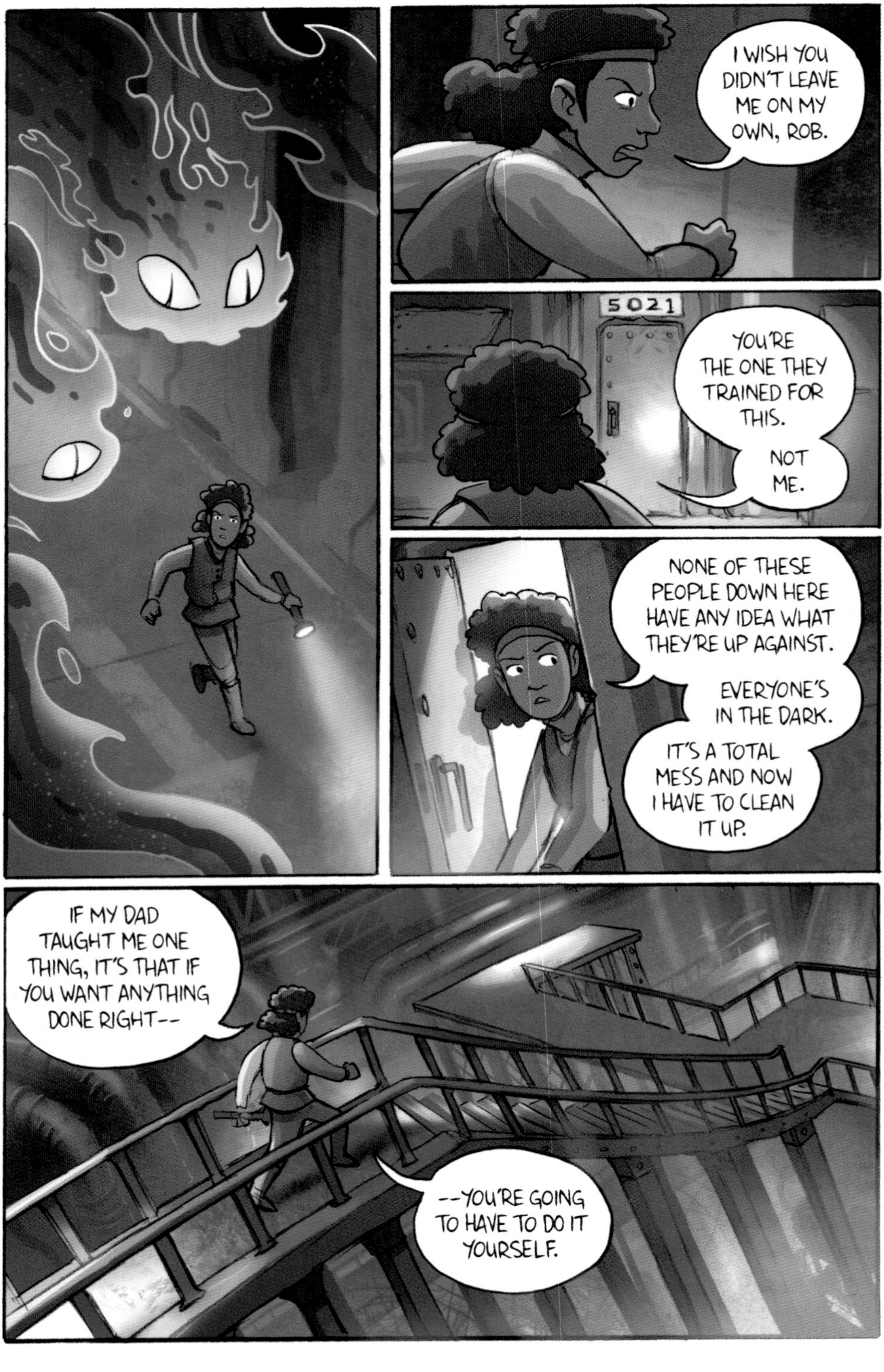
I WISH YOU DIDN'T LEAVE ME ON MY OWN, ROB.
5021
YOU'RE THE ONE THEY TRAINED FOR THIS.
NOT ME.
NONE OF THESE PEOPLE DOWN HERE HAVE ANY IDEA WHAT THEY'RE UP AGAINST.
EVERYONE'S IN THE DARK.
IT'S A TOTAL MESS AND NOW I HAVE TO CLEAN IT UP.
IF MY DAD TAUGHT ME ONE THING, IT'S THAT IF YOU WANT ANYTHING DONE RIGHT--
--YOU'RE GOING TO HAVE TO DO IT YOURSELF.

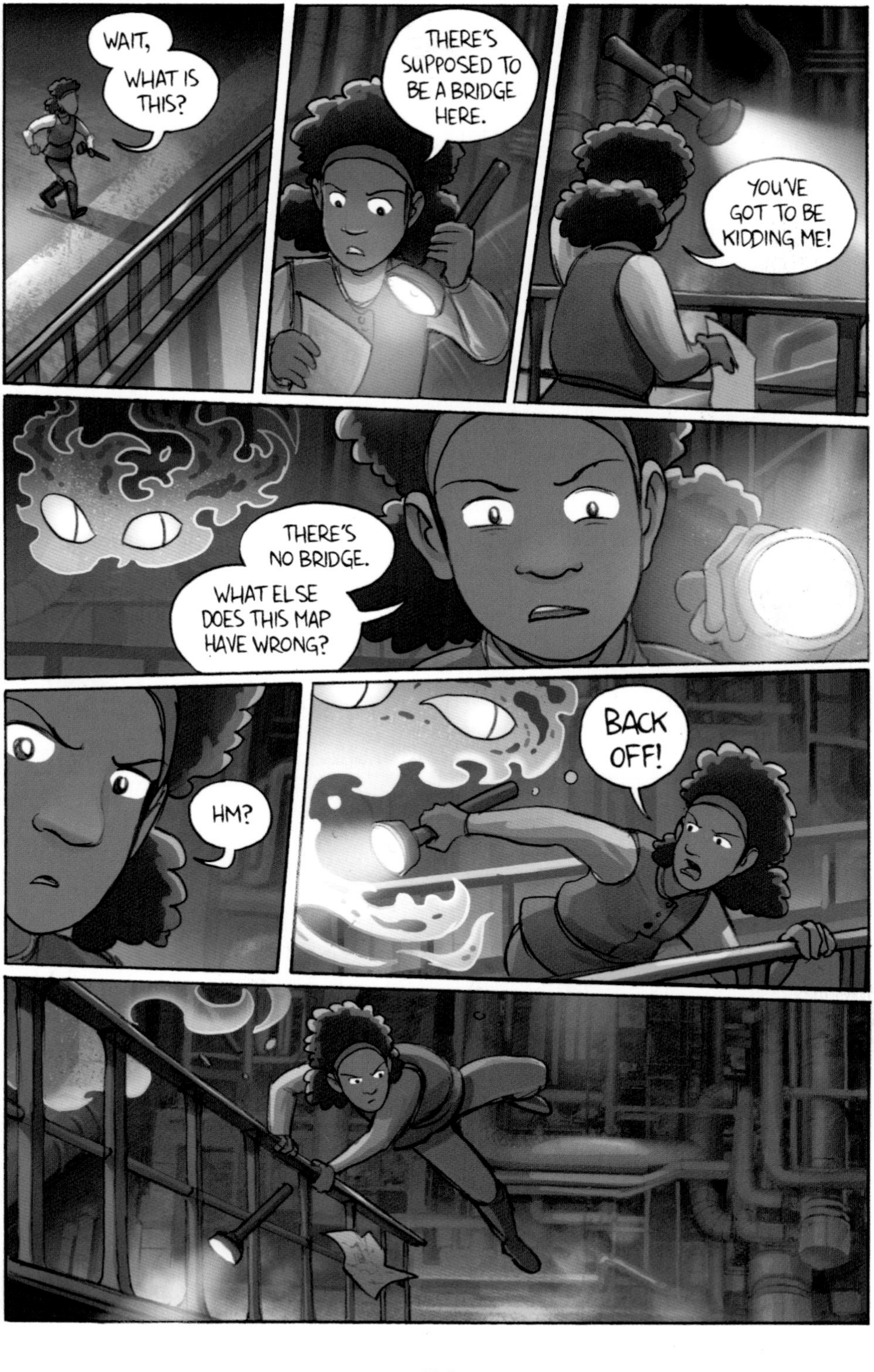
WAIT,
WHAT IS THIS?
THERE'S SUPPOSED TO BE A BRIDGE HERE.
YOU'VE GOT TO BE KIDDING ME!
THERE'S NO BRIDGE.
WHAT ELSE DOES THIS MAP HAVE WRONG?
HM?
BACK OFF!

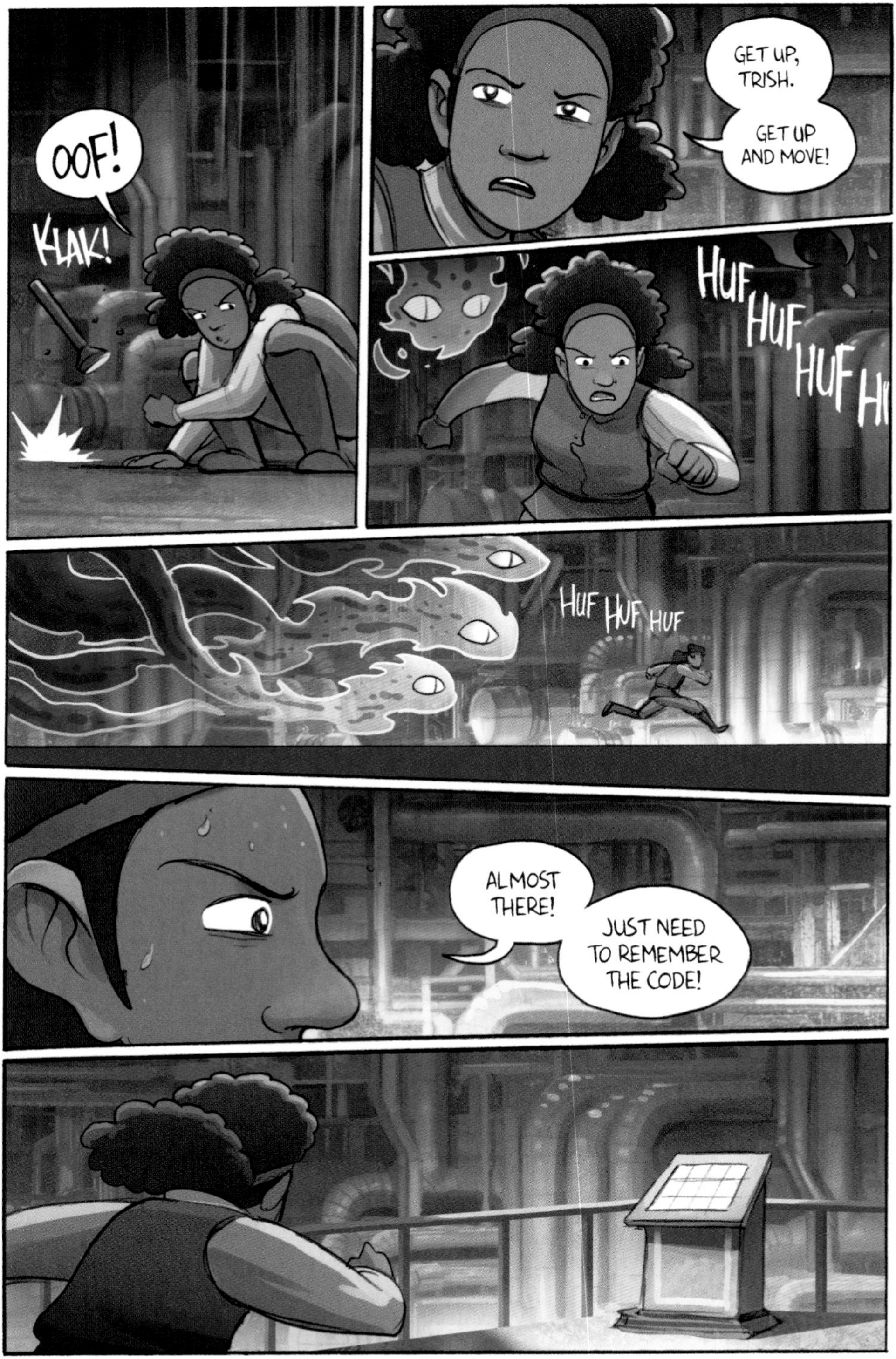
OOF!
KLAK!
GET UP, TRISH.
GET UP AND MOVE!
HUF HUF HUF HU
HUF HUF HUF
ALMOST THERE!
JUST NEED TO REMEMBER THE CODE!

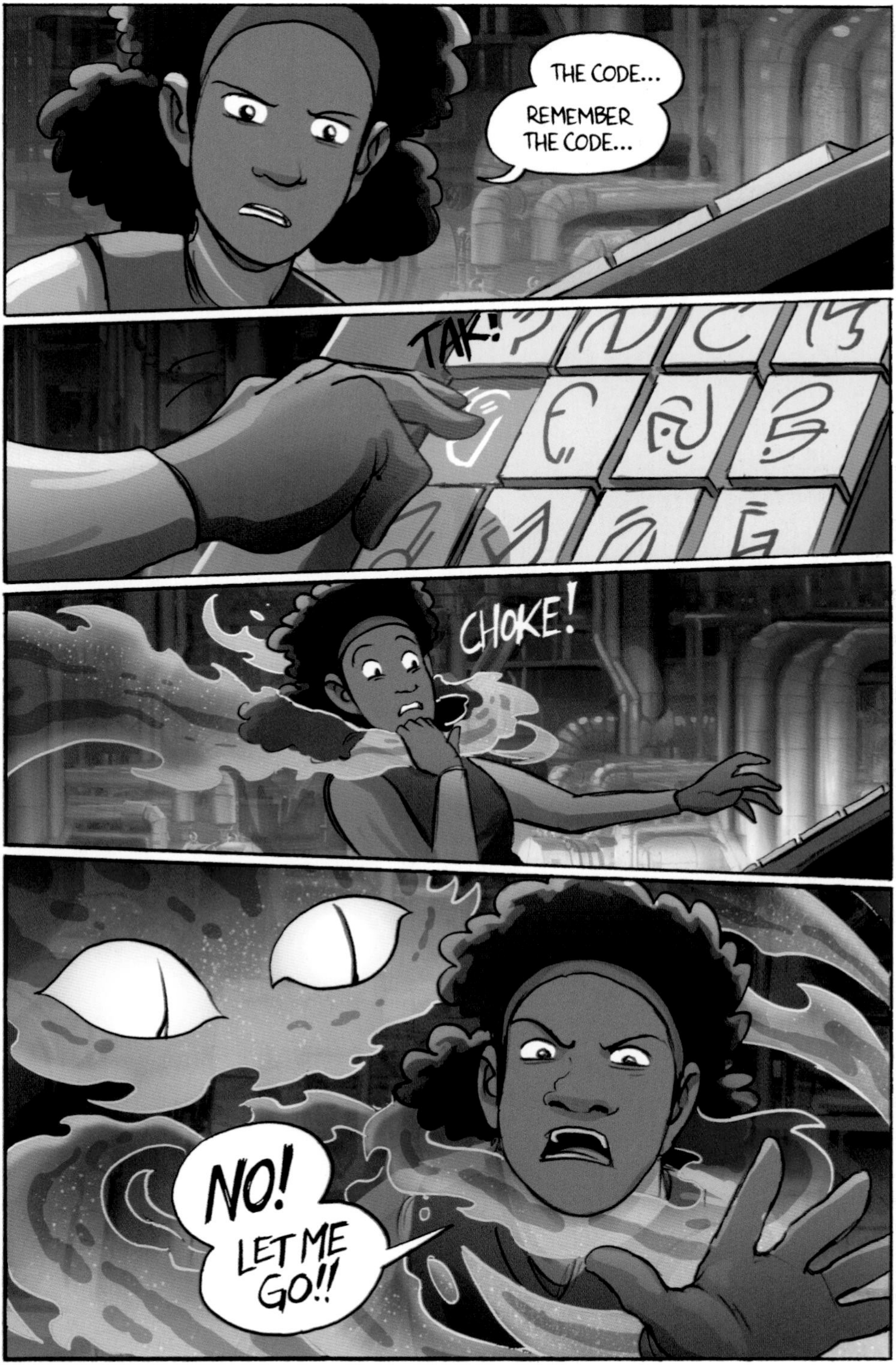
THE CODE...
REMEMBER THE CODE...
TAK!
CHOKE!
NO! LET ME GO!!

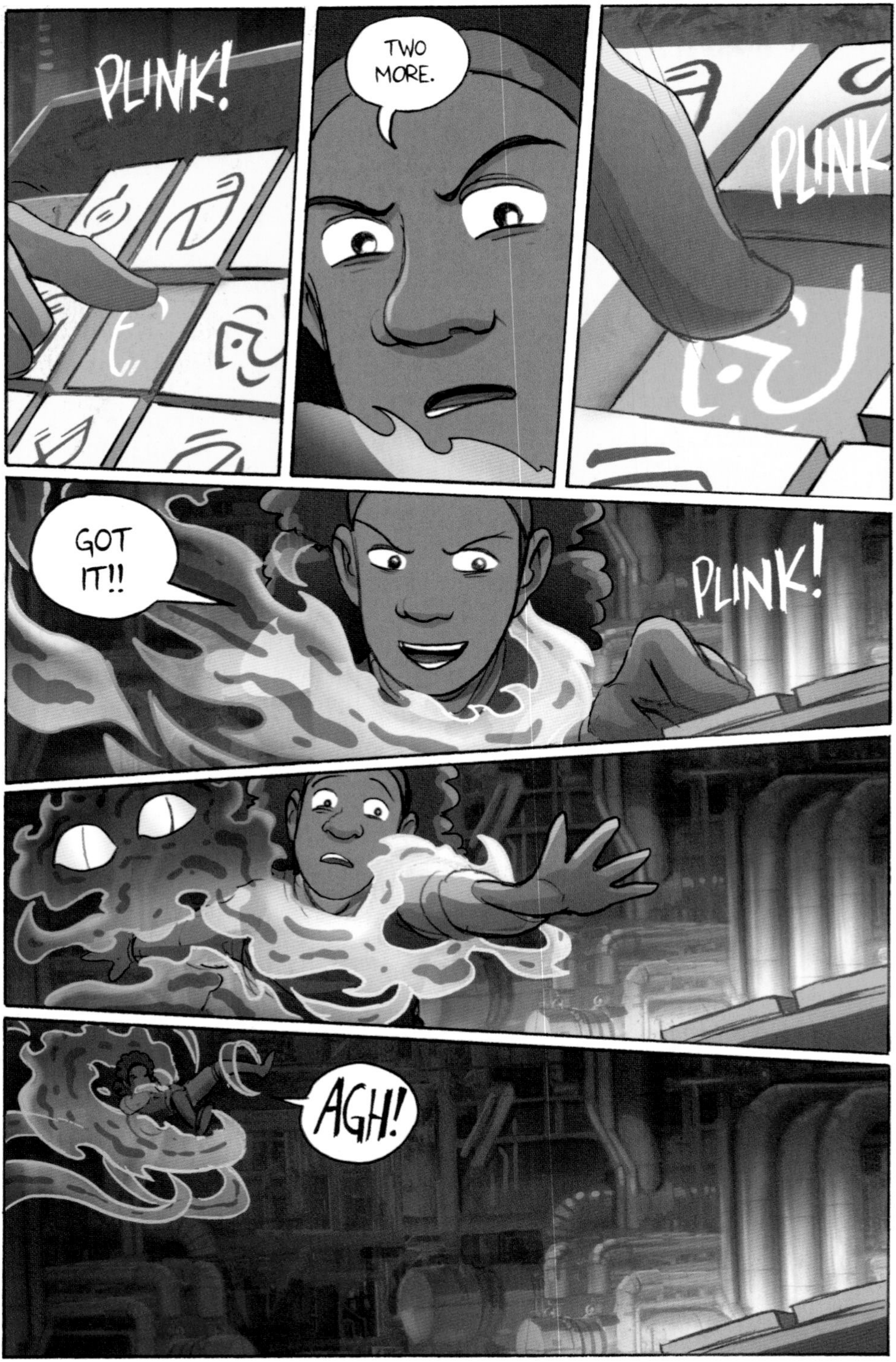
PLINK!
TWO MORE.
PLINK
GOT IT!!
PLINK!
AGH!

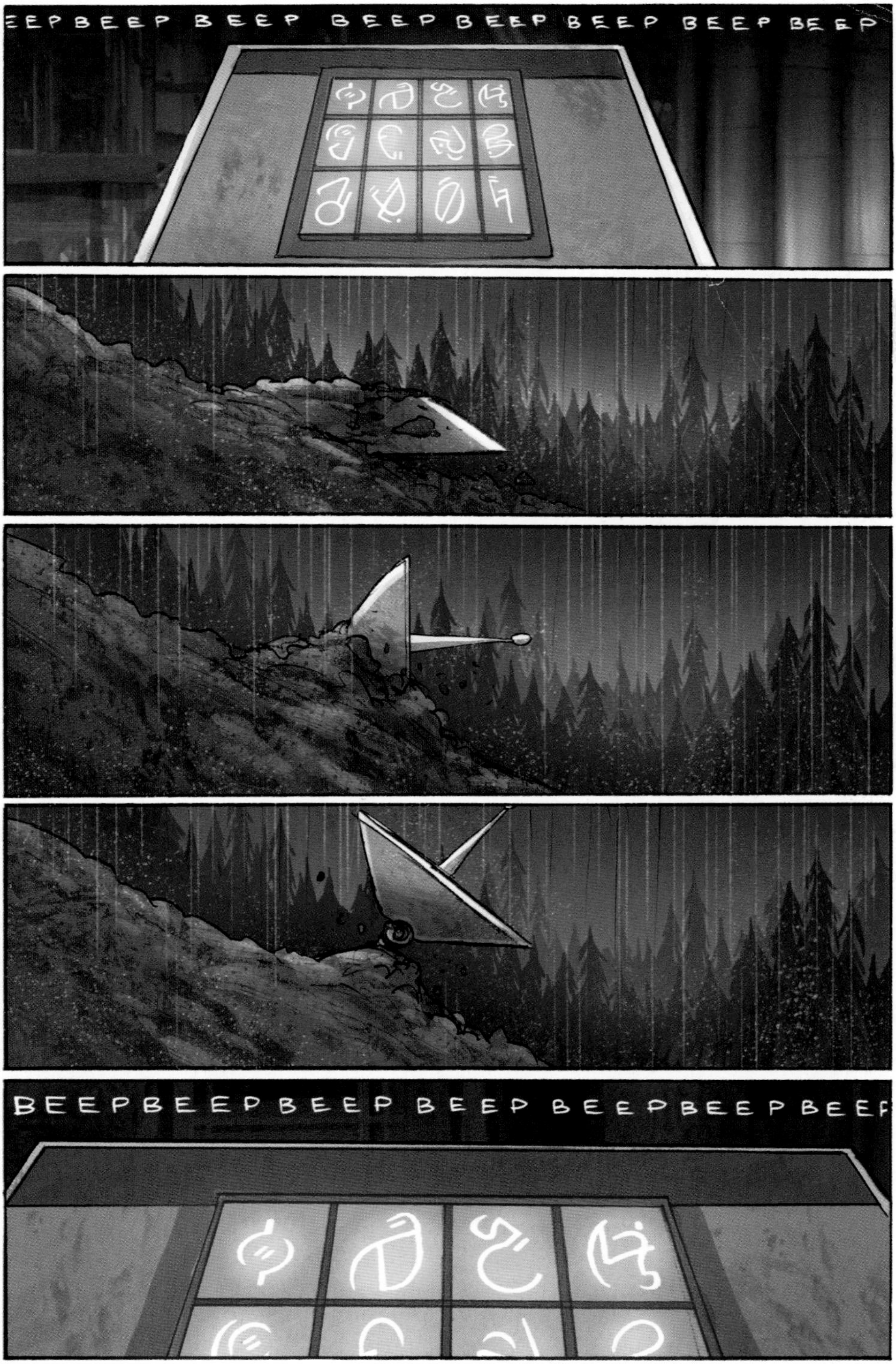
EEP BEEP BEEP BEEP BEEP BEEP BEEP BEEP
BEEP BEEP BEEP BEEP BEEP BEEP BEEP BEE

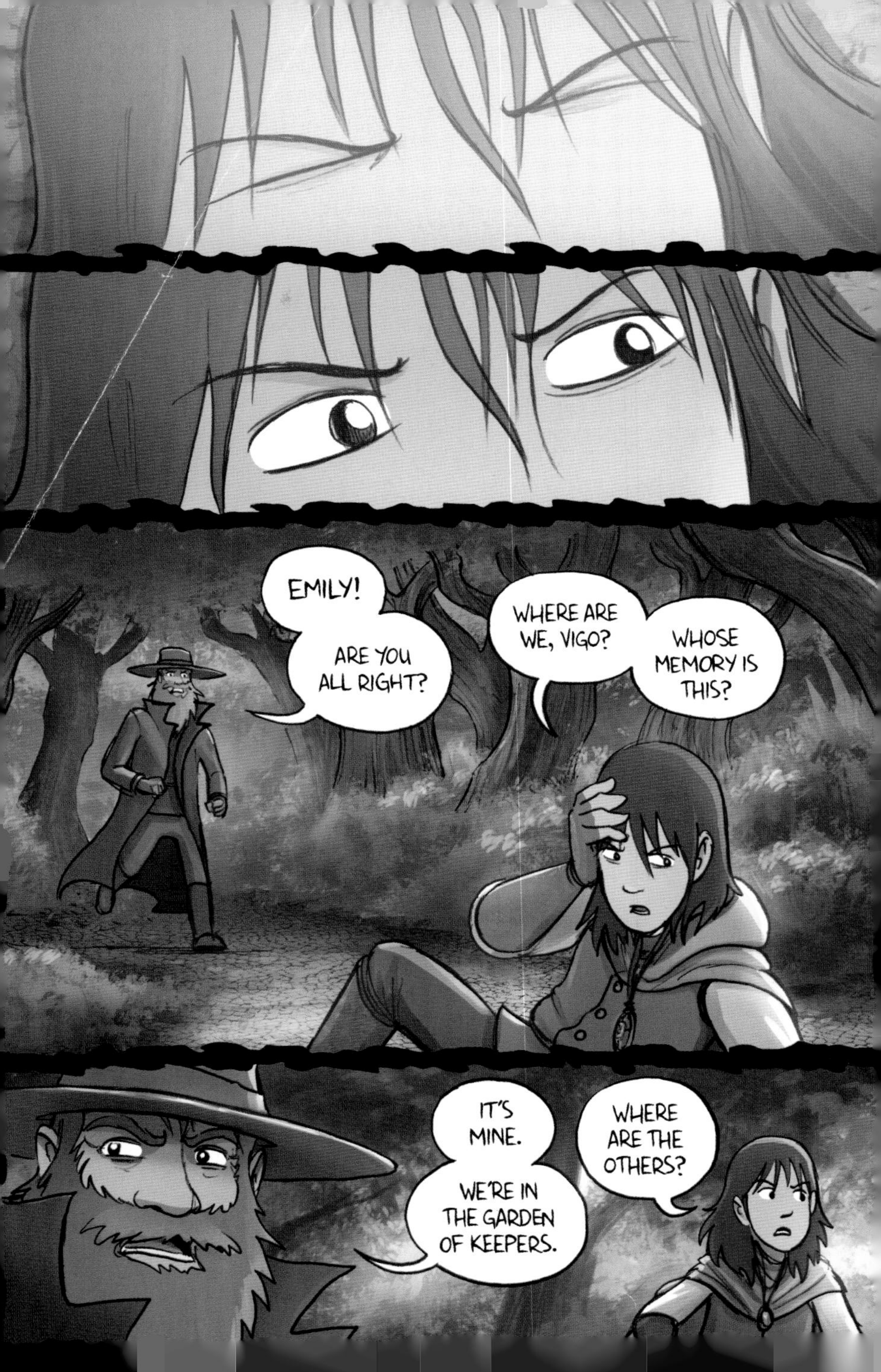
EMILY!
ARE YOU ALL RIGHT?
WHERE ARE WE, VIGO?
WHOSE MEMORY IS THIS?
IT'S MINE.
WE'RE IN THE GARDEN OF KEEPERS.
WHERE ARE THE OTHERS?

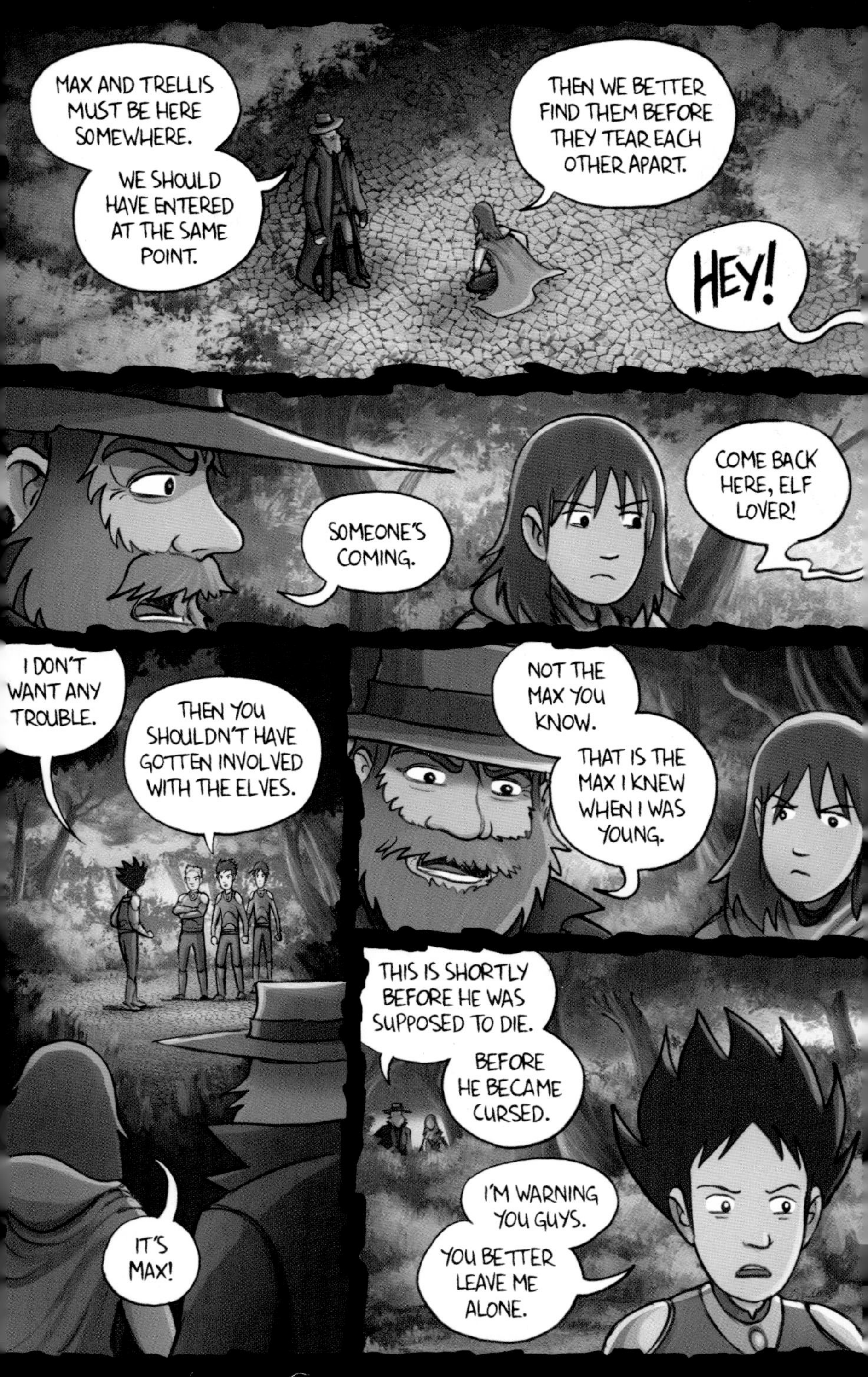
MAX AND TRELLIS MUST BE HERE SOMEWHERE.
WE SHOULD HAVE ENTERED AT THE SAME POINT.
THEN WE BETTER FIND THEM BEFORE THEY TEAR EACH OTHER APART.
HEY!
SOMEONE'S COMING.
COME BACK HERE, ELF LOVER!
I DON'T WANT ANY TROUBLE.
THEN YOU SHOULDN'T HAVE GOTTEN INVOLVED WITH THE ELVES.
IT'S MAX!
NOT THE MAX YOU KNOW.
THAT IS THE MAX I KNEW WHEN I WAS YOUNG.
THIS IS SHORTLY BEFORE HE WAS SUPPOSED TO DIE.
BEFORE HE BECAME CURSED.
I'M WARNING YOU GUYS.
YOU BETTER LEAVE ME ALONE.

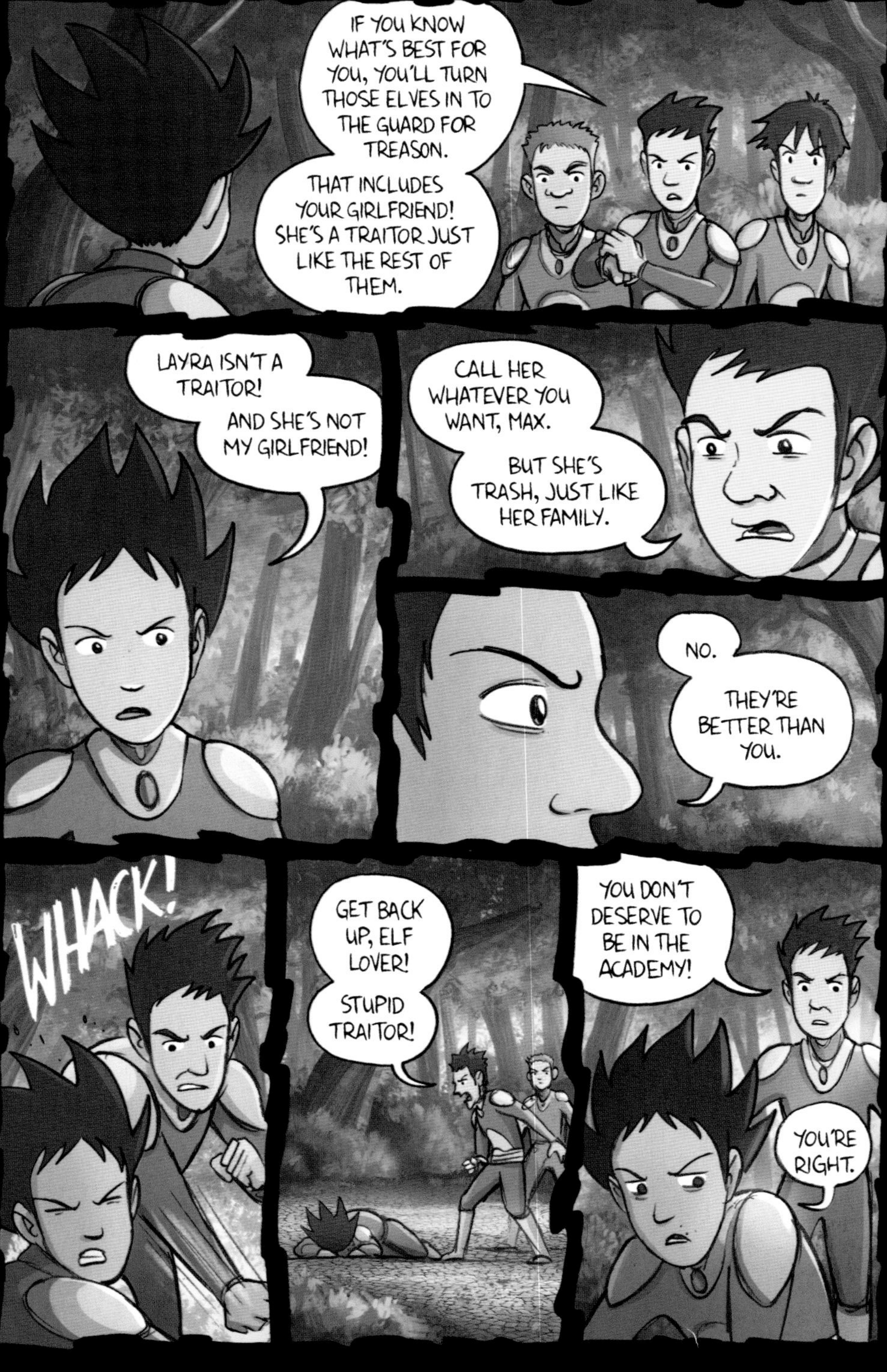
IF YOU KNOW WHAT'S BEST FOR YOU, YOU'LL TURN THOSE ELVES IN TO THE GUARD FOR TREASON.
THAT INCLUDES YOUR GIRLFRIEND! SHE'S A TRAITOR JUST LIKE THE REST OF THEM.
LAYRA ISN'T A TRAITOR!
AND SHE'S NOT MY GIRLFRIEND!
CALL HER WHATEVER YOU WANT, MAX.
BUT SHE'S TRASH, JUST LIKE HER FAMILY.
NO.
THEY'RE BETTER THAN YOU.
WHACK!
GET BACK UP, ELF LOVER!
STUPID TRAITOR!
YOU DON'T DESERVE TO BE IN THE ACADEMY!
YOU'RE RIGHT.

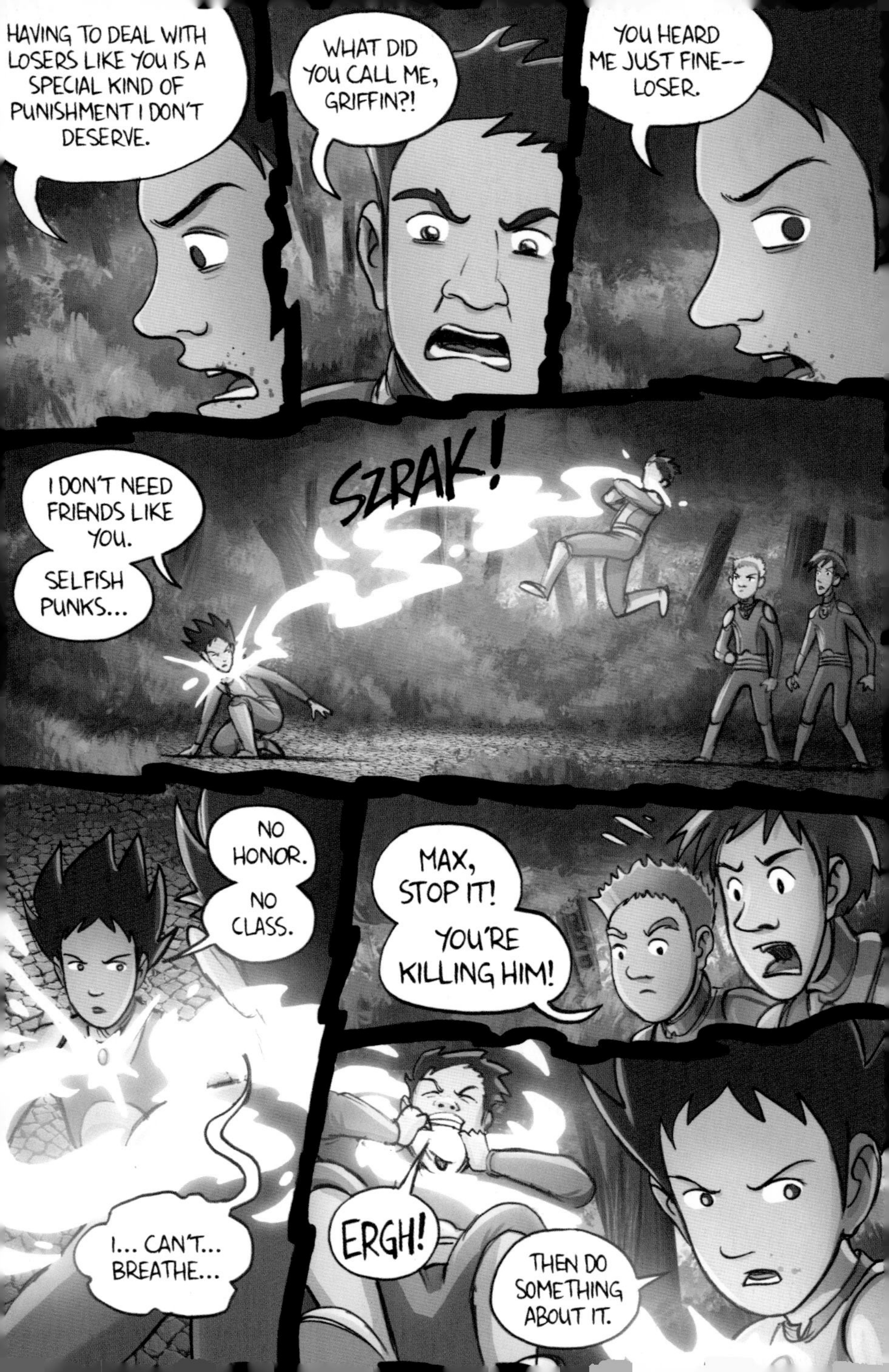
HAVING TO DEAL WITH LOSERS LIKE YOU IS A SPECIAL KIND OF PUNISHMENT I DON'T DESERVE.
WHAT DID YOU CALL ME, GRIFFIN?!
YOU HEARD ME JUST FINE--LOSER.
I DON'T NEED FRIENDS LIKE YOU.
SELFISH PUNKS...
SZRAK!
NO HONOR.
NO CLASS.
I... CAN'T... BREATHE...
MAX, STOP IT!
YOU'RE KILLING HIM!
ERGH!
THEN DO SOMETHING ABOUT IT.

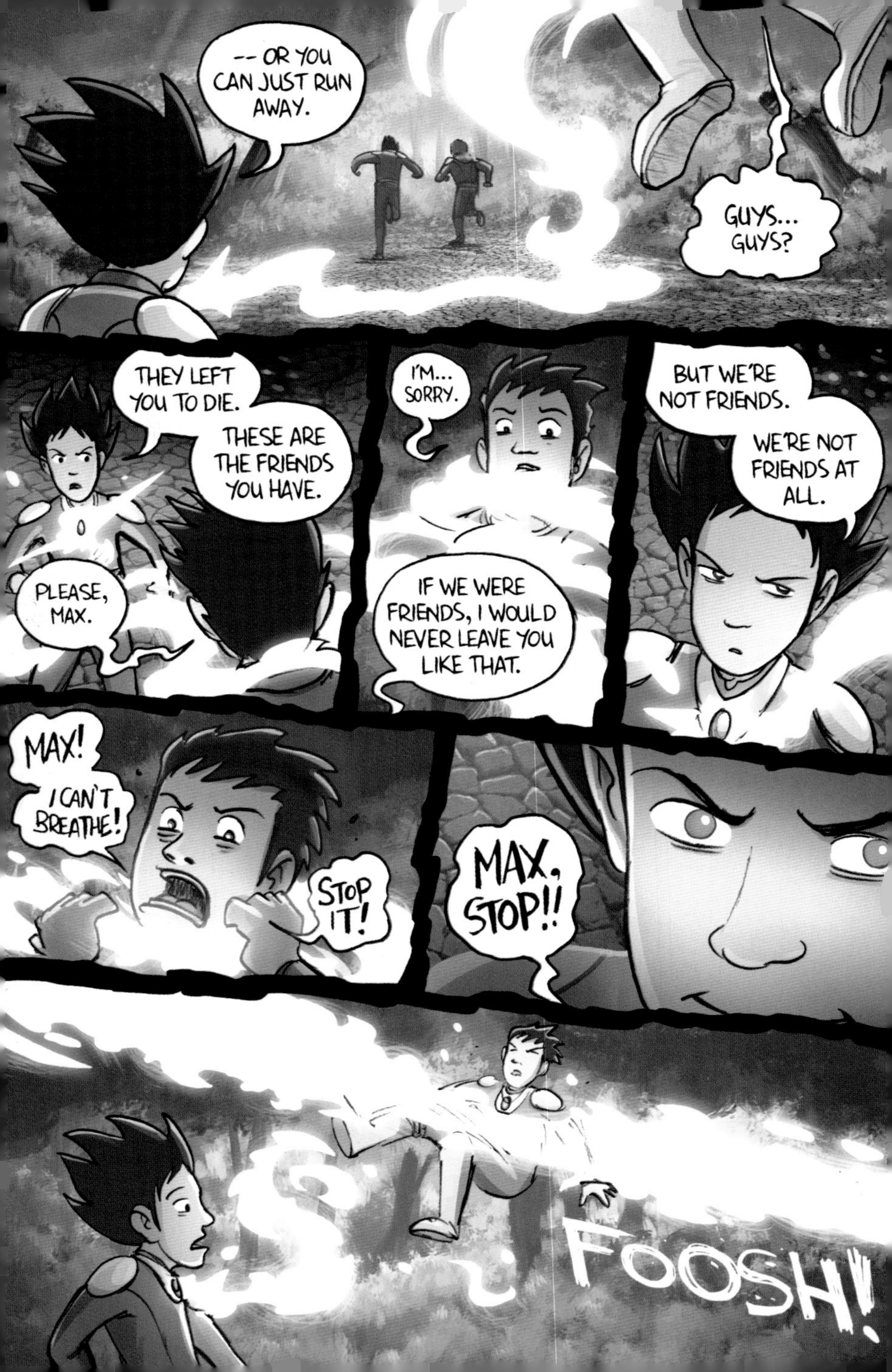
-- OR YOU CAN JUST RUN AWAY.
GUYS... GUYS?
THEY LEFT YOU TO DIE.
THESE ARE THE FRIENDS YOU HAVE.
PLEASE, MAX.
I'M... SORRY.
IF WE WERE FRIENDS, I WOULD NEVER LEAVE YOU LIKE THAT.
BUT WE'RE NOT FRIENDS.
WE'RE NOT FRIENDS AT ALL.
MAX!
I CAN'T BREATHE!
STOP IT!
MAX, STOP!!
FOOSH!

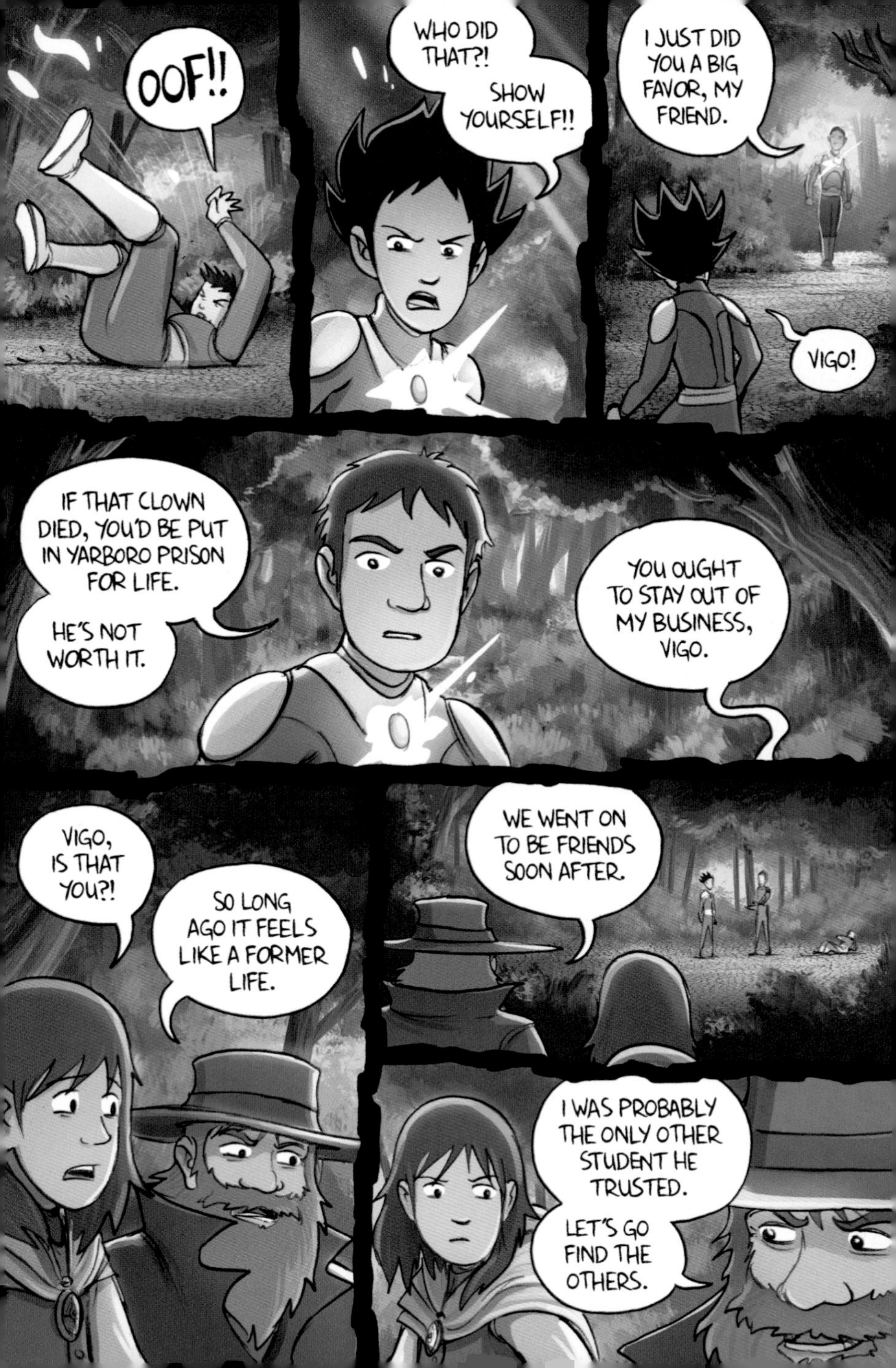
OOF!!
WHO DID THAT?!
SHOW YOURSELF!!
I JUST DID YOU A BIG FAVOR, MY FRIEND.
VIGO!
IF THAT CLOWN DIED, YOU'D BE PUT IN YARBORO PRISON FOR LIFE.
HE'S NOT WORTH IT.
YOU OUGHT TO STAY OUT OF MY BUSINESS, VIGO.
VIGO, IS THAT YOU?!
SO LONG AGO IT FEELS LIKE A FORMER LIFE.
WE WENT ON TO BE FRIENDS SOON AFTER.
I WAS PROBABLY THE ONLY OTHER STUDENT HE TRUSTED.
LET'S GO FIND THE OTHERS.

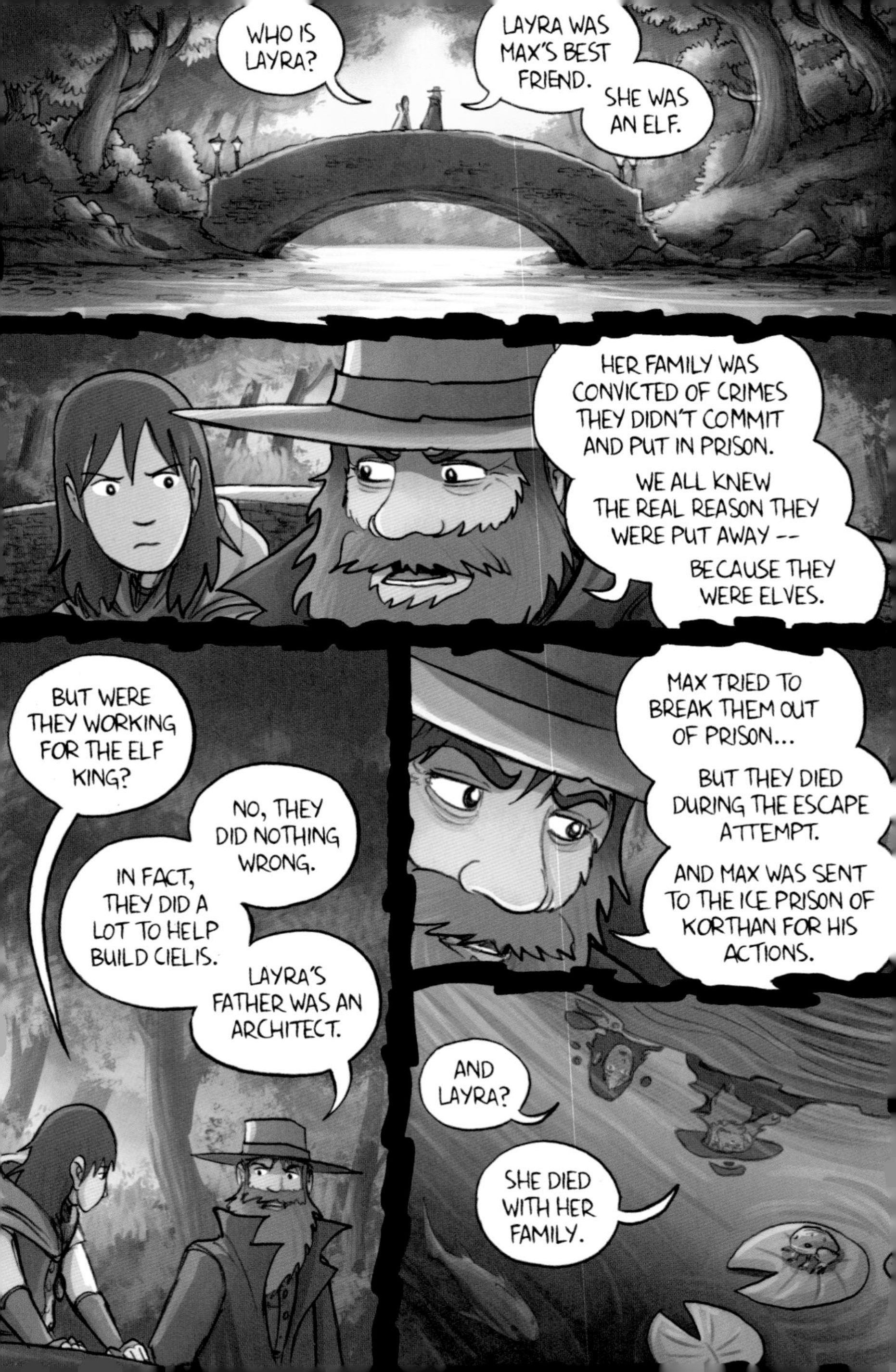
WHO IS LAYRA?
LAYRA WAS MAX'S BEST FRIEND.
SHE WAS AN ELF.
HER FAMILY WAS CONVICTED OF CRIMES THEY DIDN'T COMMIT AND PUT IN PRISON.
WE ALL KNEW THE REAL REASON THEY WERE PUT AWAY --
BECAUSE THEY WERE ELVES.
BUT WERE THEY WORKING FOR THE ELF KING?
NO, THEY DID NOTHING WRONG.
IN FACT, THEY DID A LOT TO HELP BUILD CIELIS.
LAYRA'S FATHER WAS AN ARCHITECT.
MAX TRIED TO BREAK THEM OUT OF PRISON...
BUT THEY DIED DURING THE ESCAPE ATTEMPT.
AND MAX WAS SENT TO THE ICE PRISON OF KORTHAN FOR HIS ACTIONS.
AND LAYRA?
SHE DIED WITH HER FAMILY.

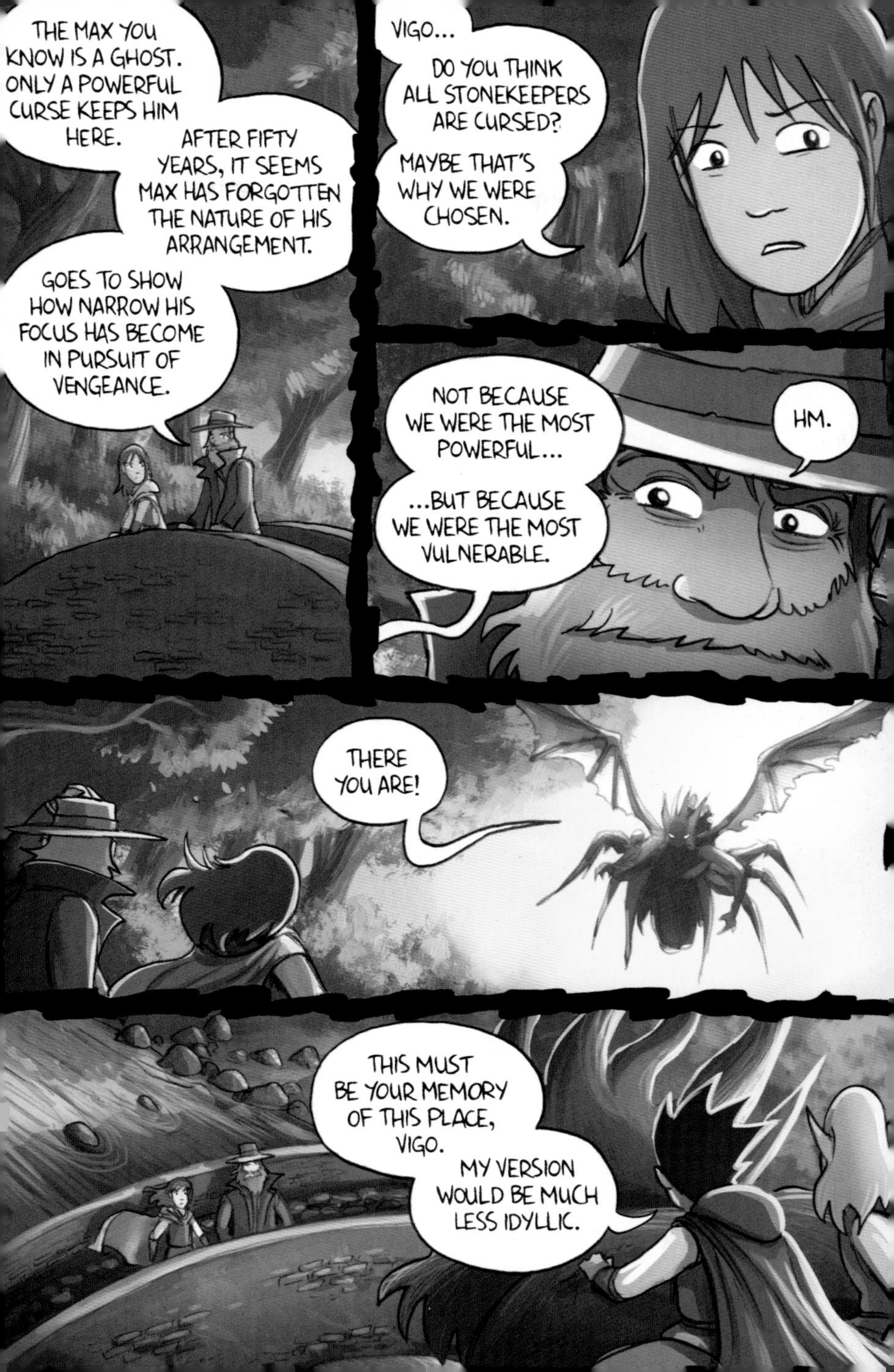
THE MAX YOU KNOW IS A GHOST. ONLY A POWERFUL CURSE KEEPS HIM HERE.
AFTER FIFTY YEARS, IT SEEMS MAX HAS FORGOTTEN THE NATURE OF HIS ARRANGEMENT.
GOES TO SHOW HOW NARROW HIS FOCUS HAS BECOME IN PURSUIT OF VENGEANCE.
VIGO...
DO YOU THINK ALL STONEKEEPERS ARE CURSED?
MAYBE THAT'S WHY WE WERE CHOSEN.
NOT BECAUSE WE WERE THE MOST POWERFUL...
...BUT BECAUSE WE WERE THE MOST VULNERABLE.
HM.
THERE YOU ARE!
THIS MUST BE YOUR MEMORY OF THIS PLACE, VIGO.
MY VERSION WOULD BE MUCH LESS IDYLLIC.

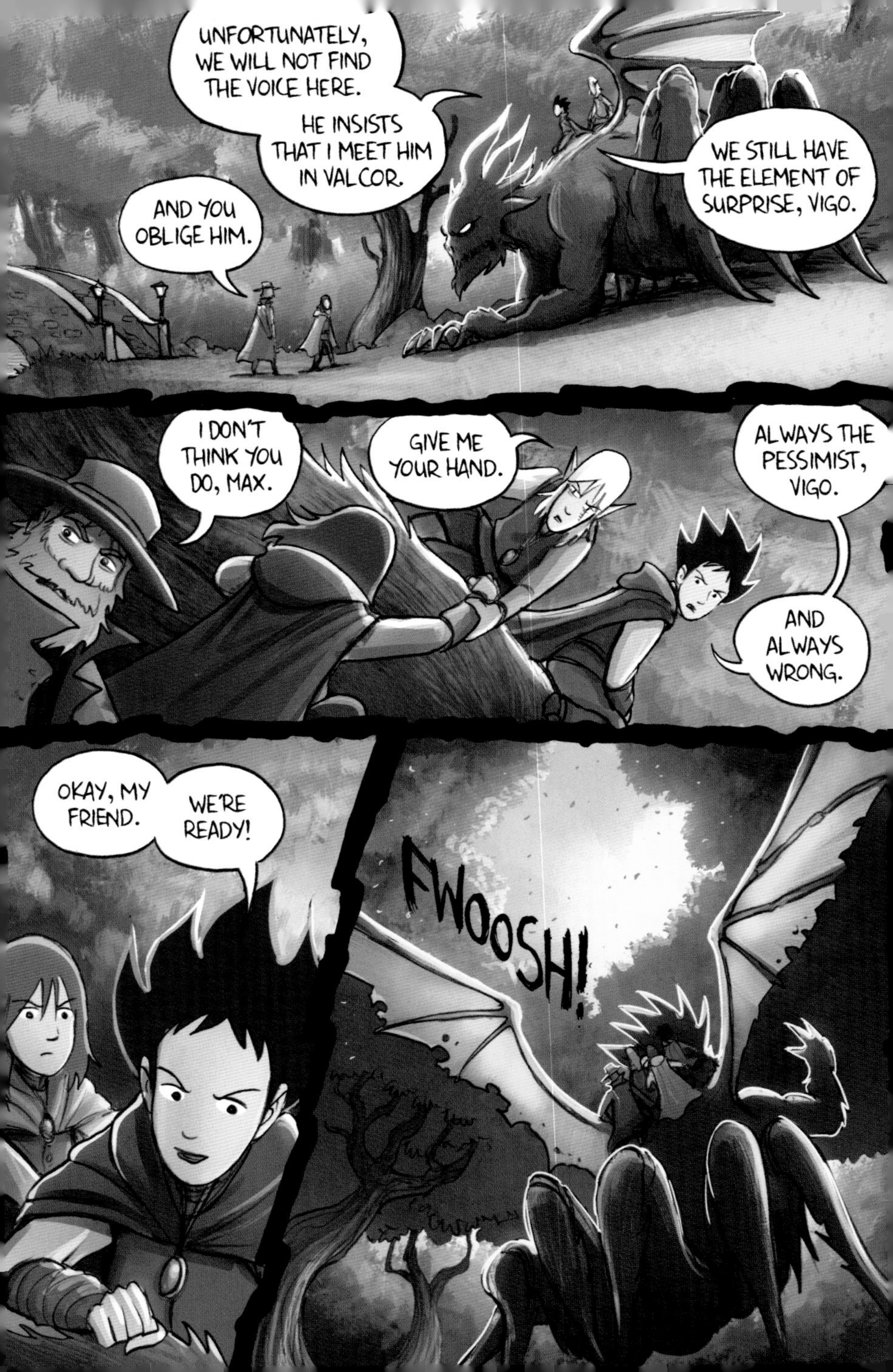
UNFORTUNATELY, WE WILL NOT FIND THE VOICE HERE.
HE INSISTS THAT I MEET HIM IN VALCOR.
AND YOU OBLIGE HIM.
WE STILL HAVE THE ELEMENT OF SURPRISE, VIGO.
I DON'T THINK YOU DO, MAX.
GIVE ME YOUR HAND.
ALWAYS THE PESSIMIST, VIGO.
AND ALWAYS WRONG.
OKAY, MY FRIEND.
WE'RE READY!
FWOOSH!

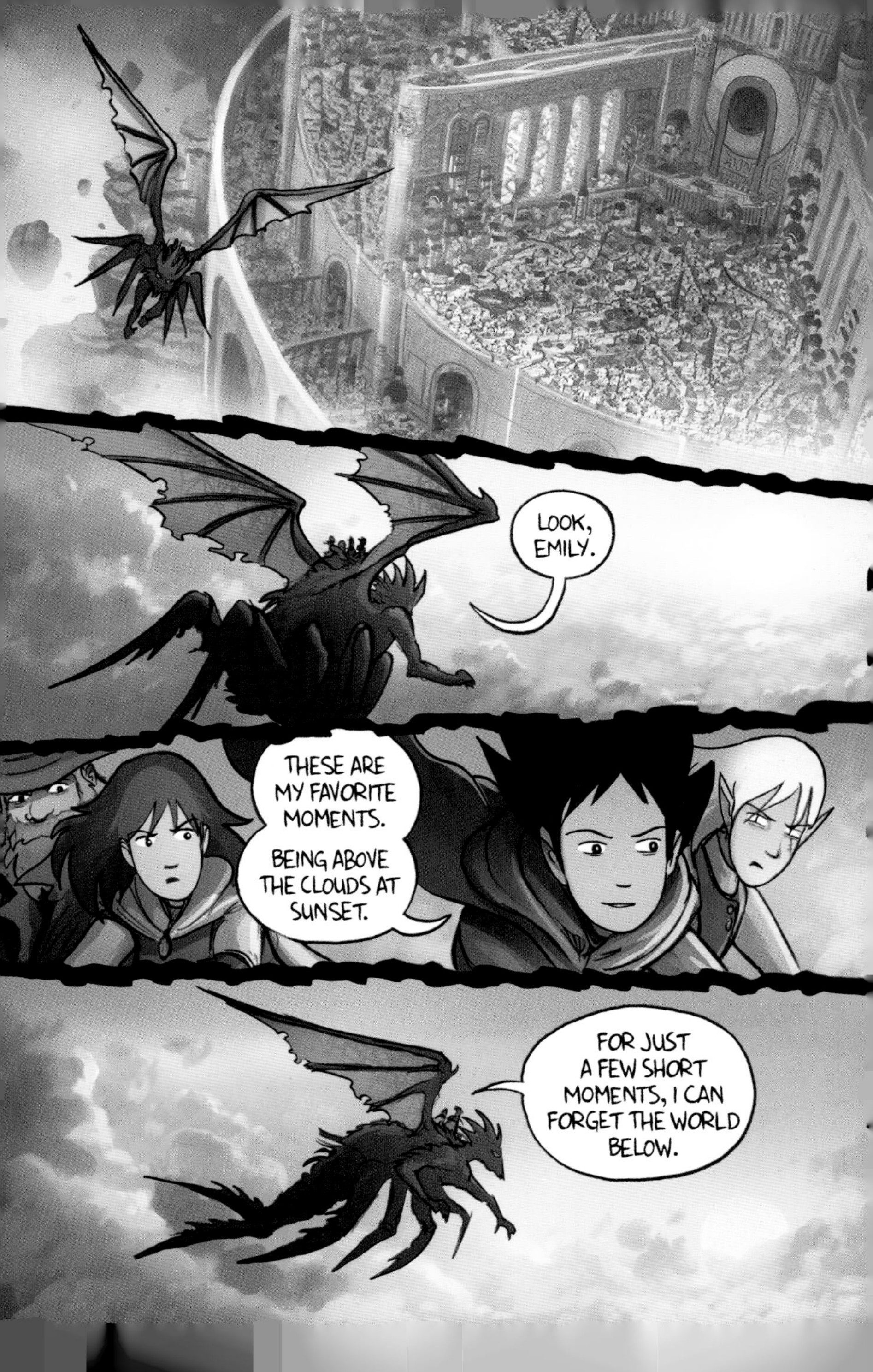
LOOK, EMILY.
THESE ARE MY FAVORITE MOMENTS.
BEING ABOVE THE CLOUDS AT SUNSET.
FOR JUST A FEW SHORT MOMENTS, I CAN FORGET THE WORLD BELOW.

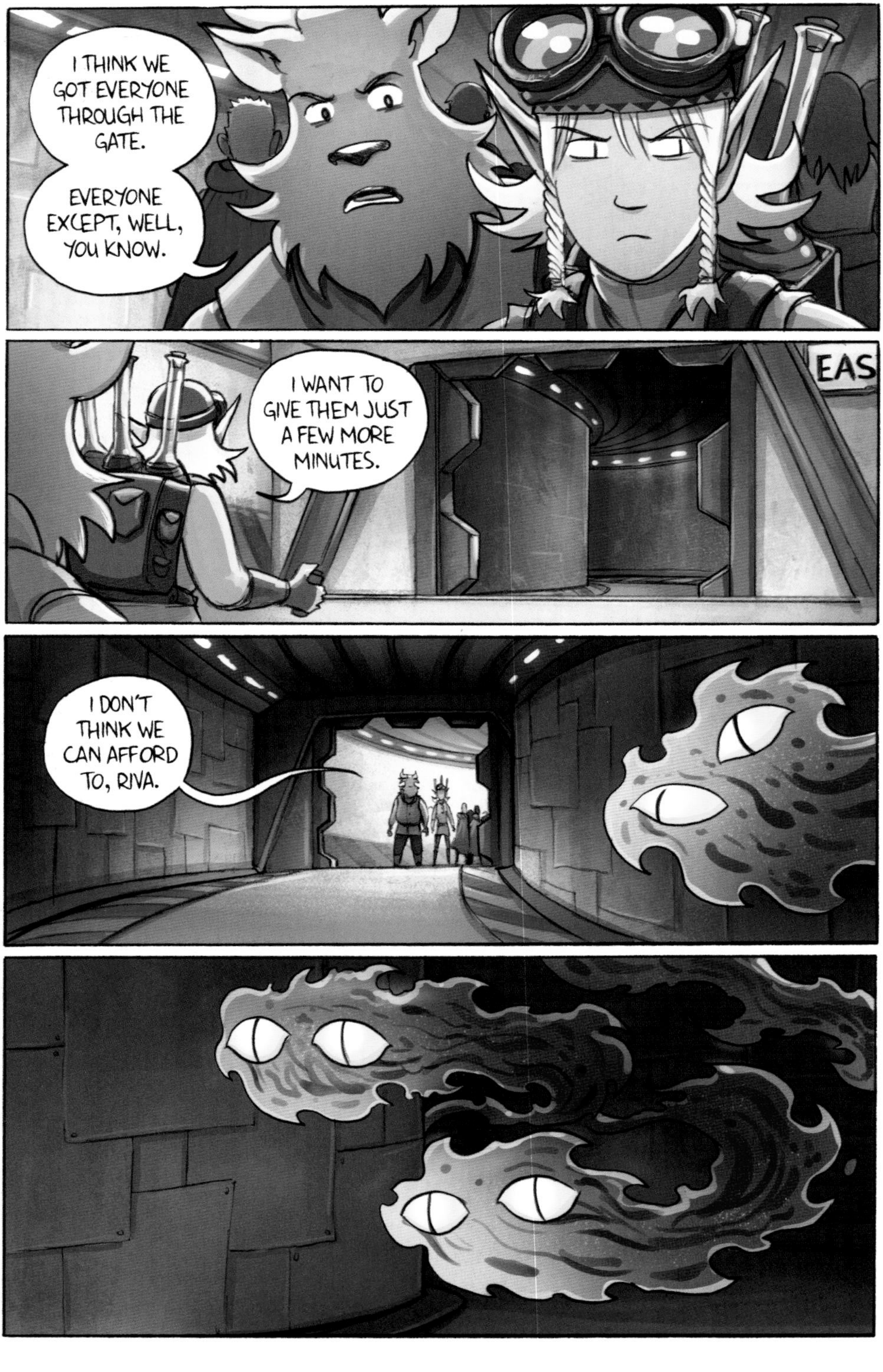
I THINK WE GOT EVERYONE THROUGH THE GATE.
EVERYONE EXCEPT, WELL, YOU KNOW.
EAS
I WANT TO GIVE THEM JUST A FEW MORE MINUTES.
I DON'T THINK WE CAN AFFORD TO, RIVA.

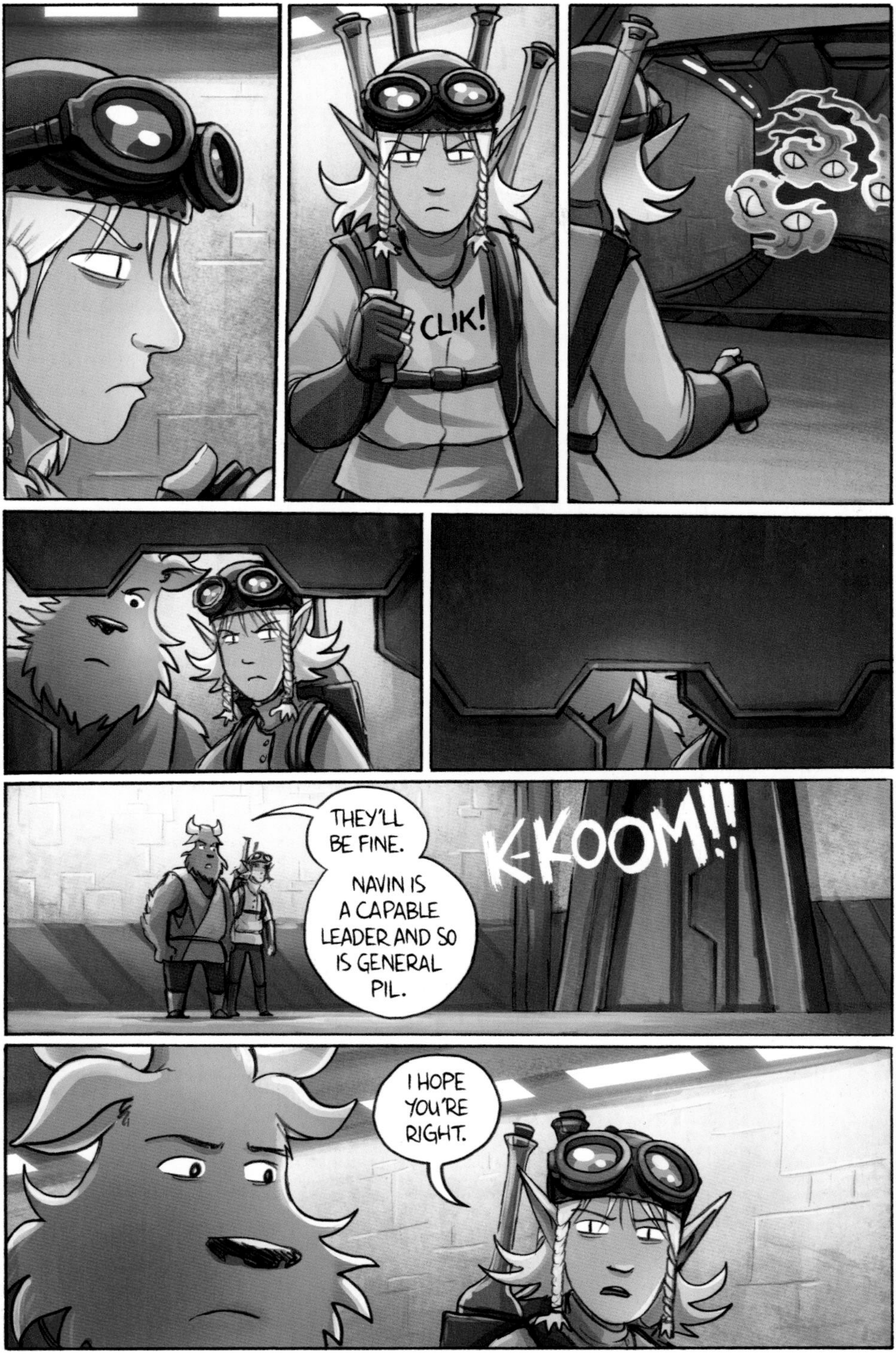
CLIK!
K-KOOM!!
THEY'LL BE FINE.
NAVIN IS A CAPABLE LEADER AND SO IS GENERAL PIL.
I HOPE YOU'RE RIGHT.

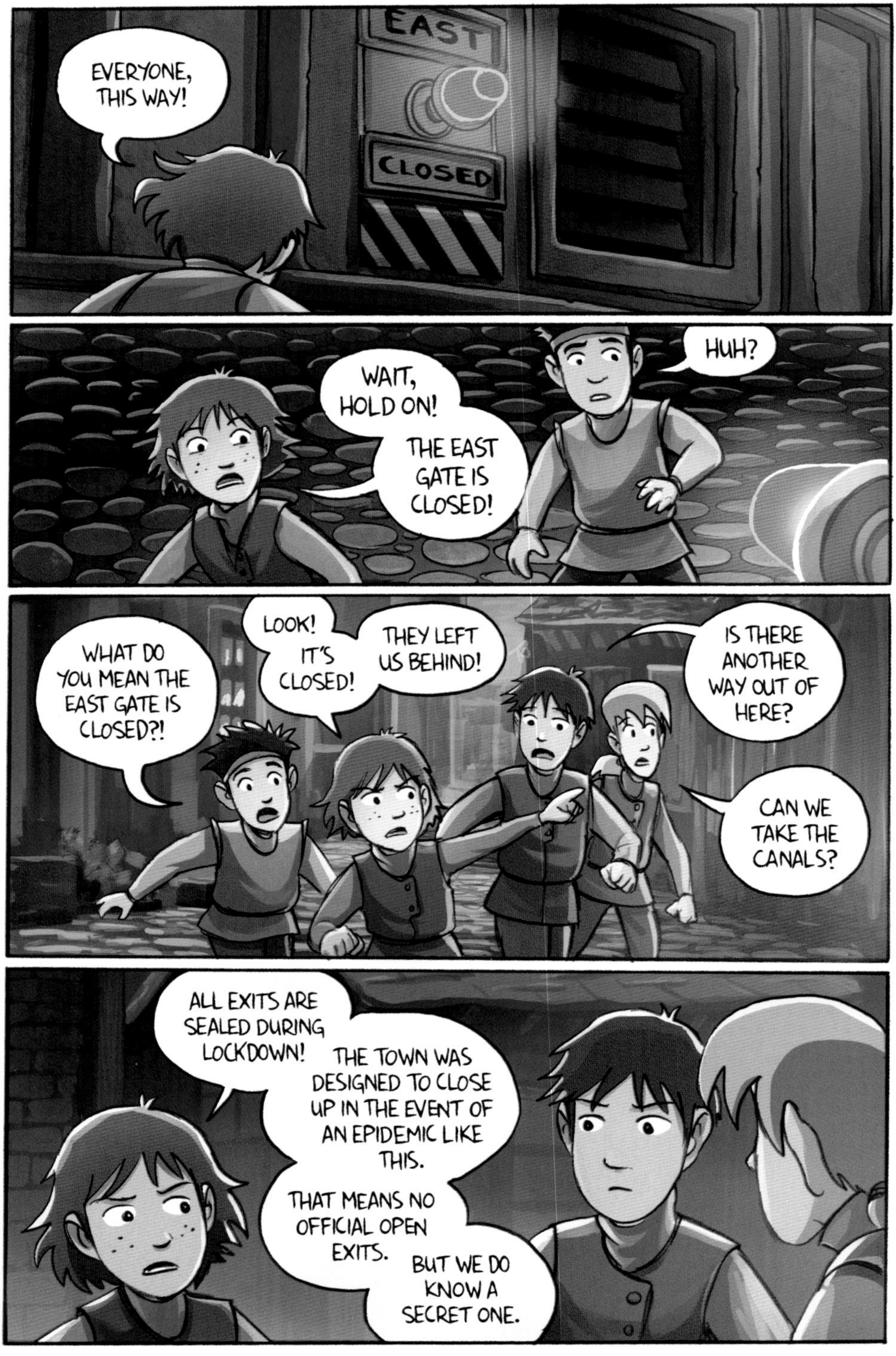
EAST
CLOSED
EVERYONE, THIS WAY!
HUH?
WAIT, HOLD ON!
THE EAST GATE IS CLOSED!
WHAT DO YOU MEAN THE EAST GATE IS CLOSED?!
LOOK!
IT'S CLOSED!
THEY LEFT US BEHIND!
IS THERE ANOTHER WAY OUT OF HERE?
CAN WE TAKE THE CANALS?
ALL EXITS ARE SEALED DURING LOCKDOWN!
THE TOWN WAS DESIGNED TO CLOSE UP IN THE EVENT OF AN EPIDEMIC LIKE THIS.
THAT MEANS NO OFFICIAL OPEN EXITS.
BUT WE DO KNOW A SECRET ONE.

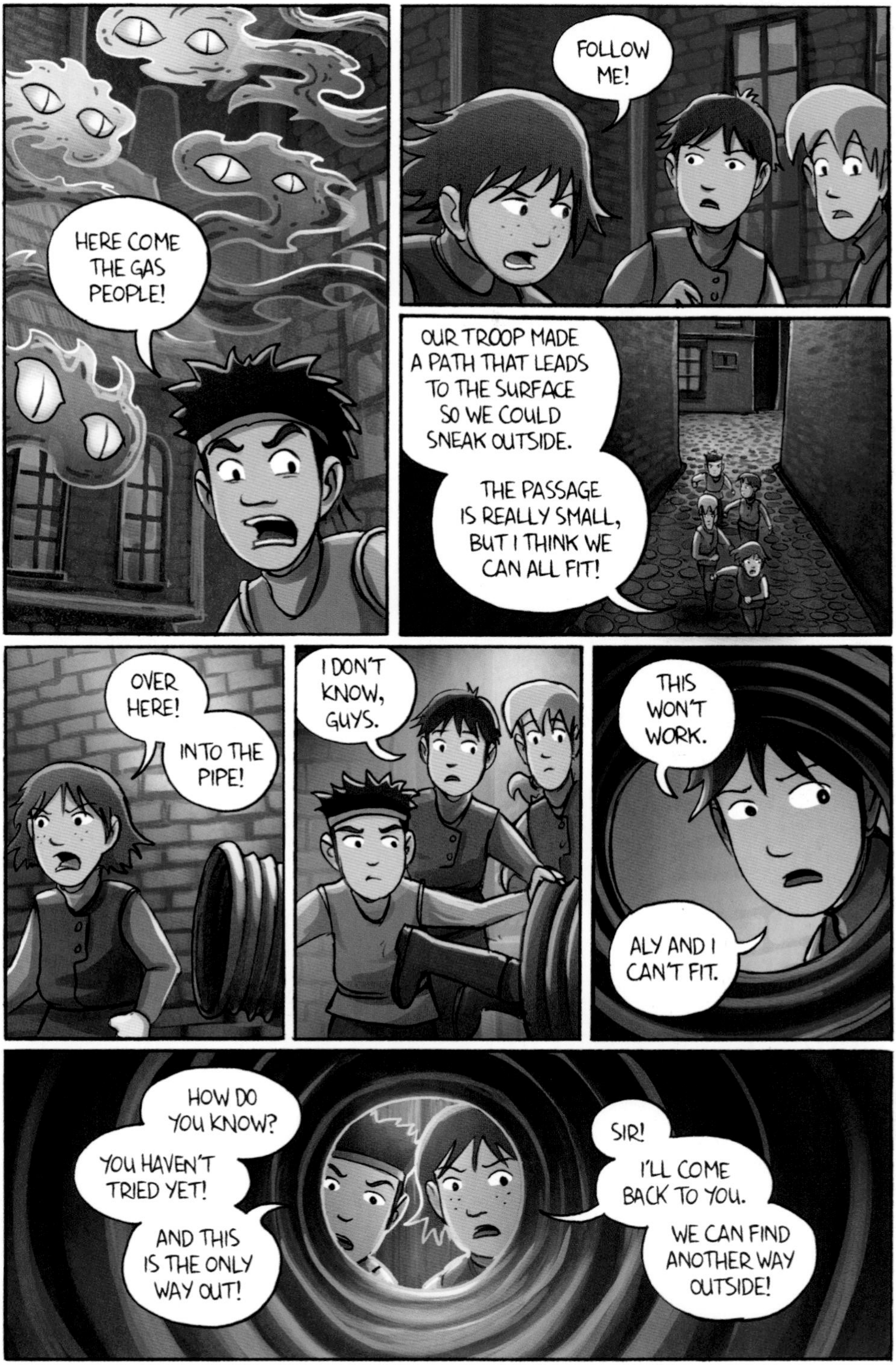
HERE COME THE GAS PEOPLE!
FOLLOW ME!
OUR TROOP MADE A PATH THAT LEADS TO THE SURFACE SO WE COULD SNEAK OUTSIDE.
THE PASSAGE IS REALLY SMALL, BUT I THINK WE CAN ALL FIT!
OVER HERE!
INTO THE PIPE!
I DON'T KNOW, GUYS.
THIS WON'T WORK.
ALY AND I CAN'T FIT.
HOW DO YOU KNOW?
YOU HAVEN'T TRIED YET!
AND THIS IS THE ONLY WAY OUT!
SIR!
I'LL COME BACK TO YOU.
WE CAN FIND ANOTHER WAY OUTSIDE!

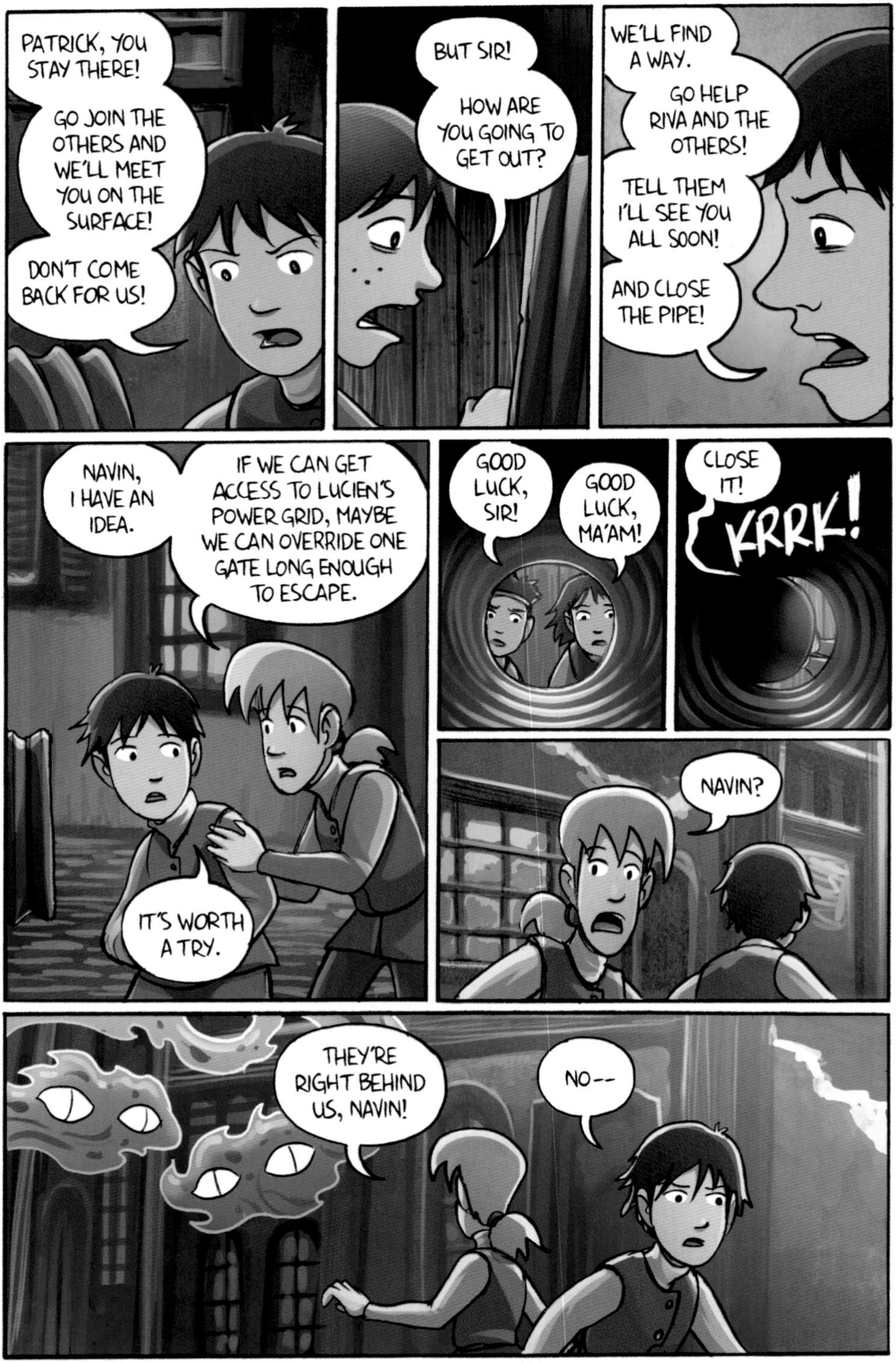
PATRICK, YOU STAY THERE!
GO JOIN THE OTHERS AND WE'LL MEET YOU ON THE SURFACE!
DON'T COME BACK FOR US!
BUT SIR!
HOW ARE YOU GOING TO GET OUT?
WE'LL FIND A WAY.
GO HELP RIVA AND THE OTHERS!
TELL THEM I'LL SEE YOU ALL SOON!
AND CLOSE THE PIPE!
NAVIN, I HAVE AN IDEA.
IF WE CAN GET ACCESS TO LUCIEN'S POWER GRID, MAYBE WE CAN OVERRIDE ONE GATE LONG ENOUGH TO ESCAPE.
IT'S WORTH A TRY.
GOOD LUCK, SIR!
GOOD LUCK, MA'AM!
CLOSE IT!
KRRK!
NAVIN?
THEY'RE RIGHT BEHIND US, NAVIN!
NO--

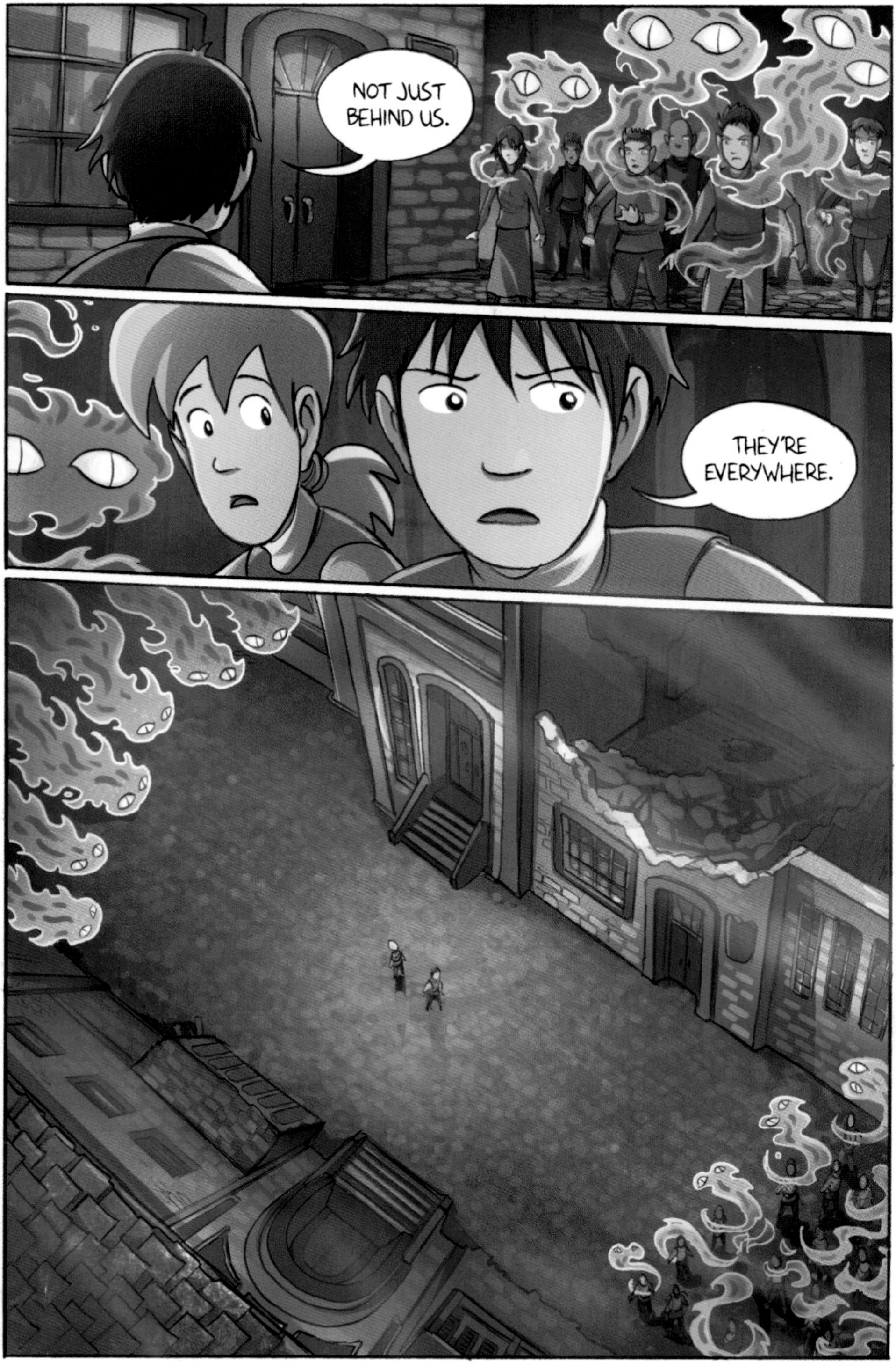
NOT JUST BEHIND US.
THEY'RE EVERYWHERE.

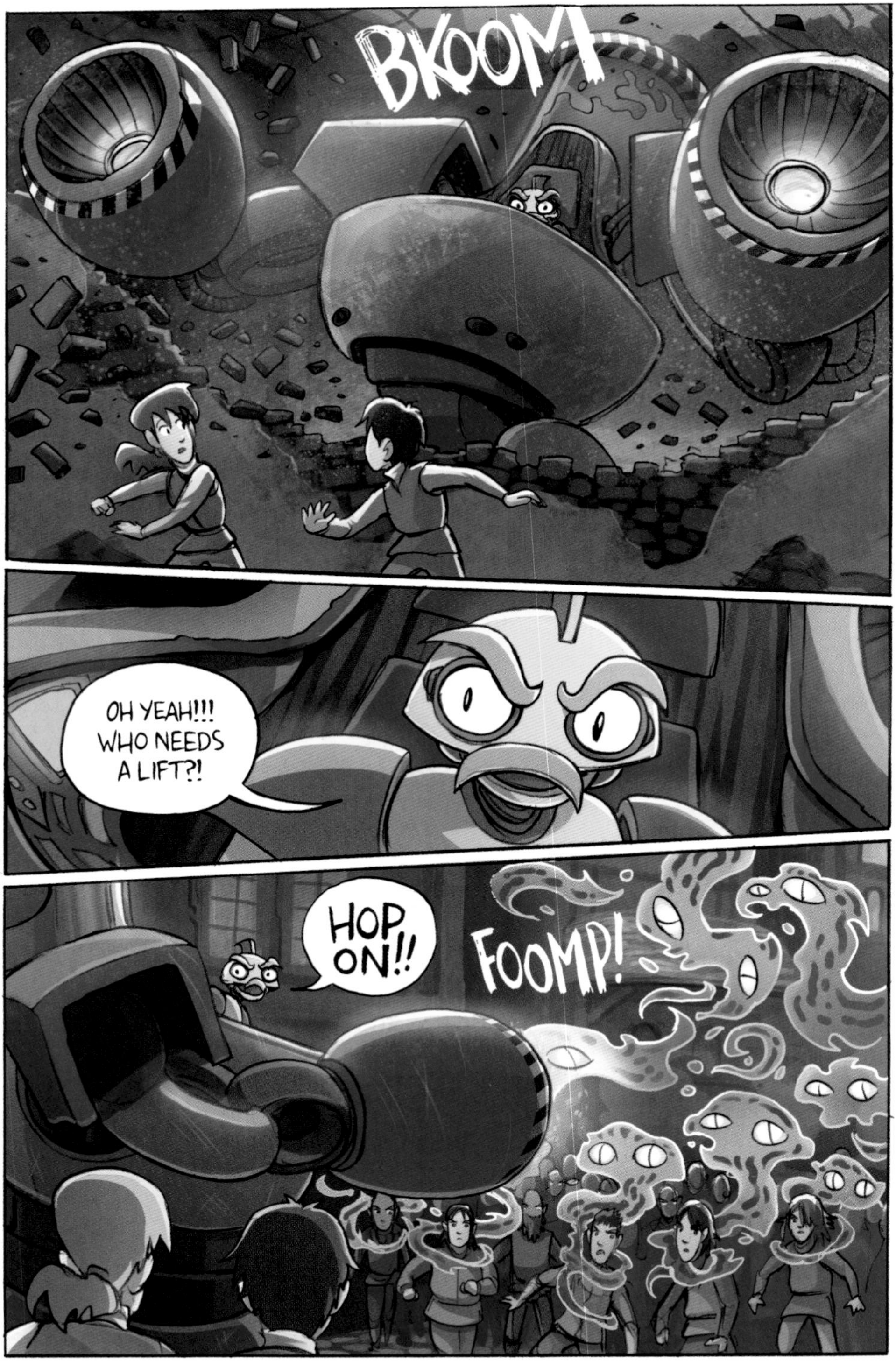
BKOOM
OH YEAH!!! WHO NEEDS A LIFT?!
HOP ON!!
FOOMP!

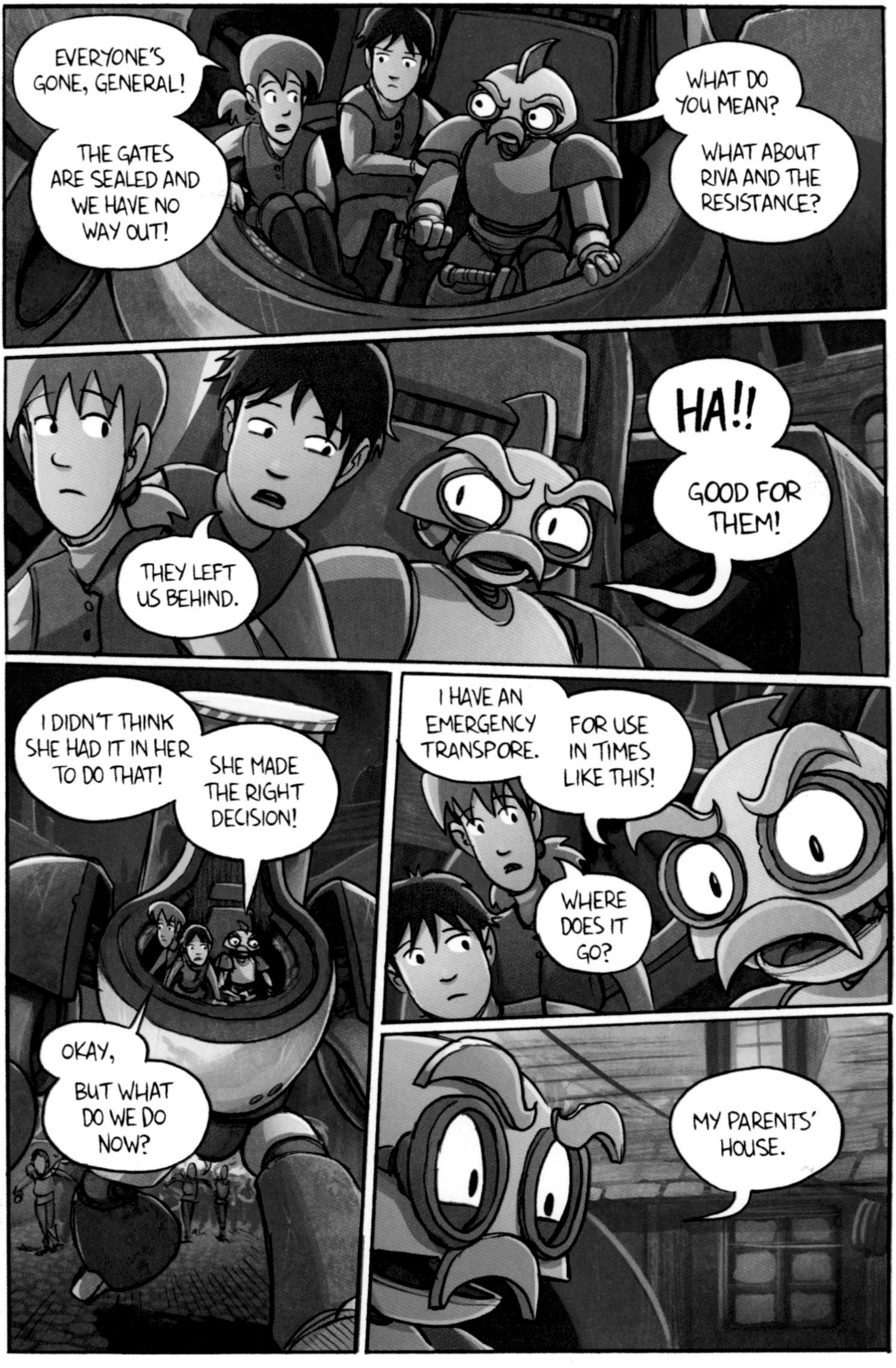
EVERYONE'S GONE, GENERAL!
THE GATES ARE SEALED AND WE HAVE NO WAY OUT!
WHAT DO YOU MEAN?
WHAT ABOUT RIVA AND THE RESISTANCE?
THEY LEFT US BEHIND.
HA!!
GOOD FOR THEM!
I DIDN'T THINK SHE HAD IT IN HER TO DO THAT!
SHE MADE THE RIGHT DECISION!
OKAY,
BUT WHAT DO WE DO NOW?
I HAVE AN EMERGENCY TRANSPORE.
FOR USE IN TIMES LIKE THIS!
WHERE DOES IT GO?
MY PARENTS' HOUSE.

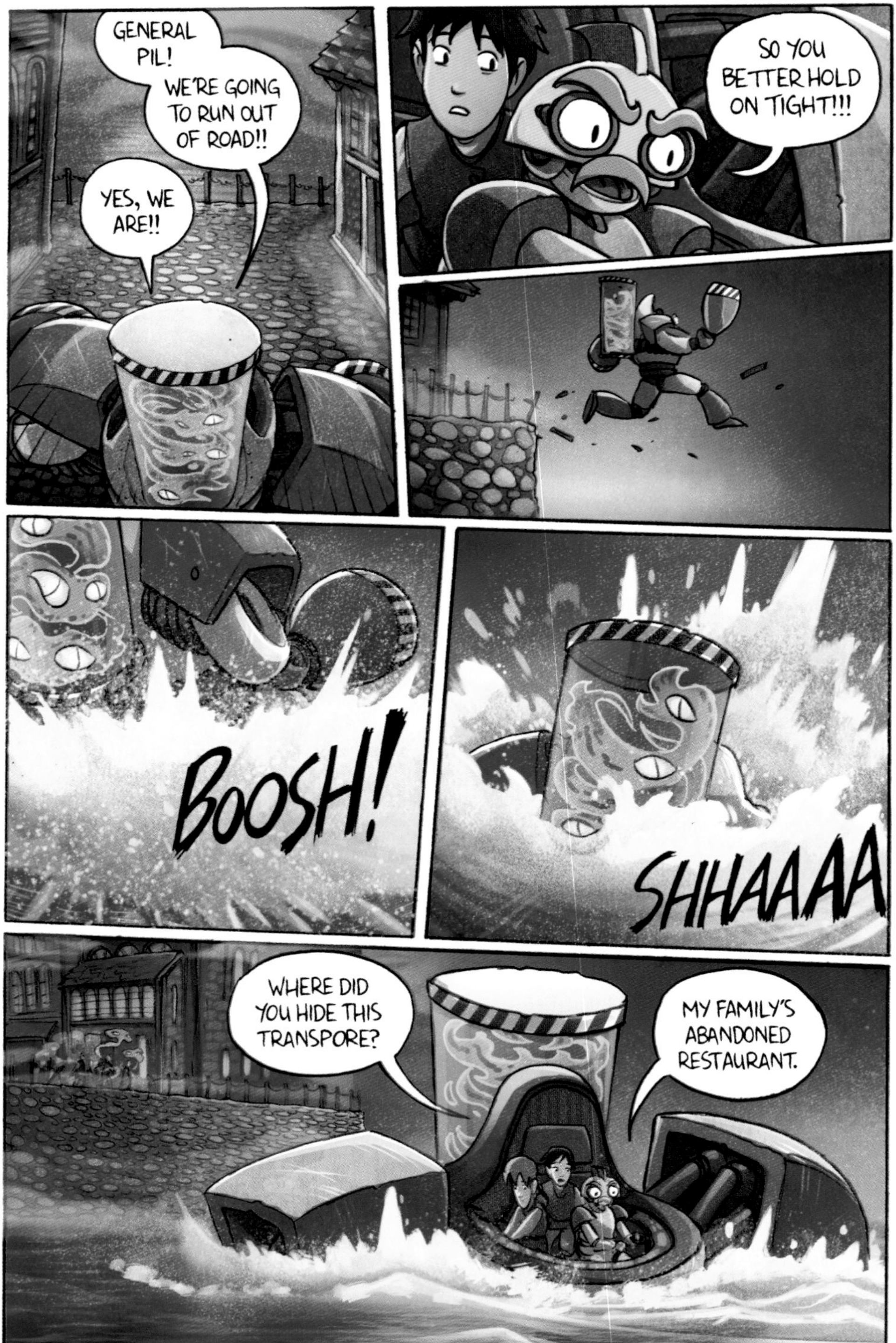
GENERAL PIL!
WE'RE GOING TO RUN OUT OF ROAD!!
YES, WE ARE!!
SO YOU BETTER HOLD ON TIGHT!!!
BOOSH!
SHHAAAA
WHERE DID YOU HIDE THIS TRANSPORE?
MY FAMILY'S ABANDONED RESTAURANT.

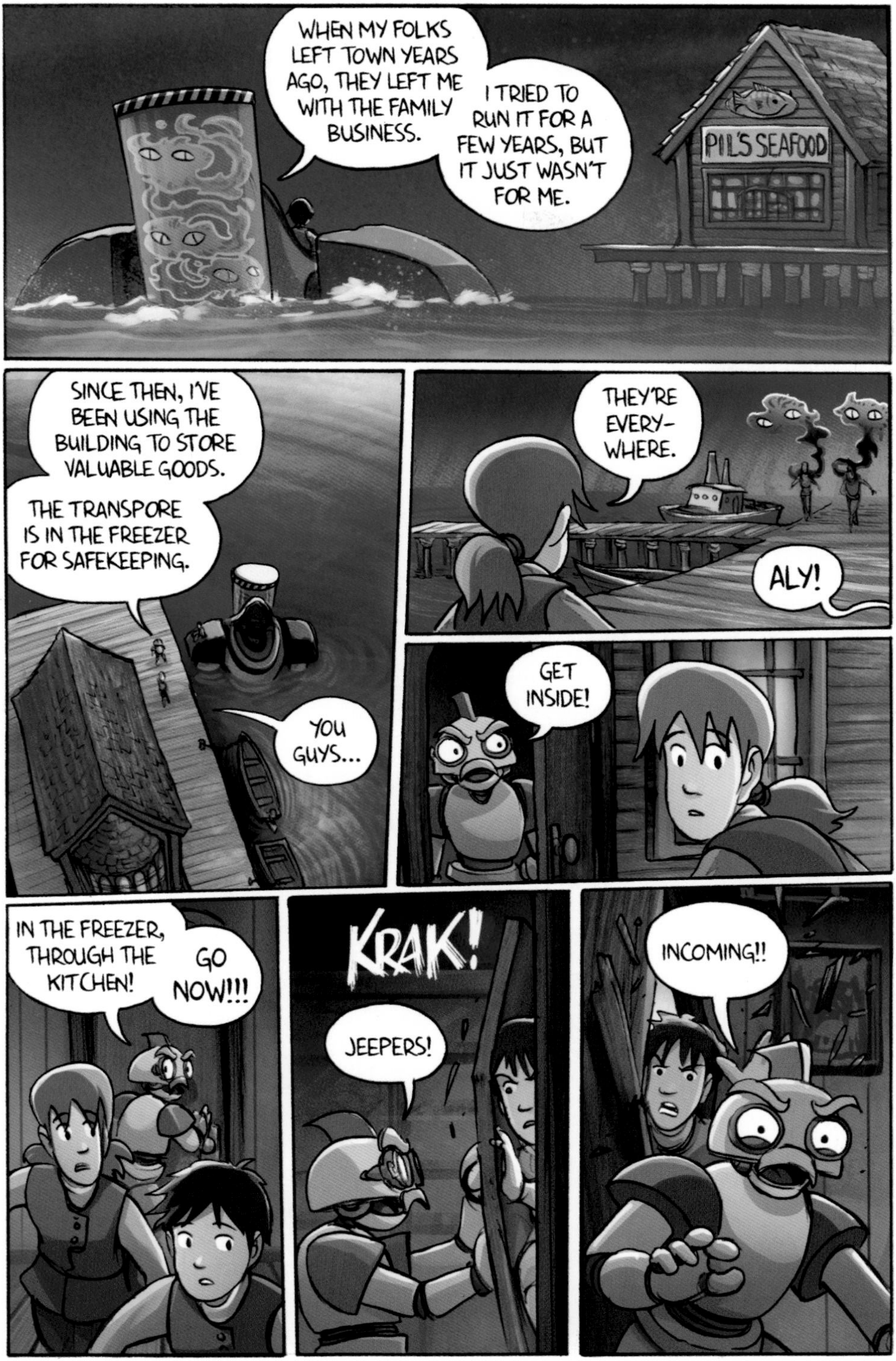
WHEN MY FOLKS LEFT TOWN YEARS AGO, THEY LEFT ME WITH THE FAMILY BUSINESS.
I TRIED TO RUN IT FOR A FEW YEARS, BUT IT JUST WASN'T FOR ME.
PIL'S SEAFOOD
SINCE THEN, I'VE BEEN USING THE BUILDING TO STORE VALUABLE GOODS.
THE TRANSPORE IS IN THE FREEZER FOR SAFEKEEPING.
YOU GUYS...
THEY'RE EVERY-WHERE.
ALY!
GET INSIDE!
IN THE FREEZER, THROUGH THE KITCHEN!
GO NOW!!!
KRAK!
JEEPERS!
INCOMING!!

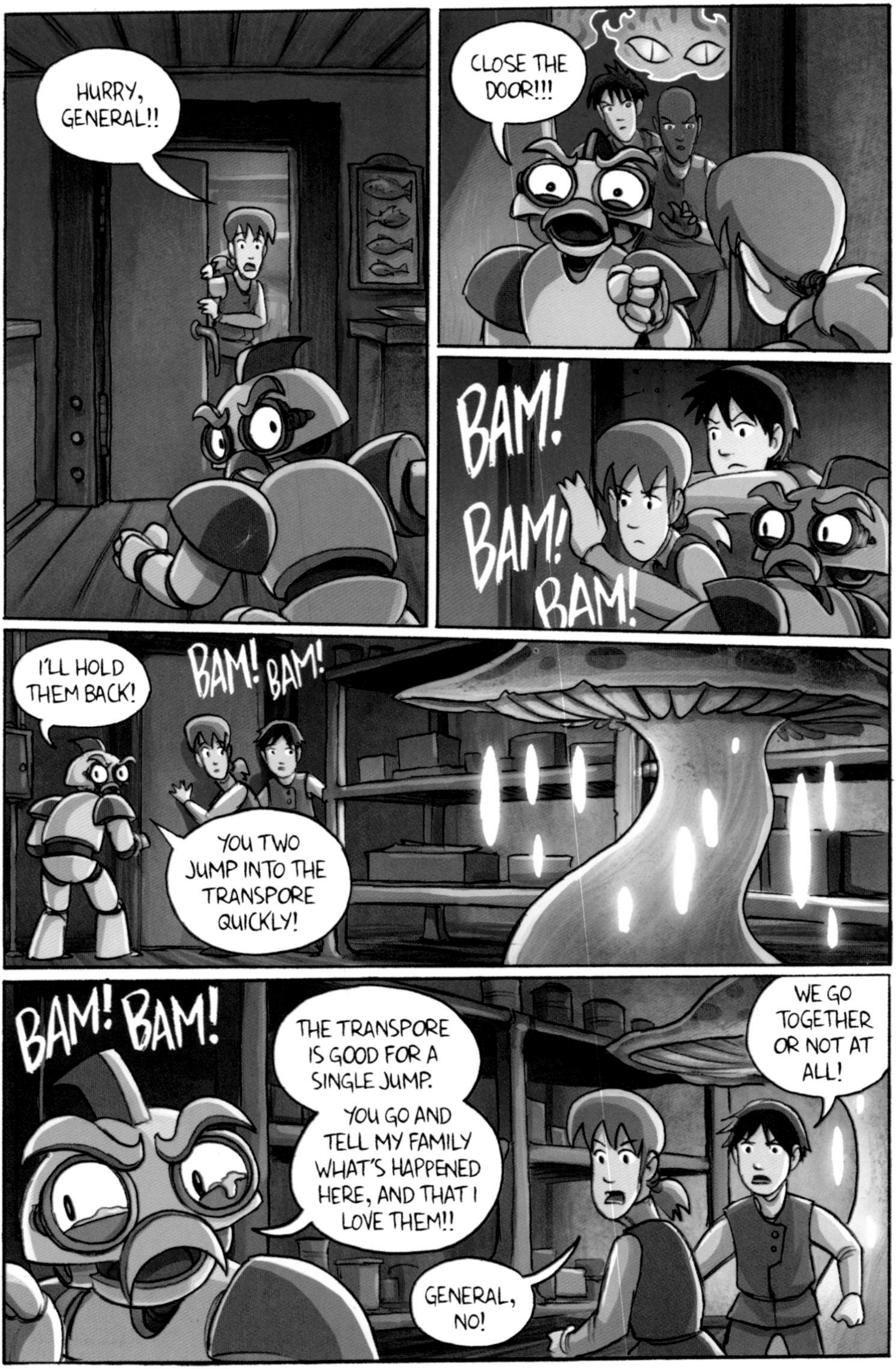
HURRY, GENERAL!!
CLOSE THE DOOR!!!
BAM! BAM! BAM!
I'LL HOLD THEM BACK!
BAM! BAM!
YOU TWO JUMP INTO THE TRANSPORE QUICKLY!
BAM! BAM!
THE TRANSPORE IS GOOD FOR A SINGLE JUMP.
YOU GO AND TELL MY FAMILY WHAT'S HAPPENED HERE, AND THAT I LOVE THEM!!
GENERAL, NO!
WE GO TOGETHER OR NOT AT ALL!

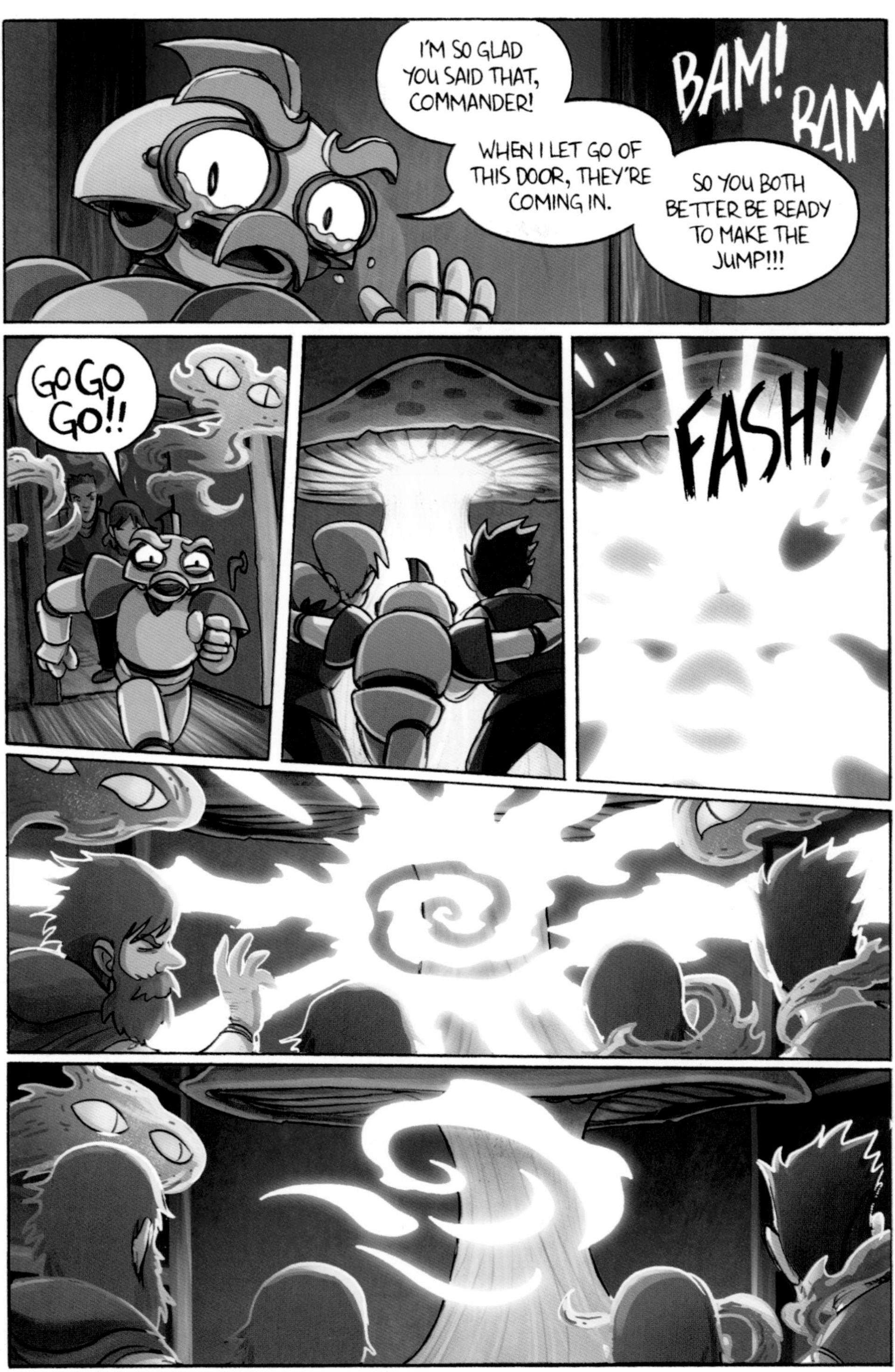
I'M SO GLAD YOU SAID THAT, COMMANDER!
WHEN I LET GO OF THIS DOOR, THEY'RE COMING IN.
BAM! BAM
SO YOU BOTH BETTER BE READY TO MAKE THE JUMP!!!
GO GO GO!!
FASH!

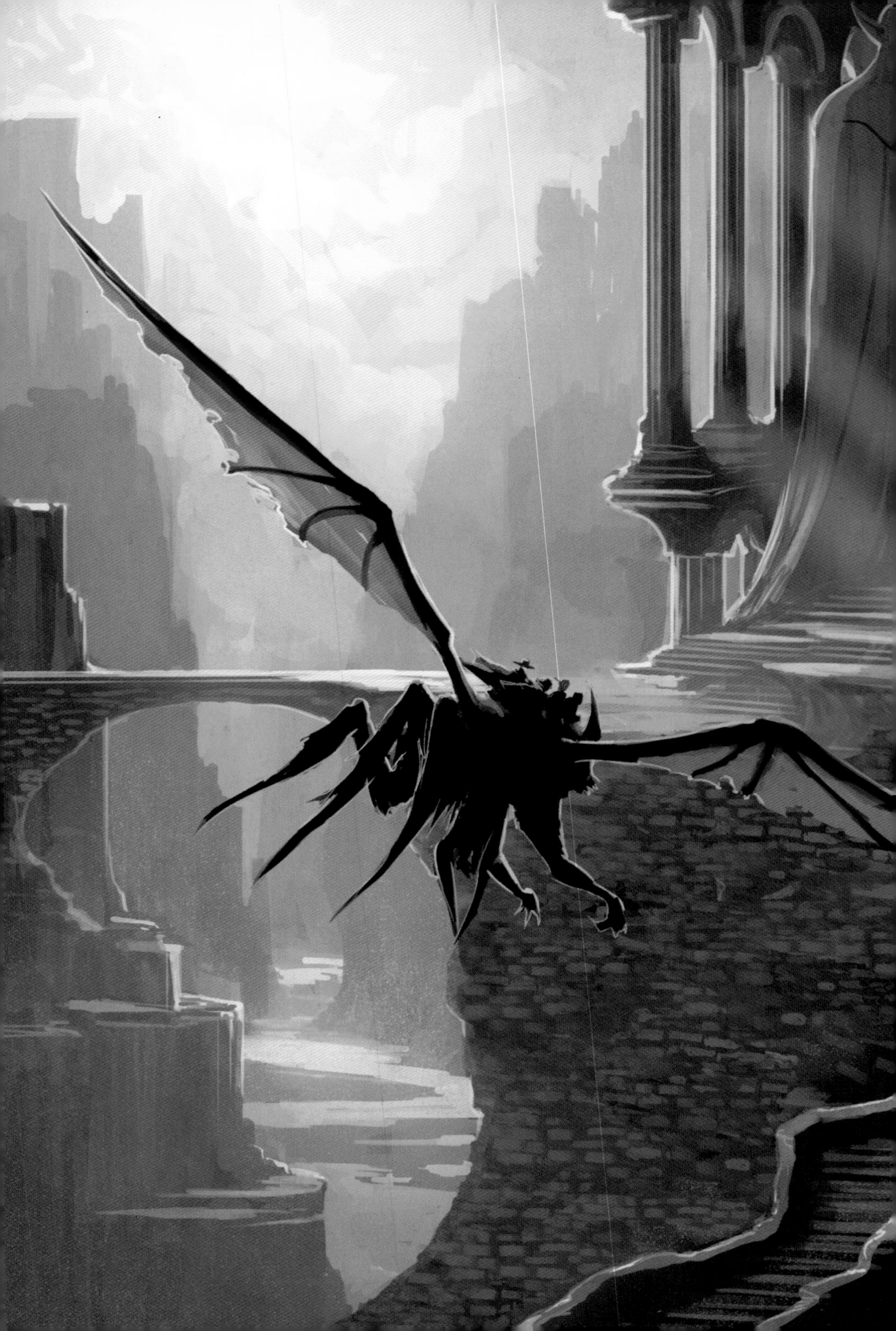

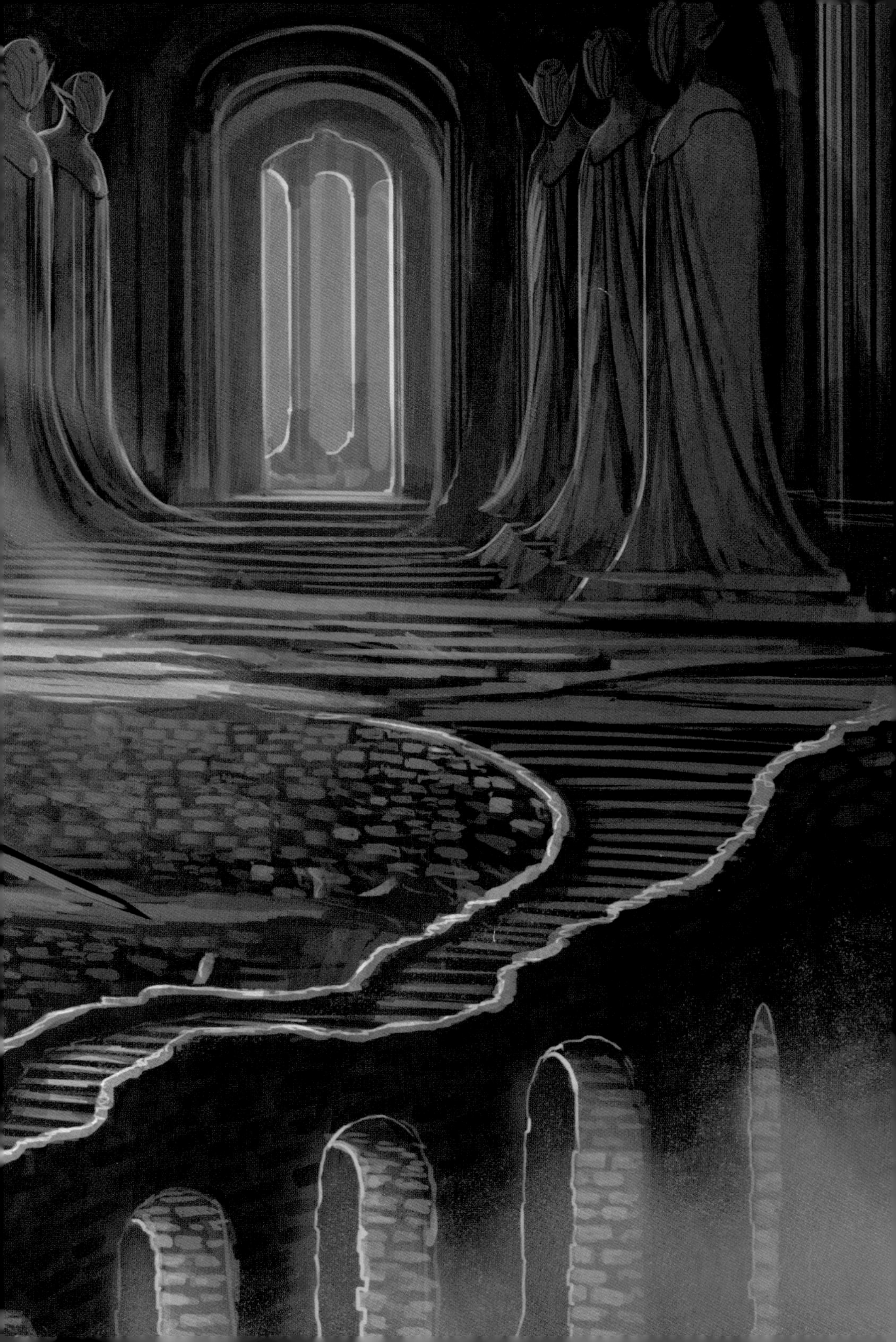

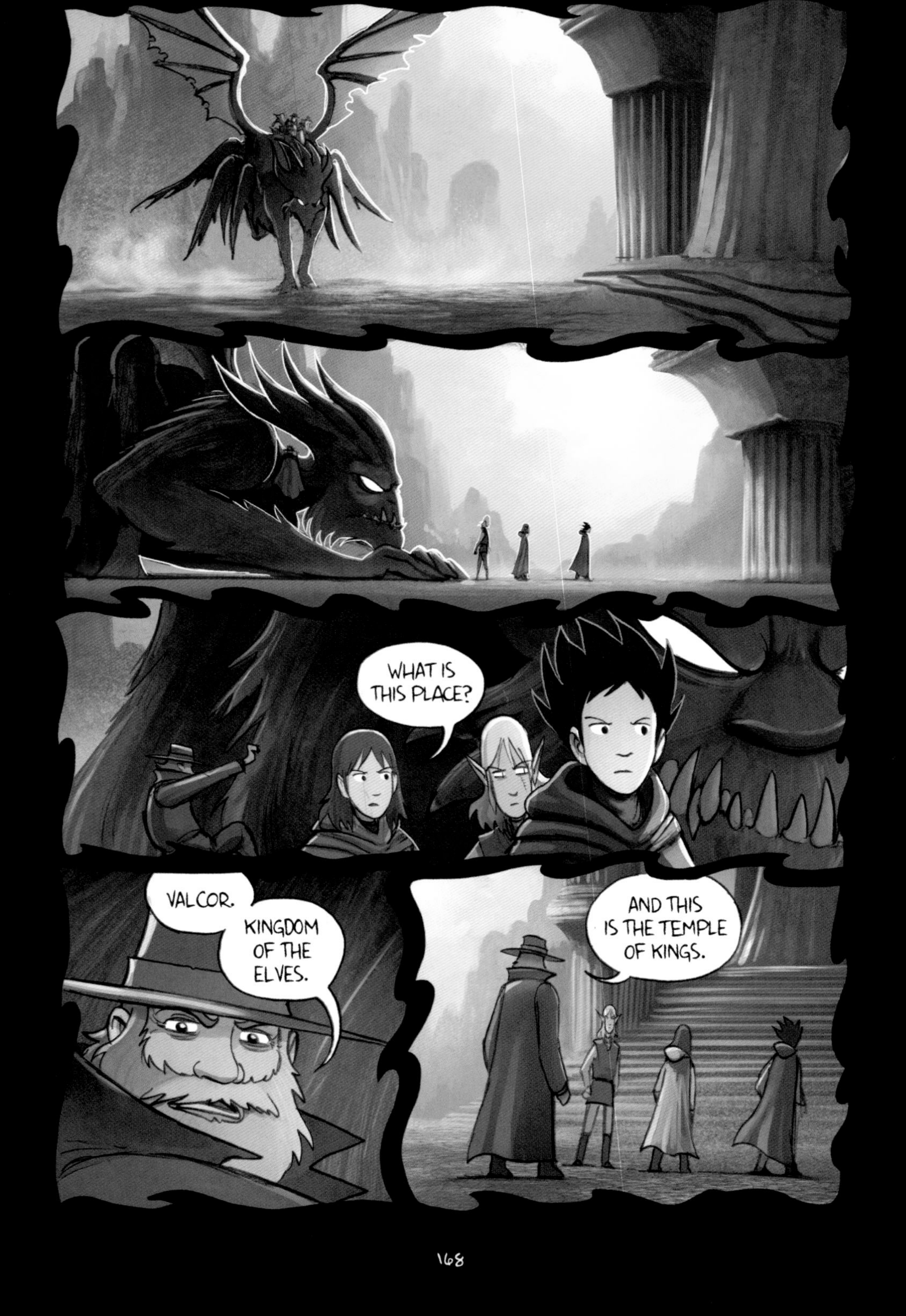
WHAT IS THIS PLACE?
VALCOR.
KINGDOM OF THE ELVES.
AND THIS IS THE TEMPLE OF KINGS.

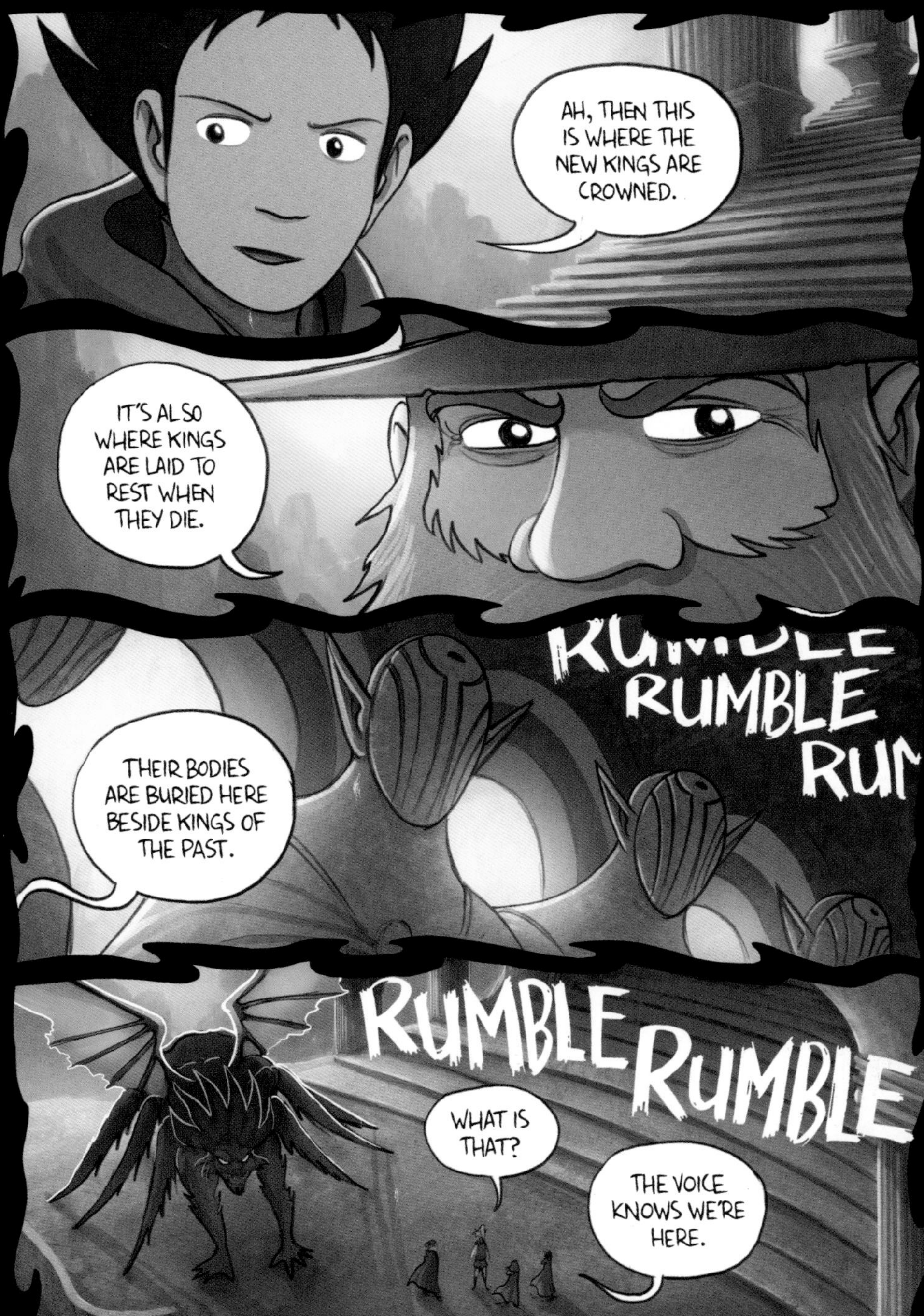

AH, THEN THIS IS WHERE THE NEW KINGS ARE CROWNED.
IT'S ALSO WHERE KINGS ARE LAID TO REST WHEN THEY DIE.
RUMBLE
RUMBLE
THEIR BODIES ARE BURIED HERE BESIDE KINGS OF THE PAST.
RUMBLE RUMBLE
WHAT IS THAT?
THE VOICE KNOWS WE'RE HERE.

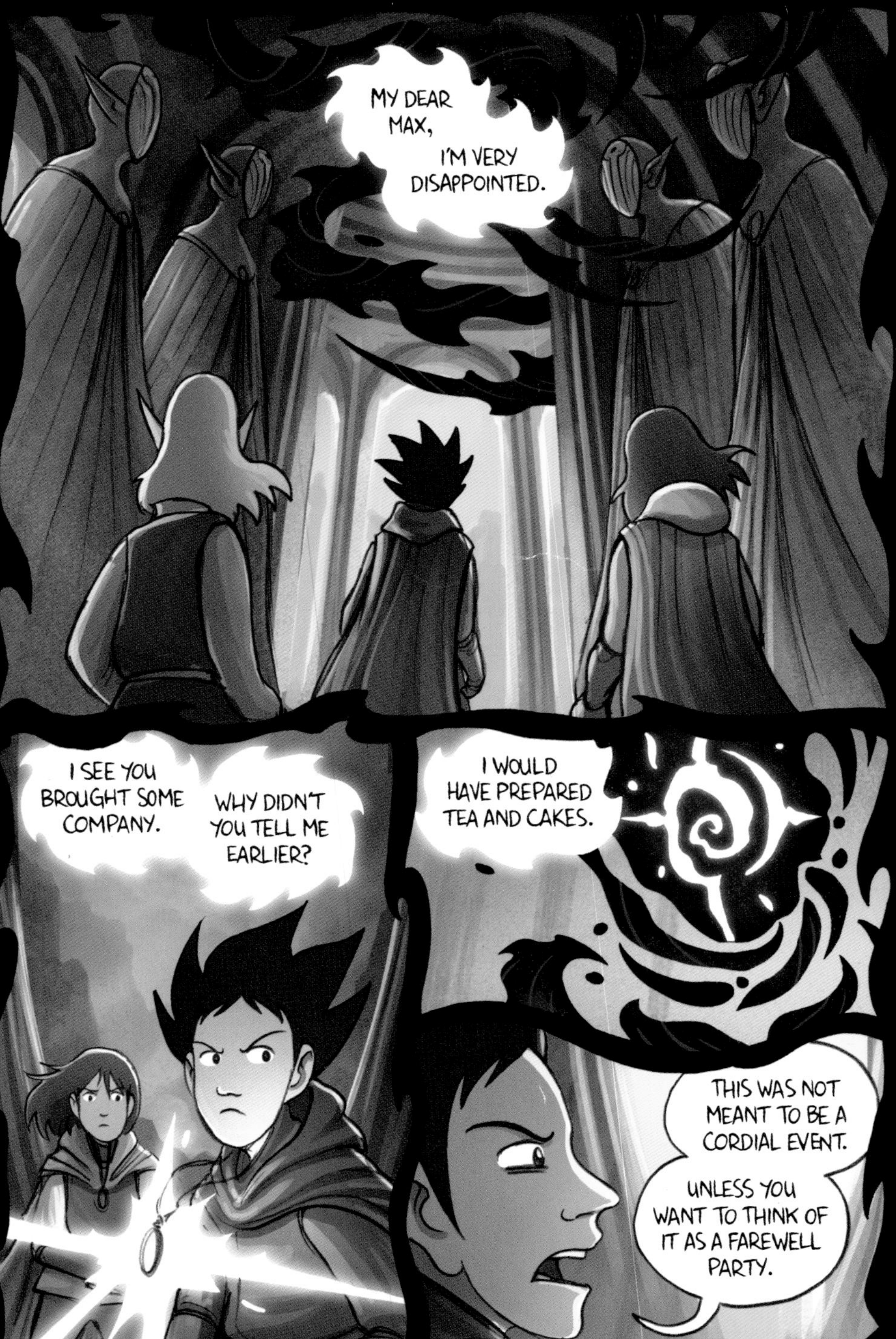
MY DEAR MAX,
I'M VERY DISAPPOINTED.
I SEE YOU BROUGHT SOME COMPANY.
WHY DIDN'T YOU TELL ME EARLIER?
I WOULD HAVE PREPARED TEA AND CAKES.
THIS WAS NOT MEANT TO BE A CORDIAL EVENT.
UNLESS YOU WANT TO THINK OF IT AS A FAREWELL PARTY.

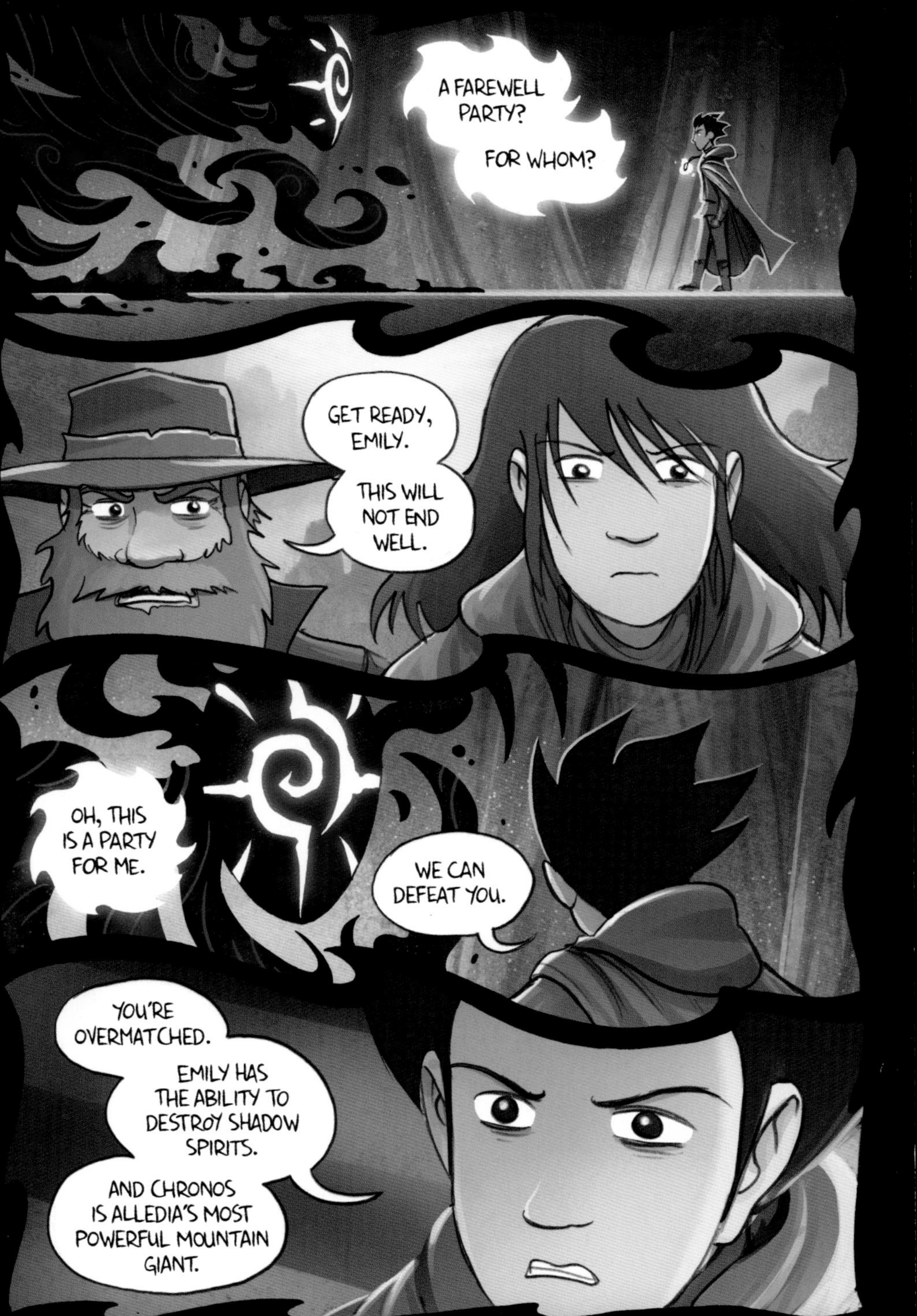
A FAREWELL PARTY?
FOR WHOM?
GET READY, EMILY.
THIS WILL NOT END WELL.
OH, THIS IS A PARTY FOR ME.
WE CAN DEFEAT YOU.
YOU'RE OVERMATCHED.
EMILY HAS THE ABILITY TO DESTROY SHADOW SPIRITS.
AND CHRONOS IS ALLEDIA'S MOST POWERFUL MOUNTAIN GIANT.

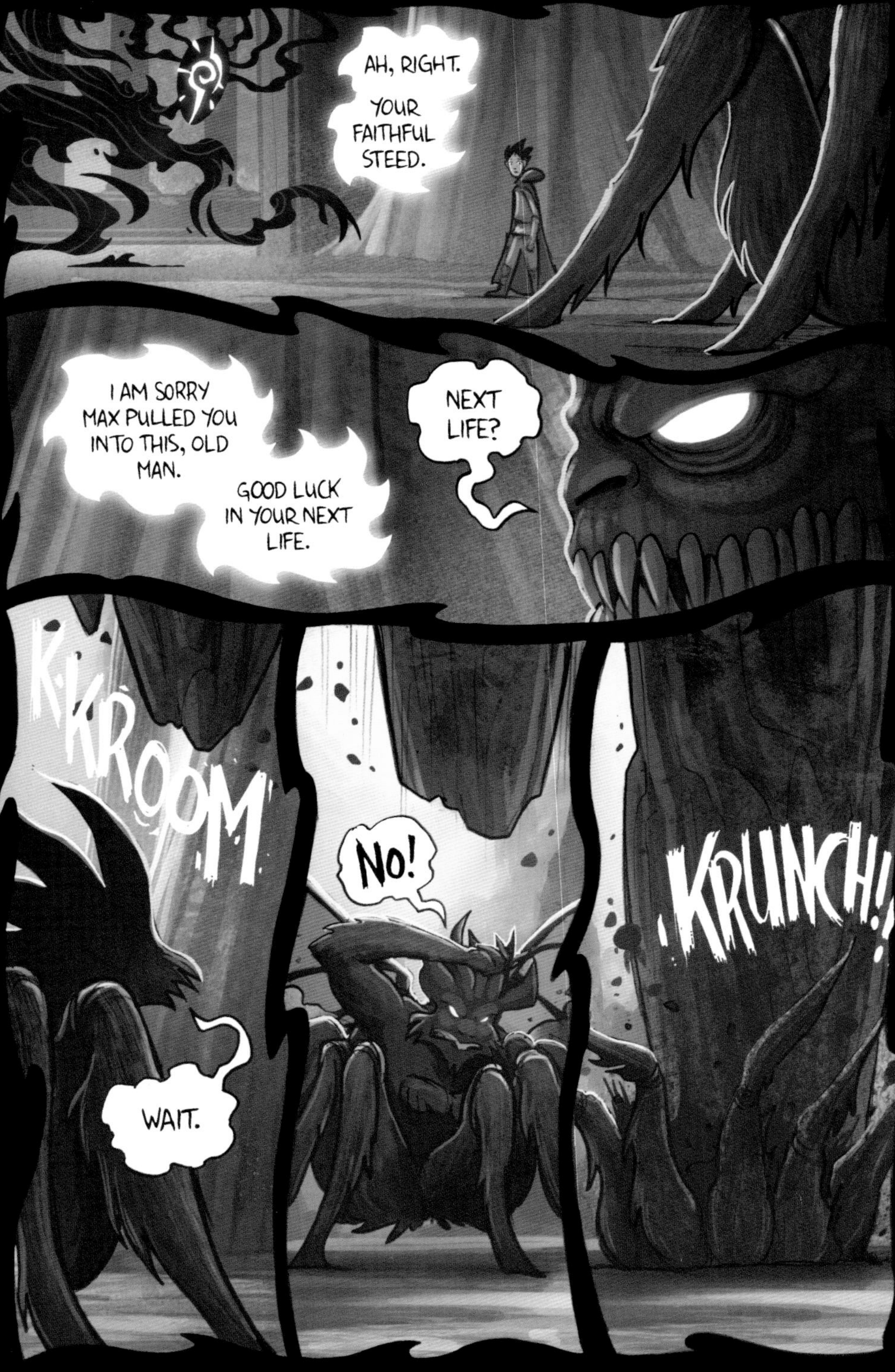
AH, RIGHT.
YOUR FAITHFUL STEED.
I AM SORRY MAX PULLED YOU INTO THIS, OLD MAN.
GOOD LUCK IN YOUR NEXT LIFE.
NEXT LIFE?
K-KROOM
WAIT.
NO!
KRUNCH!!

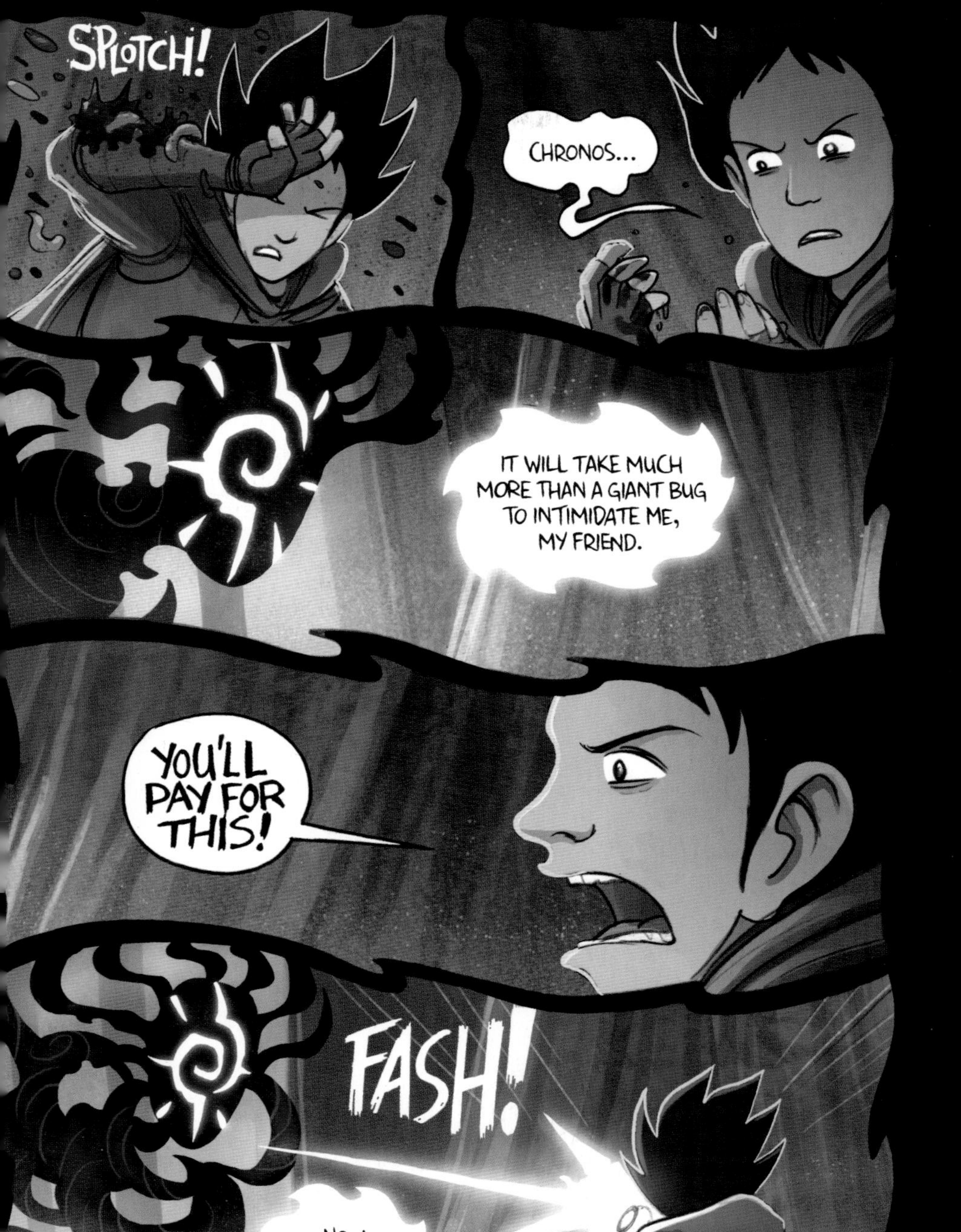
SPLOTCH!
CHRONOS...
IT WILL TAKE MUCH MORE THAN A GIANT BUG TO INTIMIDATE ME, MY FRIEND.
YOU'LL PAY FOR THIS!
FASH!
NO, I WON'T.

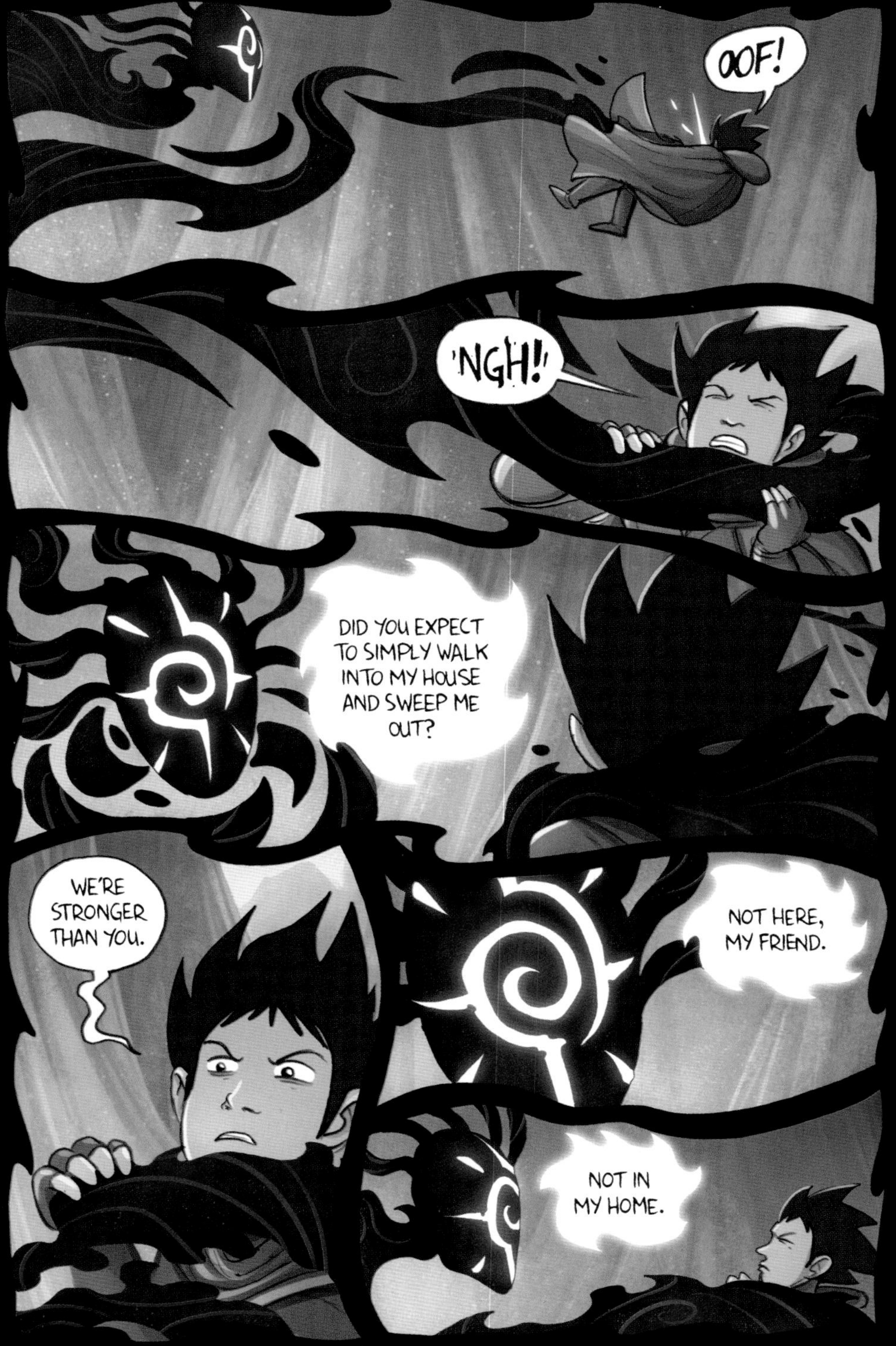
OOF!
'NGH!!
DID YOU EXPECT TO SIMPLY WALK INTO MY HOUSE AND SWEEP ME OUT?
WE'RE STRONGER THAN YOU.
NOT HERE, MY FRIEND.
NOT IN MY HOME.

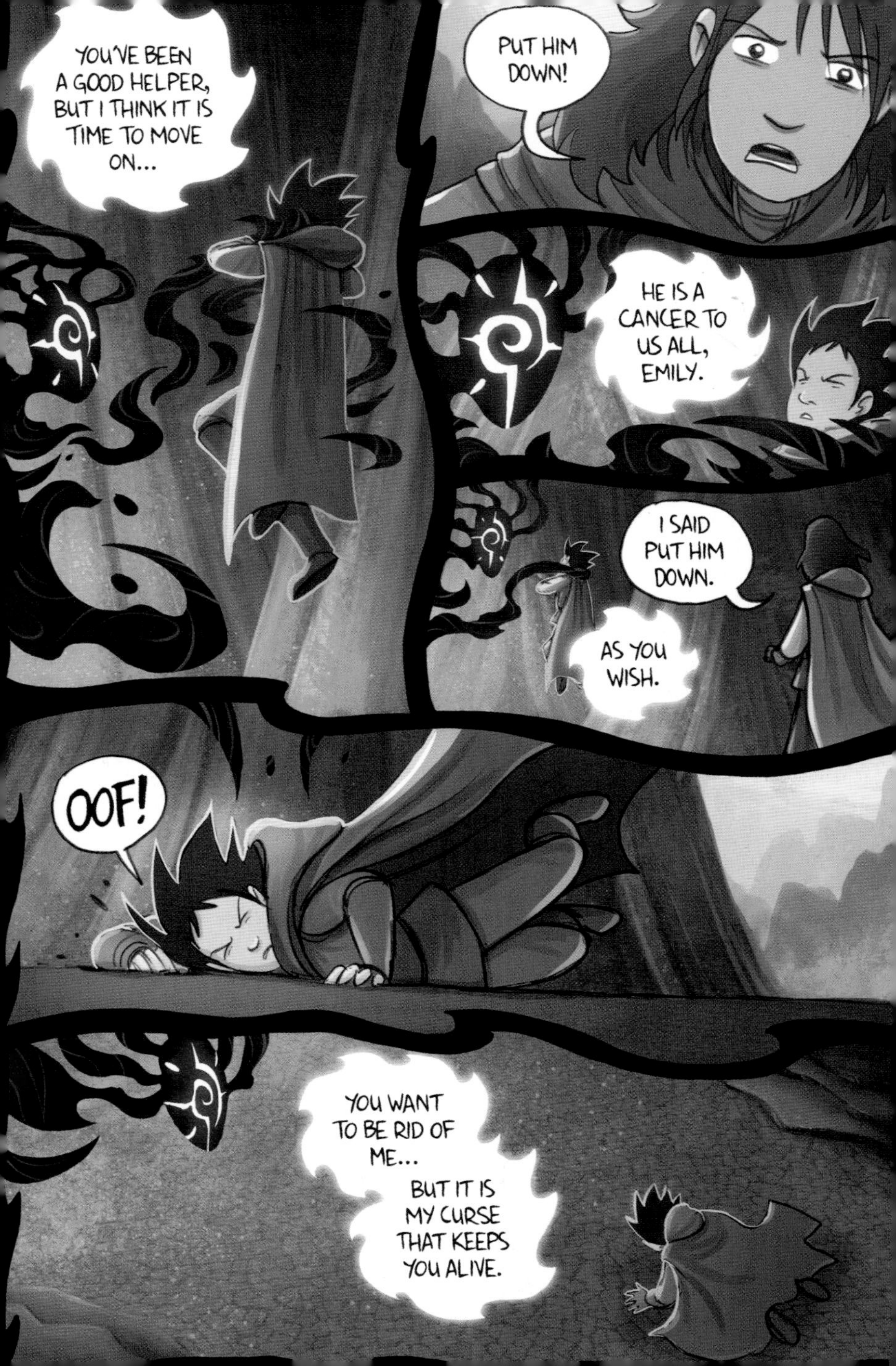
YOU'VE BEEN A GOOD HELPER, BUT I THINK IT IS TIME TO MOVE ON...
PUT HIM DOWN!
HE IS A CANCER TO US ALL, EMILY.
I SAID PUT HIM DOWN.
AS YOU WISH.
OOF!
YOU WANT TO BE RID OF ME...
BUT IT IS MY CURSE THAT KEEPS YOU ALIVE.

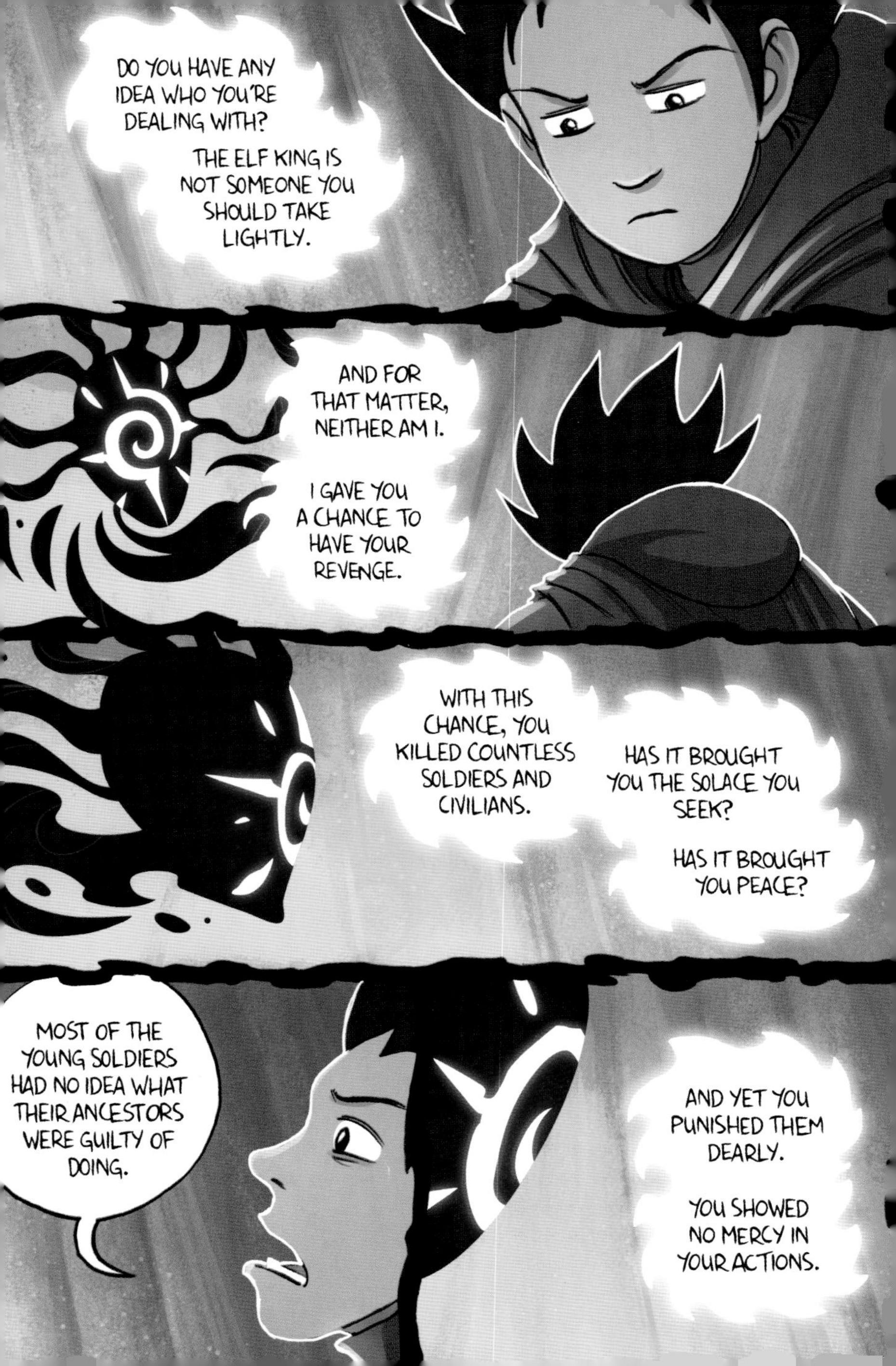
DO YOU HAVE ANY IDEA WHO YOU'RE DEALING WITH?
THE ELF KING IS NOT SOMEONE YOU SHOULD TAKE LIGHTLY.
AND FOR THAT MATTER, NEITHER AM I.
I GAVE YOU A CHANCE TO HAVE YOUR REVENGE.
WITH THIS CHANCE, YOU KILLED COUNTLESS SOLDIERS AND CIVILIANS.
HAS IT BROUGHT YOU THE SOLACE YOU SEEK?
HAS IT BROUGHT YOU PEACE?
MOST OF THE YOUNG SOLDIERS HAD NO IDEA WHAT THEIR ANCESTORS WERE GUILTY OF DOING.
AND YET YOU PUNISHED THEM DEARLY.
YOU SHOWED NO MERCY IN YOUR ACTIONS.

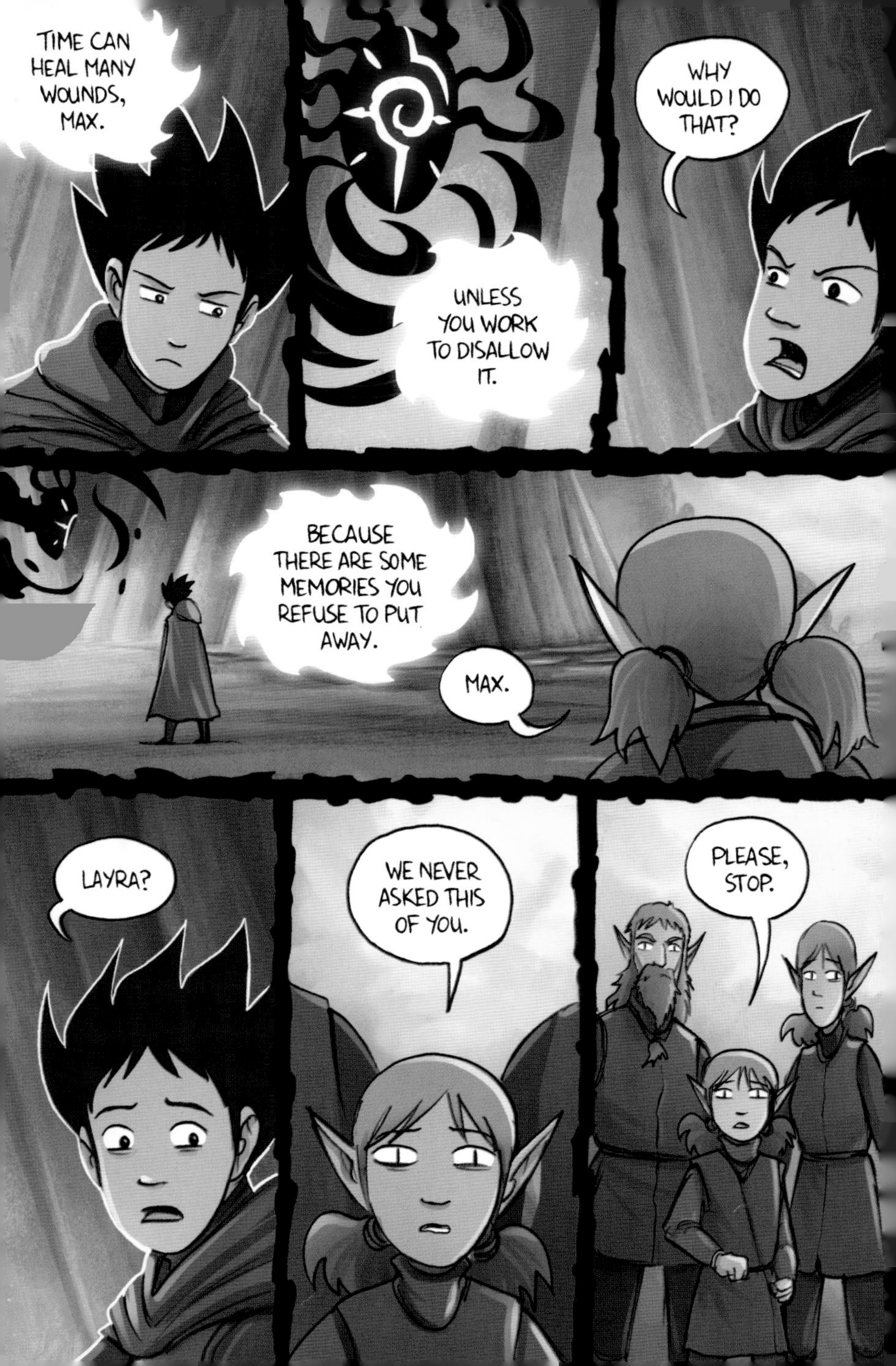
TIME CAN HEAL MANY WOUNDS, MAX.
UNLESS YOU WORK TO DISALLOW IT.
WHY WOULD I DO THAT?
BECAUSE THERE ARE SOME MEMORIES YOU REFUSE TO PUT AWAY.
MAX.
LAYRA?
WE NEVER ASKED THIS OF YOU.
PLEASE, STOP.

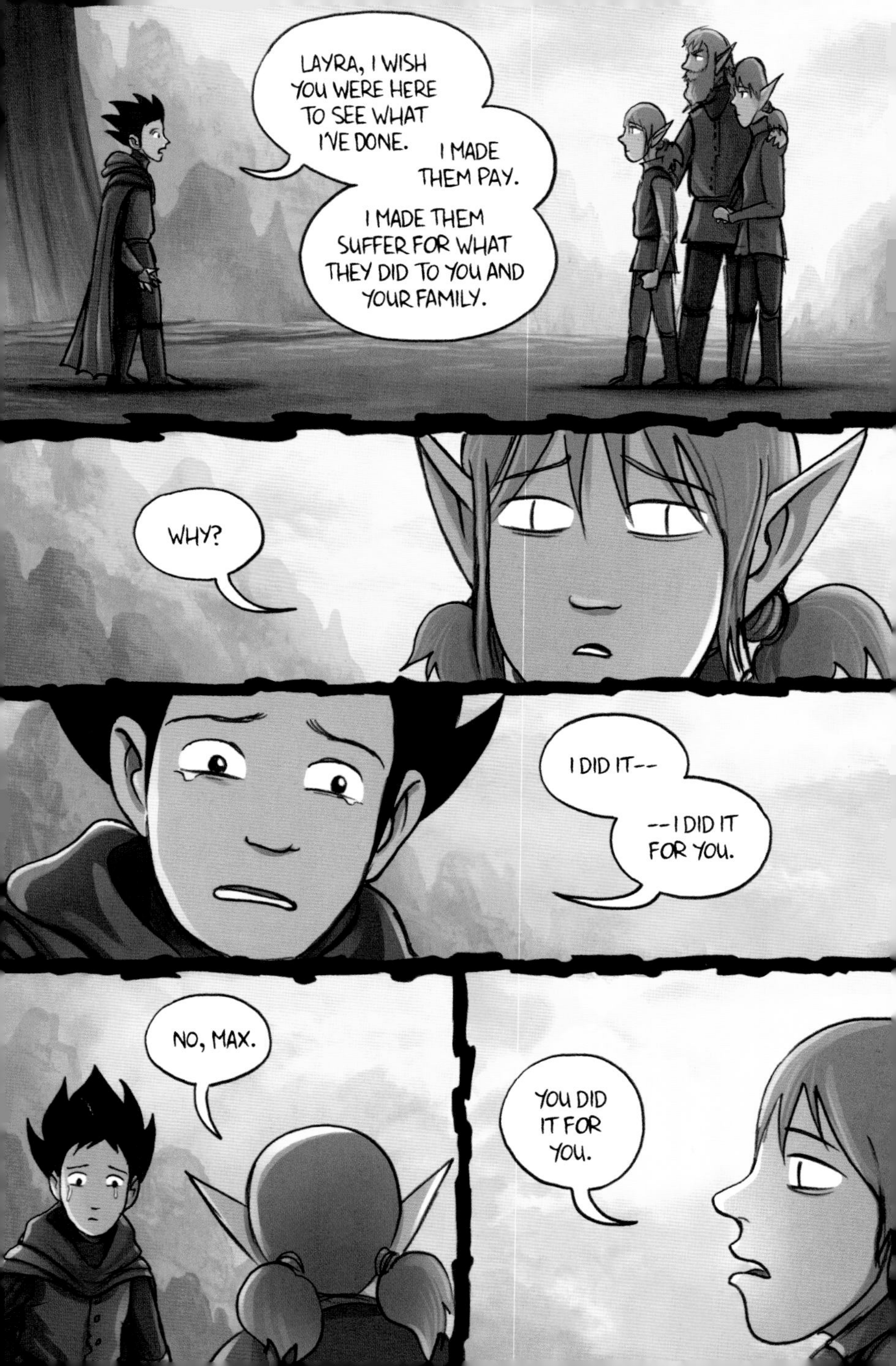
LAYRA, I WISH YOU WERE HERE TO SEE WHAT I'VE DONE.
I MADE THEM PAY.
I MADE THEM SUFFER FOR WHAT THEY DID TO YOU AND YOUR FAMILY.
WHY?
I DID IT--
--I DID IT FOR YOU.
NO, MAX.
YOU DID IT FOR YOU.

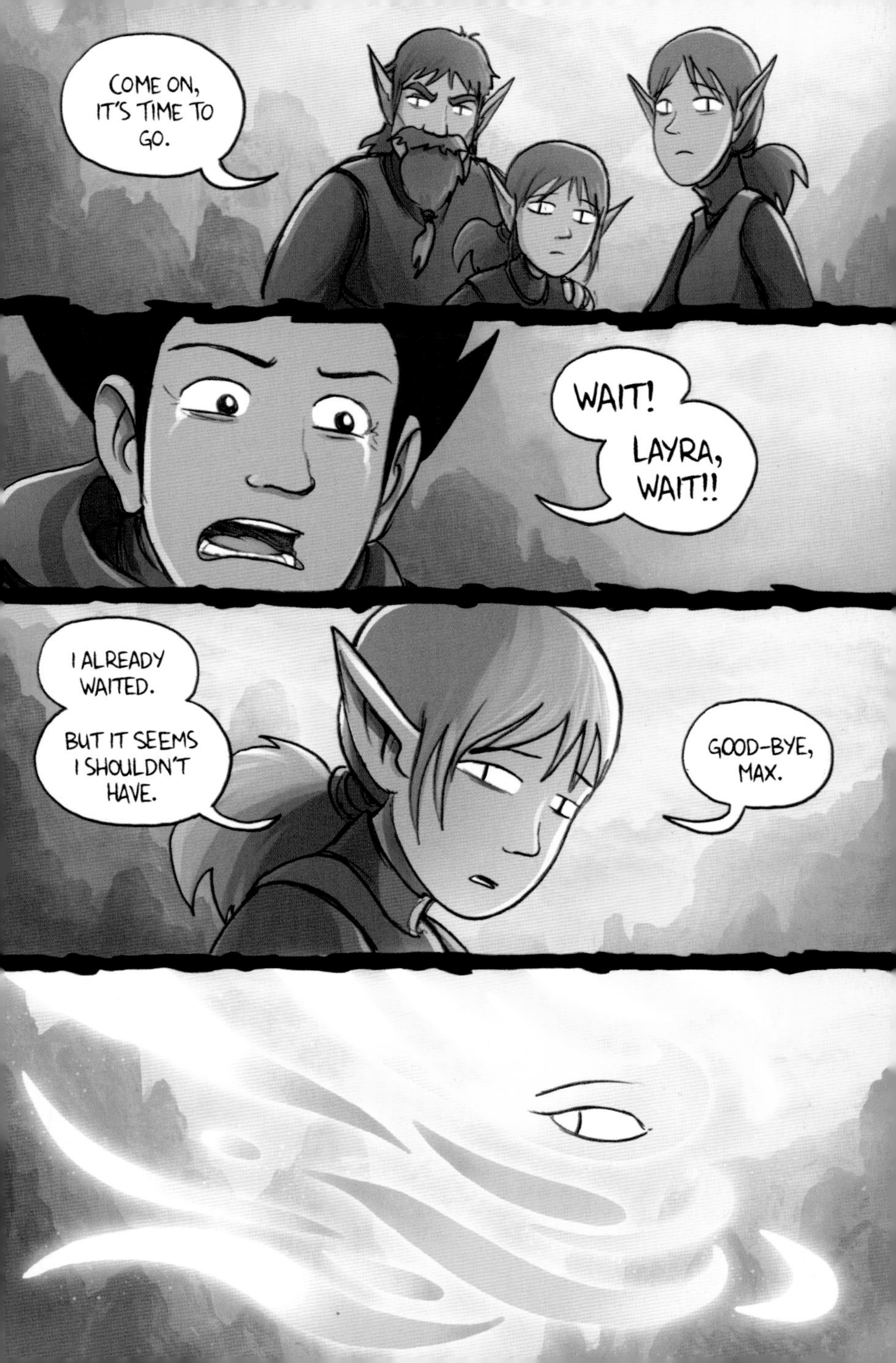
COME ON, IT'S TIME TO GO.
WAIT!
LAYRA, WAIT!!
I ALREADY WAITED.
BUT IT SEEMS I SHOULDN'T HAVE.
GOOD-BYE, MAX.

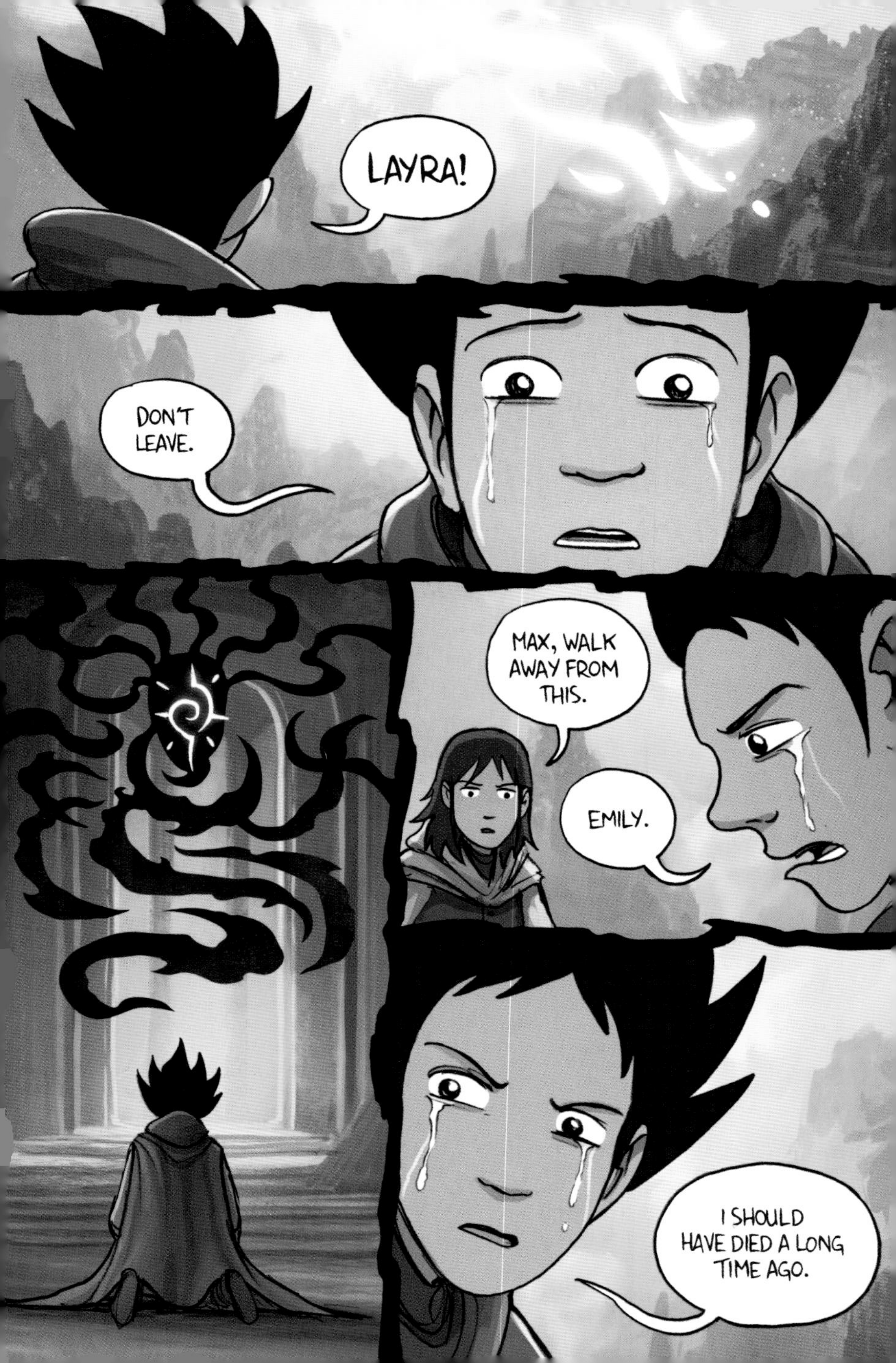
LAYRA!
DON'T LEAVE.
MAX, WALK AWAY FROM THIS.
EMILY.
I SHOULD HAVE DIED A LONG TIME AGO.

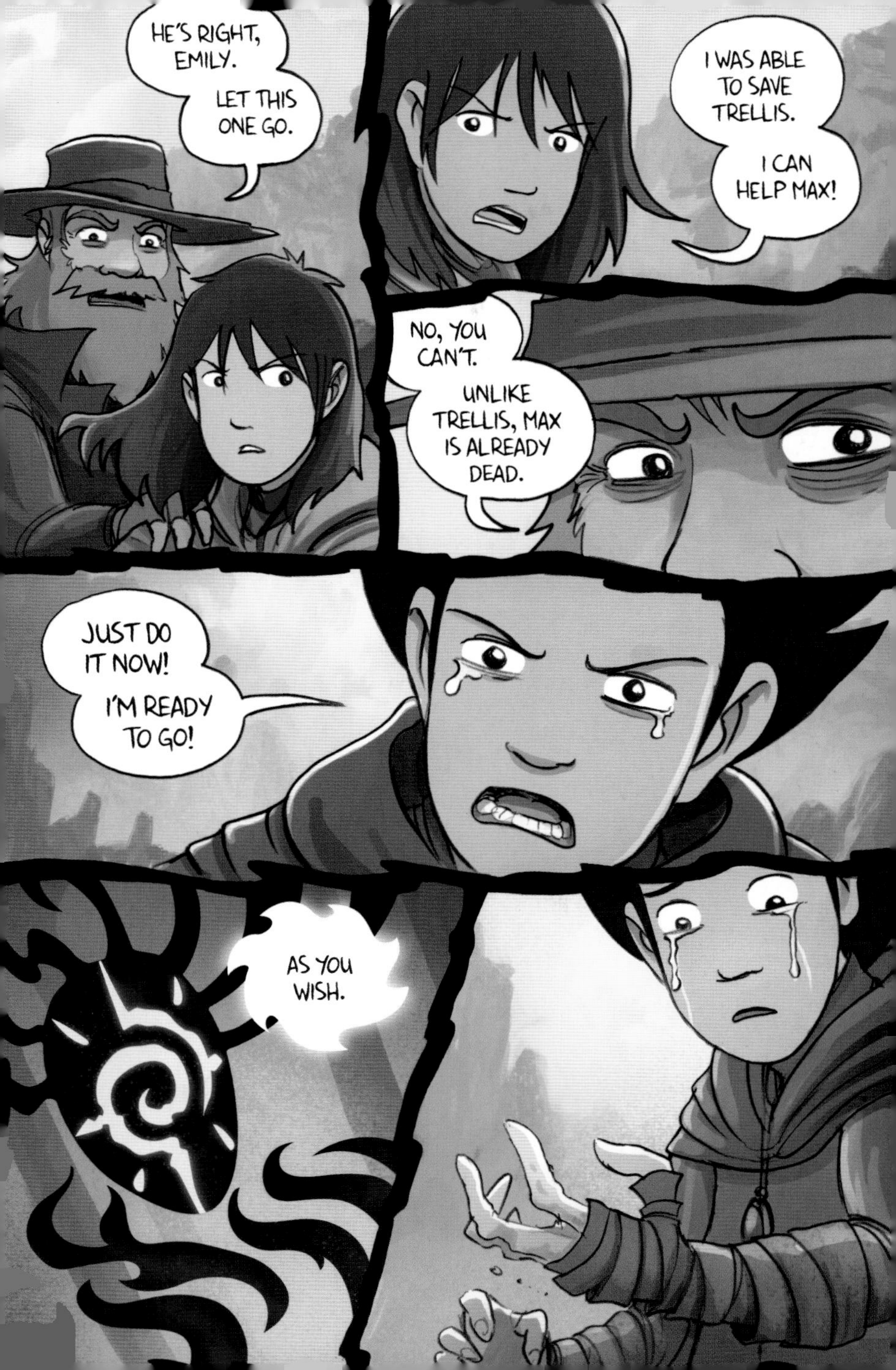
HE'S RIGHT, EMILY.
LET THIS ONE GO.
I WAS ABLE TO SAVE TRELLIS.
I CAN HELP MAX!
NO, YOU CAN'T.
UNLIKE TRELLIS, MAX IS ALREADY DEAD.
JUST DO IT NOW!
I'M READY TO GO!
AS YOU WISH.

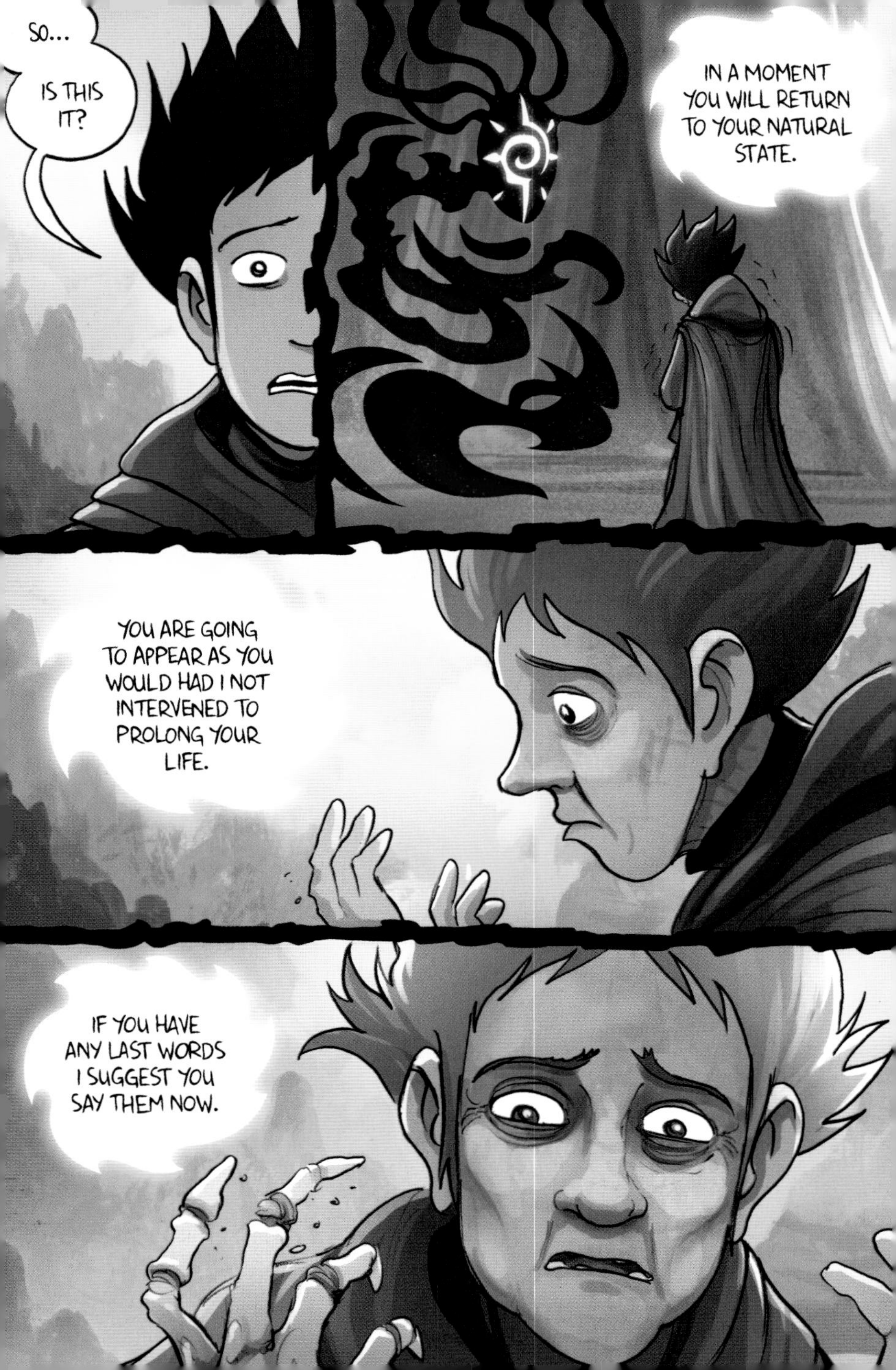
SO...
IS THIS IT?
IN A MOMENT YOU WILL RETURN TO YOUR NATURAL STATE.
YOU ARE GOING TO APPEAR AS YOU WOULD HAD I NOT INTERVENED TO PROLONG YOUR LIFE.
IF YOU HAVE ANY LAST WORDS I SUGGEST YOU SAY THEM NOW.

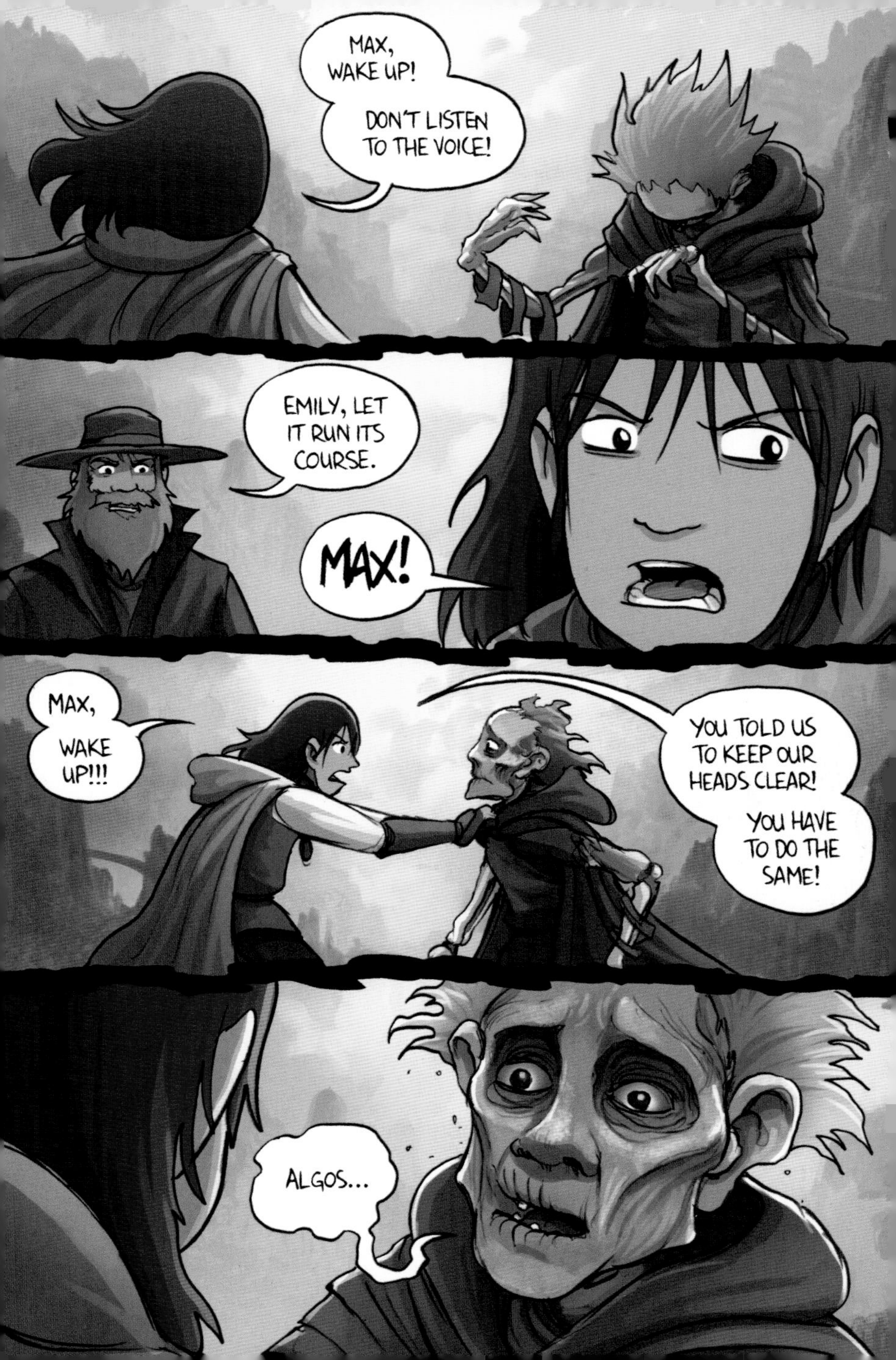
MAX, WAKE UP!
DON'T LISTEN TO THE VOICE!
EMILY, LET IT RUN ITS COURSE.
MAX!
MAX, WAKE UP!!!
YOU TOLD US TO KEEP OUR HEADS CLEAR!
YOU HAVE TO DO THE SAME!
ALGOS...

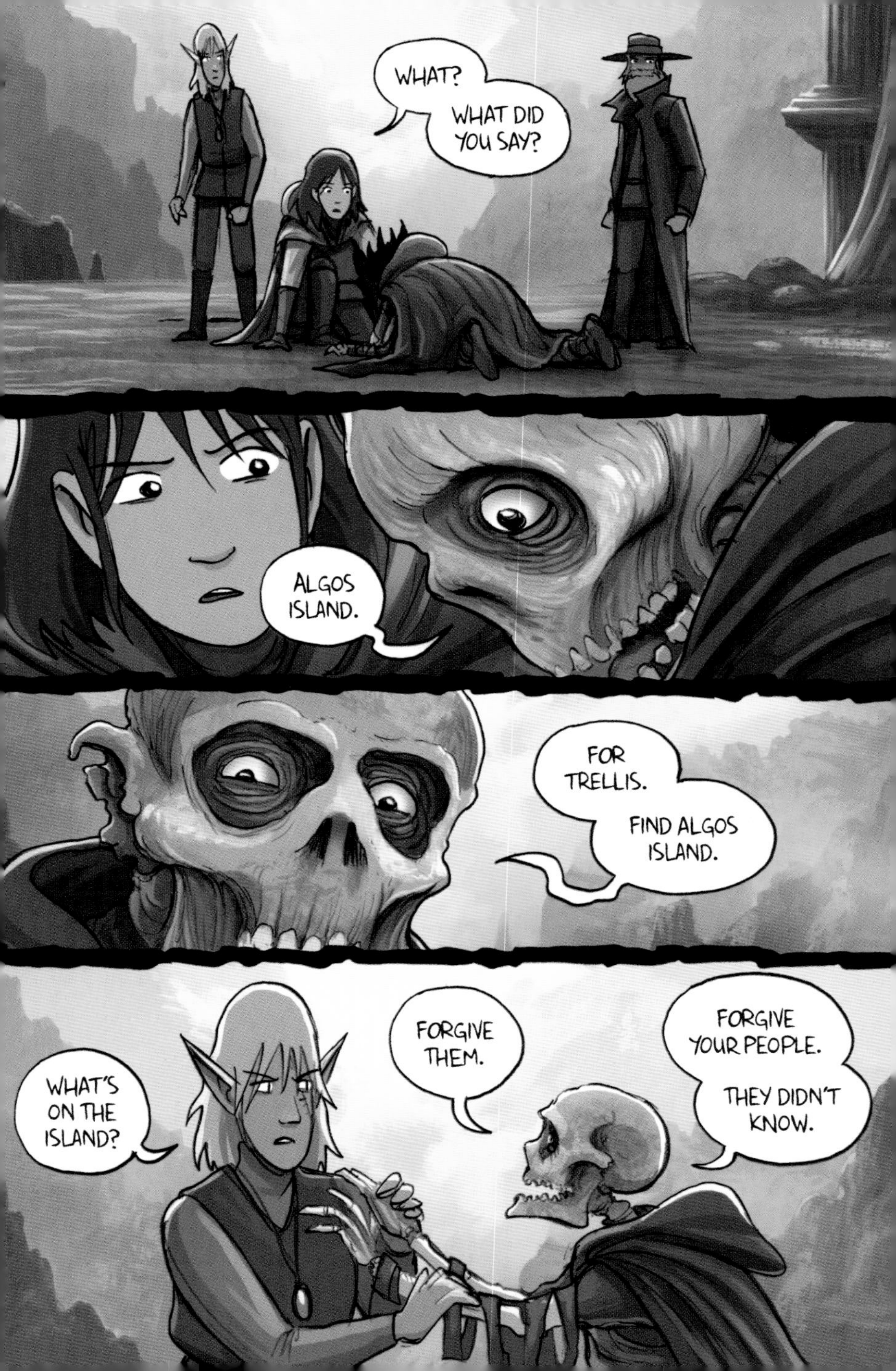
WHAT?
WHAT DID YOU SAY?
ALGOS ISLAND.
FOR TRELLIS.
FIND ALGOS ISLAND.
WHAT'S ON THE ISLAND?
FORGIVE THEM.
FORGIVE YOUR PEOPLE.
THEY DIDN'T KNOW.

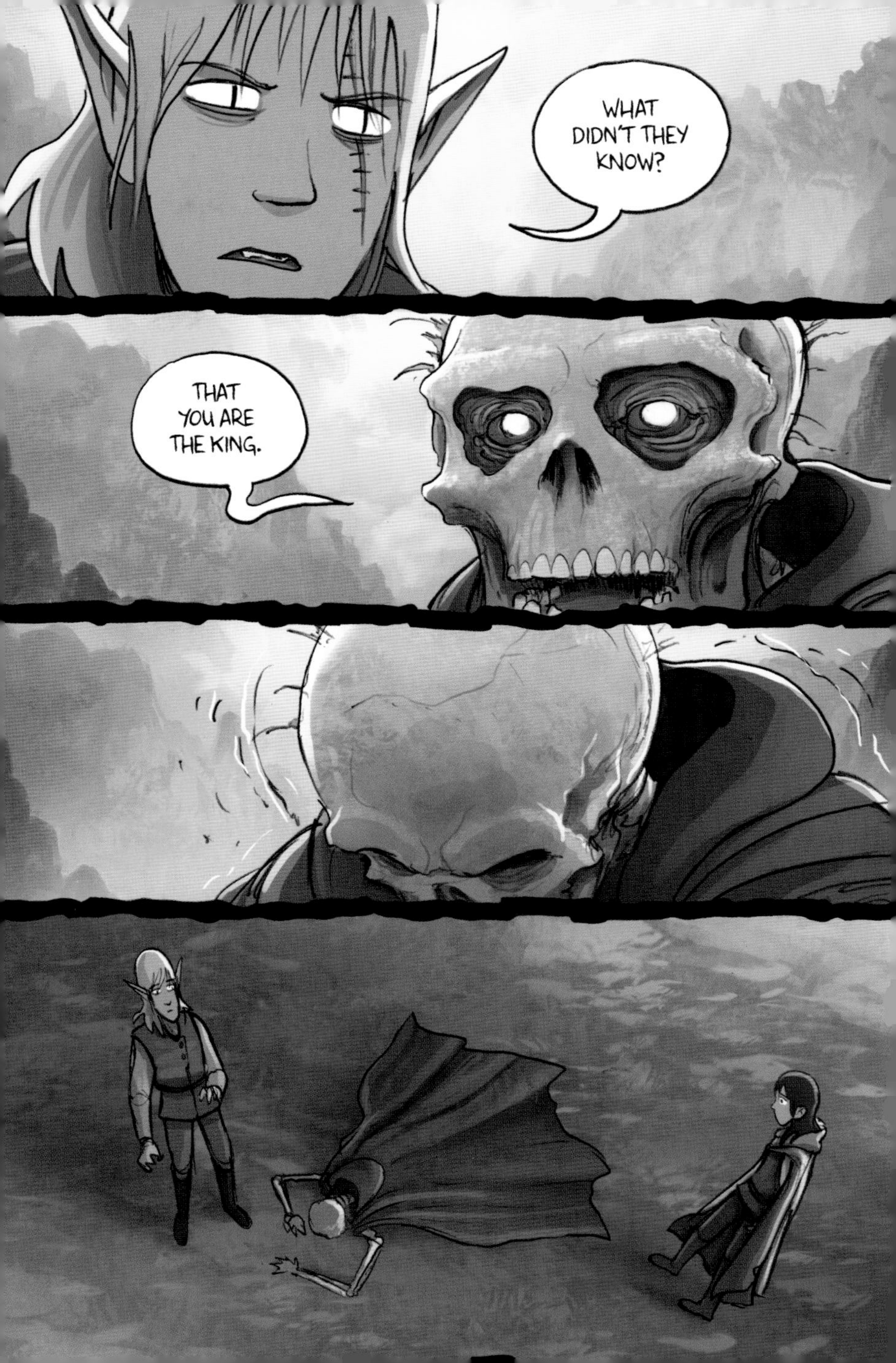
WHAT DIDN'T THEY KNOW?
THAT YOU ARE THE KING.

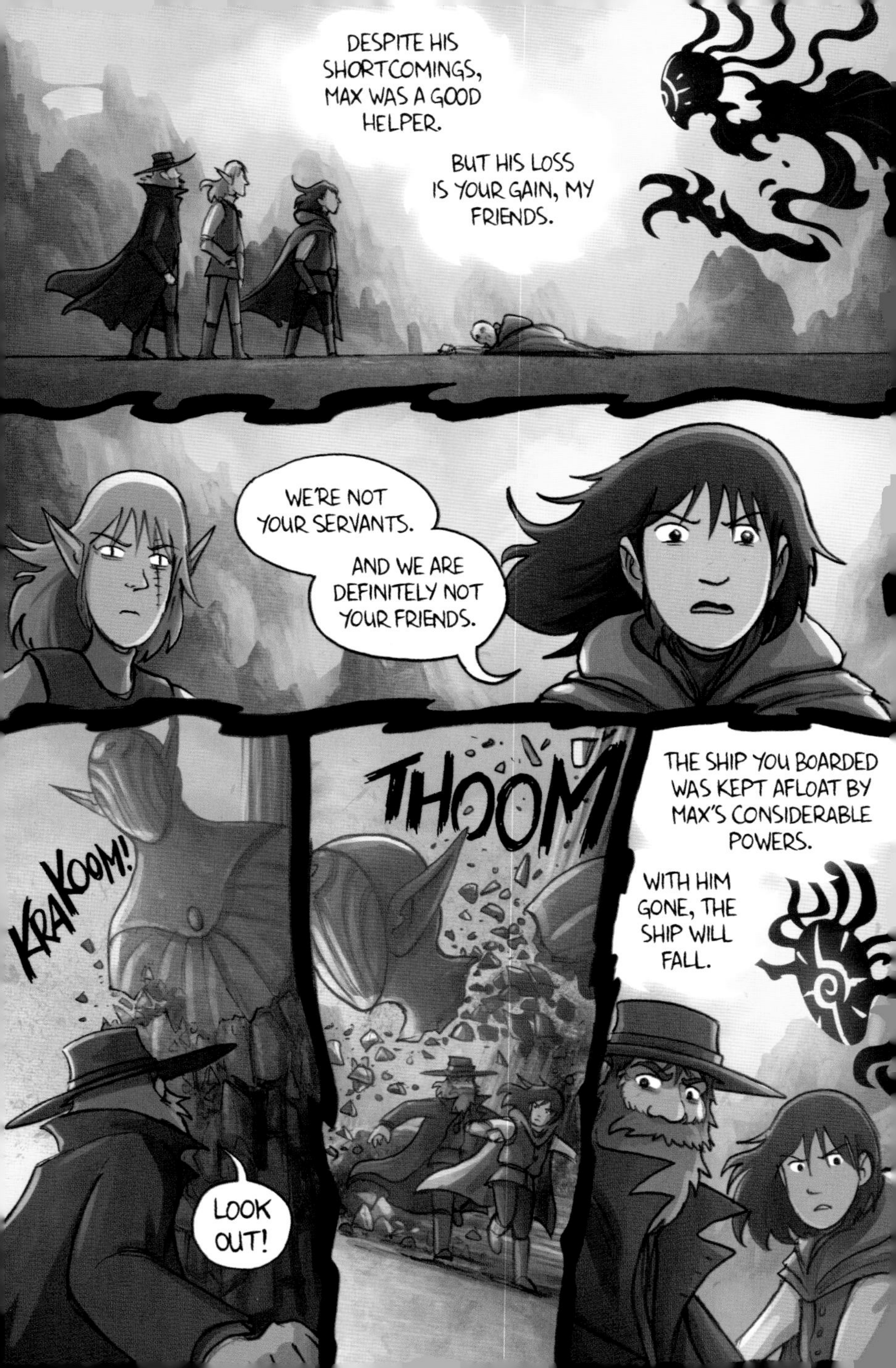

DESPITE HIS SHORTCOMINGS, MAX WAS A GOOD HELPER.
BUT HIS LOSS IS YOUR GAIN, MY FRIENDS.
WE'RE NOT YOUR SERVANTS.
AND WE ARE DEFINITELY NOT YOUR FRIENDS.
KRAKOOM!
LOOK OUT!
THOOM
THE SHIP YOU BOARDED WAS KEPT AFLOAT BY MAX'S CONSIDERABLE POWERS.
WITH HIM GONE, THE SHIP WILL FALL.

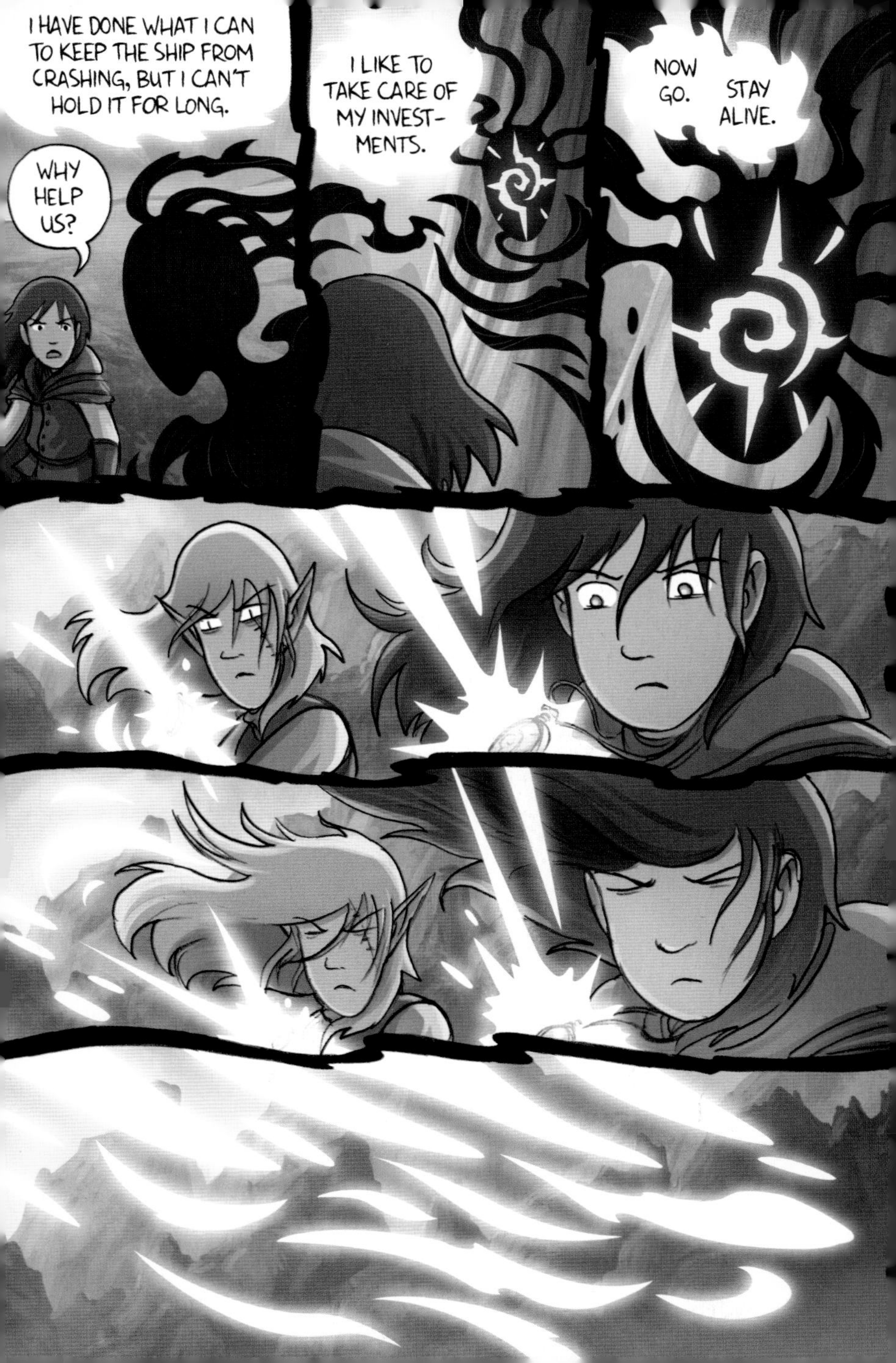
I HAVE DONE WHAT I CAN TO KEEP THE SHIP FROM CRASHING, BUT I CAN'T HOLD IT FOR LONG.
WHY HELP US?
I LIKE TO TAKE CARE OF MY INVEST-MENTS.
NOW GO.
STAY ALIVE.

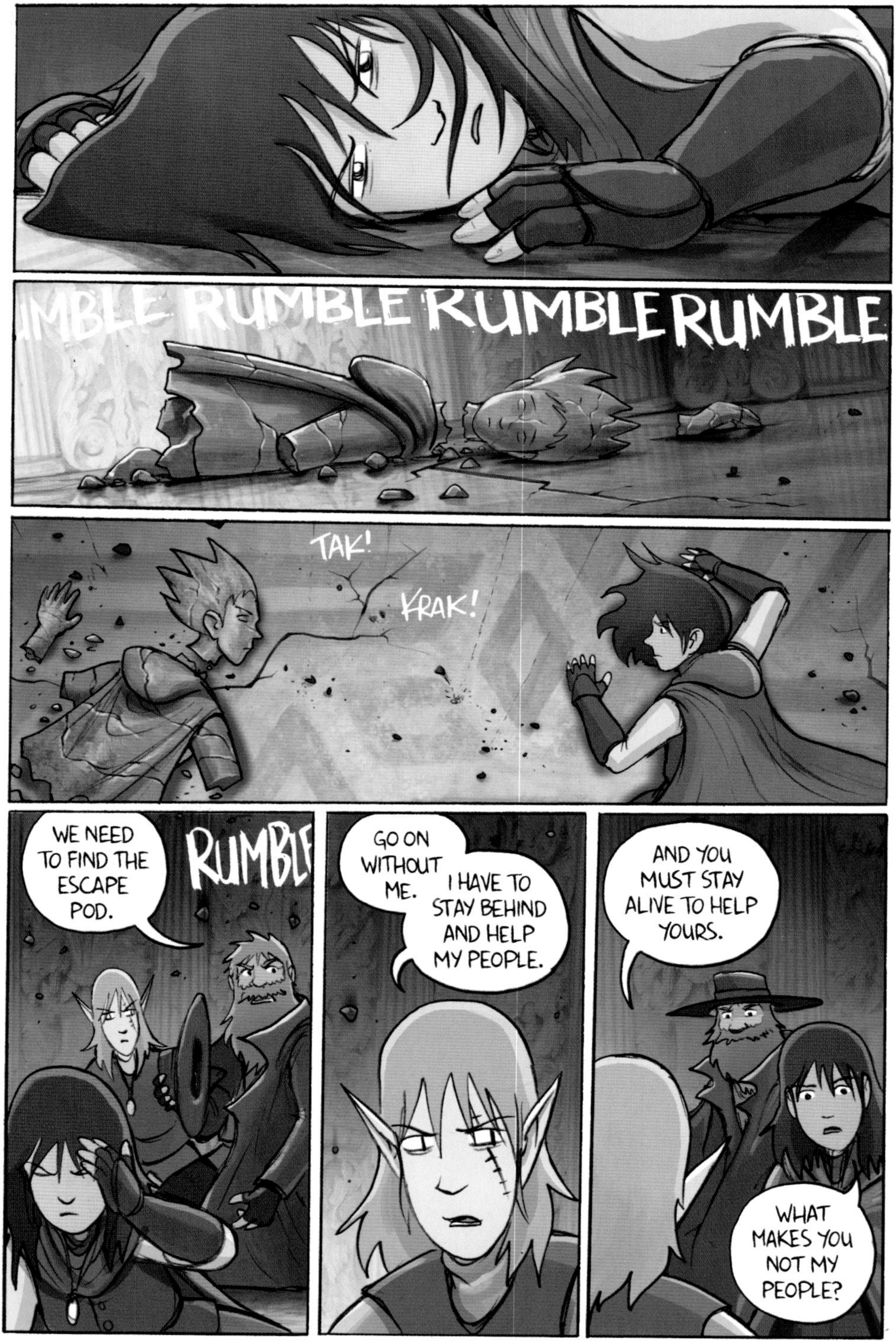
RUMBLE RUMBLE RUMBLE RUMBLE
TAK!
KRAK!
WE NEED TO FIND THE ESCAPE POD.
RUMBLE
GO ON WITHOUT ME.
I HAVE TO STAY BEHIND AND HELP MY PEOPLE.
AND YOU MUST STAY ALIVE TO HELP YOURS.
WHAT MAKES YOU NOT MY PEOPLE?

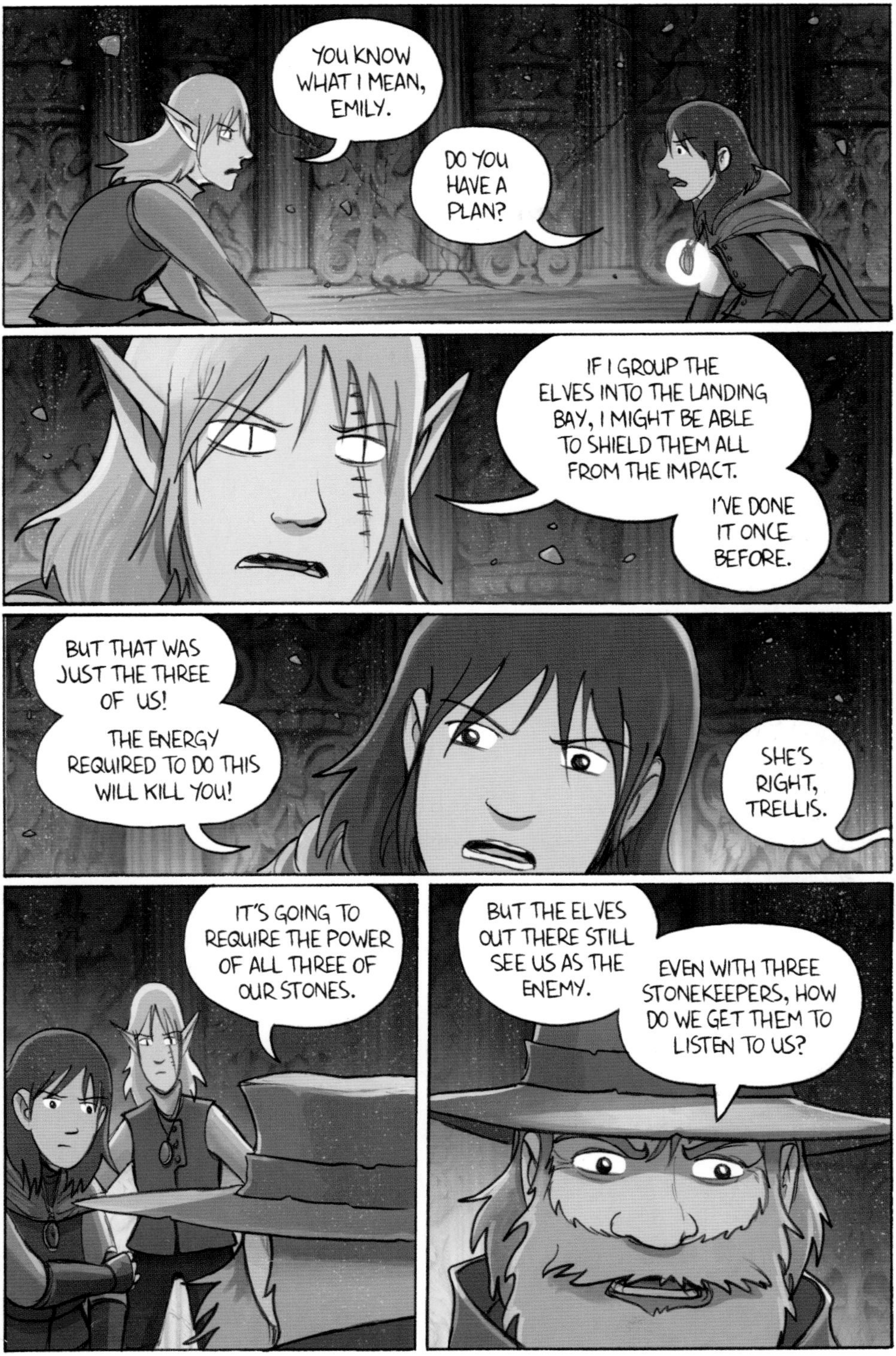
YOU KNOW WHAT I MEAN, EMILY.
DO YOU HAVE A PLAN?
IF I GROUP THE ELVES INTO THE LANDING BAY, I MIGHT BE ABLE TO SHIELD THEM ALL FROM THE IMPACT.
I'VE DONE IT ONCE BEFORE.
BUT THAT WAS JUST THE THREE OF US!
THE ENERGY REQUIRED TO DO THIS WILL KILL YOU!
SHE'S RIGHT, TRELLIS.
IT'S GOING TO REQUIRE THE POWER OF ALL THREE OF OUR STONES.
BUT THE ELVES OUT THERE STILL SEE US AS THE ENEMY.
EVEN WITH THREE STONEKEEPERS, HOW DO WE GET THEM TO LISTEN TO US?

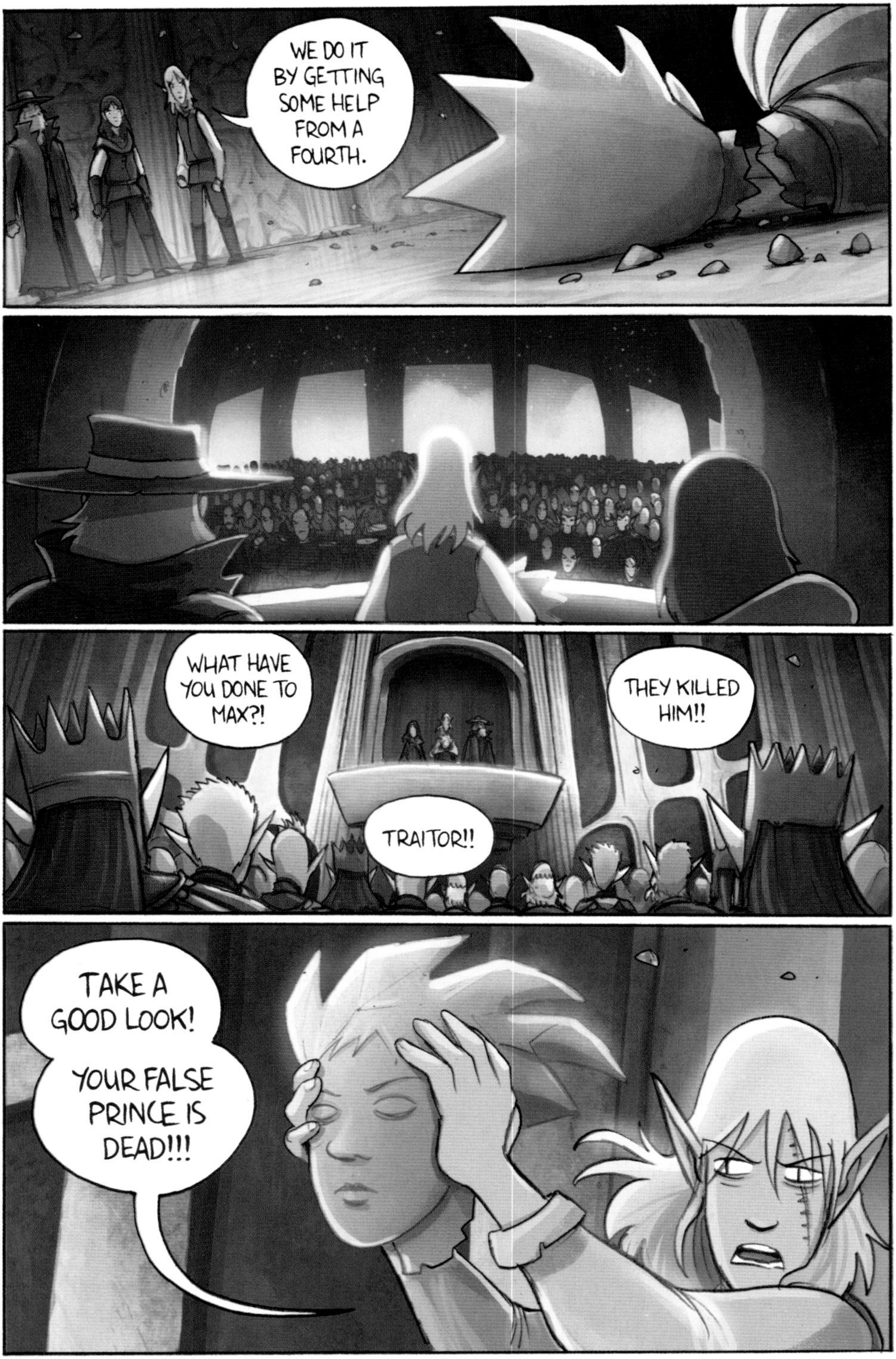
WE DO IT BY GETTING SOME HELP FROM A FOURTH.
WHAT HAVE YOU DONE TO MAX?!
THEY KILLED HIM!!
TRAITOR!!
TAKE A GOOD LOOK!
YOUR FALSE PRINCE IS DEAD!!!

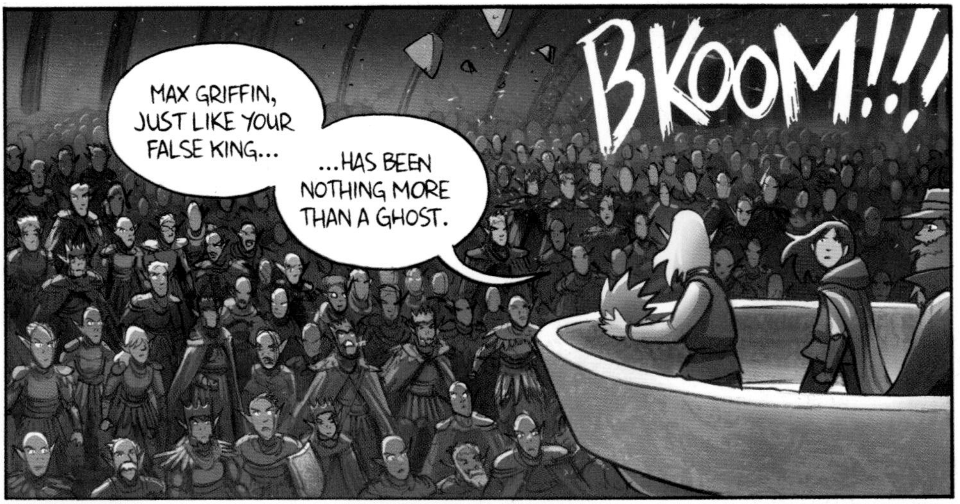
BKOOM!!!
MAX GRIFFIN, JUST LIKE YOUR FALSE KING...
...HAS BEEN NOTHING MORE THAN A GHOST.

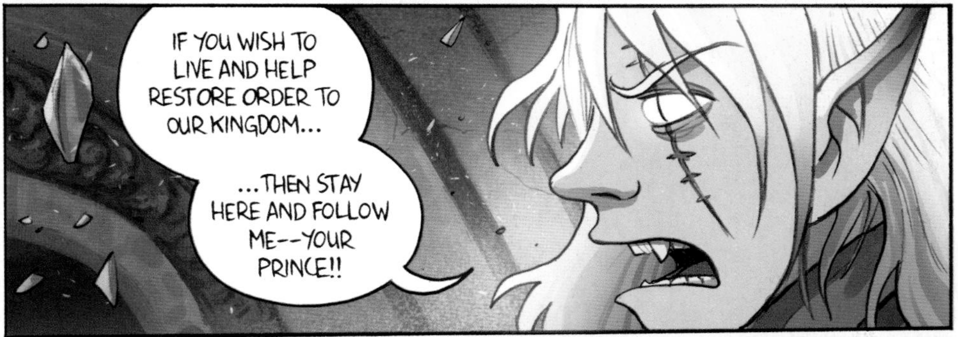
IF YOU WISH TO LIVE AND HELP RESTORE ORDER TO OUR KINGDOM...
...THEN STAY HERE AND FOLLOW ME--YOUR PRINCE!!

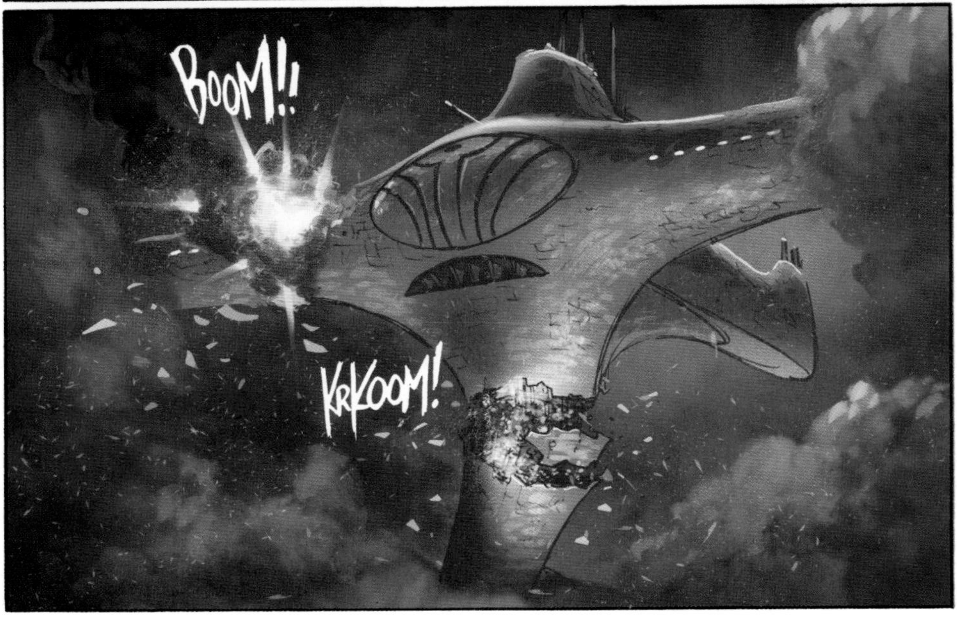
BOOM!!
KRKOOM!

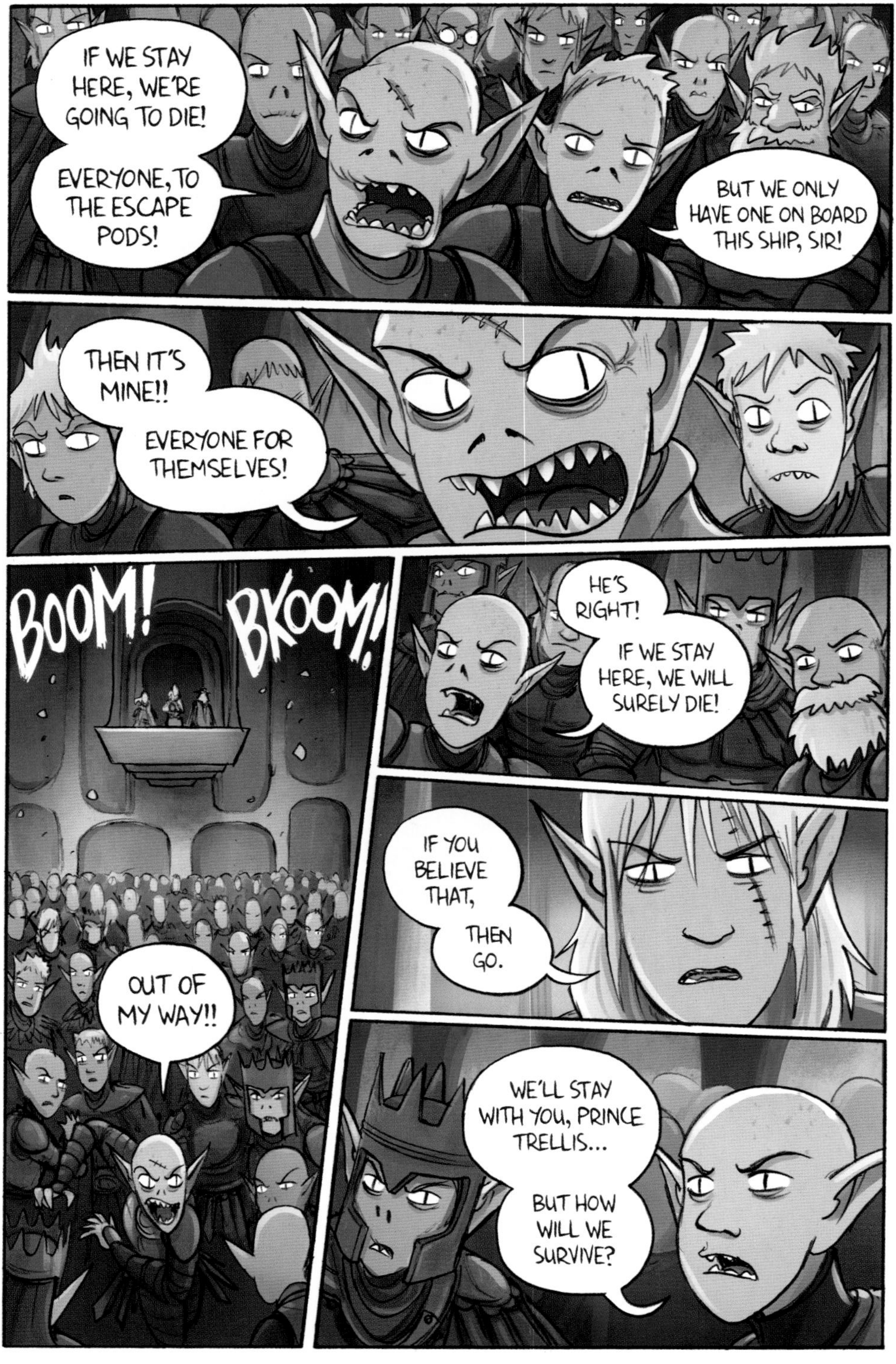
IF WE STAY HERE, WE'RE GOING TO DIE!
EVERYONE, TO THE ESCAPE PODS!
BUT WE ONLY HAVE ONE ON BOARD THIS SHIP, SIR!
THEN IT'S MINE!!
EVERYONE FOR THEMSELVES!
BOOM!
BKOOM!
OUT OF MY WAY!!
HE'S RIGHT!
IF WE STAY HERE, WE WILL SURELY DIE!
IF YOU BELIEVE THAT,
THEN GO.
WE'LL STAY WITH YOU, PRINCE TRELLIS...
BUT HOW WILL WE SURVIVE?

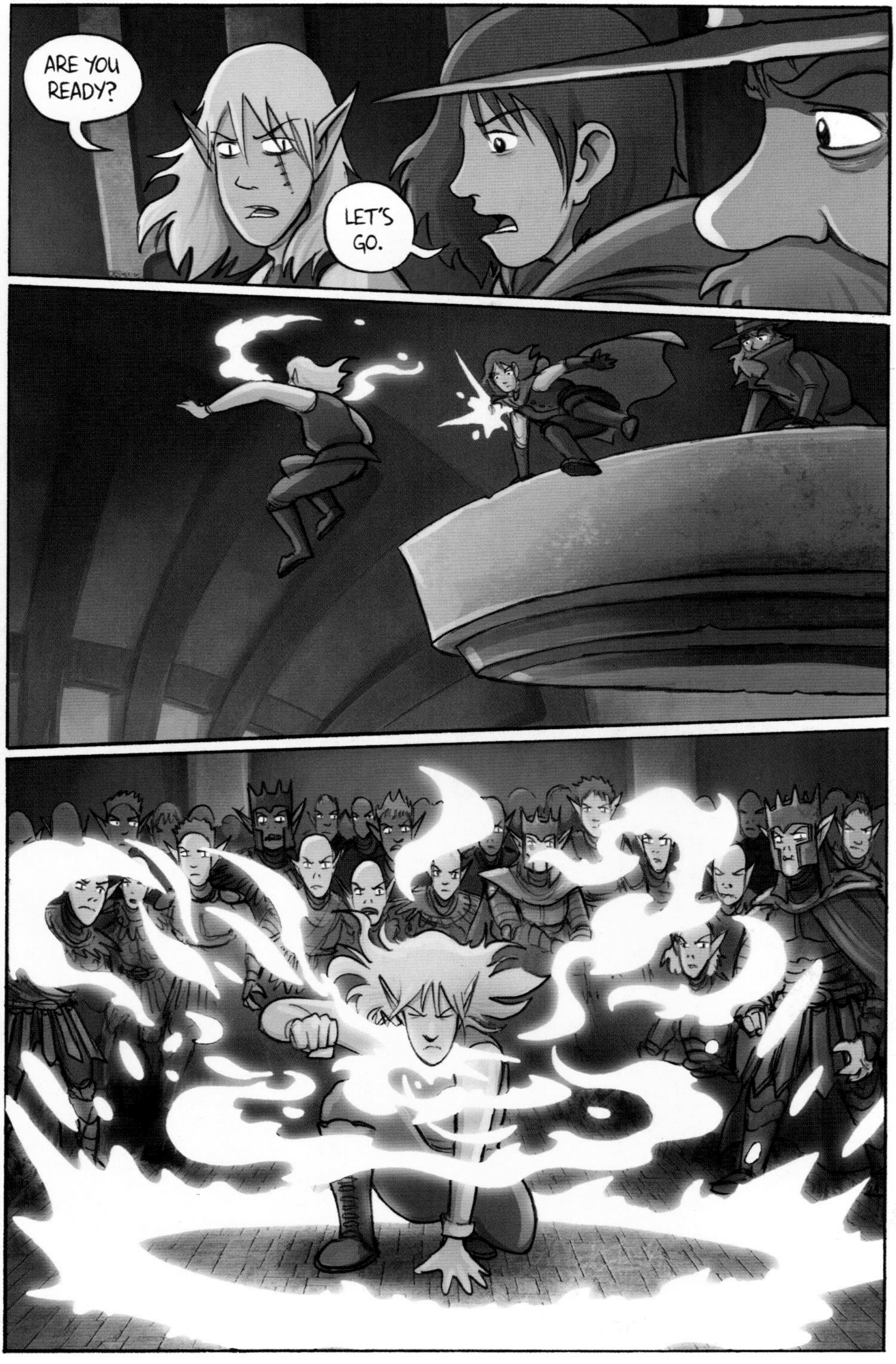
ARE YOU READY?
LET'S GO.

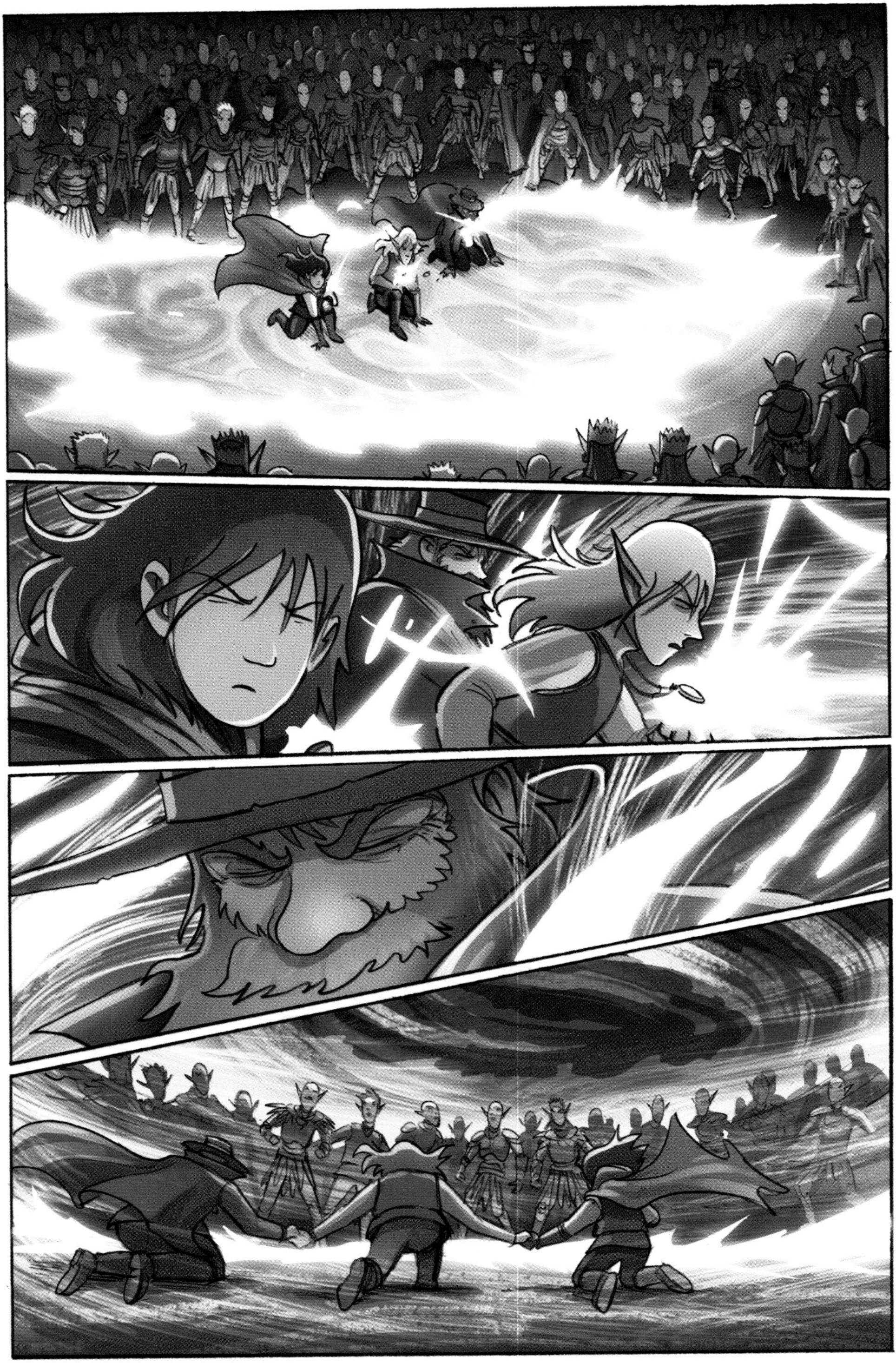

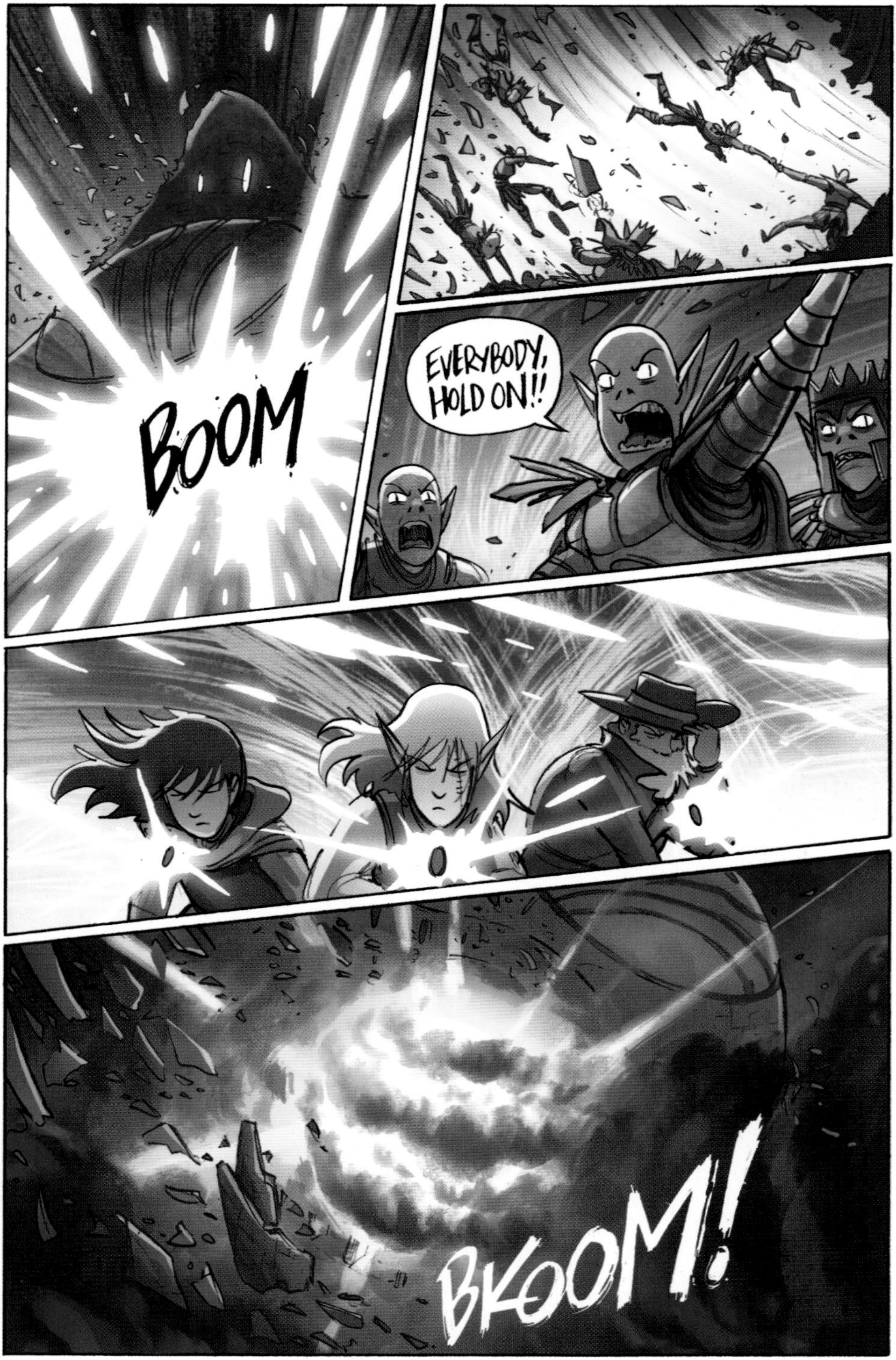
BOOM
EVERYBODY, HOLD ON!!
BKOOM!

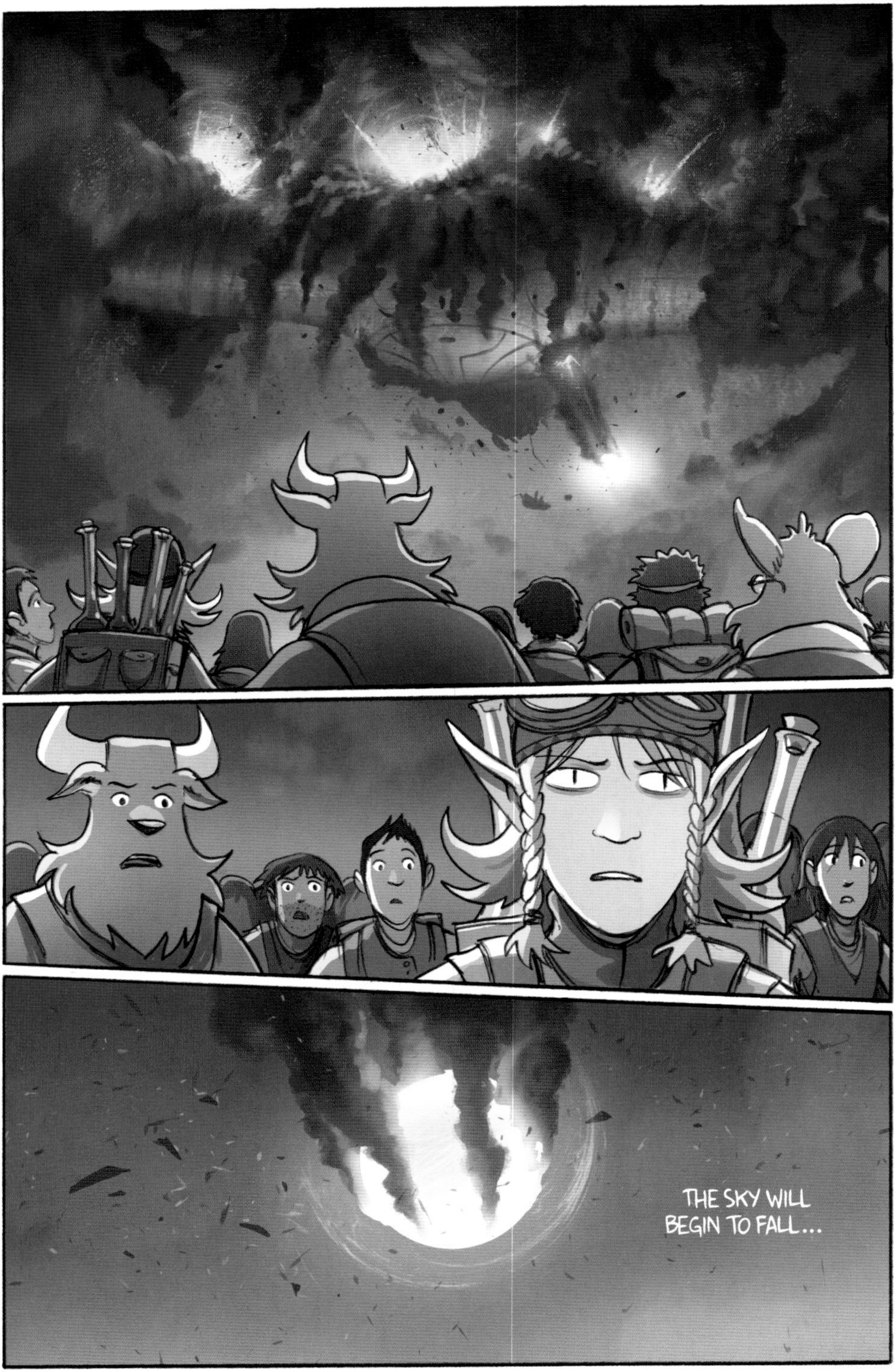
THE SKY WILL BEGIN TO FALL...

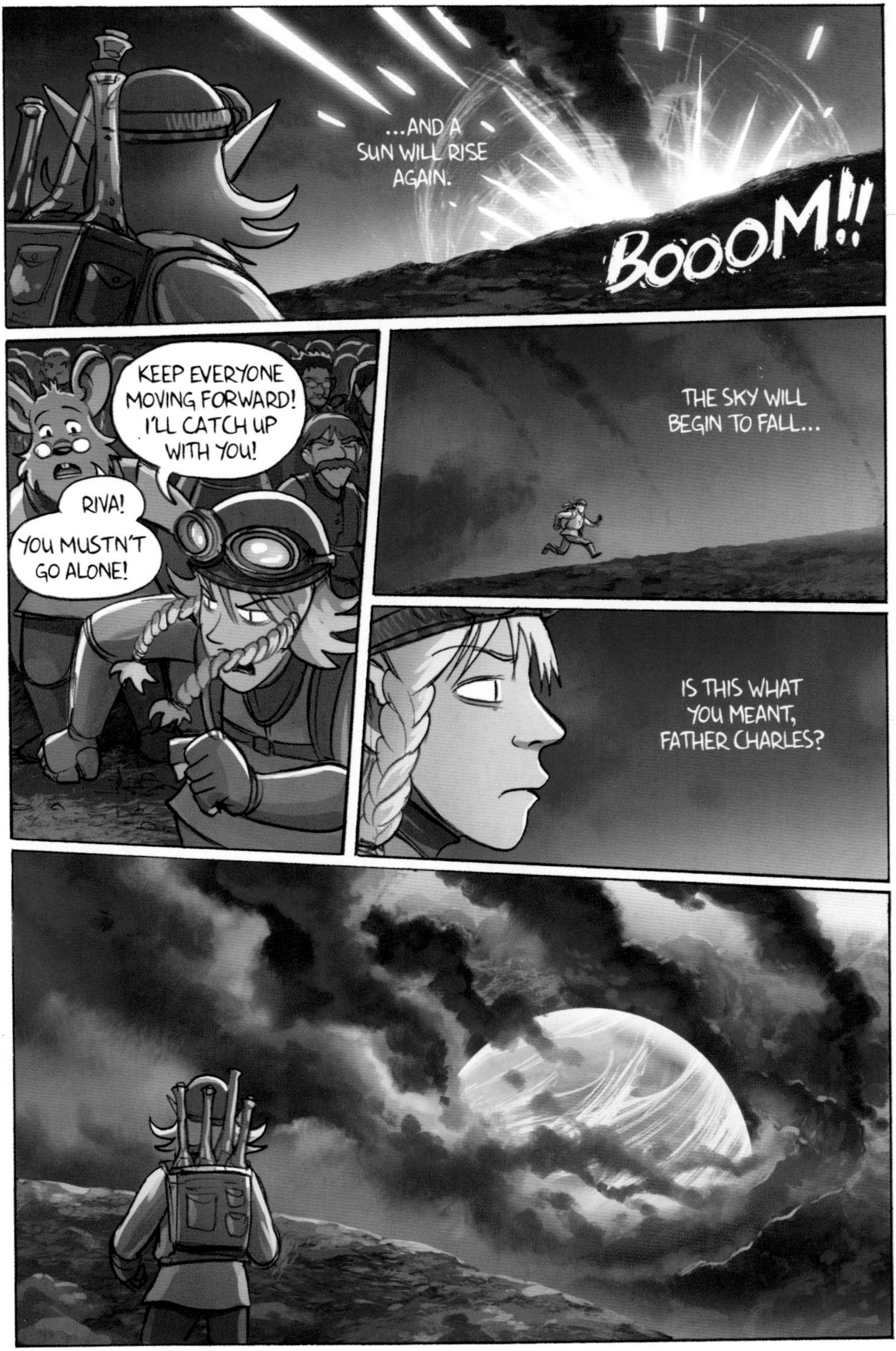
...AND A SUN WILL RISE AGAIN.
BOOOM!!
KEEP EVERYONE MOVING FORWARD! I'LL CATCH UP WITH YOU!
RIVA!
YOU MUSTN'T GO ALONE!
THE SKY WILL BEGIN TO FALL...
IS THIS WHAT YOU MEANT, FATHER CHARLES?

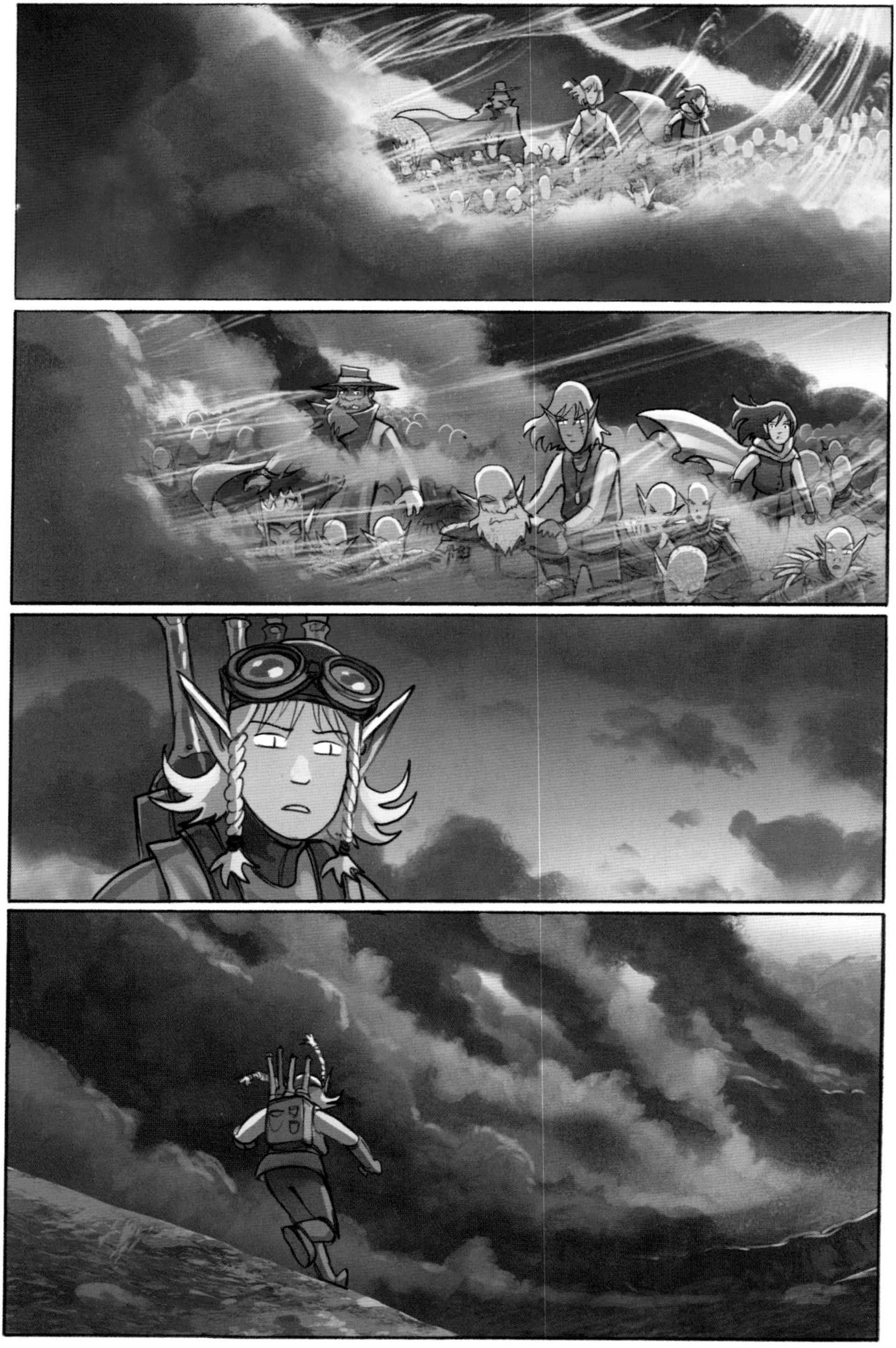

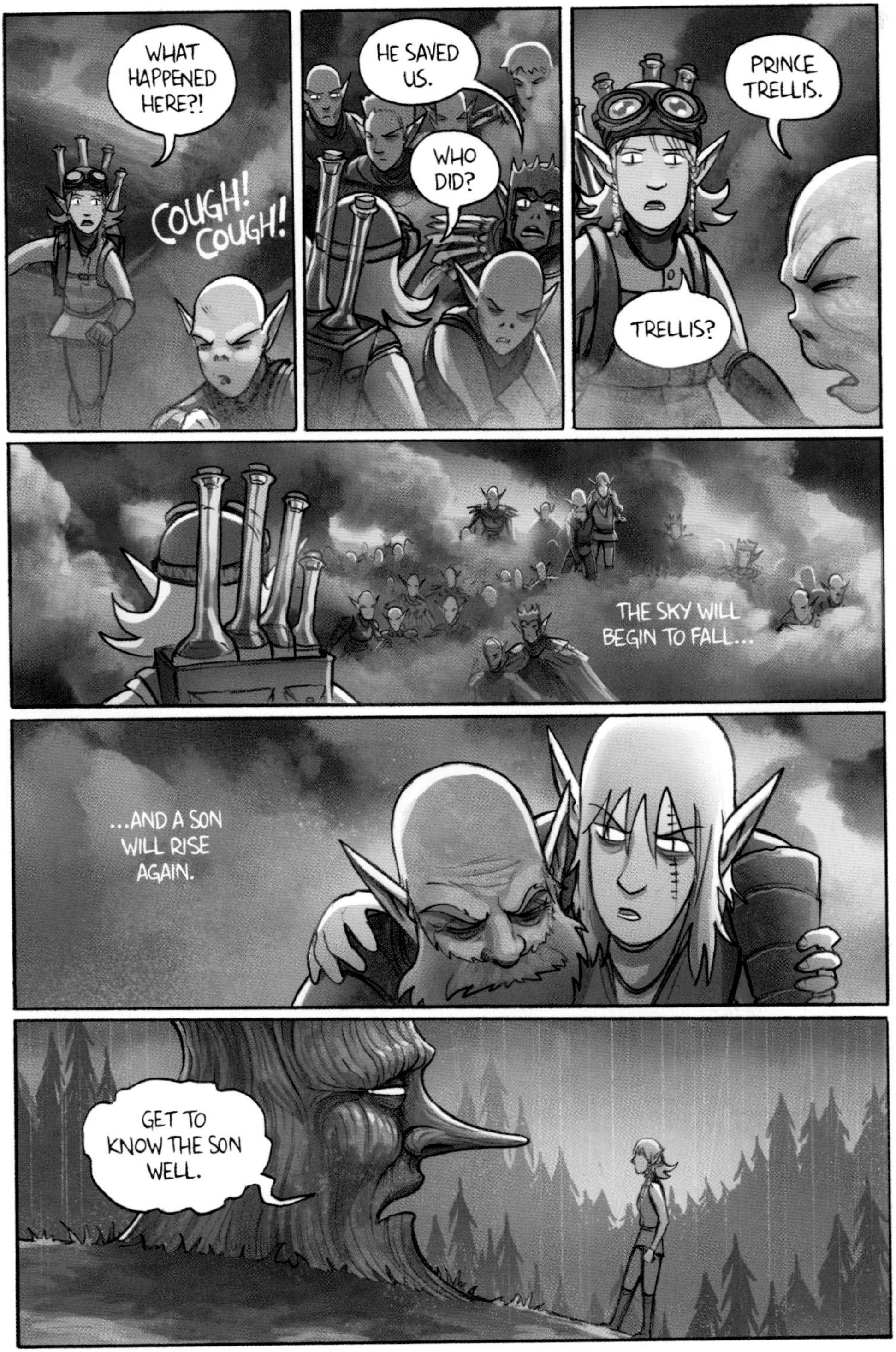
WHAT HAPPENED HERE?!
COUGH! COUGH!
HE SAVED US.
WHO DID?
PRINCE TRELLIS.
TRELLIS?
THE SKY WILL BEGIN TO FALL...
...AND A SON WILL RISE AGAIN.
GET TO KNOW THE SON WELL.

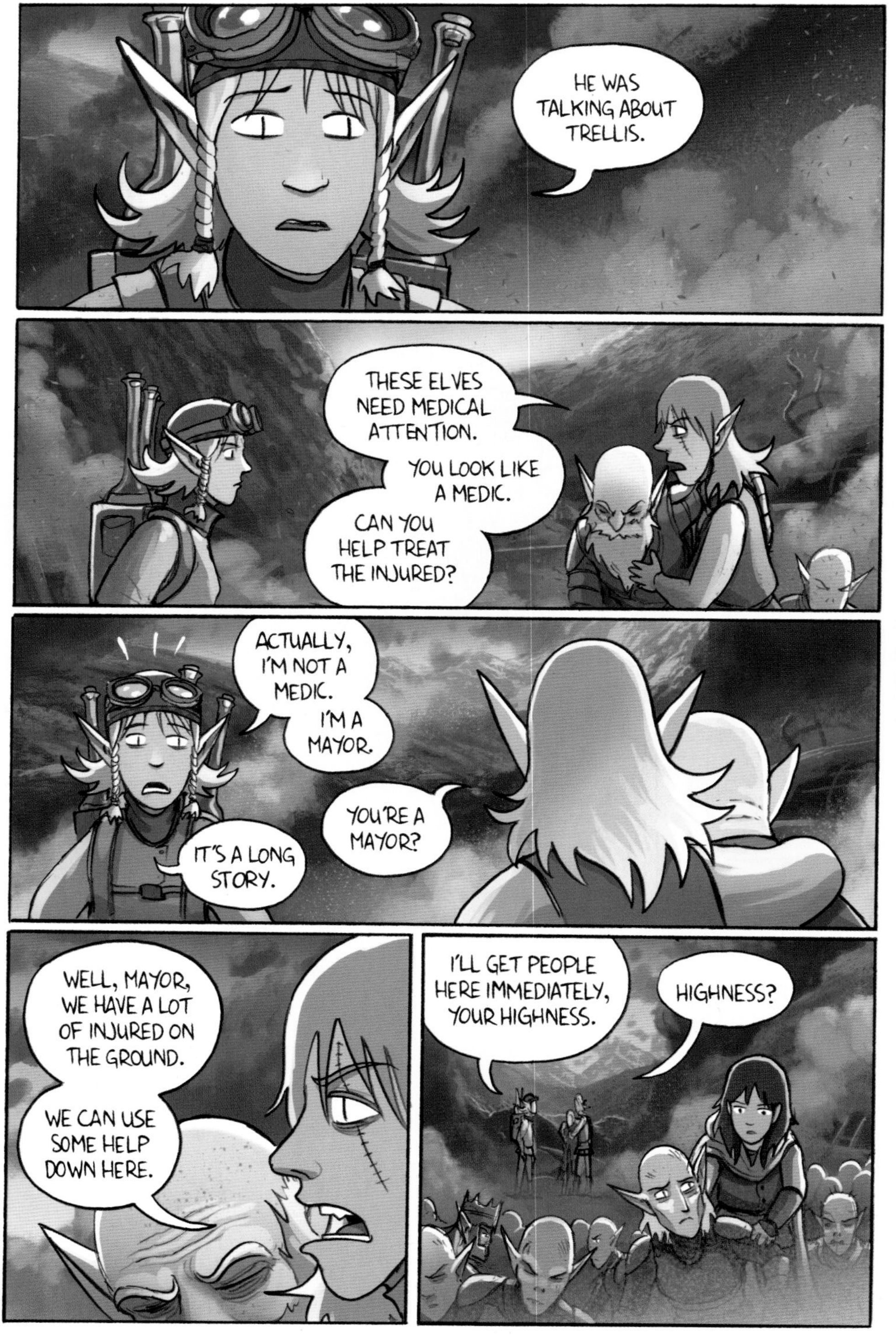
HE WAS TALKING ABOUT TRELLIS.
THESE ELVES NEED MEDICAL ATTENTION.
YOU LOOK LIKE A MEDIC.
CAN YOU HELP TREAT THE INJURED?
ACTUALLY, I'M NOT A MEDIC.
I'M A MAYOR.
IT'S A LONG STORY.
YOU'RE A MAYOR?
WELL, MAYOR, WE HAVE A LOT OF INJURED ON THE GROUND.
WE CAN USE SOME HELP DOWN HERE.
I'LL GET PEOPLE HERE IMMEDIATELY, YOUR HIGHNESS.
HIGHNESS?

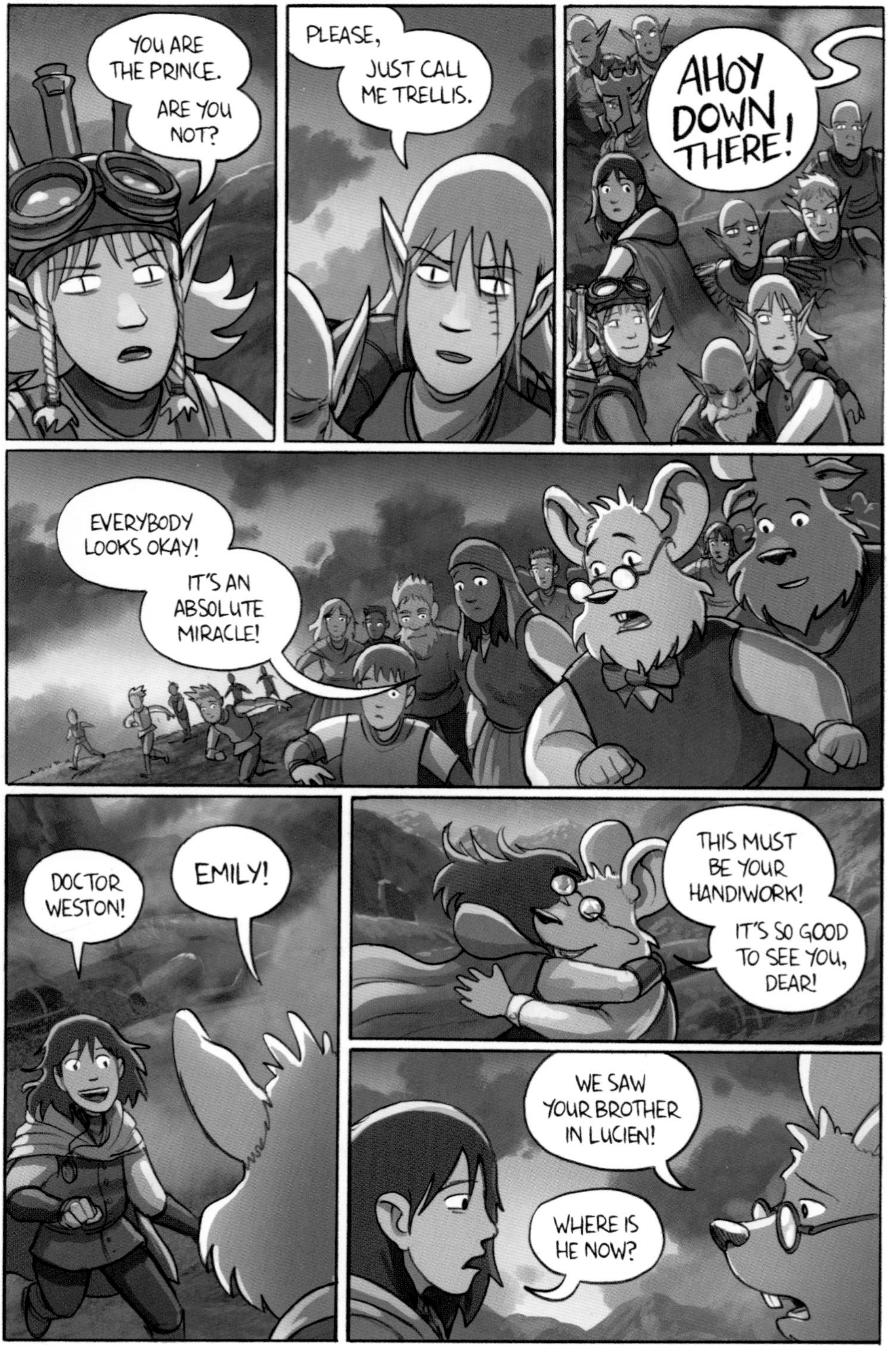
YOU ARE THE PRINCE.
ARE YOU NOT?
PLEASE,
JUST CALL ME TRELLIS.
AHOY DOWN THERE!
EVERYBODY LOOKS OKAY!
IT'S AN ABSOLUTE MIRACLE!
DOCTOR WESTON!
EMILY!
THIS MUST BE YOUR HANDIWORK!
IT'S SO GOOD TO SEE YOU, DEAR!
WE SAW YOUR BROTHER IN LUCIEN!
WHERE IS HE NOW?

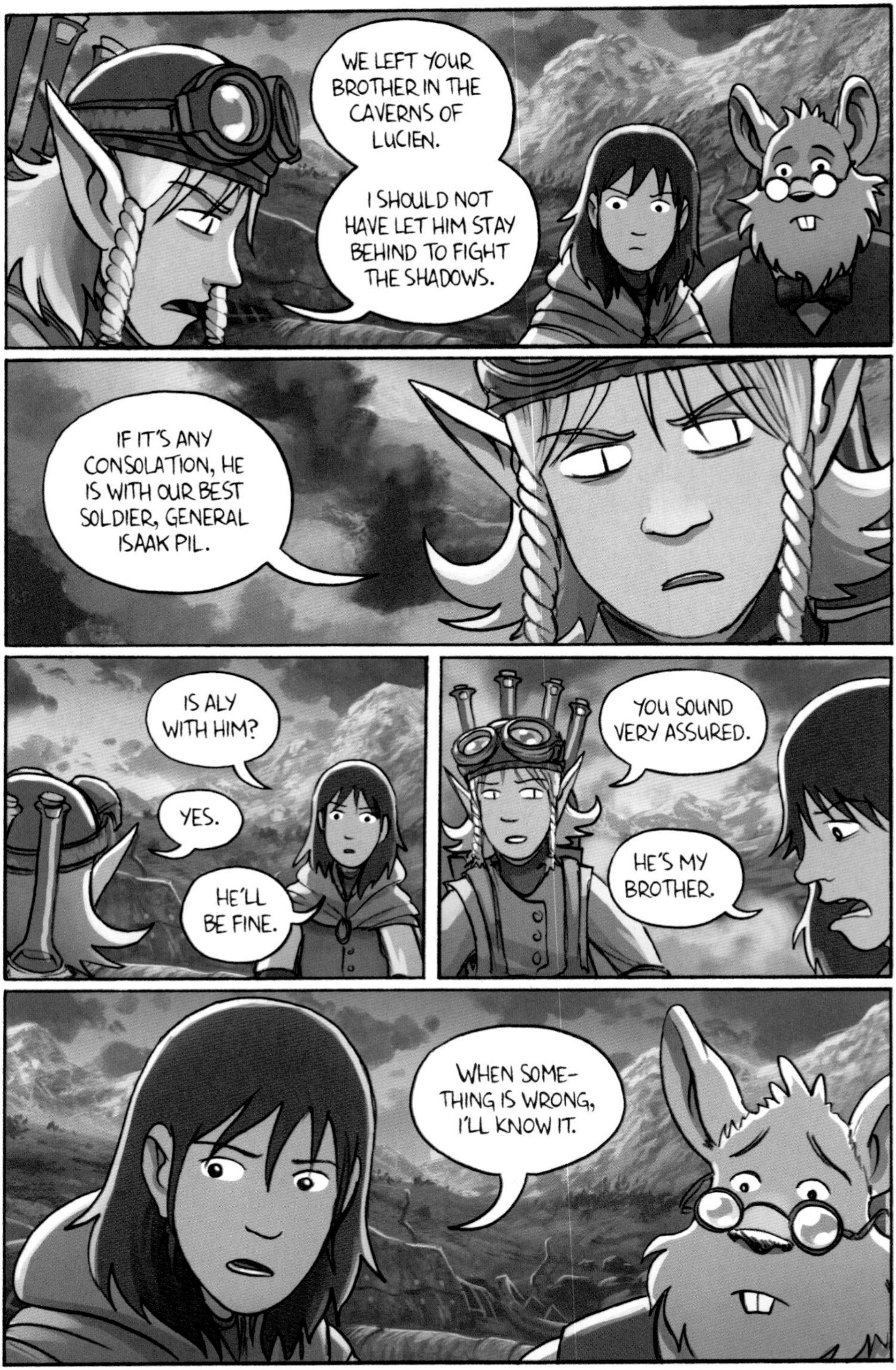
WE LEFT YOUR BROTHER IN THE CAVERNS OF LUCIEN.
I SHOULD NOT HAVE LET HIM STAY BEHIND TO FIGHT THE SHADOWS.
IF IT'S ANY CONSOLATION, HE IS WITH OUR BEST SOLDIER, GENERAL ISAAK PIL.
IS ALY WITH HIM?
YES.
HE'LL BE FINE.
YOU SOUND VERY ASSURED.
HE'S MY BROTHER.
WHEN SOME-THING IS WRONG, I'LL KNOW IT.

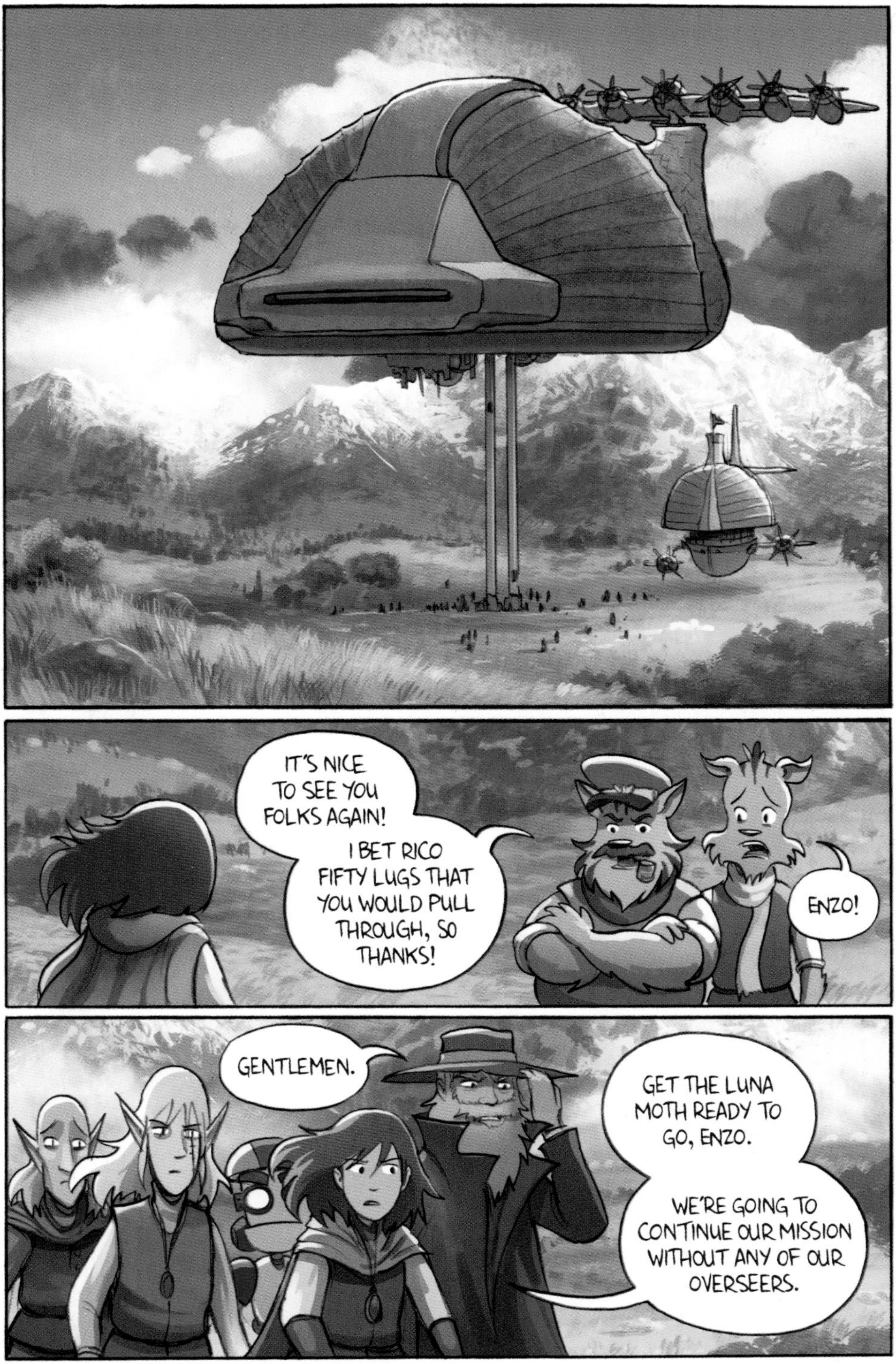
IT'S NICE TO SEE YOU FOLKS AGAIN!
I BET RICO FIFTY LUGS THAT YOU WOULD PULL THROUGH, SO THANKS!
ENZO!
GENTLEMEN.
GET THE LUNA MOTH READY TO GO, ENZO.
WE'RE GOING TO CONTINUE OUR MISSION WITHOUT ANY OF OUR OVERSEERS.

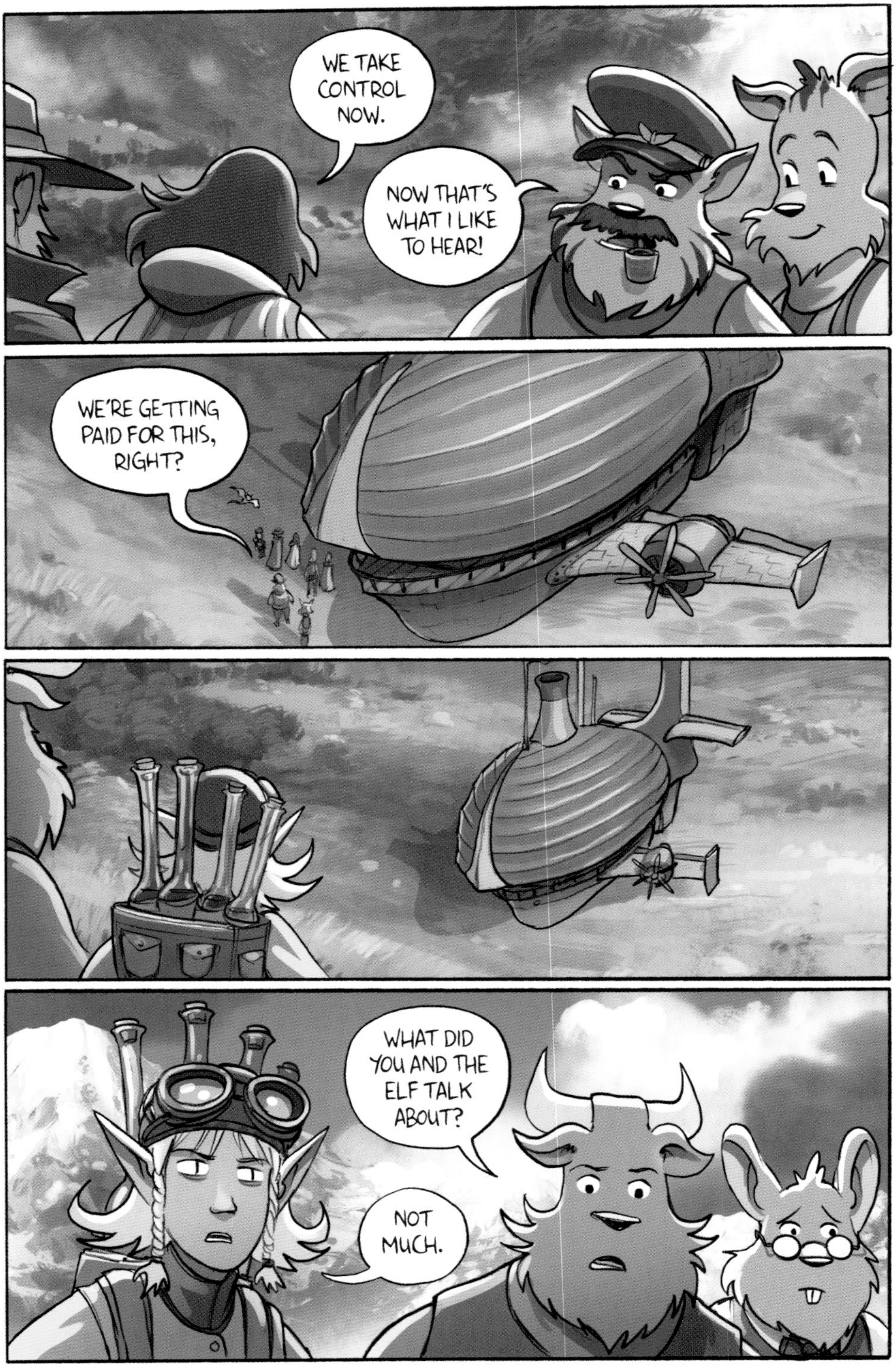
WE TAKE CONTROL NOW.
NOW THAT'S WHAT I LIKE TO HEAR!
WE'RE GETTING PAID FOR THIS, RIGHT?
WHAT DID YOU AND THE ELF TALK ABOUT?
NOT MUCH.

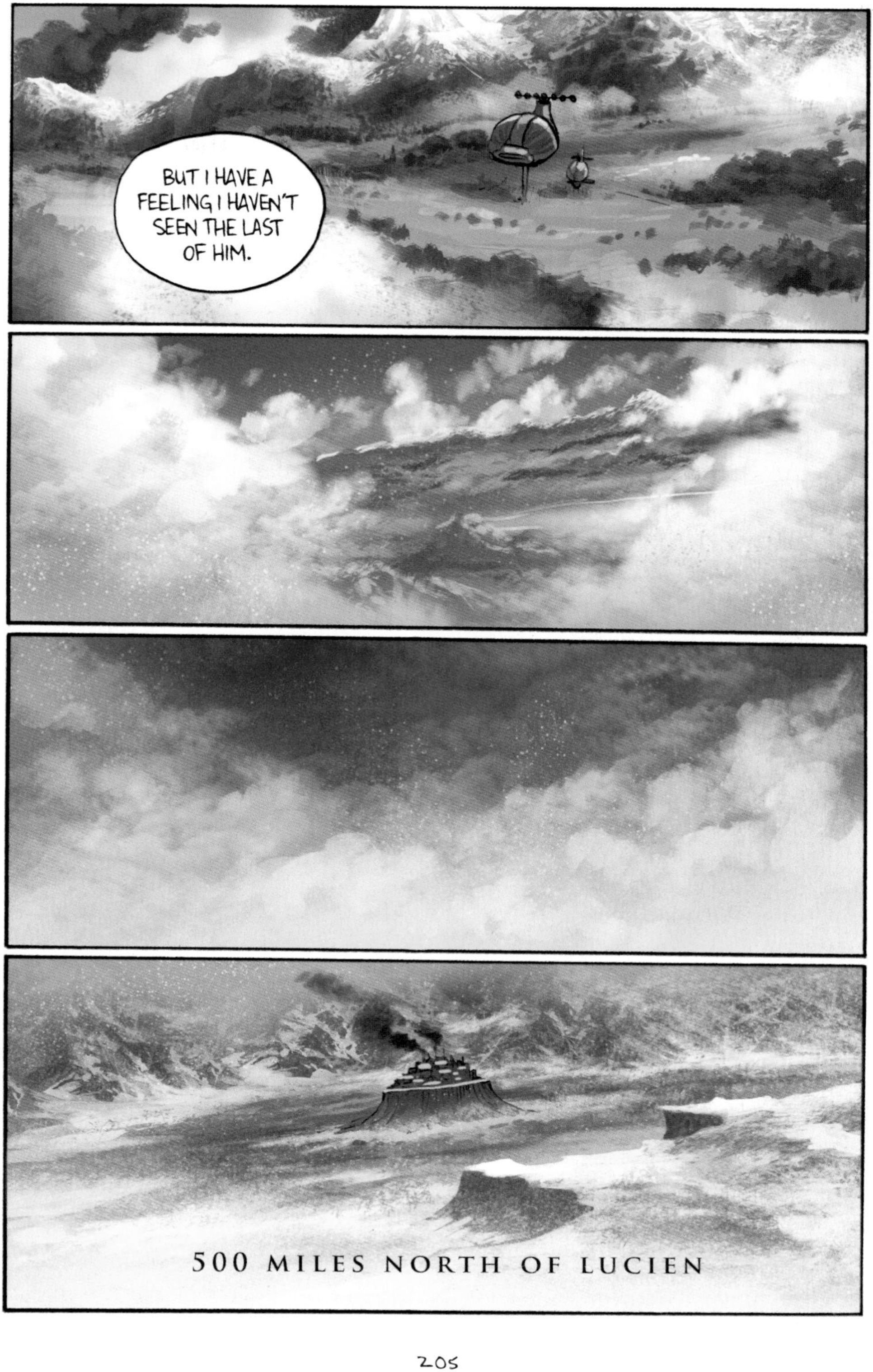
BUT I HAVE A FEELING I HAVEN'T SEEN THE LAST OF HIM.
500 MILES NORTH OF LUCIEN

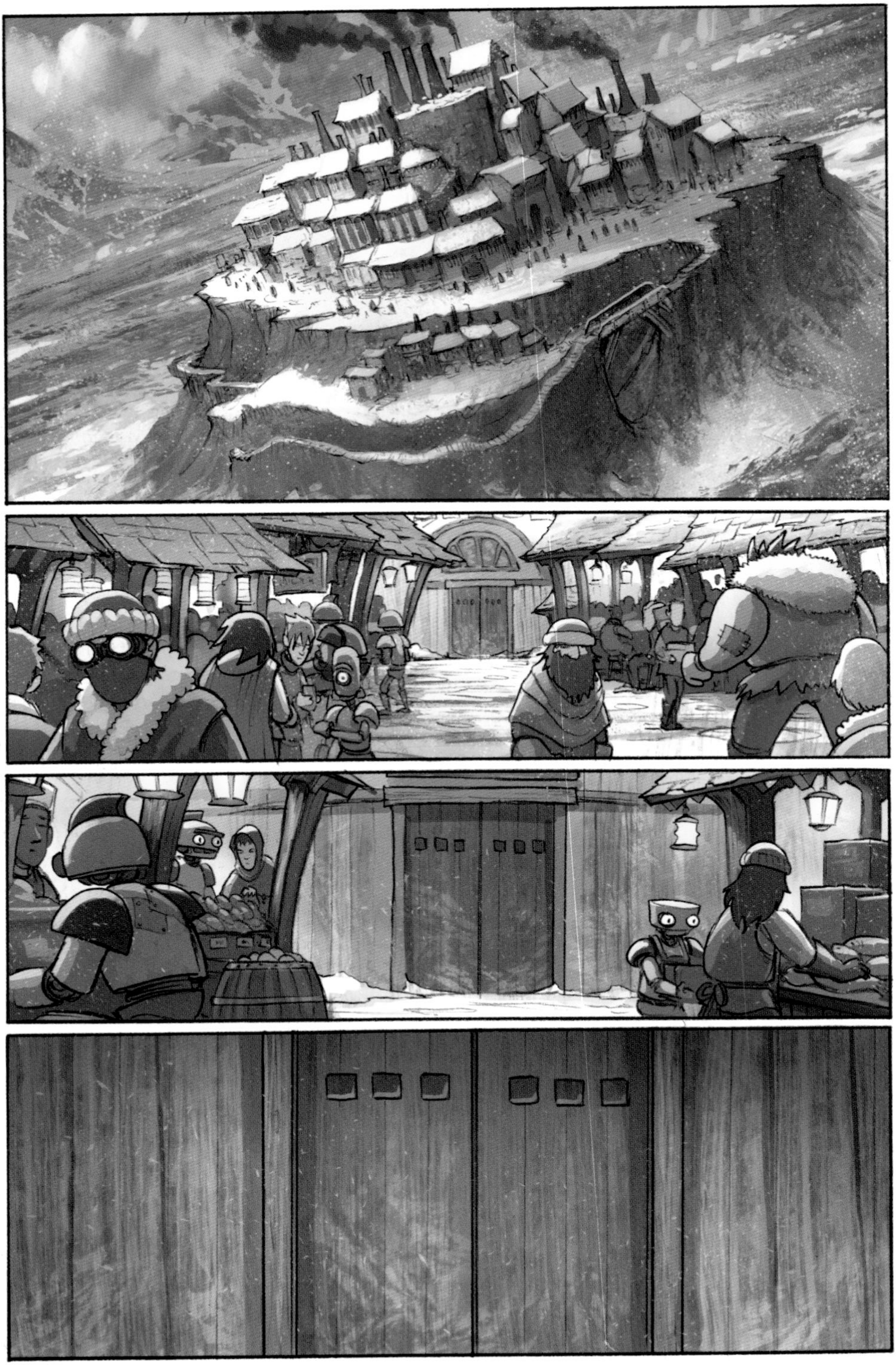

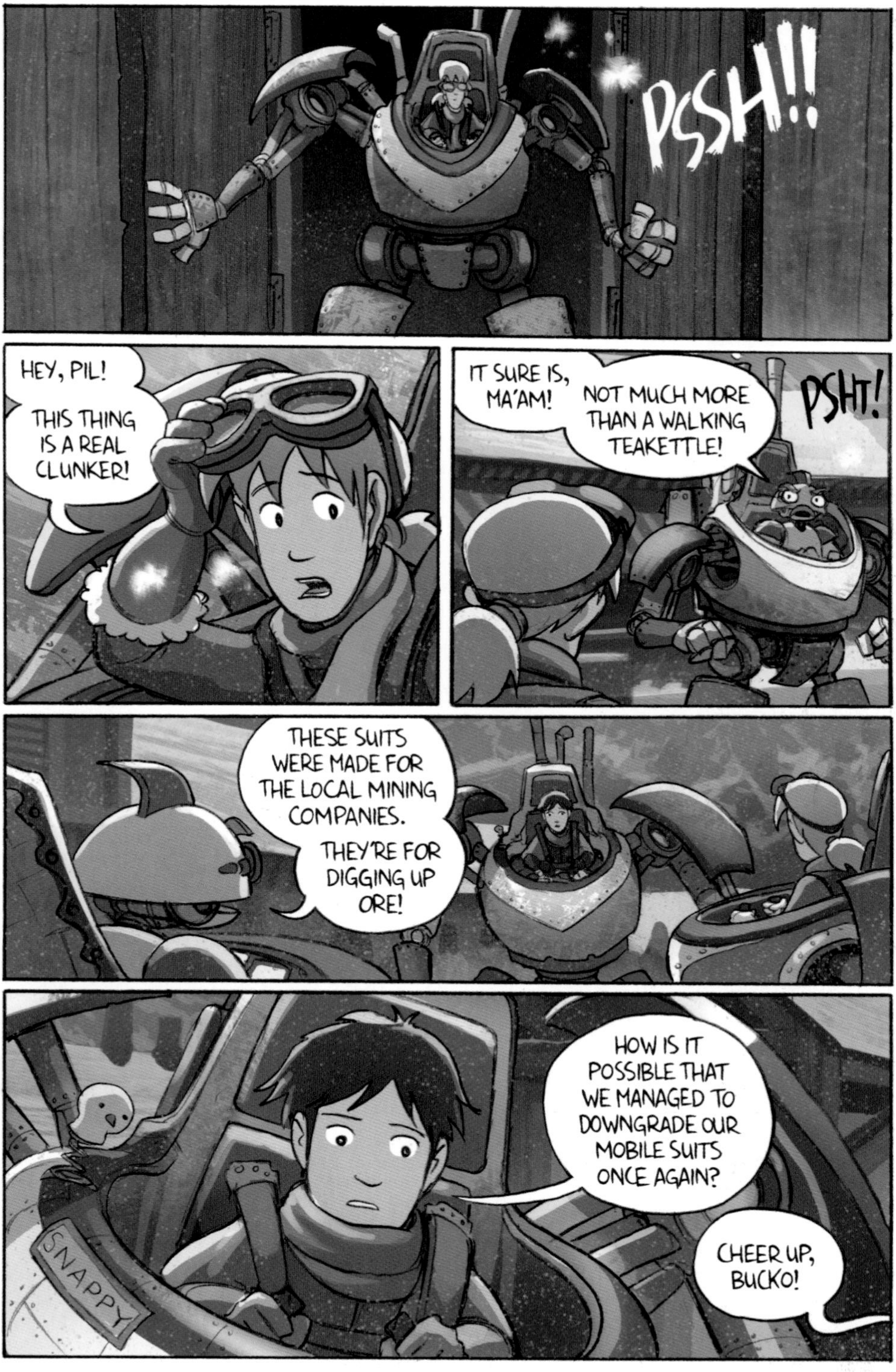
PSSH!!
HEY, PIL!
THIS THING IS A REAL CLUNKER!
IT SURE IS, MA'AM!
NOT MUCH MORE THAN A WALKING TEAKETTLE!
PSHT!
THESE SUITS WERE MADE FOR THE LOCAL MINING COMPANIES.
THEY'RE FOR DIGGING UP ORE!
SNAPPY
HOW IS IT POSSIBLE THAT WE MANAGED TO DOWNGRADE OUR MOBILE SUITS ONCE AGAIN?
CHEER UP, BUCKO!

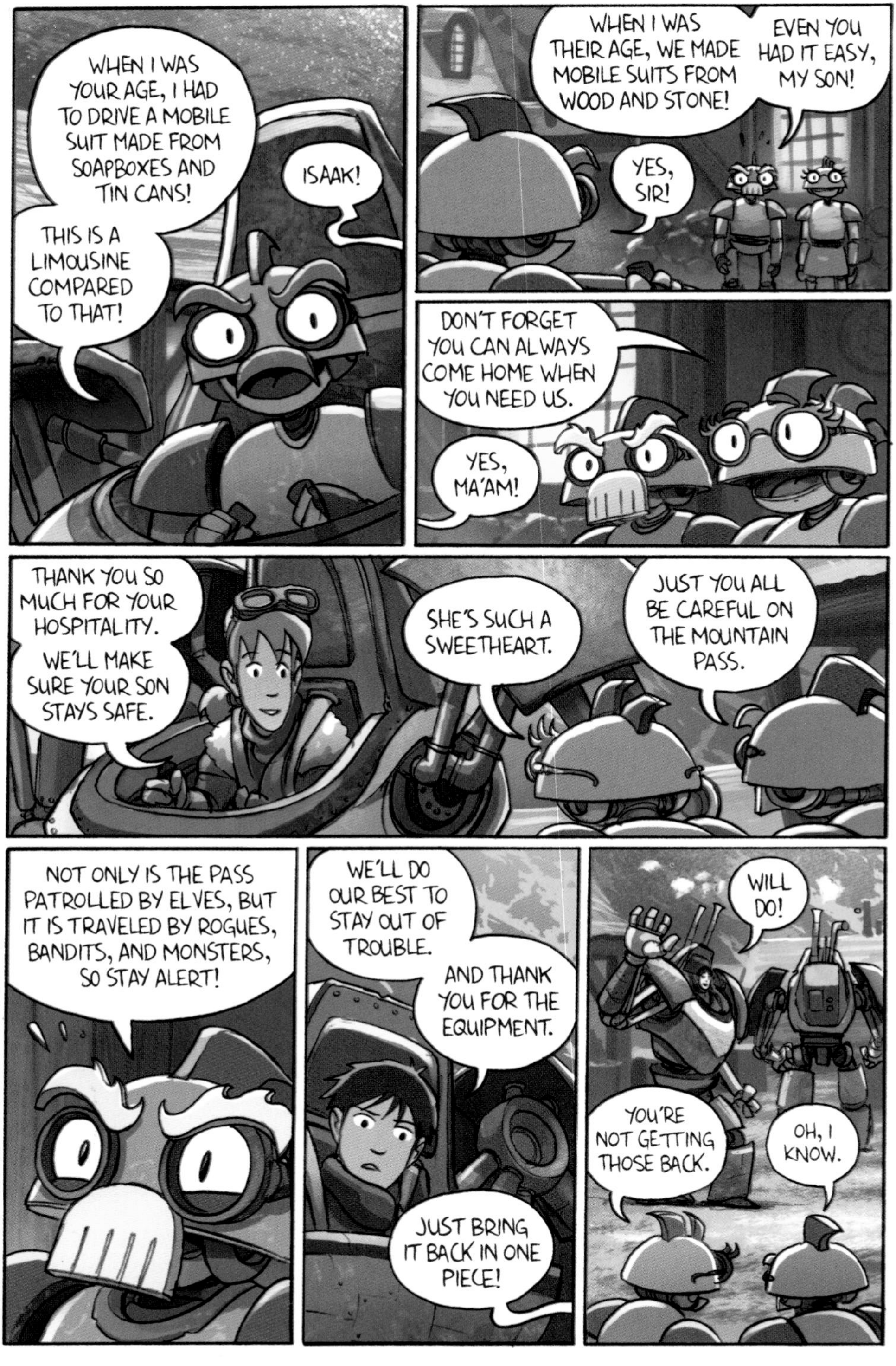
WHEN I WAS YOUR AGE, I HAD TO DRIVE A MOBILE SUIT MADE FROM SOAPBOXES AND TIN CANS!
THIS IS A LIMOUSINE COMPARED TO THAT!
ISAAK!
WHEN I WAS THEIR AGE, WE MADE MOBILE SUITS FROM WOOD AND STONE!
EVEN YOU HAD IT EASY, MY SON!
YES, SIR!
DON'T FORGET YOU CAN ALWAYS COME HOME WHEN YOU NEED US.
YES, MA'AM!
THANK YOU SO MUCH FOR YOUR HOSPITALITY.
WE'LL MAKE SURE YOUR SON STAYS SAFE.
SHE'S SUCH A SWEETHEART.
JUST YOU ALL BE CAREFUL ON THE MOUNTAIN PASS.
NOT ONLY IS THE PASS PATROLLED BY ELVES, BUT IT IS TRAVELED BY ROGUES, BANDITS, AND MONSTERS, SO STAY ALERT!
WE'LL DO OUR BEST TO STAY OUT OF TROUBLE.
AND THANK YOU FOR THE EQUIPMENT.
JUST BRING IT BACK IN ONE PIECE!
WILL DO!
YOU'RE NOT GETTING THOSE BACK.
OH, I KNOW.

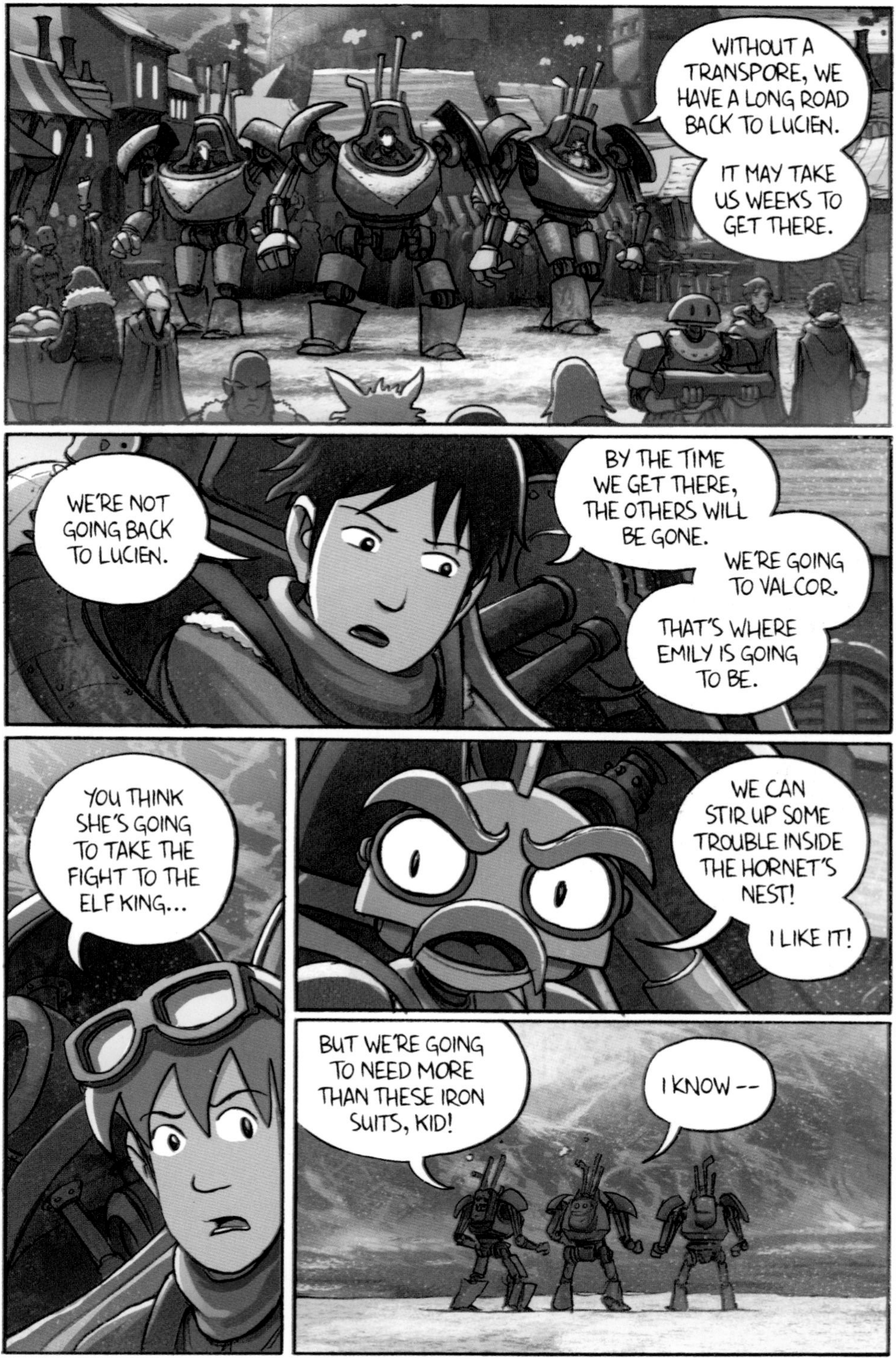
WITHOUT A TRANSPORE, WE HAVE A LONG ROAD BACK TO LUCIEN.
IT MAY TAKE US WEEKS TO GET THERE.
WE'RE NOT GOING BACK TO LUCIEN.
BY THE TIME WE GET THERE, THE OTHERS WILL BE GONE.
WE'RE GOING TO VALCOR.
THAT'S WHERE EMILY IS GOING TO BE.
YOU THINK SHE'S GOING TO TAKE THE FIGHT TO THE ELF KING...
WE CAN STIR UP SOME TROUBLE INSIDE THE HORNET'S NEST!
I LIKE IT!
BUT WE'RE GOING TO NEED MORE THAN THESE IRON SUITS, KID!
I KNOW --

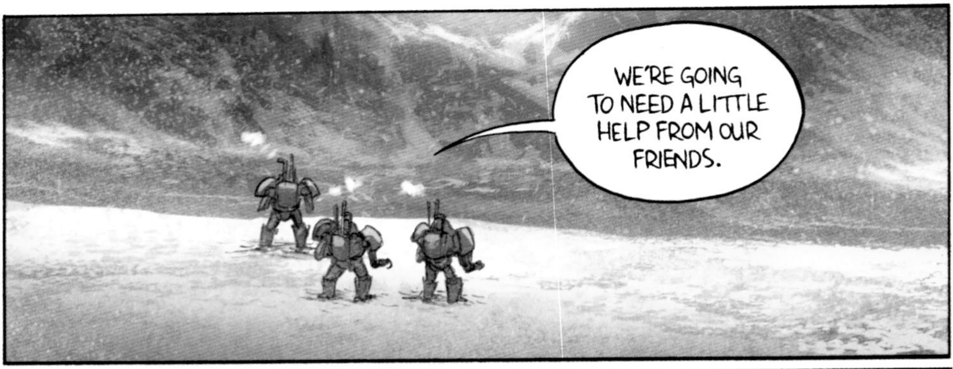
WE'RE GOING TO NEED A LITTLE HELP FROM OUR FRIENDS.

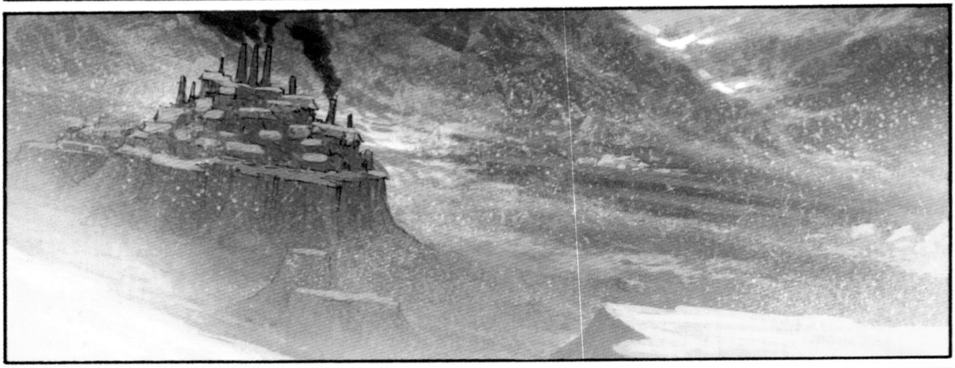

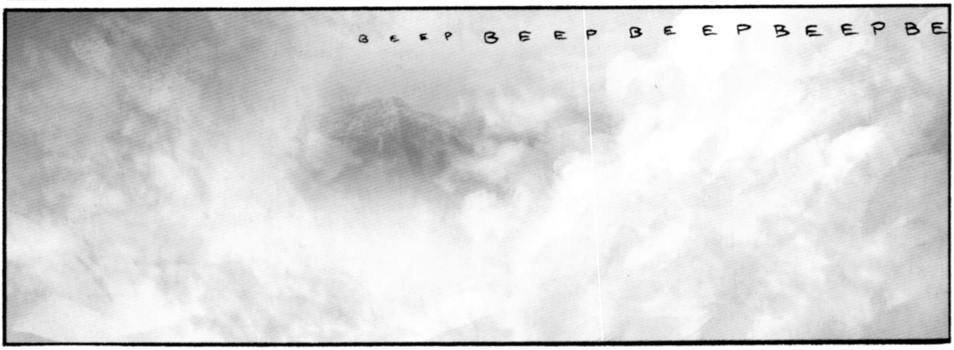
BEEP BEEP BEEP BEEPBE

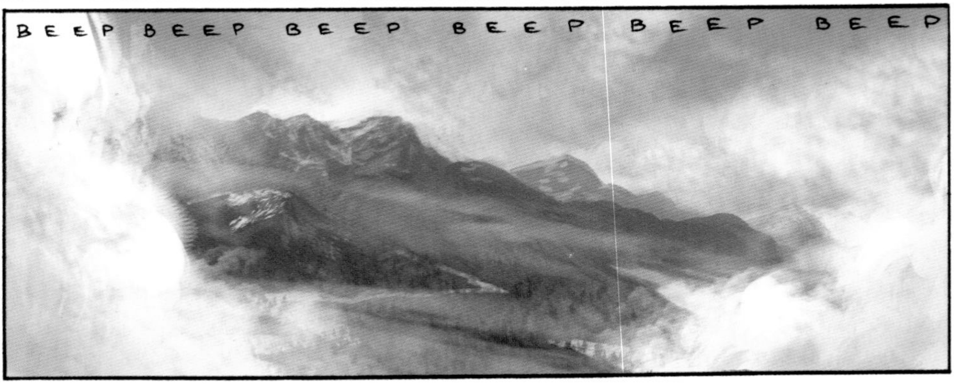
BEEP BEEP BEEP BEEP BEEP BEEP

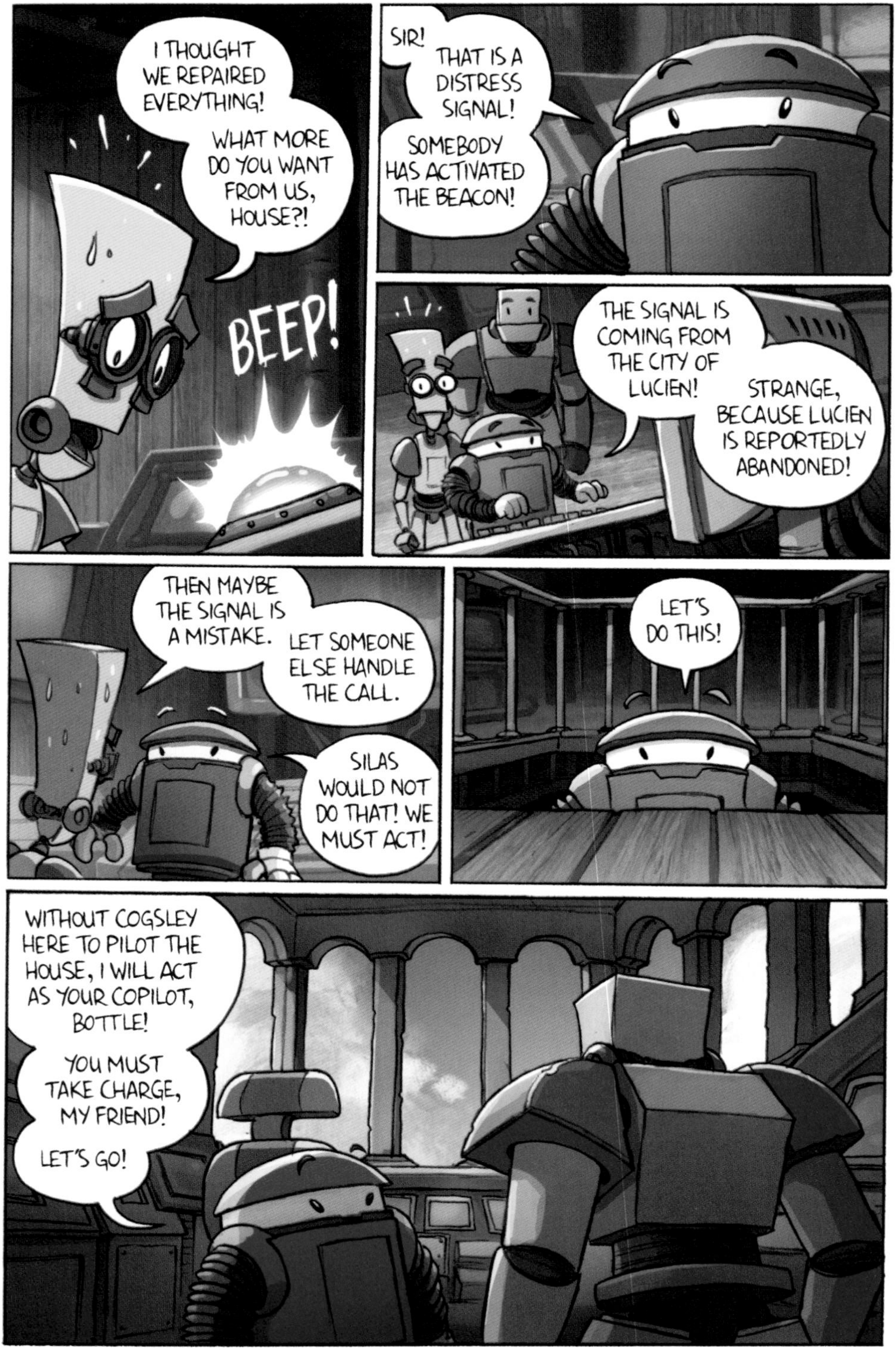
I THOUGHT WE REPAIRED EVERYTHING!
WHAT MORE DO YOU WANT FROM US, HOUSE?!
BEEP!
SIR!
THAT IS A DISTRESS SIGNAL!
SOMEBODY HAS ACTIVATED THE BEACON!
THE SIGNAL IS COMING FROM THE CITY OF LUCIEN!
STRANGE, BECAUSE LUCIEN IS REPORTEDLY ABANDONED!
THEN MAYBE THE SIGNAL IS A MISTAKE.
LET SOMEONE ELSE HANDLE THE CALL.
SILAS WOULD NOT DO THAT! WE MUST ACT!
LET'S DO THIS!
WITHOUT COGSLEY HERE TO PILOT THE HOUSE, I WILL ACT AS YOUR COPILOT, BOTTLE!
YOU MUST TAKE CHARGE, MY FRIEND!
LET'S GO!

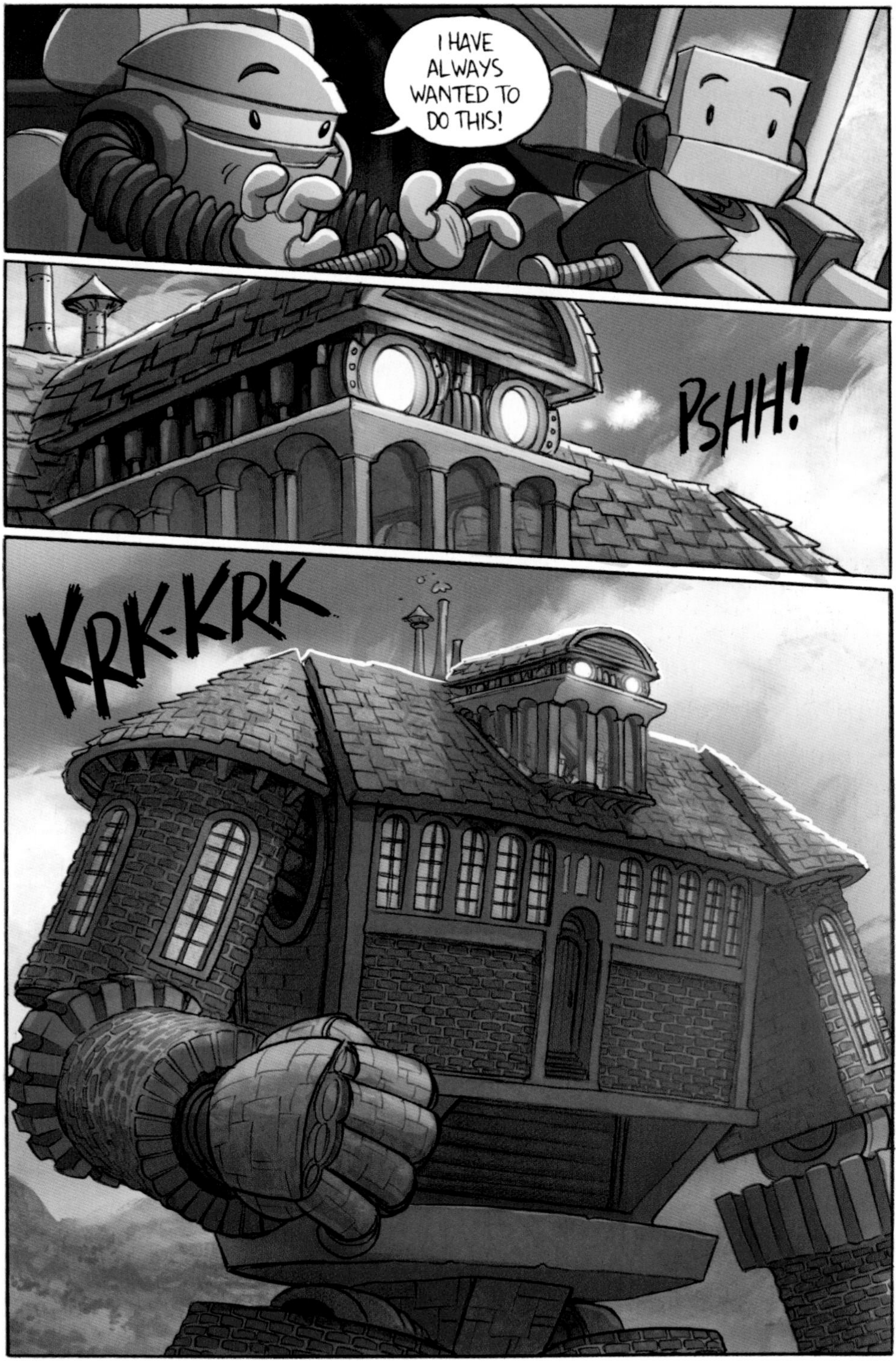
I HAVE ALWAYS WANTED TO DO THIS!
PSHH!
KRK-KRK

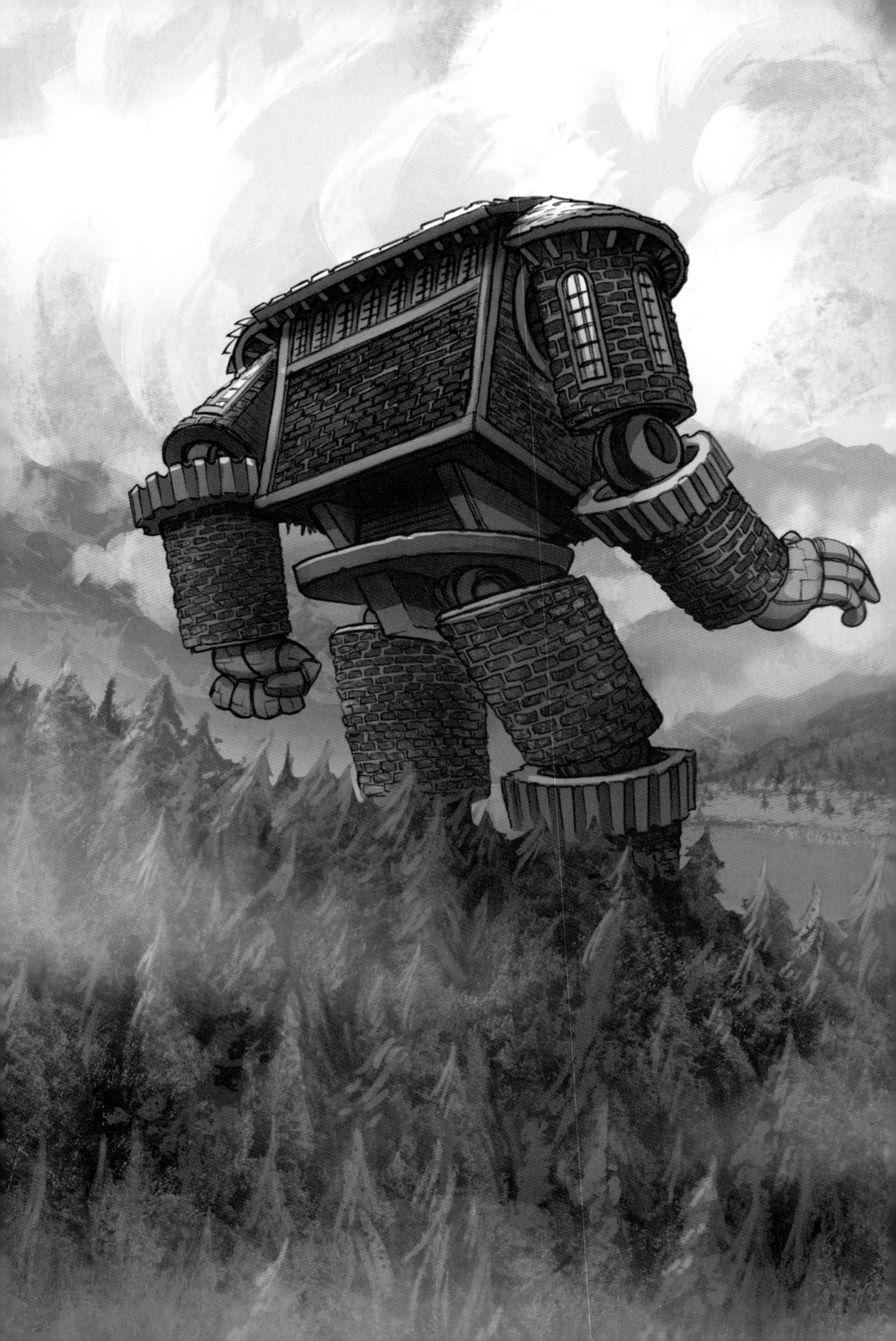

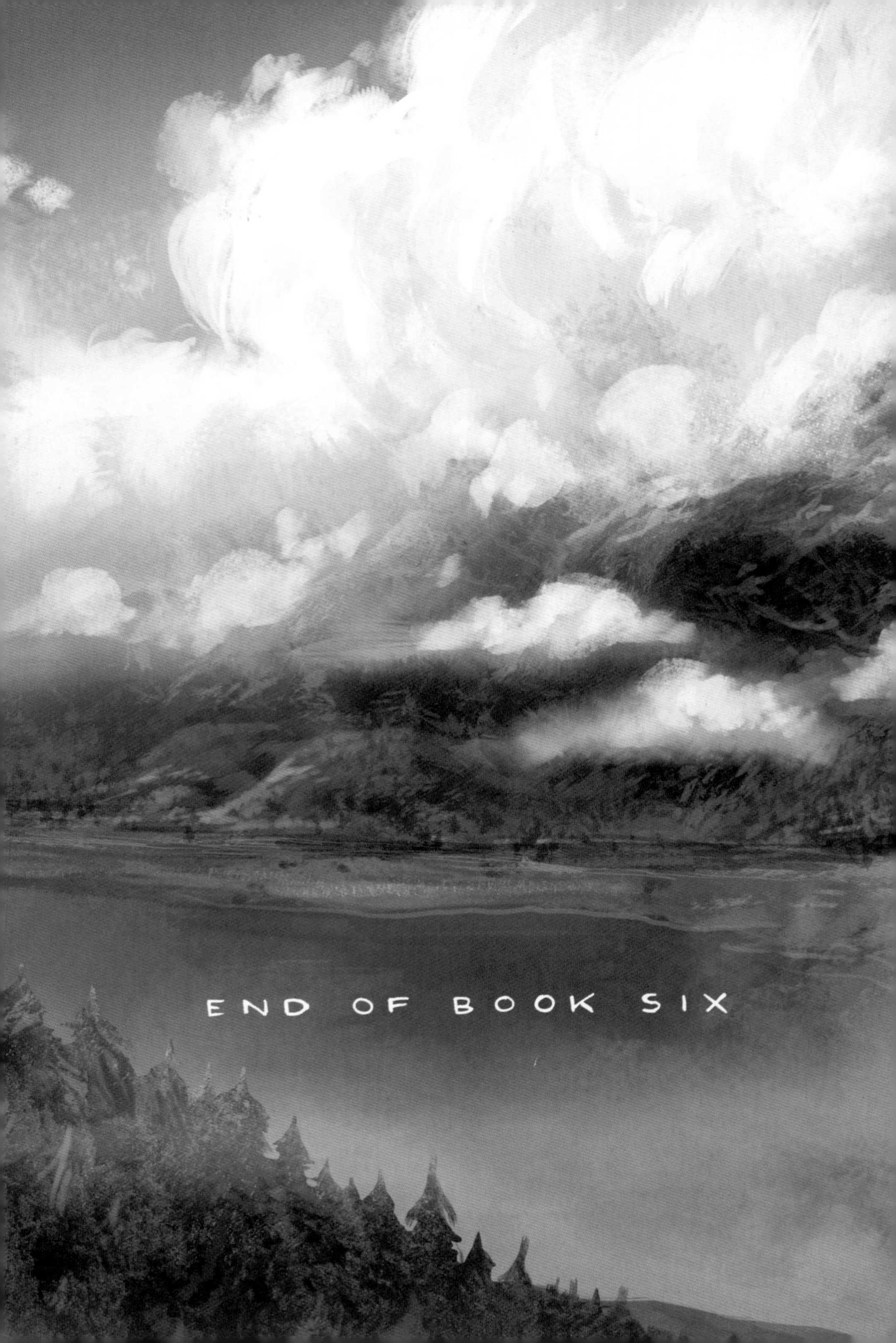
END OF BOOK SIX

CREATED AT

BOLT CITY
PRODUCTIONS

WRITTEN & ILLUSTRATED BY
KAZU KIBUISHI

LEAD PRODUCTION ARTIST
JASON CAFFOE

COLORS & BACKGROUND
JASON CAFFOE
KAZU KIBUISHI
TIM PROBERT
ALICE DUKE
JEFFREY DELGADO
DAVE MONTES
MARY CAGLE

PAGE FLATTING
MARY CAGLE
PRESTON DO
CRYSTAL KAN
MEGAN BRENNAN
STUART LIVINGSTON

SPECIAL THANKS

Amy & Juni & Sophie Kim Kibuishi, Rachel Ormiston, Nancy Caffoe, Judy Hansen, David Saylor, Phil Falco, Cassandra Pelham, Ben Zhu & the Gallery Nucleus crew, Tao & Taka & Tyler Kibuishi, Tim Ganter, Sunni Kim, June & Masa & Julie & Emi Kibuishi, Sheila Marie Everett, Lizette Serrano, Bess Braswell, Whitney Steller, Lori Benton, and Ellie Berger.

And the biggest thanks of all to the librarians, booksellers, parents, and readers who have supported us all this way. You mean the world to us.

ABOUT THE AUTHOR

Kazu Kibuishi is the creator of the #1 *New York Times* bestselling Amulet series. *Amulet, Book One: The Stonekeeper* was an ALA Best Book for Young Adults and a Children's Choice Book Award finalist. He is also the creator of *Copper*, a collection of his popular webcomic that features an adventuresome boy-and-dog pair. Kazu also illustrated the covers of the 15th anniversary paperback editions of the Harry Potter series written by J. K. Rowling. He lives and works in Seattle, Washington, with his wife, Amy Kim Kibuishi, and their children.

Visit Kazu online at www.boltcity.com.

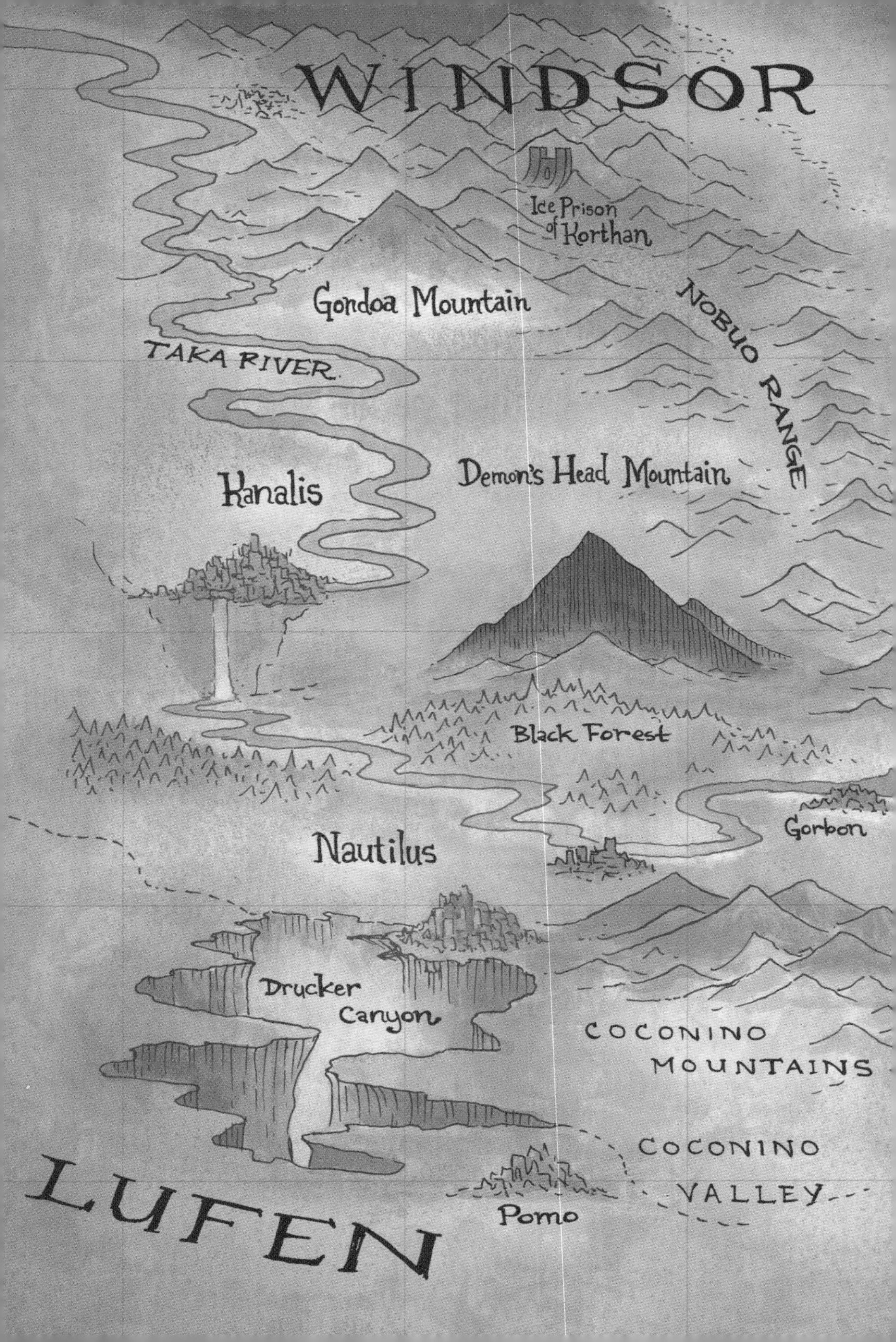
WINDSOR
Ice Prison of Korthan
Gondoa Mountain
NOBUO RANGE
TAKA RIVER
Kanalis
Demon's Head Mountain
Black Forest
Gorbon
Nautilus
Drucker Canyon
COCONINO MOUNTAINS
COCONINO VALLEY
LUFEN
Pomo

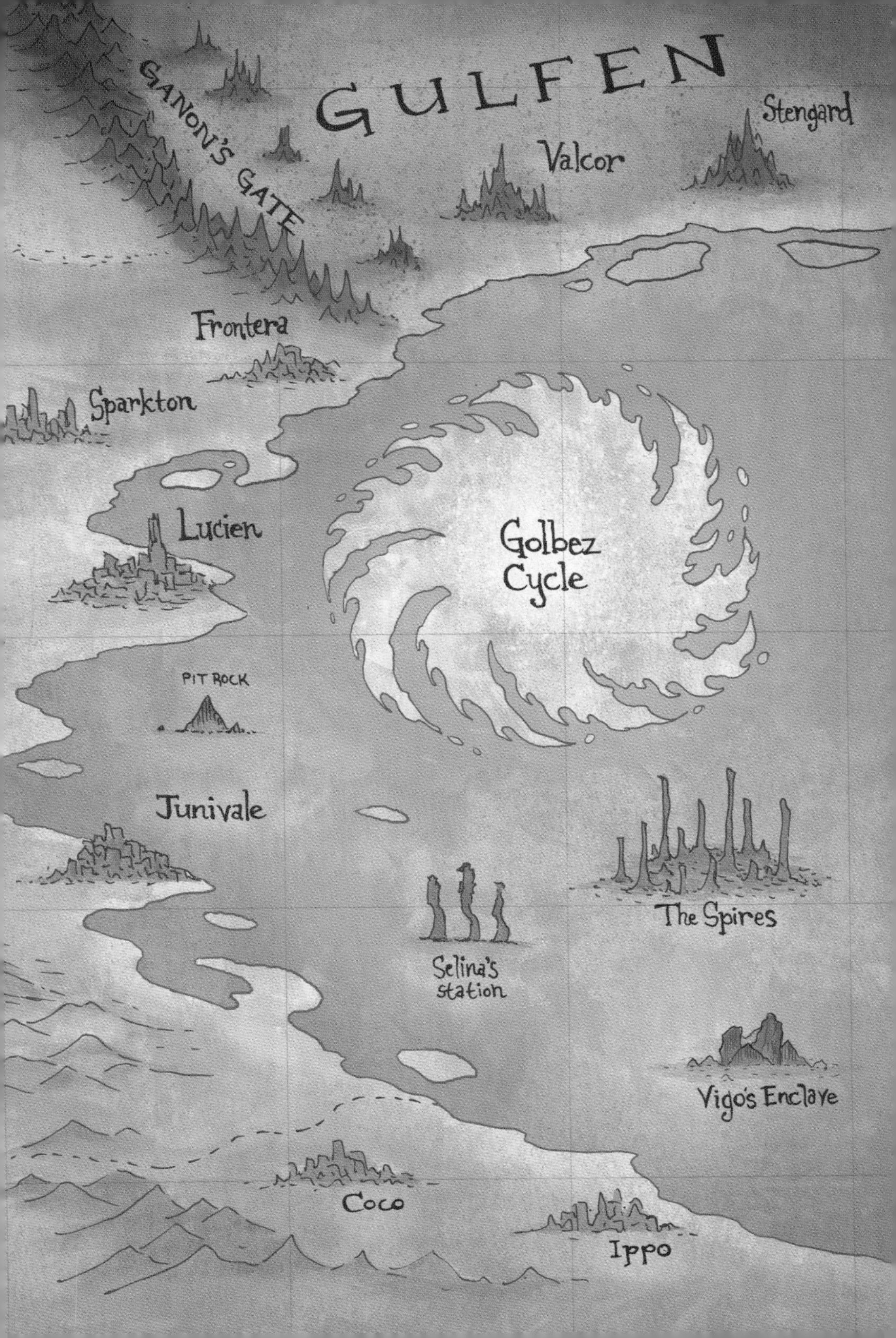
GULFEN
GANON'S GATE
Stengard
Valcor
Frontera
Sparkton
Lucien
Golbez
Cycle
PIT ROCK
Junivale
The Spires
Selina's
station
Vigo's Enclave
Coco
Ippo

Liz
May 117